"ROMANCE AT ITS FINEST AND FUNNIEST."*

Praise for Barbara Metzger and her enchanting romance novels

"Witty [and] certain to entertain."
—*Publishers Weekly* (starred review)

"Delightful [and] fun." —Under the Covers

"A doyen of humorous Regency-era romance writing. . . . Metzger's gift for re-creating the flavor and ambience of the period shines here, and the antics of her dirty-dish villains, near-villains, and starry-eyed lovers are certain to entertain."
—**Publishers Weekly* (starred review)

"The complexities of both story and character contribute much to its richness. Like life, this book is much more exciting when the layers are peeled back and savored." —*Affaire de Coeur*

"A true tour de force. . . . Only an author with Metzger's deft skill could successfully mix a Regency tale of death, ruined reputations, and scandal with humor for a fine and ultimately satisfying broth. . . . A very satisfying read." —The Best Reviews

"Queen of the Regency Romp. [She] brings the Regency era vividly to life with deft humor, sparkling dialogue, and witty descriptions."
—Romance Reviews Today

"Metzger has penned another winning Regency tale. Filled with her hallmark humor, distinctive wit, and entertaining style, this is one romance that will not fail to enchant." —*Booklist* (starred review)

A Perfect Gentleman

A Perfect Gentleman

Barbara Metzger

A SIGNET BOOK

SIGNET
Published by New American Library, a division of
Penguin Group (USA) Inc., 375 Hudson Street,
New York, New York 10014, USA
Penguin Group (Canada), 10 Alcorn Avenue, Toronto,
Ontario, M4V 3B2, Canada (a division of Pearson Penguin Canada Inc.)
Penguin Books Ltd., 80 Strand, London WC2R 0RL, England
Penguin Ireland, 25 St. Stephen's Green, Dublin 2,
Ireland (a division of Penguin Books Ltd.)
Penguin Group (Australia), 250 Camberwell Road, Camberwell, Victoria 3124,
Australia (a division of Pearson Australia Group Pty. Ltd.)
Penguin Books India Pvt. Ltd., 11 Community Centre, Panchsheel Park,
New Delhi - 110 017, India
Penguin Group (NZ), Cnr Airborne and Rosedale Roads, Albany,
Auckland 1310, New Zealand (a division of Pearson New Zealand Ltd.)
Penguin Books (South Africa) (Pty.) Ltd., 24 Sturdee Avenue,
Rosebank, Johannesburg 2196, South Africa

Penguin Books Ltd., Registered Offices:
80 Strand, London WC2R 0RL, England

First published by Signet, an imprint of New American Library,
a division of Penguin Group (USA) Inc.

ISBN 0-7394-4638-X

Printed in the United States of America

To Cousin Nancy, her new kidney,
and to organ donors everywhere

A Perfect Gentleman

Chapter One

He was, regrettably, poor. Having inherited nothing but a pile of debts, an impoverished estate, and an improvident young stepmama along with his title, Aubrey, Viscount Wellstone, was a few pounds and a diamond stickpin away from debtors' prison. He had few practical skills, no calling to the church, and no affinity for the army. He did have a gentleman's education, of course, which meant he was equally as useless in Latin and Greek. So Stony, as he was called by his many friends, turned to the gaming tables.

He was, even more regrettably, a poor gambler.

He lost as often as he won, never getting ahead of his father's debts enough to make the ancestral lands more profitable, or to make sounder investments. Before he turned twenty-six, the diamond stickpin was long gone, following his mother's jewels, his grandfather's art collection, and every bit of property or possession that was not entailed. The Wellstone fortunes were at low ebb, nearly foundering on the shoals of bad speculations, bad management, and sheer bad luck.

Then one night the tide turned. No hidden cache of gold was found behind the walls of Wellstone House in Mayfair, none of his stepmama's suitors was suddenly found suitable, nor had Stony finally resigned himself to that age-old cure for poverty: finding an heiress to wed. Neither had the viscount's skill with the pasteboards miraculously improved. In fact, he lost heavily to Lord Parkhurst that evening at the Middlethorpe ball.

"One more hand," Stony requested as politely as he could without begging, as that middle-aged gentleman rose stiffly to his feet, gathering his winnings. "One more hand to recoup my losses."

Lord Parkhurst shook his head. "I'd like to stay, my boy. Lud knows I'd play all night. But I promised my wife I'd look after her youngest sister. It's the squinty one, but the last of the bunch, thank heaven. I swore I'd make sure the girl has a partner for dinner and all that, so she doesn't look like a wallflower, you know. Not that dancing with her own brother-in-law will make her look like a belle, I swear, but my wife seems to think she'll show to better advantage on a gentleman's arm than perched on one of those spindly gilt chairs."

Everyone knew Parkhurst danced to whatever tune his pretty young wife was calling, so Stony wasted no more time trying to convince the man to stay. He scrawled his initials on an IOU and handed it over. He'd be handing his fob watch to the cents-per-centers in the morning, right before he started packing for Wellstone Park in Norfolk. He shuddered at the thought of his stepmama's tears when he informed her they would have to put the London town house up for rent. He was sincerely fond of Gwen, who was barely ten years his senior, but Lord, her tears would make the leaks in the Park's roofs seem like a trickle. He shuddered again at the thought of Gwen never finding a gentleman to wed, not among the turnip-growers and sheepherders in the shires. He took a long swallow of brandy. At least the Middlethorpes' wine was free. Maybe he'd ought to go fill his pockets with their chef's lobster patties. Heaven knew his pockets were empty of everything else.

"Damn if I wouldn't rather have you take my place," Parkhurst was saying, holding up the voucher, "than take your money."

Stony set down his glass and brushed back from his forehead a blond curl that needed trimming. "My lord?"

Parkhurst cast a longing look at the fresh decks of cards on the green baize-covered tables, the gray, smoke-shrouded room filled with like-minded gentlemen, the maroon-uniformed footmen with their decanters of brandy. Then he looked at the white scrap of paper he held. Stony held his breath.

"Why not?" Parkhurst said, a smile breaking across his lined face as he took his seat again. "My wife did not say I had to do the pretty with the girl myself, just that the chit wasn't to be left sitting alone all night. A handsome young buck like you, Wellstone, could do a lot more for her popularity. Why, if such a top-of-the-trees beau pays her court, the other chaps are bound to sit up and take notice. At least they'll ask for a dance, just to see what had you so interested." He picked up the pack of cards and started shuffling. "The more I think about it, the better the idea sounds."

It sounded too easy to Stony. "I won't marry her, you know."

"Humph. If I thought you had intentions of sniffing after her dowry, I'd have to call you out. What, let the gal run off with a pockets-to-let gamester with nothing but his pretty smile to recommend him? She might have a squint, but the gal's still my sister-in-law."

Stony was not smiling now. He stood to his full six-foot height and looked down his slightly prominent nose at the older man. "If I had wished to repair my fortunes with a wealthy bride, sir, I could have done so any time these past few years."

"Aye, and you'd have picked a female with a bigger dowry and better looks, I am sure. That's why I made you the offer. Everyone knows you ain't shopping at the marriage mart. I'm not saying that trying to repair your fortunes at the tables is any nobler than marrying a girl for her money, but at least you've got principles. And you've never been known as a womanizer, unlike so many other wastrels, trading one bit of muslin for another as fast as you change your waistcoat."

Stony had never been able to afford to keep a mistress, much less a closetful of waistcoats. The occasional willing widow, now, that was another story, one he deemed irrelevant to the current conversation.

"By George," Parkhurst was going on, "my wife would have my head if I handed the girl over to a rake. But you're not one to ruin a gal's reputation, I'd swear, not when you know you'd have to pay the preacher's price. No, you're a gentleman born and bred, one who can show an innocent girl a good time and keep the fortune-hunters and reprobates away without breaking her heart—or my wife's." He took up the slip of paper again and raised his brow in inquiry.

Stony fixed his blue eyes on that debt he could not pay. "One night?"

"That's it. One ball that's almost half over already, and you'll escort the ladies home so I don't have to leave the game in the middle. Agreed?"

Stony nodded. "Agreed."

Parkhurst ripped up the voucher.

Viscount Wellstone turned the female's squint to a sparkle.

A career was born.

A great many gentlemen of the *ton,* it appeared, would rather entrust their daughters and sisters and second cousins to a confirmed bachelor like Stony than give up their nights with the cards, their cronies, or their *amours chéris.* Lord Parkhurst confided to a friend or two how his wife's sister had had the time of her life, dancing, laughing, blushing at the viscount's attentions. Lady Middlethorpe and her dowager set noted that the young woman had shown more animation than ever before, catching the eye—slightly crossed, admittedly—of a widowed gentleman of means.

Stony suddenly had more offers and invitations than he could accept. No one was so crass as to mention terms or conditions, naturally, not in that most polite of societies. Oh, no. None of their spoiled sons had to work for a living. None of their ugly duckling daughters had to have paid male companions. No, these were favors, in the spirit of friendship and kindness, to young females finding themselves among strangers. Viscount Wellstone was the best of good fellows; that was all. And in the same spirit of goodwill, Stony found his tailor's bill paid. His account at Tattersall's was settled, his club dues discharged. Vouchers were returned, marked *Canceled,* and banknotes mysteriously found their way into his pockets. Quantities of wine were delivered to his doorstep, along with a new valet whose salary was paid for the year. A few of his family heirlooms eventually found their way home.

In return, the young ladies found the perfect escort. Viscount Wellstone was handsome and well built, with blond hair and blue eyes and a dimple to enhance his ready smile. He was polite and attentive, a superlative dancer, a practiced flirt, a knowledgeable conversationalist. He was also, the girls were warned, a sworn bachelor, so no expectations were raised. At least, they were not raised too high, for that dimple was definitely tempting. To make sure his intentions were never misunderstood by the girls or their guardians, Stony showed no female undue preference, charming the chaperones as well as his charges. So gallant was he in his new role that no one but the informed ever suspected his presence was bought and paid for.

Oh, no. It was: "Why, here is Lord Wellstone, poppet, come to beg a dance. You'd much rather take a turn with him, I am sure, than your fusty old father. He'll be able to introduce you to all his chums while I talk politics."

Or: "My friend Stony here accompanied his stepmama to the ball, but she's gossiping with the matrons, and he needs a female at his side to fend off the matchmaking mamas. Won't you take pity on him, Cousin?"

Or: "I owe the viscount a favor, Sis, so I lent him the opera box. He would be pleased if such a knowing music lover as you attended with him and Lady Wellstone."

Or even: "Don't tell anyone, Aunt Louisa, but Wellstone confided in me that he is interested in growing roses. I told him no one knew more about the plaguey—ah, precious blossoms than you."

The women, young and old, were delighted. The gentlemen, bored or busy, were relieved. And Stony? Viscount Wellstone was having fun. To his own amazement, he was enjoying himself. He liked to dance, to attend the theater, to go for drives, all the things he could not do while leaning over a dice table in some dark corner of a gaming parlor. If he never had to see a deck of cards again, he'd escort Medusa to the art museum.

Most of all, he found, he liked women, and he liked making them happy. A few of his new companions were silly or spoiled or just soured old spinsters, but he tried to find something to enjoy about them too. If he looked hard enough—and for some he needed his new magnifying glass—he could find admirable qualities to cultivate and encourage.

The fat, ugly, or stupid females offered a greater challenge than any game of chance ever had. If he could make them shine in society's light, then he was a winner, indeed. Here his stepmama rose to the challenge, fussing over his motley brood like a hen with no chicks of her own. Gwen might not make them into swans, but her fashion sense was unequaled. So was her knowledge of the latest skin treatments, the newest cosmetics, and which fat, ugly, or stupid gentlemen could not afford to be so choosy in their dance partners.

Stony's favorites were the shy, uncertain girls, the ones who bloomed under the sunlight of attention, who flowered into attractive, assured maidens. He started to take pride in all his girls, and in himself, without suffering too many regrets that he was making his living in a somewhat underhanded manner. Taking money—gifts, to put a more polite cast on his income—for saving unwilling gentlemen from Almack's and waltz parties and amateur musicales was no more, he told himself, than being treated to dinner after exercising an absent friend's horse. He chose to think of his new occupation as shadowed, rather than shady, for although he was receiving compensation for playing the courtier to unknowing females, he was also making them better women, better future wives and mothers.

Some he actually made wives and mothers. With his guidance, and his stepmama's enthusiastic assistance, introductions bore fruit, engagements were announced, marriages took place. Viscount Wellstone always received invitations to the receptions—and handsome wedding gifts for himself.

The only flies in the ointment, the ants at his picnic, the dogs in the manger, were those selfsame wives and mothers. Gentlemen trusted him to usher their proper spouses to proper functions, so they were free to conduct thoroughly improper affairs. The gentlemen should not, perhaps, have trusted their wives. Too often Stony found himself expected to accompany a bored young bride straight to her boudoir. Neglected matrons thought he should continue the dance long after the ball was ended. Even the occasional old maid sought a better bed warmer than a hot brick. A few of the more knowing ones hinted at recompense.

Stony resigned those commissions. He might be a paid companion, and the devil take him for it, but he was not a whore. His services were definitely not all for hire.

Despite these few setbacks, or maybe because he showed such scruples, the viscount received more and more requests for his company. His bank account grew, and his fame, if one could consider a knowing wink and a slap on the back to be fame. After the first Season, his club was more of an interviewing office. After the first betrothal, his new appointment calendar saw more entries than White's betting book.

Business was so good, and the male aversion to watered wine, harp recitals, and untouchable virgins so bad, that the following year Stony had to enlist two of his friends as assistants in his endeavor.

The second son of a demanding duke, Lord Charles Hammett was kept on a tight rein. One misstep and his allowance was reduced. Two and he'd be sent to inspect the family holdings in the Americas. Lord Charles suffered both mal de mer and a fear of his domineering parent, so at four and twenty he was a pattern card of respectability. Eventually he would be wed to a girl of his father's choosing, one who could advance the dukedom, of course. Meantime, Charlie was borrowing money from friends to pay his artiste of a tailor. Viscount Wellstone rescued him.

Capt. Daniel Brisbane had been a schoolmate of Stony's. Now he was returned from the army with a permanent limp, no career, and no hope but the salvation found in a bottle. Stony rescued him, too.

What female would not be thrilled with the attentions of a duke's offspring, a retired hero, and a handsome viscount? So what if Captain Brisbane could not dance and was not much for small talk or flattery? So what if Lord Charles was a mere second son with a weak chin and weaker fashion sense? So what if Lord Wellstone was below hatches, and a confirmed bachelor besides? Together they meant a girl always had a presentable partner for supper, an attractive, attentive afternoon caller, an enviable companion to whichever event her father's gout prevented him from attending.

She had an escort.

She was a success.

So was Stony.

Soon he would have Wellstone Park restored to its self-sufficient, income-producing prosperity. Soon he would have enough funds to establish a horse-breeding program, or a small shipyard on the Norfolk coast. Soon he could give Gwen the widow's portion she was due, and pray she used it for a dowry. After one more spring Season, he calculated, he'd be done with debutantes, finished with wallflowers, out of the escort business once and for all. When he reached the age of thirty, he would leave London with no regrets. But first . . .

"What do you mean, you have compromised Earl Patten's daughter?"

Neckcloth untied, coat unbuttoned, Stony was in his study going over the account books one last time before heading to bed and pleasant dreams. Then this nightmare walked in. Captain Brisbane's hand was shaking too much to pour the wine from the decanter on the viscount's desk. Stony took the bottle and filled the glass—then drank it down himself. "Damnation," he said, "you were supposed to dance with the girl, by Zeus, not destroy her reputation!"

The half-pay officer sank into the facing chair without waiting for an invitation. "She said she felt ill. I led her toward an empty room, thinking to go fetch her mother, our hostess, or a maid. Anyone. What did I know about women's ailments? But somehow when we reached the room and I steered her toward the couch, she fell against me. And my bad leg, you know."

"No, I do not know how your bad leg could have ripped her gown, dash it!"

"Well, it collapsed, and we fell to the couch. I tried to grab for the table, only I seem to have caught the lace at her bodice on the button of my coat and there was this awful sound and she screamed, and then her mother and half the guests ran in, and her father, Earl Patten, started shouting. And—"

"And you are betrothed. I wish you well. The lady might be a bit vaporish, but her handsome dowry ought to provide proper medical—"

"No."

Stony shook his head. The brandy could not have addled his wits so quickly. "No . . . what?"

Brisbane studied his shoes. "No, I will not marry the earl's daughter."

"But you're a gentleman, by all that's holy!"

"Who is going to marry the woman I love, on my honor."

"On your honor? Honor demands you marry—What is her name anyway?"

"Lady Valentina Pattendale. That is the family name."

"Right. Well, you have ruined the girl. She'll likely want to be wed on St. Valentine's Day, so you have nearly a year to grow fond of her."

"You do not understand. I love another. I am promised to her."

Stony poured another glass. This time he remembered to pour one for his guest. "And you never thought to mention the young lady to me?"

"What for? I cannot afford to marry her yet, so nothing is official. Her guardian disapproves."

The viscount let out a sigh of relief. "Well, there you have it. No notice in the papers, no ring on her finger. No, you are Lady Valentina's, all right and tight."

"No."

"Deuce take it, someone has to marry the cursed female!" Stony slammed his glass down on the desk.

The captain did not meet Stony's gaze. Silence fell like a shroud. Finally Brisbane said, "The earl is calling on you here in the morning. Or his seconds are."

"Oh, Lord. You'll have to meet him, you know."

"No."

"Gads, man, you cannot keep saying no! Everything that makes us gentlemen demands giving the earl a son-in-law or satisfaction. He is entitled to one or the other, by Harry."

Brisbane stood. He wobbled a bit on his bad leg, but held himself erect with a soldier's discipline. "War taught me how little the gentlemen's code of conduct matters. It taught me the value of life, my own included, and the horror of taking another's. Besides, I do not think the lady was taken ill at all. No, I will not meet Patten on the dueling field. Or the church steps. I am leaving London tonight. I merely came by to warn you, and to offer my regrets."

Regrets? Stony already had enough regrets to last a lifetime—or the few days he had left before Earl Patten put a pistol ball through his heart.

Chapter Two

The earl was apoplectic, understandably. Not only was his daughter ruined by a poor soldier, but Earl Patten had been paying the crippled bastard to keep her safe from fortune-hunters and libertines! To add insult to injury, the penniless, landless, untitled ex-officer refused to marry the girl!

"I don't care if the blackguard is betrothed or back at the front lines. I'll have a husband for my daughter or I'll have my pound of flesh."

The earl's face was turning redder with each pound of his fist on Viscount Wellstone's desk. Luckily the brandy decanter had been emptied long ago, so it could not splash wine on Stony's suddenly empty appointment book. The earl, it seemed, had been at his clubs shouting his displeasure all night. Canceled invitations had been arriving at Wellstone House all morning. Who would trust his womenfolk to such a reprobate? What woman wanted to be seen with a man whose services and smiles were strictly for hire?

Earl Patten had been quite thorough in his castigations. And in his violation of confidentiality. Along with the cancellations, Lord Wellstone had received two of his bouquets tossed on his doorstep, and one slap in the face. Then there were Gwen's tears. A duel was sounding more appealing.

Pistols at dawn were not harsh enough penalty for Stony's sins, it appeared. Patten shook his fist inches from the viscount's nose this time. "You! Why, you are not much better than that lily-livered soldier."

His own honor notwithstanding, Stony had to stand up for his friend. "If you are speaking of Captain Brisbane, he is one of the bravest men I know, following a higher code of honor than either of us will understand. He nearly lost his leg, almost his life, fighting for our country. How can you call him a coward?"

"He ain't here, is he?"

Stony sat down again, farther from Patten's fist and the shower that accompanied the earl's diatribe.

"Pshaw," Patten spit out. Stony reached for his handkerchief, but he'd handed his last one to Gwen. "Be damned if you are any more what I had in mind for a son-in-law than that craven was. A paid paramour, a Fancy Fred, by Jove."

Stony would have protested the epithets—hell, he would have called out any other man using those terms—except he was too relieved to be offended. "You mean I don't have to—"

Too soon.

"Good grief, my daughter will never be able to hold her head up in society. I suppose I can ship the two of you off to India. Or the East Indies. It will break her mother's heart, but better than seeing the gal a laughingstock for the rest of her life. Damn you to hell, Wellstone."

Which marriage to Lady Valentina Pattendale would certainly be. Stony took a deep breath. In contrast to the earl's furious blustering, he spoke in low, even tones. "My, ah, wife and I shall reside at Wellstone Park in Norfolk. The house is in some disrepair, having been standing empty these past years, so I hope your daughter is handy with a needle. And a mop. I'll be busy with the sheep, so I'll expect her to look after the chickens."

Now the blood drained from the earl's face and his mouth hung open. "What? My daughter? A mop?" he sputtered. "Chickens? But her dowry . . ."

"Oh, I would not live off my wife's fortune. It is a matter of honor with me, despite what you might think of my morals. I'd set any of the lady's income aside for our children. We'll want a whole parcel of them, to help on the farm, you know. But do not worry, I hope to come about in a year or two of hard work. Maybe five at the most. Then we can afford to hire more help. If we can get any of the locals to accept employment at the Park, that is. My uncle hanged himself there, if you don't recall the scandal. They say he swings from the chandelier still, but I always thought the motion was caused by the drafts in the hall. I suppose I'll have to see about fixing the windows. Or should repairing the leaking roof come first?" Stony scratched his head, deliberating.

"But . . . but this house . . . ?"

"As you said, London will be less than comfortable for your daughter, now that you have told everyone and his cousin about my, ah, vocation. Besides, I shall have to leave the London house to Gwen, my father's second wife, you know. Unless your daughter would feel more comfortable having her mother-in-law reside with us? I know my stepmama would adore having a daughter to bathe her forehead when she suffers the megrims, as the poor dear does so often."

When Patten started to wheeze and gasp, Stony took pity on the older man. He didn't want the earl expiring on his Aubusson, either. "Perhaps there is another solution to our little dilemma. If you are willing to sit and listen . . . ?"

At this point, Patten would have listened to a castrato chorus singing sea chanteys. He sank onto the seat facing the viscount's and mopped his forehead with his sleeve. The old fool must have given his clean linen to his weeping women, too, Stony thought.

In the end, the matter was resolved peacefully, to everyone's satisfaction, like the gentlemen they were. Lady Valentina's reputation was restored by an enviable betrothal; Earl Patten's honor was redeemed by a respectable alliance; Stony's freedom was secured . . . by sacrificing his other associate in the escort business, Lord Charles Hammett.

Charlie thought it a great joke, wedding a female even his father could approve, without being ordered to do it. If he waited for the duke's choice, he could do a lot worse than Lady Valentina Pattendale. The gal was pretty and lively and well dowered. What more could a second son ask?

The earl was content. So what if the young cub had no chin? His neckcloth was high enough to hide the lack, and who knew how healthy that older brother of his was, after all?

Lady Valentina was delighted. Anyone was better than the Member of Parliament her father was threatening her with if she did not settle on a match this Season. She only wished she'd thought of Lord Charles before setting her sights on that broad-shouldered wounded hero. She could have been spared an uncomfortable night and gone straight to planning her betrothal ball.

Stony told himself he was the happiest of them all, even if his future was the most in doubt. For a brief while he thought he might have to return to the card tables, and low dives at that, after such a disgrace. But he was not exiled from the beau monde, as Gwen had feared, not after accomplishing such a matrimonial coup. On the other hand, with his means of income made public, no young lady trusted his compliments or accepted his invitations. Even the plainest, shyest, doomed-to-spinsterhood misses would rather remain on the sidelines than dance with a man suspected of being paid to do so.

No one was paying him to do anything, anymore. The only ones hinting of doing so were women of a certain age or disposition whose conversations were rife with innuendo, whose bodies brushed against his too often to be accidental encounters. After one such overly familiar contact, Stony discovered a pound note tucked down his waistcoat. He found a handsome footman to return it to the lady, with his compliments. Then he cursed, kicked at a footstool, forgetting he was wearing flimsy dancing slippers, then limped home in the dark, forgetting he was supposed to drive Gwen on to another party.

Hell and damnation, he could not erase the image in his mind of some country bumpkin with food stains on his linen, slipping a coin between the sagging breasts of a sweaty barmaid in a low-cut, faded gown. That was how cheap he felt, how degraded.

Not for the first time he wondered about the lives of prostitutes, women whose only options were to sell their bodies or starve. He should have given that hot-blooded baroness's money to one of those unfortunates. Then the whore might have a choice, at least for a night or a week, or however long it lasted, if she did not spend it all on Blue Ruin, to forget.

Stony put down the fresh bottle of brandy he found on his desk. No, he would not go that tempting route. He had a choice. He'd go to Norfolk, as he'd told Patten. The house was no longer in as bad repair as he'd indicated, nor was it haunted by anything but bad memories of his parents' arguments, his father's drunken carousing. If he could not afford to set up a stud farm, by heaven, he'd learn to shear the bleating sheep himself. He'd learn to knit their blasted wool into tea cozies, if that was what it took. He was his own man, body and soul.

Then he remembered Gwen.

Sweet, silly Gwen deserved better, especially after all the support she had given Stony and his escort service. She loved filled calendars and crowded ballrooms, the latest gossip and the newest fashions. She'd hate the country. But he could not afford to maintain two establishments, much less keep her in the silks and furs and jewels Gwen had every right to, considering that Stony's father had frittered away her marriage settlements. Coming to him as a pretty young bride, she had kept the old man content for his last ten years, and kept him from falling into worse depravities. She was still a pretty female, but now she was nudging forty, about which she lied so effectively that she'd be younger than Stony in a few years. What was to become of her if Stony took up farming?

For that matter, what was to become of her if he was not in attendance at that next party? She had enough friends that she could find her own way to the ball, but what if some aged roué thought Lady Wellstone's services were for hire now, too?

Blast. Before he left to fetch his stepmama home, Stony checked the hall looking glass to make sure his neckcloth was not creased and his hair was not tousled. He'd be damned if he'd go to a dance looking like he was ready for his bed—or fresh from someone else's. He also checked the tray where the mail was placed, hoping against hope for an offer of honest employment, if one could call playing the cavalier for coins an honest occupation. Stony no longer knew if he was any better than an organ grinder's monkey dancing for pennies.

One letter caught his eye from among the bills and Gwen's correspondence. For a moment . . . No, his name and address were written in a feminine script. He tossed the letter back on the pile so fast it almost skidded off the table. With any luck the cursed invitation, or assignation or whatever it was, would fall behind the furniture, never to be seen again.

His luck holding true to form, the letter appeared at the breakfast table, along with the eggs and toast and bills.

Gwen was opening her own mail, exclaiming over

Lady Walsh's first grandchild, Mrs. Mallory's husband's gout, and the come-out ball for Miss Nathania Fisk-Hamilton. Stony was not listening. He was reading. And calculating how much dancing a monkey had to do for one hundred pounds.

"Gwen, do you know a Miss Ellianne Kane?"

Gwen was trying to decipher another of her letters, this one written both down the page, then up, reversed, to save postage. She could barely make out the salutation without resorting to her detested spectacles. "I don't think so, dear. Should I?"

The viscount silently passed her his quizzing glass.

"Thank you, Aubrey, dear. Oh, my. Lady Farnham's daughter has given birth to twin daughters. I thought her husband has been serving with the army on the Peninsula this past year. Or was he the one in the navy? Of course, he may have had leave that no one told me about. . . ."

Stony took back the magnifying lens. "Gwen."

"Yes, dear? What was that you were saying?"

"A Miss Kane has written to request my escort about Town for her and her aunt." The reassuring, respectable reference to an aunt had kept Stony reading.

Gwen rotated the page of her own correspondence, trying to make out another line. Frustrated, she set it aside until she was in her own chamber, with no one to see her wearing glasses. She started to butter a slice of toast sparingly, ever mindful of her figure. "I don't suppose the woman heard about . . . But she must have, to write to you so openly. Although no one in polite society would have put it so boldly." Gwen set the knife down, her forehead creased by a frown that she quickly erased lest it leave a permanent line. "Oh, dear. She must be a dowdy, rag-mannered, provincial miss thinking you can find her an eligible *parti*. With our own credibility somewhat diminished, we might not . . . That is, perhaps you should not accept such a forward, encroaching kind of girl, although you have been worried about—"

Stony interrupted, as he had learned to do when his stepmama was thinking aloud. "She sent me a bank draft for a hundred pounds, in advance."

"Why, how lovely. I am quite looking forward to meeting dear Miss Crane. I am certain we can do something for the poor girl, unless she is terribly ineligible. But how ineligible could she be if she has a hundred pounds to hire a . . . Um. And I suppose I must not refer to her as poor, if she—"

"That is Miss Ellianne Kane, not Crane, and the hundred-pound check is drawn on Kane Bank, in Devon."

Gwen forgot all about her figure in light of the figure Stony named. She reached for a sweet roll instead of the dry toast. "That Miss Kane! Why did you not say so! Oh, my. She has to be one of the wealthiest heiresses in all of England, if she is Ellis Kane's elder daughter. She must be, if she is named Ellianne, wouldn't you think? Such a pretty name; she must be quite attractive. Whoever heard of an ugly heiress, anyway? I swear I never have, although that Lady Frederica Sniddon who came out the year I wed your father did bear an unfortunate resemblance to her own lapdog, but—"

"But you do not truly know anything about her? Miss Kane, that is, not that other female."

Gwen looked affronted. She knew something about everyone who was anyone. Miss Ellianne Kane was someone. "Now that I think of it, there was another Kane girl in town not so long ago. Isabelle, I think her name was. Or Annabelle? No, Annabelle was the mother, Lady Annabelle Chansford she had been, the daughter of the Marquess of Chaston. I do believe that to be so, although she was before my time, of course."

"How much before?" Stony was trying to gauge the woman's age, and thus the daughter's.

Gwen waved her hand in the air. "Oh, ages."

Which meant, Stony understood, that Lady Annabelle could not be all that many years older than his stepmama. The daughter must still be a young woman.

Gwen hurried on before he could ask her to be more specific. "They say it caused quite a stir when Lady Annabelle ran off with a banker's son. The families became estranged. The younger Kane daughter—I am fairly certain it was Isabelle—was staying this winter with Lady Augusta Chansford, however. Lady Augusta was Lady Annabelle's spinster sister, so they must have reconciled, don't you think?"

She did not wait to hear Stony's opinion. "They must have, for Lady Augusta was not one to take in strays, you know. A squeezecrab," she added, whispering as if watching one's pennies were a sin. "Your young lady must be another of the nieces, so you need not worry on that score. About her being a social-climbing mushroom, that is."

Toadstools were the least of Stony's worries. What he had to do to earn that hundred pounds was of far more concern.

"Lady Augusta might have been a nipfarthing," Gwen went on after taking a nibble of her roll, despite Stony's impatience, "but she was good *ton*. Kane was nothing but a Cit, of course. Except he *was* knighted. Not that it would matter, with all his—"

" 'Was'?"

While Stony tapped his fingers on the table, Gwen had to take a sip of her sugared tea. And another bite of a sweet roll that was not half as sweet as the smile she wore, thinking of Ellis Kane's fortune.

"He was?" Stony repeated, interrupting her daydreams.

"What's that, Aubrey? Oh, yes. Ellis Kane. He was knighted some years ago for his service to the Crown. He must have paid some of Prinny's debts or something. That's the only way a man of his upbringing could be elevated, I suppose, if he wasn't a war hero. Money works miracles," she added, as if Stony did not know.

He sighed. "I meant, you said Ellis Kane *was* a Cit, that Miss Kane *was* an heiress, Lady Augusta *was* good *ton.* Sir Ellis Kane is dead, then?"

"Oh, yes, he died some years ago. And the mother well before that, too. Lady Augusta passed on just last month. It was the same week as that little difficulty with Lady Valentina, so I did not pay her final departure much mind. She had been ailing for some months, now that I recall, which might explain why we never saw the younger Kane girl about. The funeral must have been in the country, for I do not remember mention of it in the newspapers, although they hardly mentioned anything but the Pattendale problem. Do you remember it?"

Stony did not make a habit of reading the obituaries. Or the *on dits* columns. He shrugged and picked up the letter once more.

Gwen was all smiles again, as if they were not speaking of a whole family's demise. "Just think, those poor dear girls are all alone in the world. Except for us, of course."

"The letter did not mention anything about a sister."

"Perhaps Miss Isabelle stayed in the country after the funeral, grief-stricken, although I cannot imagine who could mourn that old . . . Hmm, I wonder if the girls inherited Lady Augusta's town house. I cannot recall any other relations visiting with her. The rest of the Chansfords, the current marquess and his family, never come to Town. Yorkshire, I believe. Or perhaps Berkshire? Unless it is part of the marquess's holdings. Now that would be a shame. For Miss Kane, of course."

Stony reread the few brief, neatly inscribed lines of the page in his hand. "Miss Kane requests that I call on her at Number Ten Sloane Street." It sounded more like an order to him, couched in terms of minimal courtesy.

Gwen clapped her hands. "That is Lady Augusta's direction. I was invited there once for tea. The most meager spread you can imagine. Why, I had to stop at Gunter's on the way home, I was so hungry."

Stony cleared his throat.

"What? Are you waiting for me to pass the— Oh, you want to know more about Miss Kane. Well, if she did inherit the house, which she might have done, being the eldest niece, it is a very neat residence indeed. Very nicely kept, too, despite all the tales of Lady Augusta's miserliness. If she is taking up residence in the house, your Miss Kane must have inherited Lady Augusta's fortune, too, which should be considerable, since the woman kept every cent she ever came by. Unless she found a way to take it with—"

"She is not my Miss Kane."

Gwen anxiously added another lump of sugar to her tea. "But you will call on her as she requested?" And another lump. "Won't you?"

"Then you think I should consider accepting Miss Kane's check? Fending off the fortune-hunters might prove difficult if what you say is true, but if the chit is at all presentable, it should not be too hard a piece of work to get her fired off."

Gwen took a sip of her tea, then set it aside with a grimace. Stony started to pour her a fresh cup as she answered, "No, dear, I do not think you should become Miss Kane's paid escort. I think you should marry her."

The tea landed in his lap.

Chapter Three

Thunderation!" the viscount yelled, jumping up and grabbing for an extra napkin. "That is not funny, Gwen."

"I am not joking. That letter and the Kane heiress just might be opportunity knocking."

"Opportunity has knocked many times, and I have never yet opened that particular door. I see no reason to do so now, no matter how much gold waits on the other side."

"Well, I see a great many reasons not to let Miss Kane slip through your fingers. You are nearly thirty and not getting any younger, for one thing."

"That is two things. I am barely nine and twenty, and only you seem to have discovered the knack of subtracting years from your age instead of adding them."

"We are not discussing my age, thank you. Not at the breakfast table. But you . . . you have to marry eventually anyway."

"I do?"

"Of course, as you well know, dearest. You have not been working so hard to restore Wellstone Park just so the Crown might claim it when you die with no male heirs. Why, you do not even have a distant cousin with any kind of claim. Not a prolific lot, the Wellstone ancestors, were they? At any rate, the only way to beget those heirs—legitimate ones, I will have you know—is by marrying a proper young woman. Of course, there was that lord who claimed his dead brother's son as his heir when everyone knew the boy was his, but that is another story."

For once Stony did not mind Gwen's digressions. She could have repeated every tale of every bastard born, with his blessings. Damn if she did not get straight back on course, though.

"And since you need to marry sooner or later," she persisted, "why not sooner, as Lord Charles decided to do?"

"Charlie had other reasons for his betrothal, spiting his father being first among them. I have no such compunctions to wed for the sake of convenience."

"No such compunctions? What do you call a broken-down estate and all of those who depend on it for their livelihoods? Or that shipyard you speak of building, to make jobs? Or that home for unwed mothers I know you support, even while you preach economy to me? Why, we have not opened the guest rooms here in ages. I am still mortified to think of my cousin and his wife putting up at a hotel when we have—"

"I shall not marry a woman for her money. Not ever."

"Fine, then you will marry for love, although I never supposed you to have a romantic bent like one of those poets. But, Aubrey, dearest, you have been squiring females of all types and temperaments for the past three years at least. Beautiful, intelligent, and talented girls among them . . . to say nothing of their dowries, which any sane man has to consider. Not even you could be such a nodcock as to ignore a bride's portion. Could you? No, do not answer that."

He did not, pretending to inspect his trousers for tea

stains. Gwen went on: "Not a one of those females has caught your fancy. If you do not choose a bride soon you are liable to settle into a lonely old bachelorhood. Or else you'll wait till you are quite old, then marry a girl barely out of the schoolroom, as your father did the second time, making a May game of his dignity."

"Marrying you was the best thing my father ever did, and no one ever teased him over his beautiful young bride. All his friends were too envious."

Gwen blushed and said, "Thank you. You always know just what to say, dear. Except for now. Say you will consider Miss Kane."

"I am considering her. And her offer of employment."

"Bah! Haven't you been listening? You need to marry, not be matchmaking for another desperate miss."

"What, is Miss Kane such an antidote, then, that she has to purchase a husband?"

"Of course not! For all we know she might already be betrothed, or promised to one of her father's wealthy partners. Or she might be waiting to fall in love with the perfect gentleman. You."

Stony made a rude noise. "Oh, I am fairly certain she is not on the lookout for a pockets-to-let peer."

"Oh? And if you are so certain you know what Miss Kane is seeking, perhaps you might tell me just what the . . . the devil you are looking for in a wife?"

Stony was walking from the sideboard—without making a selection from the covered dishes—to the window, without noticing the sun breaking through the morning clouds and fog. "I do not know, but I will recognize it when I see it."

"Rubbish. That is like your father saying he could recognize a winner from the horses in the paddock. He never could, you know. Of course you know, having been paying off his debts for years. And do stop pacing, dear. You are making me lose my appetite."

His was long gone. "I am not pacing. I am drying

my trousers. By the way, don't you have anything better to do this morning? A dress fitting or a book to return to the lending library? Perhaps you need to consult with your maid about a new wrinkle cream. I thought I saw a—"

"Oh, no! Where?" She tried to see her reflection in the silver teapot.

"I was merely teasing, Gwen. You are as beautiful as ever."

She sighed in relief. "Wrinkles or not, nothing is as important to me as seeing to the future of my late husband's son. I vowed that I would."

"What, you promised my father to look after me?" He had to laugh. "The old rip made me swear to take care of you."

"As you have." Gwen nodded regally, or as regally as she could with her hair still tied in curl papers. "And now I am trying to do my part to ensure your happiness."

"Do you really think that Miss Kane, a woman neither of us has ever met, will ensure my happiness?"

"Why not? You wouldn't have to fret over money, and you could have that horse farm at last. You could travel or collect paintings or fund a hundred charity homes. Anything you want, and you would not have to do what you do not want."

That last sounded the most tempting: no more harp recitals, no more bowing to the bitches who ruled Almack's, no more juggling the household accounts between candles and coal. Still, he could not. He shook his head. "I will not live off my wife's money."

Gwen was losing patience—and politeness. "Well, living off your wits has not filled your coffers, and living off your charm seems to have reached its limits." She gasped when she saw the white line around his mouth. "Oh, I am sorry, Aubrey. I never should have said such hateful things, especially when you have worked so hard to keep this roof over our heads. And I am sure I have not helped, with my expensive dresser and that new bonnet I simply had to have. And the—"

"Dash it, Gwen, I have never begrudged you your fripperies. And I am well aware how an advantageous alliance could brighten my life and yours. But, by Jupiter, I do not want a marriage like my parents'. They could barely tolerate each other in their perfectly suitable union."

"Yes, but their match was arranged. Yours will be by your own choice. And Miss Kane's, of course. You would know long before the betrothal whether you could rub along well together. You might even find that you like her."

"Next you will be recounting how much we have in common. Nonsense! Miss Kane is a provincial heiress, a financier's daughter with no social graces, as evidenced by her letter and the fact that she needs to hire a gentleman companion. And I? I am a scattergood viscount's wastrel son, a Town beau with nothing to recommend him except what you call a degree of charm, and his prowess on the dance floor."

"Nothing but the most handsome visage in all the *ton*."

"You forgot your spectacles again, goose."

"I do not forget your gentle kindness, and your lovely blue eyes, and that devastating dimple. Why, I doubt any female could resist your smile. Miss Kane will fall in love with you in an instant, with the least encouragement."

"A wealthy heiress, smitten by a smile? You have been reading far too many Minerva Press novels, Gwen. And even if she did happen to topple into love with my baby blue eyes"—not even Gwen could miss the scorn in his voice—"her trustees would never let Miss Kane throw herself and her fortune away on a ramshackle gentleman of little repute or regard."

"Well, you are far out there. No one but Earl Patten ever had anything but the highest praise for you, and he came about. And do not dismiss the viscountcy as a mere bauble hanging off your waistcoat pocket. A girl with more than enough money but no entrée to higher social circles just might wish to elevate her standing. I doubt there are any unattached earls half so handsome, nor any marquesses with your sense of honor. As for the royal dukes, the less said the better."

"What, Miss Kane has gone from a silly chit whose head can be turned with a smile to a greedy, grasping social climber? Either way, she sounds unappealing."

"She sounds like a practical woman to me!" Gwen insisted. "Females are raised to make good marriages, not find grand passions. A thrilling lover might make a girl's toes curl, but she needs her feet firmly on the ground to find a responsible provider, a companion in her old age, a decent father to her children. My grandchildren." Gwen's eyes filled with tears. "You would be a good husband for Miss Kane. I know it. No one could not love you," she added with a stepmother's prejudice and a sniffle.

Lord, she wasn't going to start crying, was she? Stony handed her his handkerchief and a new subject as quickly as he could. "What about you, Gwen? Why haven't you found a new husband? I know any number of decent chaps would have been happy to take you off my—that is, to take you to wife, with or without any kind of dowry."

Gwen stopped crying instantly. "There were quite a few, weren't there?" she asked with pride in her voice.

"Yes, and you made me refuse all of the ones who approached me. Heaven knows how many asked you directly. Why?"

"I suppose because they thought you were too young to be head of the family, or I was too old to need a guardian's permission."

Stony rubbed at his aching temples. "No, I mean why have you refused so many respectable offers? Any of those men could have provided for you far better than I can. Lud knows, better than my father did. If, as you say, women are taught to be practical, you must have realized you could have had comfort and security and all the luxuries you deserve. Endless parties, summers in Brighton, a wardrobe full of new frocks. You might have had children of your own."

"I did try with your father, you know," she said with a blush. "We tried very hard, in fact."

"Yes, but another man, a younger one . . . Never mind." Some things he was not prepared to discuss with his stepmama, especially when she looked like a mere girl with her brown hair up in curl papers and pink ribbons flowing from her robe. She was more a sister to him—a younger sister, at that—than anything else. He would have wanted a better life for his sister, too. "You could have become a famous hostess, instead of having to tell your cousins to put up at a hotel."

"Oh, but I could not leave you, Aubrey. You would have retired to the country with your horses and your sheep and your account books. You'd have become a hermit, forgetting how to be gay. Then one day you would realize you were all alone, and you would have married a milkmaid or a shepherdess. I could not let you do that, could I?"

Gwen wouldn't accept another husband because she would not abandon Stony, and here he'd stayed in London because he couldn't abandon his father's wife. How absurd, Stony thought, and how typical of tenderhearted Gwen. But what if she had truly cared for one of her suitors but had remained a widow for his sake? Devil take it, he felt guilty enough not providing her with jewels and furs. Had he kept her from finding her heart's content?

He stepped closer, took up her hand and squeezed it, then tilted her chin so she had to look up at him. "Tell me truly, Gwen, was there a gentleman you would have accepted if you were free to choose? One whom you regret turning down?" If the fellow wasn't already married, Stony would have him on his knees in Gwen's parlor before the gudgeon knew what happened to him. "One that you could love?"

She patted his cheek, then frowned, for he had not shaved yet. "Silly boy, you must know I would have seen you married by hook or by crook if I had found a gentleman I was that desperatc to wed. But no, I never met a man I liked half as well as your father."

"What, an old reprobate who gambled away your dowry, as well as my mother's and his own inheritance, on horses and the Exchange and every mad scheme that came along? He left you with nothing."

"He left me with you. And he was so good to me for the years we had together. I did not have to marry him, you know. My parents were not very well off, but they were not pushing me to make a match that Season. No, I chose your father for myself, and I never regretted that decision. I know we were irresponsible with the money that should have come to you, but we had such good times until . . ."

Stony reached for his handkerchief before he realized he'd already given it to her. He usually carried two, for such emergencies, but was not fully dressed yet.

"You are very much like him, you know," Gwen said, dabbing at her eyes.

Stony leaped back, stung. "I am?"

"Yes, you have the same ability to make whatever woman you are with feel like the only woman you wish to be with, if that makes sense."

It did, after a moment. "But he meant it. Father didn't need a young bride. He already had an heir, and he had his wom— That is, he was not bored or lonely. He truly loved you."

"I know. That's why none of those other gentlemen measured up. And that is what I was always waiting for you to find with your next dance partner, the next pretty passenger in your curricle."

"The next heiress?"

"Why not?"

* * *

Why not? Because he already disliked the woman, sight unseen. Her manner was brusque and authoritative, as though she were used to having her every command obeyed on the instant. Arrogance, that was what Stony deduced from Miss Kane's short note, and arrogance was his least favorite trait in a female. Why, the very brevity of the message was somehow condescending, as if she were too busy with matters of more serious concern to be bothered with a mere paid companion.

Lord Wellstone, it began, without a courtesy salutation. That lack alone spoke more than any words could have.

I wish to engage your services to escort my aunt and myself about London. Well, that was to the point. Trust a banker's daughter to get to the bottom line in a hurry. The woman obviously did not believe in subtlety, veiling her request in pretenses of prior friendship or mutual acquaintanceship or some such to preserve his pride. Obviously his dignity held no place in her reckoning.

Worse, she had included a handsome fee, as if he'd already accepted. Or would not think of refusing. Or could not. The research she must have done to discover his name and the nature of his services might also have uncovered his financial difficulties. Lud, for all Stony knew, Miss Kane had a complete accounting of his bank statements, as a favor from one banking establishment to another. Then again, the servants' grapevine might have been enough to reveal his so-called profession and his so-real insolvency. Damn.

Please call at Number Ten Sloane Street as soon as possible. At least she had written *please,* so the female was not entirely without manners. She had not, however, mentioned his earliest convenience, an invitation to tea, or the possibility of his declining. She was hiring a blasted servant, by God, and saw no reason to be polite.

Unless she spoke to all men that way, Stony speculated. Perhaps the heiress was so accustomed to toad-eaters and fortune-hunters that she despised the entire male species. That was it, he decided. Miss Kane had to be one of those starched up females who thought all men were swine, good only to serve as obedient butlers and strong-backed blacksmiths. The only reason she was not content to have a footman shadow her on her sightseeing and shopping excursions was that no footman, no mere servant, no matter how bent on catering to her every wish, could get her access to the exclusive entertainments of the London social Season.

With the aunt dead, the banker's daughter had no one to make her known to the important hostesses, no one to seek vouchers to Almack's exclusive Wednesday assemblies for her. With the stink of trade fumigated by her father's knighthood, masked by the marquessate connection, and perfumed by a fortune, Miss Kane could be accepted by all but the highest sticklers—with the proper introductions. Without them, she could never get to look over the latest crop of highborn bachelors, if she was indeed husband hunting.

The aunt had never married, and this female, if Gwen's information was correct, had even more brass at her fingertips, therefore less need to put herself under some gentleman's thumb. Stony could not picture the author of this note taking her place as the demure bride of some overbearing boor.

Yet why else would the woman come to London? If her reasons were legal or financial, to do with her aunt's estate, say, her man of business would be ample attendant. Fashions? She could have the finest dressmaker in the kingdom come to her. The opera? The theater? Possibly, and both of those venues truly were more comfortable with a gentleman escort. But a countrywoman craving culture? Stony doubted it. No, Miss Coin must be shopping the marriage mart, likely looking for the highest title, connected to the weakest backbone.

He went back to the letter.

Yrs., she signed the note.

His?

Hah!

Chapter Four

All of Stony's theories about Miss Kane, he acknowledged, were no more than idle speculation. And a way to avoid actually calling on the woman.

He even convinced himself that he had to do more research before accepting this prospective employer, that his antipathy toward her was merely a product of his resentment at his own situation. He hated being dependent on the whims of anyone, man or woman. A woman at the reins was worse, he admitted to himself, but he should not hold that against Miss Kane.

He could not convince himself to look forward to meeting her, no matter how he tried. No, what he actually, honestly felt was that the woman was too deuced sure of herself. She could dashed well wait another day before he dutifully presented himself in her drawing room. Unless she expected him to use the trade entrance. He would use the time to gather information, as she seemed to have done about him.

The lending library might have stacks of reference books, but the best, most reliable knowledge, he knew, was to be found at pubs patronized by servants, smoking rooms frequented by gentlemen, and anywhere three or more females congregated. Stony sent his valet off to the taverns, and accompanied Gwen to the latest ball honoring Sir Charles and his newly affianced bride, Lady Valentina Pattendale.

Before getting down to the serious business of playing at detective, Stony had to dance with the guest of honor. Gwen insisted he had to partner Lady Valentina, and look like he was enjoying himself, to boot, to put an end to any gossip about her betrothal. His own reputation could be polished up a bit too, she claimed, by showing no hard feelings or ill will.

Stony did not have to feign his pleasure as Charlie's rosy-cheeked intended giggled and gurgled her way through the contra dance they shared. The chit was a lively, bouncy, cheery sort, one who would make Charlie a merry partner as they danced through life together.

Lady Val, as she asked Stony to call her, danced quickly, talked quickly, and was quick to hasten her marriage.

"I would not wish to move the date so far earlier that anyone will question the hurry, you understand, but as soon as can decently be."

Stony understood perfectly. Odd, but he had never thought of weak-chinned Lord Charles as one to inspire burning, yearning need in a young girl's breast. Charlie did not, or at least Lady Valentina did not confide such intimate itches to Stony, thank goodness. No, the conniving wench was trying to persuade her parents to an earlier wedding date for another reason altogether.

"Then I can put off these insipid whites and pastels considered de rigueur for maidens. Charlie is going to help pick out my trousseau." She grinned over at Lord Charles, who was beaming at them from the sidelines.

Charlie was wearing yellow pantaloons with red heeled slippers. He had on a green waistcoat embroidered with at least a flock of hummingbirds, and a wasp-waisted green coat the color of spinach. Ah, a match made in haberdasher's heaven!

Stony left the ballroom with the famous Wellstone smile on his handsome face. One young miss swooned to think the smile was for her. One older woman almost ripped her gown, tugging the bodice lower in case it might be. The viscount did not notice either of them. He was smiling simply out of happiness. He was happy that he had not consigned his friend to a lifetime of misery with a designing minx. He was happier even that he was not the one wedding the artful bit of . . . aristocracy. What made him really smile, though, was that he could now take himself off to pursue his own pleasures. With no obligation of employment, no commitments to partner the unpopular, and his duty dance finished, he was free to leave the ballroom.

When—if—he accepted Miss Kane's offer, he would be at her beck and call. Tonight he was off duty. Free. No more suffering the stifling heat, the overpowering perfumes, the jostling, or the jigs and reels. He could spend the rest of the evening, until Gwen was ready to leave, propping up a pillar, watching the other capering fellows make fools of themselves. Or he could stand by the refreshments table eating all the lobster patties and drinking himself insensible. He could blow a cloud or bet on the sex of Charlie's first child, or lose his pocket money at cards. He could even wait for a waltz and a willing widow.

By George, he could leave the carriage for Gwen and go visit that new house of accommodation, or the Green Room, or a gaming hell with dainty, available dealers. Instead of having a woman, he could go to his club and listen to gentlemen talk of politics, the military, and having a woman.

Somehow, none of those pastimes appealed to Stony. A good book and his own fireside sounded far more inviting. Perhaps he was getting old, as Gwen had hinted. Maybe he *should* settle down, before he settled into his dotage, too ancient to dance at his own wedding. He'd think about it, Stony resolved, as soon as he was through thinking about the Kane affair.

He wandered to the room set aside for gaming, but did not take a seat at any of the card tables. Once he had given up wagering for a living, games of chance did not interest him at all. Instead he walked around, a drink in his hand, chatting with various friends and acquaintances, laughing over Charlie's plunge into parson's mousetrap, the way bachelors were wont to do, as if their own time would never come.

Every once in a while, he asked one or another gentleman if he knew anything about the Chansford residence on Sloane Street. With Lady Augusta gone, he said, he was wondering if the place was for sale or to let, for those cousins of Gwen's.

He found out about three other houses recently come on the market, the names of two reputable land agents, one shabster to avoid, and the address of Lady Augusta's man of affairs. Other than that, not much information was to be had.

One of the cardplayers, Godfrey Blanchard, did guess that the niece must have inherited the place.

Stony sipped at his drink. "Oh? I never met any of Lady Augusta's nieces. I thought I knew most of the young females in Town."

Blanchard laughed as he waited for the next hand to be dealt. "I don't know about any others, but you sure as Hades wouldn't have known this one. Lady Augusta kept the chit as close as bark on a tree. Afraid of the likes of you and me, I suppose."

Blanchard's pockets were emptier than Stony's. The only reason he managed to remain in Town was that his family would rather pay to keep him there than have him at home. He tossed some chips across the table and said, "I think the chit's hand was already promised to someone, anyway. At least that's what the old cheeseparer's housekeeper told my landlady, explaining why she wasn't giving the girl a proper presentation. Too cheap, more likely, to foot the expense."

"Any idea who the lucky chap might be?"

Blanchard shrugged. "Never heard. At any rate, the old lady grew too sickly to take the gal around much. Then she stuck her spoon in the wall."

"I heard there was some question about that, too."

One of the other men at the table answered as he shuffled the deck. "The magistrate looked into it, as I recall. But he decided that since Lady Augusta was ailing, it did not matter if she hit her head and her heart stopped, or if she hit her head because her heart gave out. No one cared much either way, I suppose."

"The niece must have cared."

The dealer did not answer, and Blanchard shrugged again and turned his attention to his new cards. If an heiress was out of bounds or out of reach, she was of no interest to him. A good hand was.

Stony waited through the deal to see if anyone remembered anything further. When the play paused again, he started to leave, but Blanchard called him back. "Hold a minute, Wellstone. All this interest in the house and the heiress . . . You haven't heard anything I should know, have you?"

Stony was not about to toss Miss Kane to the wolves, no matter what he felt about the woman. Blanchard and his oily ilk were too hungry, too quick to slaver over a tender morsel. They were just the kind of scoundrels Stony steered away from the young misses in his care, when he had young lambs—ladies—to shepherd about. He waved a casual farewell. "No, nothing you should know, I am sure, Blanchard. It was just something I recently read."

Gwen learned nothing Stony did not already know, to her chagrin. Stony's valet was nearly as unhelpful. A closemouthed household was the Sloane Street residence, he reported, with mostly female servants, as befitted a single gentlewoman's establishment. Most had found new employment since the mistress's demise. There was no valet for Stony's man to chat with, naturally, and the old butler was said to be an odd chap who kept to himself since Lady Augusta's passing. He should have been pensioned off, the neighboring servants all agreed, resentful on his—and their futures'—behalf. But old Lady Lickpenny must have died the way she lived, hoarding every shilling.

Stony's valet had also found out that Miss Isabelle Kane had left the Sloane Street dwelling on the very night her aunt's body was discovered, which fact led to a lot of conjecture on the servants' part. Time, not the coroner's jury's ruling of death by natural causes, slowed the flood of gossip to a trickle. Oh, and Blanchard's man admitted that Lady Augusta's door had been slammed in the gambler's face when he tried to call there.

Neither Gwen's coterie of gabble-grinders nor the servants' grapevine had heard so much as a whisper of Miss Ellianne Kane's arrival in the metropolis.

Well, she was here now, and waiting for Stony to call. He had used all the delaying tactics he could think of by the next afternoon: exercising his gelding, then needing a bath; leaving his card of thanks at last night's hostess's door, and a posy at Lady Valentina's; sending a letter to his bailiff at Wellstone Park, and another to a schoolmate he had not seen in ten years; shaving again, closer, which meant tying a fresh neckcloth; selecting a bouquet of flowers to bring so he did not arrive like an applicant for a position, then putting back half the blooms so he did not look like a suitor; deciding which one of the extras he should wear in his buttonhole.

Oh, he could have wasted another whole day deliberating if he should send a note around first, if he should ride, drive, or walk, or if he should take Gwen along. He would gladly have sent Gwen alone, if he could have, which would have been everything proper, one gentlewoman welcoming another to the city. Unfortunately, Miss Kane was not precisely a lady born—and Gwen was too liable to have him in leg shackles before he could say Jack Rabbit.

Stony had to go. He had to accept the heiress's offer. That one hundred pounds had one hundred good uses.

He hated the necessity, all hundred of them, and was growing to hate Miss Kane, too, knowing that she knew that he had to accept her terms.

Stony swallowed his pride and, hat in hand along with the bouquet, he set off to see how he might serve Miss Ellianne Kane. His only consolation was that his hat was a fine curly-brimmed beaver, not a little red cap with bells on it like the organ-grinder's monkey wore. He was dancing to her tune, but doing it as a gentleman, by Jupiter.

The stooped butler who opened the door at Number Ten Sloane Street was so frail that Stony feared the weight of his beaver hat would topple the old relic. The ancient retainer certainly should have been retired, and Stony's contempt for Miss Kane grew at the omission. The aunt might have been a miser, or she might have gone on to her reward before she could reward her loyal servitors, but Miss Kane ought to know better. She ought to act better. A true gentlewoman, titled or otherwise, would have.

The old fellow seemed to know his business, however, carefully placing Stony's hat and gloves on a well-polished table and holding out his trembling hand for Stony's card. His powdered wig and black suit and white gloves were as proper as any majordomo's in Mayfair. He bowed over the coin Stony proffered with as much punctilio as any of the prince's staff, if one ignored the slight wheeze and groan as he straightened.

Then he drew a pair of thick-lensed spectacles from his coat pocket. Even with the glasses he had a hard time reading the small calling card.

"Aubrey, Viscount Wellstone," Stony said to save the man the effort and the embarrassment, "to see Miss Ellianne Kane. She is expecting me to call."

Timms, as the butler introduced himself, placed his spectacles on the hall table, missing by mere inches. He smiled when Stony bent to pick them up, showing a perfect pair of gleaming dentures. Then he stiffened his spine, which took years off his age, making him seem a mere ninety, instead of one hundred. He stared over Stony's left shoulder and started praising the Lord. Not Lord Wellstone, but the Lord.

"Ah, our prayers are answered. Thank you, thank you on high. Your blessing has arrived."

Stony looked around. High or low, he and Timms were the only ones in the marble-tiled hallway.

Timms noticed. "Ah, but He is everywhere. His grace knows no boundaries. His mysteries and goodness are equal."

"He?"

"The Almighty, of course, who saw fit to bring you into our lives at our time of need and despair."

Almighty gods, were they so religious here? No wonder the woman had not been seen at the opera or at card parties, if such were the case. Hell, she would never find a husband if she were Bible-bound. Sunday morning sobriety was about all the lip service the *ton* paid to piety.

"May He shine His light down on your shoulders. May His infinite wisdom guide you on the path to righteousness. May—"

"May I see Miss Kane?" Stony asked in a hurry, praying—well, not literally, as Timms seemed to be doing—that the woman was no zealot. He'd rather waltz a wallflower around Almack's than ferry a fanatic to every church in London. He'd be damned if he got down on his . . . That is, he'd be darned if his trousers' knees needed darning again.

The butler placed his card on a small silver salver. "If you would be so good as to wait here, my lord, I shall see if Miss Kane is receiving." Timms turned, but could not resist a parting "God bless you" on his way.

Stony had not sneezed, but his breathing was definitely obstructed.

He took the opportunity to look about him. Lady Augusta had not stinted on her own comfort, it appeared. The entry was elegant, with expensive furnishings gleaming with polish. One table held a priceless Oriental urn filled with so many exotic blooms that his own floral offering looked like a handful of wayside wildflowers. Two small portraits that Stony would love to have examined closer hung beside an exquisite—and undoubtedly expensive—marble statue of Apollo, a naked Apollo. No puritanism here, then, Stony was relieved to see.

He was about to reach for his looking glass to identify which Old Master had painted the portraits, when he heard Timms's slow, stately tread coming back down the hall. Actually, the tread was slower than it was stately, with a shuffle here and there, and a pause to rest against the carved newel post at the foot of the stairs.

Stony heard another noise coming from that direction, too. At first he could not make out the words; then he could not believe the words.

"Numb-nuts nobility, I say. Numb-nuts nobility."

The butler's hearing must have been better than his eyesight, for spots of color appeared on his gaunt cheeks. "Pardon, my lord. It is the, ah, parrot. Yes, the parrot. No telling what they will say, eh? All God's creatures, you know."

Timms looked like he would cheerfully strangle that particular evidence of the Creator's sense of humor, but he did say, "Do follow me, my lord, this way."

Stony did not shuffle, but he walked as slowly as Timms, like a tired old man, or like a condemned convict walking toward the gibbet.

Chapter Five

"Aubrey, Viscount Wellstone."

Stony could not recall when he had been announced with such solemn, heartfelt fervor.

"Oh, botheration, Timms. I told you to wait. I still have glue on my fingers."

Stony could not recall when he had been greeted so rudely. He would have backed out of the small, sunny parlor, to wait on the lady's convenience, but Timms had shut the door at his back. He took a few steps into the room, waiting for his eyes to grow accustomed to the light. "Miss Kane?" he asked, addressing the woman who was scrubbing at her hands with a handkerchief.

She was tall and thin, of indeterminate age. Hell, he thought, she would have been of indeterminate gender under all the yards of black that shrouded her from her bony neck to her narrow feet. What looked like a black lace sack covered her head and her hair, and was tied under a pointed chin. He'd forgotten she was in mourning, but this was beyond proper grieving for a mere aunt. How the devil did Miss Kane expect to attract a gentleman while she looked like a crow—or a corpse?

She bobbed a slight curtsy without looking up from her scrubbing. "I am sorry I cannot offer my hand." She raised her right one. The handkerchief was stuck to it. Despite that, she gestured toward a spindly ladies' desk in the corner. "I am trying to make some order out of things here."

He looked toward the desk and saw that she had been affixing small pieces of paper to a larger one. From where Stony stood, her project made no sense. He doubted it made sense at any distance.

As he looked, he noticed another woman sitting in the other far corner. This one was definitely old, also black-clad, with a black scowl on her face. She had an embroidery frame in front of her and kept right on jabbing her needle into the fabric, pulling it out, jabbing it in. This must be the aunt who accompanied the heiress to Town.

Stony looked back at Miss Kane, one blond eyebrow raised as he waited to be made known to the older woman.

"Oh, of course. Please forgive my manners."

Stony was relieved to discover she had any.

Miss Kane fluttered her hand, free now of the clinging linen. She rushed through the introduction. "My aunt Lally, that is, Mrs. Lavinia Goudge. Lord Wellstone."

Stony bowed and stepped closer, expecting the aunt to offer her fingers for him to salute. The needle went in. The needle came out.

"My aunt, um, does not speak," said Miss Kane, pouring water from a pitcher on the desk onto the handkerchief.

"She is mute?"

"Drat." Now the handle of the pitcher seemed stuck to Miss Kane's hand. "What's that? Mute? Oh, no. She has, um, taken a vow of silence."

Good grief, they were Papists after all. That enveloping black must be some sort of habit, then. Miss Kane was taking herself, her fortune, and her sticky fingers to a nunnery. The fortune would be missed. "Which, ah, religious order does she follow?" Stony asked out of politeness.

"Religion? That is Timmy's new hobby. Aunt does needlework. She just, um, took her vow in memory of her beloved husband. She spoke unkindly to the dear captain before his ship sailed. He never returned."

Stony nodded in the widow's direction. She appeared to be choking back tears. "My condolences, ma'am. But a sea captain. That would explain the parrot."

"The parrot?"

Miss Kane was looking at Stony as if he were queer in the attic. Hah! That was the kettle calling the pot black if he ever heard it. "Your butler said the distasteful language I heard was from—"

"You heard . . . ? Oh, that parrot. We, um, put it away when guests call. In a closet. With a blanket over the cage. Polly is not fit for company, you see."

Mrs. Goudge was choking again, most likely at the reminder of her lost sailor. Stony wondered if he should offer his handkerchief to her, or to the heiress, whose own cloth was now hanging off the front of her skirt like a flag of surrender. No one had offered him a seat or refreshments, and he still held the bouquet. No one seemed liable to take charge, either, with the aunt not speaking and the niece's fingers stuck together. "Won't you sit down?" he asked finally, when Miss Kane stopped staring at her hand like Lady Macbeth.

"Of course." She did, on a comfortable-looking armchair, immediately tucking her offending fingers in her skirts, out of sight. That left him to choose between a low, pillow-strewn sofa and a hard-backed chair with claw-foot legs. He chose the sofa.

Mrs. Goudge made gagging sounds and Miss Kane leaped to her feet. "Oh, no, not there!"

Before Stony could react, a brown-and-white pillow detached itself from the sofa, yawned, stretched, and unfolded into the fattest, ugliest, smelliest bulldog Stony had ever encountered. He held out his fingers, in hope that at least someone in this household knew what to do with a gentleman's hand. The dog sniffed, snarled, then lunged, trying to launch a drooping, drooling jaw toward Stony's throat. It fell short, on its short, bowed legs.

"Yi!" Stony yelled.

"Don't worry. He has no teeth."

"He has my blasted hand!"

"I'll ring for tea."

Was the woman totally insane? The cur had a death grip—toothless or not—on Stony's wrist and refused to let go, and *now* she was serving refreshments?

She ran toward the desk and a small silver bell there, which of course immediately stuck to her hand. It rang anyway.

Timms must have been anticipating her call, for he wheeled in a tea cart before the last chime. Actually, the old butler leaned on the cart as it rolled. He took one look at the situation and fell to his knees.

"Now is not the time to pray, man!" Stony shouted.

But Timms wasn't praying. He was tossing tiny cucumber sandwiches at Stony. That is, he was trying to get them near enough for the lockjawed dog to notice, but without his spectacles . . .

Then Miss Kane reached into her pocket and pulled out a small . . . boiled potato. Stony's mouth would have hung open, except he was too busy yelling and trying to shake the barnacle bulldog off.

"Here, Atlas. Your favorite."

The dog's name was Atlas? It should have been Attila. But those steel-trap jaws did open, and the beady, bloodshot eyes did follow the path of the falling potato, which, luckily, did not stick to Miss Kane's hand.

Stony did not know whether to wipe his wet, aching hand on his handkerchief, or use the linen square as a bandage. Should he ask for hot water to get rid of the slime, or a piece of ice to hold against the swelling? One thing he was not going to do was put his fingers in his mouth to ease the pain, not after where they'd been.

No one was hurrying to his assistance, anyway. The aunt was making henlike cackling sounds in her corner. Stony could not be certain if she was trying to smother her advice or her laughter.

Miss Kane was on the floor beside the butler, patting his back, then helping him to stand. Why, Stony could not help wondering, did she not pension the old man off, if she was so solicitous of his well-being? He did not understand, and he decided that he did not wish to understand anything about this odd household that kept a four-legged piranha as a throw pillow.

Miss Kane must have noticed his uneasy glance toward Atlas, on the floor. "Oh, he will not bother you anymore. You were just in his place, you see."

"The sofa is his?"

The heiress fussed over Timms instead of answering, straightening his neckcloth and likely leaving it permanently glued together. "He is content on the floor for now."

Of course he was. Having gobbled up all the fallen sandwiches, the brute was now devouring Stony's bouquet that had landed on the floor. Stony chose not to argue with him over it.

Timms was standing on his own now. "I'll just go fetch more refreshments, Miss Kane," he said.

She looked at the empty plate on the tea cart. "Thank you, Timmy, that would be lovely. And somc wine?"

"Thank you, miss. Don't mind if I do. The good Lord always blessed the fruit of the vine, didn't he?"

When the butler left, Stony could not stop himself from asking, "Why do you keep him?"

"Timmy? He has been with the family for generations. What would you have me do, toss him out on the street just because he is old?"

And slow, decrepit, half-blind, and a psalmist? "No, I meant the dog. Why would you keep an animal like that in the house?"

"It's his house." She sat down in her armchair again. Stony sat in the hard wooden chair, just to be safe.

"Oh, I doubt the inheritance would stand in a court of law," Miss Kane went on when Stony offered no comment. "But Aunt Augusta left her home to Atlas. I could not neglect my aunt's wishes, could I, especially when she left five copies of her will? Besides, the house will come to my sister and me eventually."

Not soon enough by half, in Stony's estimation. "Does he bite you?" he wanted to know.

"Not since I started carrying treats for him."

"You know, I don't think I have ever seen a dog eat a potato before, or a cucumber sandwich."

"Aunt Augusta was a vegetarian, you see. She did not permit any flesh in her kitchen. At least she did not write that into her will."

Timms brought in another tray of refreshments and a fresh pot of hot water. Miss Kane was busy brewing the tea and rearranging the food and serving her aunt. Timms offered Stony a delicate cut-crystal goblet and a half-filled bottle of wine. The Madeira was so fine, and the bottle so bare of excise labels, that Stony could not help wondering if the sea captain was other than a naval officer, as he had assumed. He savored his glass and some excellent biscuits, finally relaxing.

Miss Kane nibbled on a narrow slice of watercress sandwich. No wonder the woman was so thin, he considered. She ate like a bird. "The macaroons are delicious," he mentioned between bites. "Have you tried them?"

She did, at his urging. He felt better for that, for some reason.

The dog was snoring, or was that the aunt? Either way, it was a peaceful, normal scene, one Stony was reluctant to disturb with mention of business matters.

To delay, he asked for a cup of tea, since Timms had taken himself and the bottle away.

"Sugar? Milk? Lemon?" Miss Kane was everything polite. She'd do, he decided, watching her graceful moves. He would not be embarrassed to take her out in public. Not too public, of course, for she still looked like a pallbearer. A bit of sightseeing, a few shops where he was unknown . . .

Miss Kane was finished with her repast. The macaroon lay half-eaten on her plate. As soon as she handed Stony his cup, she cleared her throat. "About my request for your escort," she began, straightening the spoons on the serving tray.

Stony let go his plans for tomorrow. "Yes?"

"I do not think we will suit."

For the second time in as many days, Stony's trousers were tea spattered. Not suit? How could a worldly, fashionable gentleman like himself not suit this dowdy, eccentric female? Hell, he was not going to marry her—at which Gwen would be delighted instead of disappointed, once she met the woman—just take her touring! How arrogant, how presumptuous. How could he change her mind?

Stony was thinking of that check in his pocket. The devil alone knew what Miss Kane was thinking as she stuttered and sputtered through an apology for taking his time, for letting Atlas savagely gum his hand, for letting the dog eat his lovely flowers.

"For heaven's sake, madam, just say what is wrong and I shall try to fix it."

"Oh, there is nothing to fix. Nothing at all, to be sure." She refolded the extra napkins, her head down so that black abomination on her head hid her features and her expression. Then she cleared her throat, as if to gather her resolve. "You are simply not what I had in mind."

Before Stony could ask for an explanation, she continued: "You see, Timmy thought I should do better with a gentleman's escort, but I find you . . ."

"Yes?"

"Too . . . too . . ."

"Young?" He gave his best Wellstone smile, wondering again at the female's age. Her skin appeared good, from what he could see of it, clear and unlined. "I assure you, my stepmama thinks I am nearing my dotage."

"Too pretty."

"You think I am too . . . pretty?"

"Well, polished then, if the other offends. I would feel like a lump of coal next to a faceted diamond. Worse, at your side I would feel that every eye was upon me, which is far from my intention. I much prefer my anonymity."

Stony could understand that a shy girl might shun the notoriety of public scrutiny, but Miss Kane did not appear bashful. Buffleheaded, perhaps, but not bashful. He could even recognize that an heiress might cherish her privacy, away from fortune-hunters and hangers-on but, even coming from the country, she had to know that a nabob's daughter was news, no matter how she looked, or with whom she danced. "I do not see how—" he began, but she interrupted him.

"Furthermore, I have two other gentlemen in mind to assist me during my stay in London."

"I am glad to hear that," he lied, wondering what young buck or enterprising pauper was trying to take over his escort business. "You and your aunt should not be going about unprotected here in town. It is different from what you are accustomed to in the country, where you know everyone."

"Yes, that is what Timmy said."

"If you are also unfamiliar with the other gentlemen you are considering, at least I might be of assistance in your choice." Or he might have words with the dastards, for hunting on his preserves.

"Well, I doubt that you would know Mr. Edward Lattimer. He is a Bow Street Runner."

"What, you think he can take you to balls?"

She blinked and said, "I have no intention of attending balls." Stony noticed, now, that she had fine green eyes.

Then the parrot—it had to have been the parrot, for the auntie was asleep and sworn to silence—squawked, "No balls at Bow Street. No balls, a'tall, I say."

Stony looked around but did not see the creature. Miss Kane's cheeks were awash with color, but she managed to say, "Thin walls, don't you know," before hurrying on. "The other with whom I thought to consult is Lord Strickland. Perhaps you do know him."

Stony did, but not out of choice. Strickland was a hard-drinking, heavy-gambling widower of middle years and middling intelligence. He was a known frequenter of some of the less discriminating brothels, which were not the London landmarks Miss Kane would be desirous of seeing. "If the baron is an acquaintance of yours or a friend of your family's, I must apologize, but I do not consider Lord Strickland the best of company for a young female."

"As if I didn't know that," Stony thought he heard her mutter. He also thought the parrot in the next room said "Prickland," but perhaps Mrs. Goudge was mumbling in her sleep about jabbing her hand with the needle.

Miss Kane had taken up her teacup again and was swirling the tea dregs around in it as if she could read her future there. She was not pleased with what she saw, Stony thought, for she said, "Tsk. And he has not bothered to answer my letter either."

She'd summoned the baron, too? Stony wondered if Miss Kane had been as peremptory with Strickland, or if she had also sent him a bank draft. Strickland was not known to be plump in the pocket; neither was he rumored to be below hatches enough to go into trade. The thought of a bank draft reminded Stony of the check in his pocket. He took it out and handed it to her. Better it stick to her hand than his conscience. "Your retainer."

"Oh, no, you must keep it. For your time and trouble."

Stony shook his head and stood to go. "No, I cannot accept what I have not earned. I assure you it has been no trouble, and a pleasant time."

Miss Kane stood too, to walk him to the door. "Please keep it. If not for your efforts, then for your boots."

"My . . . ?"

The dog had cast up his accounts, and a few expensive hothouse flowers, on Stony's feet. The viscount had to bite his tongue to keep from using the vocabulary that kept the parrot banned.

Miss Kane was shaking her head as if she were reading his mind now, which was a great deal easier than the tea leaves. "I know what you are thinking," she said, "but my aunt did love him."

Or her aunt did not love her niece. It was none of his affair, thank goodness. Stony was halfway to the door when he stopped. "Miss Kane, I really hate to say this"—he hated himself more for not fleeing when he had the chance—"but I truly think you should reconsider."

She looked at the check in her hand. "I suppose you would think so, if you need money as badly as— That is, I thank you for coming."

"It is not just the money. I do not believe either of the men you mentioned can serve you as well, or look after your interests. I greatly fear you might be taken advantage of or misled. I would feel negligent if I did not warn you of the pitfalls awaiting a . . ." He wanted to say ninnyhammer, but that was no way to ingratiate himself with a potential employer. "A newcomer to our city."

Miss Kane was listening, head cocked to the side, but not nodding her agreement, so he went on: "As you must know, I have looked after other young women, and none in my care has ever come to harm." Except for Lady Valentina, who landed in clover. "I do not wish you to be any less well attended."

"Thank you, my lord, for your caring about my welfare as well as the fee. And I shall reconsider. Why, if I do not hear from either Strickland or Mr. Lattimer in a sennight, I shall be at my wits' end."

Oh, it would not take half as long, Stony was positive, not with her wits. They'd never stretch so far. "I think you should send me a note after two days, rather than waiting any longer, or venturing out without escort. That way, you can see something of the city, and I shall know you are safe."

She agreed and Stony left, wondering why he had tried so hard for a position he did not want. The only place he'd feel safe escorting Miss Ellianne Kane to was Bedlam. The only question was which of them would return.

Chapter Six

"By Saint Homobono's ballocks, Ellianne, what were you thinking, dismissing that prime goer before you'd tried his paces?"

Miss Ellianne Kane looked around to make sure none of the housemaids would be embarrassed by her aunt's speech. Ellianne was not surprised that Aunt Lally was talking; nor was she surprised at the vulgarity. Her aunt was known throughout Devon for speaking her mind, in whatever terms she saw fit. Her freebooter husband had encouraged the freer speech, and Ellianne's father had laughed at his sister's eccentricities. Lavinia Goudge, née Kane, was old enough, wealthy enough, and uncaring enough of anyone's opinion. Hence the phantom parrot. And hence the occasionally practiced vow of silence. Without it, London would have been an impossibility. They'd have been shunned by everyone, from high society to shopkeepers. As it was, they were nearly housebound, but that was by choice.

No, what surprised Ellianne was that her aunt seemed to have approved of Lord Wellstone. "I thought you wanted me to have nothing to do with the viscount," she said. " 'A useless bit of pomp' is what you called him."

Aunt Lally had called the viscount a lot worse, and the rest of the British peerage along with him. In fact, she had urged Ellianne to toss Lord Wellstone out on his aristocratic arse.

"Faugh, that was before I saw him," Aunt Lally declared, setting aside her needlework. "I have changed my mind."

Ellianne was back to working on her charts and scraps of paper, being more careful with the glue this time. "So have I. We need not engage a highborn squire. If Mr. Lattimer cannot help, or Lord Strickland will not, we shall go about our business on our own. Timmy can hire extra footmen, that's all. I should feel uncomfortable explaining our situation to his lordship, or accepting his escort."

"Uncomfortable? Is that what you called that mealymouthed performance you put on for him?"

"I was not mealymouthed. I was simply embarrassed by the glue and the dog and the parrot and—"

"Rubbish. One smile from that handsome jackadandy and your knees went weak, admit it!"

Ellianne spilled the glue again. This time she kept her fingers out of the mess, using the blotter instead to rescue her bits of newspaper clippings. "I shall not! My knees did no such thing. They performed just as they ought."

"Well, mine turned to blancmange, I swear. If I were ten years younger . . ."

"Ten?"

Aunt Lally ignored the insolent query. "I suppose you are going to tell me that you never noticed the bonny breadth of his shoulders, or how his breeches hugged those muscled thighs. No, you don't have to tell me. I can see the red in your cheeks."

"A lady does not notice such things," Ellianne insisted.

"Is that what they taught you at that fancy academy? To go deaf, dumb, and blind? Of course you noticed. You're a female, ain't you?" She frowned at the encompassing black her niece wore. "For all anyone can tell, in that crepe sail you're wrapped in. But that is beside the point. If his smile did not set your pulse racing, and his physique did not knock you to flinders, why did you turn muckle-minded when he walked in the room? And why, by Saint Cecilia's corset, did you let him walk *out* of the room?"

Ellianne stuck down another list of names on her chart, to delay answering. Finally she sighed and said, "Because I am not blind. You saw him. He is the handsomest man I have ever met."

"So what? You've seen pretty fellows before. In fact, you've dealt with good-looking men your whole life, at the bank. You've hired and fired scores of them. And at the local assemblies you danced with any number of fine specimens. Maybe not as well rigged as Wellstone, but I never saw you go arsy-varsy over one before."

"Well, I was never dressed like this when I met them, with my fingers stuck together! I meant to change, of course. I thought he would send a message setting a time for an interview."

"Instead of paying a proper call, with flowers, no less."

"But that is just it. I do not want an elegant escort with perfect manners and a perfect knot in his cravat. That is not why I wrote to him. Lord Wellstone is too much the Town beau for my purposes."

"Then change your fustian purposes," Aunt Lally muttered. "Or else ignore his looks." She laughed at her niece's inelegant snort of disbelief. "And think of his connections. That's what you said you needed."

"And you said a member of his elite circles would be as useful as teats on Atlas." The dog was back on the sofa, wheezing in his sleep. "He would not want to assist one of my birth in such a havey-cavey matter."

"A lady shouldn't repeat everything she hears. Besides, I think that young bucko might be ripe for a challenge. He plainly thought you'd be better off with him than with Strickland or the Bow Street fellow."

"You think he wanted my company, after he saw me and Atlas?"

"He said so, didn't he?"

"That was the money speaking. Anyone could tell he was dreading the notion of being seen with either of us. He wanted my business, that was all. We always knew Lord Wellstone needs to earn an income."

"I don't hold that against him, and neither should you. Your own father was a self-made man, as was Mr. Goudge. I admire a chap, especially one with a title to his name, trying to make something of himself, not being a barnacle on the backside of society. The fellow's got b—"

Ellianne cleared her throat.

"Bottom," Aunt Lally amended.

"I do not hold ambition against anyone of any class. I simply feel that Lord Wellstone's sincerity can be had for sixpence."

"Perhaps. But he does know his way around a lady's drawing room. Bedroom too, less'n I miss my guess, but he just might be a help in finding that featherheaded sister of yours. The sooner the peagoose is back in the nest, the sooner we can go home."

"I am sorry if you are missing your cottage, Aunt Lally."

"It ain't just the cottage or my cats. At home a woman can walk wherever she chooses, can entertain as she pleases." It pleased Lavinia Goudge to entertain her husband's first mate, who had taken over Captain Goudge's ships and lucrative smuggling routes. "And at home a rich young female doesn't have to hide herself away for fear that every caller is a rake ready to kidnap her to force a marriage or a ransom."

"Until we know what happened to Isabelle, we ought to take care, is all."

"Is that what you are doing? I thought you were hugging shore to avoid being swamped by fortune-hunting swells."

Ellianne cut another article from a newspaper and pasted it down under the appropriate date, pressing firmly enough to tear a hole in the page. "Oh, bother." She glued another scrap atop the first. Her project was a mess, and it was all that man's fault. "I did not enjoy my last encounter with London's bachelors. I do not intend to repeat the experience."

"Well, at least Wellstone is aboveboard in his goals. No secret that he sails under whatever flag is paying him. For what it's worth, though, to my ears he did sound like he cared about leaving you on your own."

"Perhaps he did, a little."

"Well, you think on it, Ellianne. To my mind, he'll do."

"Do for what, Aunt Lally?" Ellianne asked, peering at her aunt over yet another newspaper. "You would not be trying to matchmake, would you? You know I do not intend to marry."

If Aunt Lally had her own views about her niece's intentions of remaining single, she was, for once, wise enough not to speak them. "Promote a match between you and Wellstone? Zounds, no. A blueblood like the viscount will marry one of his own kind when he gets around to it. An earl's brat or better, I'd wager. You've too wise a head on your shoulders to expect anything else. If I thought the bounder would break your heart I'd not be encouraging you to keep him on, would I?"

"I should hope not. There is no chance of my heart being remotely involved, at any rate. It would take a great deal more than a handsome face"—and a devilish smile, a Greek god's build, and a courtier's glib tongue—"to change my mind."

Timmy agreed with Mrs. Goudge. "He'll do, miss."

Contrary to popular opinion, the two households,

the Kanes' and Lady Augusta's, were on long-standing terms of familiarity. The rift had been between Ellianne's mother, Annabelle, and Annabelle's father, Lord Chaston, not the two sisters. Like her father and then her brother, the current marquess, Lady Augusta, never chose to socialize with Ellis Kane, but she did invite her nieces to spend school holidays or summer vacations with her in London or at the seaside. Lady Annabelle, Mrs. Kane, was pleased to send her daughters, perhaps to counter the influence of their other aunt, Lavinia Goudge. So Ellianne and Timms were old friends. Mellowed by the Madeira, the ancient butler sat in the kitchen, his aching feet up, his false teeth out, his spectacles on. Ellianne sat across from him, her charts spread on the table and her heavy, mantilla-like head covering spread on another chair. Her hair trailed down her back, and her shoes were back in the parlor. She too swirled a glass of wine between her hands.

"That is what my aunt says, that the viscount might help find Isabelle."

"You should listen to her. Not in the general way, of course," Timms quickly added. "But his lordship seemed a decent sort, bless his soul and hopes for heaven." Timms recalled the second coin the viscount handed him, on his way out this time, while everyone knew the young peer's own pockets were to let. Timms blessed him again.

"But he is so very elegant," Ellianne complained.

"Aye, top of the trees, as they say. A Nonpareil."

"Precisely. He'll think I am a desperate spinster, so starved for male attention that I have to pay for it."

"Now, missy, no heiress has to pay to have men at her feet, especially one as pretty as you, and Lord Wellstone is sure to know that. A downy one, he is, and right as rain, they say. You'll not find a more honorable gentleman in all of London, as God is my witness. And discreet, which is what you need to save Miss Isabelle's reputation if you find her."

"When I find her," she corrected him.

Timms looked at her over the rims of his spectacles. "You don't fear she met her maker, then? That Bow Street fellow, he seemed convinced of it."

"I refuse to believe that. We shall get her back, wherever she is. You must have faith too, Timmy."

"Oh, I do. And I get down on my knees and pray for Miss Isabelle every night, and most mornings when my old knees aren't too stiff."

Ellianne reached out and touched his age-spotted hand. "Thank you, Timmy. I do not know what I would do without you."

Neither did Timms, and he was afraid to find out. He wanted Miss Ellianne and her sister provided for before that time came. Oh, they had enough blunt between them to be merry as grigs, but that did not suit the butler's opinion of the proper futures for young ladies. Hadn't the Lord commanded His children to go forth and multiply? For all Miss Ellianne's ability to add and subtract, to manage an entire bank as well as other women balanced their household accounts, she knew nothing about the world. She needed a man to teach her, and hadn't the Savior provided the perfect one? Unlike Mrs. Goudge, who was firmly entrenched in the merchant class, Timms had a romantic fondness for misalliances, for marriages made for love. Stranger things had happened than a handsome lord falling in love with a beautiful heiress. He'd wager it could happen again, if he got these youngsters together.

Well, he would not wager. He'd given his word to Miss Ellianne. Right after he'd had to confess losing his entire pension at the races. She'd reinstate it, the darling promised, as soon as he proved he was cured of the gambling disease. With the good Lord's help—and fear of the poorhouse—he was. Now the sooner they found Miss Isabelle and got both girls hitched, the sooner he could retire to that little cottage he'd found, right near Epsom Downs. To that end, he tried to puff up the viscount's virtues.

He pointed to her charts and said, "My old memory is no help to you with those, but Viscount Wellstone is bound to know everyone on your lists. In addition, he has been squiring ladies about town for three or four years now, and no one ever knew it, he was that circumspect."

"You knew it."

"I am a butler, missy. It is my job to know everything."

She smiled, as Timms knew she would. "But everyone knows it now, you told me. All of London knows Viscount Wellstone was taking money to act as escort to young ladies so their fathers and brothers did not have to."

"A very unfortunate affair indeed," Timms said, needing another swallow of wine to rid himself of the bad taste of such a social debacle. "Orchestrated entirely by that scheming Pattendale female and her mother, I'd lay odds—that is, I would lay my soul in the hands of the Almighty. Then with that officer friend of his shabbing off, Lord Wellstone's own reputation was blown to bits. He was frequently lampooned in the scandal sheets, where they said his services went far beyond dancing with the ladies. A Fancy Fred, they were calling him."

"Why Fred?"

"They say it came from a farmer's hog what got hired out to service the sows. The farmer had Fred all washed and combed, fancified, as it were, as if the pigs cared one whit." Timms recalled he was not at his local pub, from which he was exiled, along with the racetracks, by his vow to his young mistress. "Pardon the indelicacy, Miss Ellianne."

She brushed that aside. "I am no green girl, you know. Go on. Tell me more about Lord Wellstone and his situation."

"It got worse. One cartoonist even portrayed his poor lordship as Othello, the Moor of Venice. Except the newspaper captioned his likeness, 'the M'whore of London.' A male whore, you know. It was despicable, and not true, on my word as a true believer."

"The poor man," Ellianne said, sympathetic to the viscount's plight, as Timms had intended. Then she thought about it, and the blue-eyed Adonis with a smile that could tempt birds out of trees, or ladies into his bed. "How can you be sure it was all untrue?"

Timms pushed his spectacles back on his nose. "I told you, butlers know everything. Besides, it is simple, really. He'd have been caught long since, were he visiting the paddock with the fillies before the races, so to speak. If he'd been serving the old mares, he would not have needed to keep half his house shut up to save money."

"So you think he can be trusted?"

Timms nodded. "He'll give good value for your coin or have me to answer to, miss. As for your father's money—if that is what you are worried over, that he's seeking more than temporary employment—his lordship could have wed an heiress anytime." Granted, few with so large and tempting a fortune as Miss Ellianne Kane, but the principle was there. "He didn't. The lad is no fortune-hunter, and bless him for that."

"Good, because he'll only be disappointed." Ellianne sat up straighter on her chair. "I do not intend to marry, as I told you."

And she told him again, to Timms's disgust, and once again after most of the wine was gone.

"No, I am better off single," Ellianne finished with a yawn, "than with a man who likes my money better than he likes me. Besides, the spinster life was good enough for Aunt Augusta."

Timms emptied the bottle into his glass. "Who left her house to a blessed dog."

* * *

So Ellianne consulted the dog. "What did you think of Lord Wellstone?" she asked as they went for a short walk in the small walled garden behind the house, all the old dog was capable of before he wheezed himself into a faint. "Will he do?"

Atlas had no tail to speak of to wag. He did raise his leg, though.

"Well, you liked his flowers."

So had she, before the dog ate them, anyway. Despite what she'd told her aunt, she still liked the fact that Lord Wellstone had thought to bring her a token. Ellianne had received flowers before, of course. At eight and twenty, she had enjoyed her share of suitors. Unfortunately, she had not truly enjoyed them. She always doubted their sincerity, wondering how many would call, how many would bring flowers or sweets, if her dowry were less generous. Lord Wellstone did not have to bring a bouquet to win her regard; he already had her check.

None of those other gentlemen, the well-born ones who deigned to honor a banker's daughter with their attentions, or the ambitious ones who thought to ally themselves with her family, had impressed her. Not the way Lord Wellstone had.

Ellianne reassured herself that she was far past the age of being swept off her feet, not that the viscount was wielding a broom or anything. He was simply devilishly attractive, and she could appreciate that—the way she could admire a painting in a gallery without having to own it, or touch it, or sit staring at it for hours like a moonling.

She was in no danger of falling for his practiced charm, of course, flowers or no flowers. Aunt Lally was right about that. Along with the bouquets and bonbons, she'd had more than her share of hot, wet, horrid kisses from men claiming ardor while calculating her income. She'd been pawed at and pressed into corners by men claiming affection while trying to compromise her into marriage. They had shown her how revolting, how self-serving and sycophantic a man's attentions could be. The charming ones had been the worst, for she'd almost believed them, especially when she was younger and less experienced. Now she wanted nothing to do with men or their passions or their promises.

All she wanted was her sister back.

She had everything else: a busy, rewarding life, a respected place in her community, friends who shared her interests, and the wherewithal to help better other women's circumstances. Her charities were making a difference, not just holding meetings. She ran orphanages and training schools and hospitals. Ellianne Kane answered to no one and feared no one.

No, that was not true. She did fear being forced into marriage by some man unscrupulous enough to abduct her, as she feared had happened to Isabelle. Kidnapings were not that uncommon, according to Mr. Lattimer of Bow Street. No ransom note had been received, however.

Lord Wellstone would know the people she had to speak to about her sister's disappearance, and he would know just which greedy, groping gentlemen Ellianne had to avoid meanwhile. If he was not one of them, he would certainly recognize their kind. According to Timms, his lordship was circumspect in his dealings, so could protect both her and Isabelle's reputations. His size and strength alone afforded physical protection.

"So what do you think, Atlas? Will he do?"

He'd have to. If Lattimer was no help, and Ellianne could not get in to speak to Baron Strickland, Lord Wellstone was her best hope.

Atlas growled at his own shadow.

Chapter Seven

"So, will she do?" Gwen wanted to know.

"Do for what?" Stony replied. "For the farce between dramas at Drury Lane? For the interment of a truly despised relation? You may send Miss Kane to star in either, with my blessings."

"For your wife, silly! You know that is what we intended."

"No, that is what you intended. I would rather marry the old auntie. At least she does not speak."

The two were attending a musical evening at Lady Woodruff's, not a particular friend, and not a favorite form of entertainment. Gwen, however, had decreed that they had to go, to show their faces so no one thought they were ashamed of anything or in retreat. One of the Misses Woodruff—the unfortunate Lord Woodruff had been presented with four frilly tokens of his wife's affection, with nary an heir—thought she could play the flute, to another of her sisters' accompaniment on the pianoforte. Neither could follow the other or the musical score, so Stony was suffering through two horrible renditions instead of one. All he had to look forward to was the other untalented pair, one singing, the other on the harp. Or was that the harpsichord?

"What was so awful about Miss Kane? Nothing that cannot be improved, I am convinced," Gwen whispered, but a matron on her other side glared at her. An aunt of the Woodruffs', undoubtedly.

Stony waited for the obligatory applause between pieces. "Even you would be appalled. She is a long Meg, for one, thin as a rail, and with the fashion sense of a simian. I have no idea of her age, but she might be rather old for childbearing, which renders her useless to a man seeking an heir. She has manners, but only when she remembers to use them. She is awkward and addlepated, at the least."

"Yes, but money can fix a great deal."

Stony raised his eyebrows. "Her height? Her age? Her lunacy? I think not."

Gwen's eyes started to fill with tears of disappointment.

"Deuce take it, you are not going to cry here, are you?" Stony pulled out his handkerchief. "Cough instead."

So Gwen coughed, and Stony excused themselves to those seated nearby. The viscount and his stepmama fled to the adjoining room, where servants were setting out bowls of punch. Gwen's tears instantly disappeared, fortunately. They could still hear the music, unfortunately.

Placed in a much more comfortable chair than the hard-backed wooden seats in the music room, Gwen tried again. "Surely the young woman cannot be totally ineligible, dear. You have always been able to discern and enhance the best qualities of those females in your care."

"The best quality about Miss Kane is that she is *not* in my care. Rid yourself of the notion of her as a daughter-in-law, Gwen. Even if I were interested, which I swear I am not and never could be, were her father King Midas or a coal miner, she is not looking for a husband. She says she has no intention of attending balls and such, and the way she dresses could only discourage the most ardent suitor, rather than attract any."

"Then what does she want with your escort?"

"I have no idea, and never will find out, now. That is, Miss Kane does not want me as an attendant." Which still rankled, despite his relief. "She decided not to engage my services after all."

"Oh my. She must truly be peculiar to decline your company."

Stony patted Gwen's hand in thanks for her gratifying but biased opinion. "Worse yet, she seems to prefer the attentions of a Mr. Lattimer, who is nothing but a Bow Street man."

Gwen had never met one of the new policemen. "Perhaps she developed a *tendre* for the gentleman who was investigating her aunt's death, and that is why she has no interest in finding another suitor. After all, the Kane Bank heiress can wed wherever her heart wishes, without needing to consider income or social standing."

"But a Runner, who is hardly considered a gentleman? No, I do not think Miss Kane bears affection for the fellow." Stony had seen signs of infatuation aplenty in the young girls he'd chaperoned. Miss Kane showed none of those indications: no lilt to her voice when she mentioned Lattimer's name, no blush of color at the thought of her beau, no oblivion to any other gentleman's existence.

"Worse," Stony went on, "I believe she is considering that old reprobate Strickland to fill whatever need she has."

"The baron? He is not so bad."

"How can you say that, Gwen? Everyone knows he gambled away his entire estate years ago."

"As your father would have done, if the property

were not entailed to you. And, as you say, that was years ago. He has never been in debtors' prison, has he?"

"He has been in enough houses of ill repute to make up for that."

Gwen did not need to mention Stony's father again, or as he was before her time, of course. "No more so than many gentlemen."

Stony frowned. "Why are you defending the man, Gwen?"

She fanned herself, so that anyone coming into the room would believe she had been taken ill. "He has always treated me courteously enough, the few times we met. He looked lonely, I thought. If your Miss Kane is as old as you think, she might find Lord Strickland attractive."

"He is fat, in his fifties, and wears his breakfast to dinner. Great gods, how could any woman be attracted to him?"

Gwen fanned harder as the applause became louder and more enthusiastic, signaling the intermission. Soon the other guests would pour into this room for much-needed—and well-deserved refreshments. "If Miss Kane is as odd as you say, she cannot afford to be so choosy."

Stony bowed and nodded to the members of the audience who'd run fastest out of the music room. Gwen coughed a few times, discouraging anyone who would have approached them. "Still," she said, behind her fan, "it is a shame, your not securing her confidence." Or her hand, although Gwen could not like an attics-to-let spinster for a stepdaughter-in-law. If they were barely holding on to their position in society now, who knew what a vacant-headed viscountess would do. "I know you could have used the money. But just think, dear, that if Miss Kane is so impossible, you are well rid of her."

"Who said I am rid of the woman? I have every intention of returning to Sloane Street in a day or two."

Now tears truly came to Gwen's eyes. She hated the thought of her dear stepson debasing himself, begging for work from a harebrained heiress. "If it is about the money, I could sell—"

"It is not the money," Stony said, surprising himself more than Gwen. "It is the woman. I think she needs help."

"Oh, Aubrey, not another lost lamb?"

He nodded. "How could I sleep at night, thinking of what could happen to a woman of great means but little sense? You said it yourself, but she would not be a lamb going off to slaughter here in London. She would be stew. Once I see that someone honorable is looking after Miss Kane, then I can rest easy."

No matter what Stony said, he slept perfectly fine, despite a green-eyed crow flying through his dreams, screeching in distress. That screeching was Miss Woodruff's singing, yet he managed to sleep right through the second half of the musical program.

The day following Lord Wellstone's call, Ellianne tried once more to speak with Baron Strickland. She had gone to his house the first day she arrived in London, of course, since he was the most logical person to ask about Isabelle. Hadn't he been a friend of Aunt Augusta's? Hadn't Isabelle mentioned his name in her last letter? Hadn't he seemed a slimy toad eight years ago when Ellianne came to town for her own so-called presentation?

Two conversations with the baron and one with her aunt had convinced Ellianne she was better off home. They were intending to see her wed to his lordship, no matter her own wishes. Aunt Augusta was determined to see her niece marry into the aristocracy, with the least expense to her. Lord Strickland wanted to get back the estate he had forfeited years earlier to Kane Bank, lands that now belonged to Ellianne and her sister. Marrying the heiress seemed the quickest, easiest, cheapest way to redeem his property. He seemed to think that slobbering on her would hasten the engagement. Ellianne thought differently, and thought she would be happier at home in Devon, single.

Of course, she was a great deal less experienced then or else she might have been able to discourage the baron's attentions without kicking him in the groin, but so she had. Which was no reason, she felt now, for him to refuse to see her.

She knew he was home that first day. The insolent servant who answered her knock had almost slammed the door in her black-veiled face.

"But I am an acquaintance of his lordship's. He will wish to see me."

An old hag, accompanied by an older one and a stooped chap who was older than the two of them added together? Country relatives or collectors for charity, he decided on the spot. No, Lord Strickland would not want them in his house, not by half. Kimble's job did not pay much, or often, but he wanted to keep it. " 'Is lordship ain't to home."

Ellianne had seen draperies on the upper level pulled aside when her hired coach pulled up. Someone was there. She took a coin out of her reticule. She almost took the small pistol out, to wipe the grin from the servant's face, but thought that might be premature. She was right. For the glint of gold, Kimble agreed to take her card up to his master.

Lord Strickland could not see her, the man said with real regret, seeing the gold turn to copper. "He is, ah, indisposed."

"But he is home? We shall wait." Ellianne handed him two coins, one to tell his master that he had guests, the other to bring refreshments, for her man Timmy needed a restorative.

"Wine will do, my good man," the old chap said, "and God bless you for the effort and a good year."

Ellianne sighed and handed over another coin.

Wine and some slivers of toast arrived, but not

Strickland. They could hear feet hurrying down the stairs, some muffled shouts, and a rear door slamming.

"I am that sorry, ma'am," the servant reported, not looking at her, "but 'is lordship was called away on business."

"I see."

So did Aunt Lally, whose vow of silence lapsed. "Ran off, did the old bugger? You should have kicked him in the brainbox, Ellianne. Bigger target than his b—Ooph." Aunt Lally rubbed at her side, where her niece's elbow had connected.

Ellianne held out yet another coin. "What about the lady of the house?"

"There's never been a lady in this house, not since I came, ma'am. Some of the other sort, but none you'd be a-wishing to meet."

"Now? Is Lord Strickland entertaining any female company? Did anyone leave with him, or is there a woman still upstairs?"

The baron's man eyed the coin. Lud, the master would have his hide for sure. Kimble was torn between fealty to the gent who paid his pitiful pittance of a wage, or another coin to join its jingling fellows in his pocket until he could get to Sukey Johnson's rooms. Loyalty might have stood up to greed, but not when lust entered the lists. "No, he ain't brought no fancy piece here in an age. Why sup at home when the menu somewheres else is bigger, better, and changes every night?" He licked his lips, thinking of Sukey Johnson's tender morsels.

Ellianne was really tempted to use that pistol—on Strickland or his man, she did not care which. She handed over a last coin instead. "This is to see that your employer gets my message. I would like him to call on me in Sloane Street. At his earliest convenience, is that clear?"

It could not be clearer, nor could Strickland's guilty conscience. He had not called. Nor had he answered the notes she sent 'round. Why would the man refuse to see her if he had nothing to hide? He could not still be angry over that kick, could he? After all, if he were still visiting houses of accommodation, he could not have been permanently discommoded.

This time Ellianne and her aunt took two footmen, determined to gain entry by bribes or by brawn. The knocker was off the door, however, signaling that Lord Strickland was out of town, out of range of her questions. No one answered the door, no servant to bribe, not even a caretaker.

"Limp-rod loped off," Aunt Lally said, and Ellianne did not have the heart to chide her for the language.

She went home and sent for Mr. Lattimer, the Bow Street man she'd hired to find Isabelle. Now she wanted him to locate the baron too.

He was not encouraging. With no crime committed, he could not get warrants and such. Not to investigate a titled gentleman. Everyone knew Bow Street's funding depended on the votes in Parliament, votes by other gentlemen who considered themselves and their cronies above the law.

"But he is guilty of something. I know it," Ellianne insisted.

Lattimer would ask around. That was all he could do, no matter how much of a reward Miss Kane promised. As a young, ambitious man, there was nothing Lattimer wanted more than to please his employer. Finding a lost heiress would be a feather in his cap and a promotion in his career, to say nothing of the blunt in his pocket.

He was not quite ambitious enough to think that Miss Kane's gratitude, if he found her missing sister, would extend to more than pay and praise. But he could hope. For now he was nothing more than a hired investigator, paid to make inquiries without making a byword of Miss Isabelle Kane's name. Why, he was not even supposed to tell anyone the identity of his employer. His superiors knew, of course, but they did not want her presence in London spread through the newspapers, either, for fear they'd have another abduction on their hands. Bad business, they said, when rich young women were not safe in the streets. Another kidnaping would prove their uselessness.

Of course, none of his superiors believed the girl was stolen from her home. A ransom note would have been received long ago, or a tearful bride would have been returned from Gretna Green, with a new husband ready to claim her dowry. They did not believe she was dead, either, or they'd have found a body.

No, what Lattimer's bosses thought, and what he was tending to believe, was that the young woman, barely nineteen, had run off with a gentleman of whom her aunt disapproved. They'd fought, the aunt died, the girl ran into the arms of her lover. Now she was hiding, and would not be found until she was deuced well ready—or until a bright, talented investigator outsmarted her.

The problem was that Lattimer could not get to speak with the young ladies Miss Isabelle might have confided in. He could not question the matrons who might have noted her dance partners. He could not ask the gentlemen at White's if one of them had an heiress stashed in his attics. Hell, without the proper papers, he could not get past the door of White's or into a lady's drawing room. Without a body, or evidence of a crime, he could not get those papers.

Stymied, that was what Lattimer was, and more disappointed at disappointing Miss Kane than anything.

"I am sure you are doing your best," Ellianne told the earnest young man who was flipping the pages of his daybook over and over, as if he could find answers at the next shuffle. He was near her age, with thick brown hair and ears that only protruded a bit more than they should. He was polite and intelligent, neatly dressed and hardworking, the kind of man she would have welcomed at the bank. The problem was that Lattimer's best was not good enough.

Isabelle could be held captive somewhere. She could be stranded in Scotland. She could be on a ship bound for the white slave trade! Ellianne had to find her. She'd promised her dying mother to look after the baby, and she had promised her dying father to keep his beloved little girl safe. She had worked so hard to keep Isabelle's fortune protected from unscrupulous trustees, to keep Isabelle herself protected from unworthy suitors. The nine years between them might have been nineteen, so careful was Ellianne of Isabelle's health and happiness. Why, she had even urged the girl to accept Aunt Augusta's invitation, so that Isabelle might see more of society, in case her future lay in that direction.

Ellianne herself was nearly as disdainful of the idle upper class as Aunt Lally was, but she would not have discouraged Isabelle from marrying a title, not if the man was a true good and gentle man and their affections were truly engaged. The fellow would be the father of the nieces and nephews Ellianne was eager to dote upon, so she would come to love him too, for her sister's sake.

That man, whoever he was, would not have been cad enough to run away to Scotland with Isabelle. No, Ellianne would not believe that her sister was staying away out of choice, not without telling Ellianne. That was too cruel. Isabelle was as selfish and spoiled as any wealthy miss of nineteen years, but she was never mean. She loved her older sister, and knew that Ellianne loved her.

Ellianne would not believe her sister dead, either. After all, Isabelle had sent one water-stained, illegible letter—from who-knew-where. No, something was wrong, terribly wrong, and something had to be done about it. Ellis Kane's daughter had not been raised to sit back and let others take charge, or wait for them to act. Hadn't she dismissed those embezzlers at the bank and increased its holdings threefold herself, until she could hire responsible managers? Hadn't she started that school where poor girls could learn to sew and cook, as well as read and write, so they could make something of their lives? She might not have built the structure with her own hands, by heaven, but she had made sure the thing got done. She'd hired the best architect and the best brickworkers. She'd found the most accomplished, dedicated instructors for the school and the most astute, honest financiers for the bank.

Then as now, if she could not accomplish her goals herself, she would hire the best man for the job.

Chapter Eight

Ellianne decided to sleep on her decision. The problem was, she couldn't sleep. She was in a strange bed in a strange house, and she was about to entrust herself and her sister to a strange gentleman. Not that Lord Wellstone was peculiar; he was simply unknown to her. And she could not help still feeling intimidated by the viscount's physical appearance, his air of assurance, those smiling blue eyes that might be laughing at her, even as he took her money.

On the other hand, he needed her money. Knowing his motives was almost as much protection as the pistol under her pillow. She was paying the piper; therefore she was calling the tunes. She would not be taken in by Wellstone's charm, but she would demand his loyalty. She'd have to make that clear. And the need for discretion. And speed.

She got up to make a new chart. If she was going to deal with Lord Wellstone, it would be on her terms, all business, like at the bank. When entering into a transaction, one listed the clauses and provisions so both parties understood the agreement. Just so would she spell out the conditions of Wellstone's employment. That way, she felt, she would be treading familiar ground, instead of hurtling into the unknown.

On one side of her paper she listed the duties she expected his lordship to perform. On the other side she wrote what seemed fair compensation for his time. Of course, she could not put a monetary value on loyalty, but introducing her to girls of Isabelle's age could not take a great deal of effort on Lord Wellstone's part. Helping her break into Lord Strickland's house might be a bit more difficult.

She tallied the sums instantly in her head, as always, then readded the column. Now she was satisfied with her calculations and efficiency, confident that Wellstone would recognize her as a creature of logic and maturity instead of the blithering ninny of their first meeting. Then she reminded herself that she was the one in charge. He would be working for her, not doing her favors. It should not matter what he thought of her.

It did. She climbed back into bed, mentally writing the note asking him to call in the afternoon, so she had time to wash her hair. She planned what she would wear when he arrived, and what to have Cook serve. There. Now she could face Lord Wellstone with poise and dignity.

And shadows under her eyes. Ellianne still could not sleep. She tossed and turned for hours, it seemed. Then she took the pistol from under her pillow and placed it on the night table.

She awoke early, long before Aunt Lally arose, and composed her note, at least five times. She had to admit that she was reconsidering hiring Wellstone, but not that she was desperate for his assistance. When she felt she had the right tone, not too imperious, not too humble, she enclosed the same check, then affixed her seal.

Having inquired when she wrote the first letter, Ellianne knew that Timmy would have to send a footman across the square and over a few streets. The day was too young to have her messenger wait for a reply, though. Goodness, if Wellstone was like other London gentlemen, he would not be out of bed yet. He might not have returned home from his evening's revels until a mere hour or two ago. Ellianne could have to wait for hours for a reply, unless he simply appeared at her doorstep again. Or simply did not answer. After all, she had rescinded her offer of employment. Perhaps he had taken another post.

Well, the sooner the letter got to him, the sooner she would know. And how foolish to take a servant away from his tasks when she had nothing better to do but fret. She could use the exercise and fresh air besides, since she was used to walking to the bank every morning. Then, too, she could still change her mind along the way, or once she saw how imposing the viscount's town house was, or if his servants treated her disrespectfully.

So early, in such an elegant neighborhood, she did not fear being accosted by hoodlums. Since few people knew of her arrival in Town, she did not worry over being approached by so-called gentlemen either. She was tired of being so cautious, so afraid. It was time she took her own life back, instead of hiding in the house like some forest creature trembling in its burrow against unnamed dangers. Writing the letter to Lord Wellstone was a first step; delivering the letter herself was the second.

Making the decision to hire the viscount—if he accepted her terms—might have bolstered her confidence, but it did not make her a fool. Aunt Lally was asleep, and toothless Atlas was useless, so she took her maid . . . and her pistol.

Stony was going to wait three days, rather than two, so he did not appear desperate for Miss Kane's blunt. No, he decided, the peagoose could get into too much trouble in another day. He'd stop by this morning on his way to Gentleman Jackson's Boxing Parlor and speak with the butler, Timms. Miss Kane would likely be asleep until noon, anyway, like most other females of his acquaintance. Old Timms seemed knowledgeable despite his age, and Stony needed to learn the lay of the land before he threw himself into the fray. He doubted Miss Kane could tell him what he wanted to know, if she even understood the perils of her situation. He was certain to get a better idea of conditions at Sloane Street from the butler than from the bacon-brained heiress. Hell, he'd get more coherent answers from the parrot!

He liked walking. He could be halfway to his destination before his curricle was brought 'round from the livery stable, and why should he pay the price of a hackney cab when he had legs of his own? What was the point of driving to an exercise session, anyway? This early in the morning he could enjoy the streets before they were filled with carriages and strolling Society. Stony noted that the trees were well budded, that the gardeners had been busy in the squares and the side yards of some of the houses, that one of the maids polishing the brass stair rails had a fine singing voice. The Woodruff sisters could have taken lessons from her. He tipped his hat to the soprano, and she gave him a friendly wink and a wave with her cleaning rag. Yes, he enjoyed mornings, especially ones like this when the sun was out and his fellow men were in. No blather, no bother with yesterday's scandal or tomorrow's gossip. No, the only ones out at this time of day were servants, tradesmen, and working people—like him.

His pleasure in the day faded.

Then it evaporated completely when he spotted two women on the steps of what was once Lady Augusta's town house and now belonged to an imbecilic, ill-favored . . . dog. Miss Kane did not own the residence, he recalled. She was leaving it, though. Even from this distance he could recognize her height and spare form, and the black skirts.

Stony was not pleased to see the woman going abroad so early. Didn't she realize there was no one about if she needed help? At least she had a maid with her, so the woman did have a shred of care for her safety and her reputation. He was also pleased to see that the maid, identified by a drab gray gown and a serviceable cloak, knew her trade, or had some pride in her employment. Today Miss Kane wore a fashionable green pelisse with black trim in the current military style over her black gown. She also wore a black satin bonnet, but at least the dreariness of the deep-brimmed, concealing hat was relieved by a green feather.

The same brim that hid Miss Kane's face from view also kept her unaware of Stony's approach. He could wait for her to leave before speaking with Timms, or he could follow to see where she was going so early, before the shops were open. Church? An assignation? He thought Timms would accompany her to the first, and could not imagine who would join her for the second.

In the end, he decided on candor, if not complete honesty. He quickened his pace to intercept her before she reached the corner. "Miss Kane, how delightful to see you out and about."

"Lord Wellstone?" Ellianne was stunned. The ink on her letter was barely dry, much less delivered, yet here he was. She hid the letter in a fold of her skirt, which was not the gown she'd intended to wear for their next interview. Nor was her hair styled properly. He, of course, was looking magnificent in fawn breeches and gleaming high-topped boots. The slight breeze had ruffled his hair and brought a healthy glow to his fair complexion. His eyes were even bluer than she recalled, bluer than the sunlit sky. "That is, good morning, sir."

"It is, is it not? My favorite time of day. As a matter of fact, I was on my way to pay you a call."

Ellianne frowned. Even she knew that proper morning calls were made after twelve o'clock. "So early?"

"Actually, I was going to ask Timms the best hour to stop by. But this is better. May I accompany you on your errand, whatever it is?"

What, let him walk her to his own house? Ellianne crumpled the letter into a ball in her fist. "Oh, we were just going to the park," she replied, the maid's start of surprise giving away the lie.

"Excellent," he said, "that was my next stop." He placed her gloved hand on his arm and turned in the opposite direction from where she had been headed. "Unless you mind my escort? I wished to know how you were getting on in town, and if matters were working out to your satisfaction."

He meant Mr. Lattimer or Baron Strickland, she knew, and was being diplomatic for the maid's sake. Ellianne could be diplomatic, too. "They are now."

For the rest of the walk to the park, Lord Wellstone kept up a steady stream of conversation, pointing out this notable garden, that impressive architecture. He remarked on the Thoroughbreds being ridden past for their morning gallops, and the drayhorses pulling their loads. Since Ellianne only had to nod and add the occasional "Oh?" she had a chance to think. If she was going to engage his services, she ought to be honest with the man. After all, she expected nothing less in return. And what happened to her resolve to be masterful, assured, in command? She refused to turn into a fluttering, flea-brained fool just because her companion was tall and handsome and charming and intelligent and built like a Roman warrior and . . .

"Millie," she addressed her maid as soon as they were on the pedestrian path in the park and near some benches, "why do you not sit and enjoy the rare sunshine awhile? His lordship and I will stroll a bit farther, but not out of sight."

There, she was acting decisively, while showing her acceptance of the rules for polite behavior, rules she expected the viscount to follow. Proud of herself, she held her head high and marched down the path until she found another bench, set on a higher rise, away from the foot traffic. "This offers a lovely view, does it not, my lord?"

All Stony could see was that wretched black bonnet, but he agreed, and took his seat beside her, not close enough to be suggestive, not so far away that their words could be overheard.

There were no words. Miss Kane was staring at the vista, wadding her handkerchief in her hands.

Finally Stony said, "Perhaps we should start anew."

"Yes, I would like that."

He nodded. "I am pleased to make your acquaintance, Miss Kane. I am Aubrey, Viscount Wellstone, but my friends call me Stony, and I am at your service." He held his hand out, and she dropped her handkerchief into it. Deuce take it, the woman still had no idea how to shake hands, or offer her fingers for a polite tribute. No, it was a letter, crumpled into a ball.

He looked at her, or what he could see under the brim of her bonnet, but found no answers there, only pale cheeks and shadowed eyes, so he smoothed out the folded, sealed page and saw his own name on the outside.

"I was going to call at your house to deliver this."

When he broke the seal with his finger the bank draft fell out, much creased and crumpled, but still legible, still worth one hundred blessed pounds. Stony raised one blond eyebrow.

"I need your help," was all she said.

"You have it."

"But there are conditions," she said at the same time he added, "Depending on your requirements."

"That is only fair," Ellianne agreed. "You should

not commit yourself until you know what is expected of you."

"Nothing illegal, I trust," he said with a smile, to think of this sober-sided spinster asking him escort her to gaming hells and bordellos, the worst he could think of her expectations.

"I cannot promise that."

Which wiped the smile right off his face. "Perhaps, since we have begun anew, you should begin at the start."

"Very well. To put it simply, my sister is missing. I will do anything it takes to find her, including hiring a—"

"Bow Street Runner?"

"Precisely. Mr. Lattimer. Except that he cannot go the places you can go. He cannot introduce me to members of society who might recall meeting her, or remember whom she spoke to, or who was the particular gentleman who took her fancy. He cannot make inquiries at the gentlemen's clubs about who left Town, or who needed money so badly he might have abducted an heiress."

Stony let out a deep breath. "Is that what you think happened to your sister?"

"I do not know. No ransom note has been sent, nor a wedding announcement with a demand for her dowry. I do not know what to believe anymore."

At the quaver in her voice, Stony started to reach for his handkerchief, but Miss Kane gathered her composure and said, "Nevertheless, I do believe I will find her."

Gwen would have turned into a watering pot by now, Stony knew. He was glad Miss Kane was made of sterner stuff. She would have to be, to face such a crisis. Now he felt bad about the disparaging thoughts he'd had of her. No wonder the poor woman was ready for Bedlam. Anyone would be, he supposed.

"Why don't you tell me what you know, so I can better understand what you want me to do?"

So she did. She explained how Isabelle had come to London at their aunt's invitation—and Ellianne's own urging—to see something of Town, to meet eligible gentlemen and attend parties. She was under no obligation to find a husband, not at nineteen years of age, not with her substantial income. She had left home four months ago, well before the start of the social Season, so she might shop and see the sights.

Her first letters were of the places she had seen, the stores and the commotion that was London. Then she mentioned paying calls with Aunt Augusta, and receiving invitations. Their aunt's health was deteriorating, she wrote, so they did not accept as many of those as they had hoped, but Isabelle was content. Not used to having three entertainments every evening or changing her outfits four times a day, Isabelle was happy enough to have made some new acquaintances. One was a special friend, she hoped, but would not dare put her emotions on paper, not even to her sister, until she was certain her feelings were reciprocated.

"Ah, the unnamed suitor."

Ellianne nodded. "She never mentioned him by name, only as her special friend, and that Aunt Augusta did not encourage his interest."

"Which might have meant your aunt knew the fellow was unworthy."

"Or it might have meant she had another choice in mind for Isabelle, one of higher birth."

"Not . . . ?"

"Yes, Baron Strickland."

"But he is far too old for a young female, far too worldly for an innocent maid. Surely your aunt could not have promoted a match between them?"

"I assure you she could, despite my remonstrances. Isabelle's next-to-last letter was about a drive she took with his lordship. Aunt Augusta declared herself too ill to leave the house, and Strickland was the only escort she would permit my sister."

"No wonder the chit disappeared."

"No, she did not leave because she feared marriage to Lord Strickland. She knew I would never allow her to be wed against her will. And he knew that I controlled her dowry, so he would never get his greedy hands on the property he craved."

"Unusual, isn't it, for one young woman to manage another's estate?"

"Unusual, but not unheard of. When I turned one and twenty, I decided to examine our inheritance more carefully. I found that the bank's trustees, our trustees, were embezzling funds. With proof, I had the courts make them surrender their guardianship—and replace the funds, of course—or face imprisonment. No one was named in their stead."

Stony was impressed and said so.

She thanked him, saying, "I have a head for figures."

Which made up, he decided, for the fact that she had no figure. "So you have been managing Kane Bank?"

"Not the day-to-day operations, of course, for which I found honest managers. But yes, I oversee the bank. And our investments, and Fairview. That is our estate, which used to belong to Baron Strickland, until he forfeited on a mortgage loan before Isabelle was even born."

"You say you control your sister's dowry, but could not a desperate man force your hand?"

"You mean force Isabelle to the altar? I do not think so. I taught my sister how to discourage importunate suitors, and how to defend herself against those like the baron who might become, ah, amorous."

"You taught her from experience, I take it?"

"To my regret. I was Baron Strickland's first choice

of bride, naturally, being older and less well protected than Isabelle."

Stony was going to get to practice his boxing skills today after all, on Strickland's face! "But you avoided his efforts. Since your sister is not now Lady Strickland, nor betrothed to be, we must assume she did too. So what then?"

"Then nothing."

"Damn. I beg your pardon."

"No apologies necessary. That is my sentiment exactly. Damn."

Chapter Nine

Stony could not sit still any longer. He got up and started to pace around the bench. "My word, what a coil. Did you not hear from your aunt?"

"The next letter I received from London came a month ago, from Aunt Augusta's solicitor, notifying me of her death. Her remains were being taken to Chansford Fold in Yorkshire, he wrote, so that she might find her final resting place beside her parents. He was kind enough to enclose a copy of my aunt's will."

"And your sister?"

"She was mentioned in the will, of course, but not in the solicitor's message. I expected her home in a matter of days, or a letter telling me she had been invited to a friend's home. I did get one letter, forwarded to me here in London from home: It was so spotted and smeared, I could not read it. She knew she could not stay on in Sloane Street with no one but servants as chaperones. When I did not hear more, I thought the mail must have gone astray, that she was enjoying herself at a house party somewhere. I even wondered if her sense of duty had forced her to accompany our aunt's remains to the Marquess of Chaston's seat."

"Would you have gone?"

"To a family who never acknowledged my mother's marriage? Who did not bother to send condolences on her death? To an uncle who did not wonder at his own nieces' welfare when they were left orphans? No, I would not have traveled to Yorkshire. I did send a messenger."

"While you came to London." Stony's mind was coursing ahead like a hound on a scent, seeking answers. "What did the servants say?"

"Aunt Augusta's dresser had, indeed, accompanied her body to Yorkshire, where her own family resides. The housekeeper had taken her pension and Aunt's silver candlesticks, and emigrated to Canada. The maidservants left for other positions, heaven knows where. And Timms . . . well, he was not much help."

"Surely he knew who called, where the ladies visited, which gentleman was to be refused entry."

"He should have, but he was letting the maids act as butler while he spent most of his days in the wine cellar."

"Not at church?"

"Oh, no, that is a much more recent calling, since losing my aunt." And losing his pension, but Ellianne saw no need to mention dear Timmy's fatal flaw. "Her death was devastating to him. They had been together for over forty years, you see. He suffered a crisis of the nerves."

"And found religion?"

"No, that was not until I promised to restore his pension if he stopped drinking and gambling." So much for protecting the old man's pride. Ellianne was still angry that he could not name Isabelle's beau. "He remembers nothing, except that Aunt Augusta and my sister were shouting the last night. My aunt was found dead in the morning by one of the maids, and my sister found missing by another."

"With her clothes?"

"Some of them, what could fit in two valises and a hatbox. Her jewels. So Isabelle did not rush out in a panicked frenzy." Ellianne looked over at him, where he had stopped pacing to lean against the bench. "She did not kill our aunt. I doubt Isabelle knew Aunt Augusta was dead when she left."

"The magistrate was satisfied?"

"Aunt's solicitor was thorough—and generous."

Stony started pacing again. "Very well. Your aunt is dead, the butler lost his memory in a bottle, the servants are scattered, and your sister is still missing. Bow Street cannot find her. What does Strickland say?"

"He refuses to say anything. He does not answer my messages, and when I called at his house—"

Stony stopped dead in his tracks, turning to face her. He disordered his fair curls even more by running his fingers through them. "You called at his house? The man who might have caused your sister's disappearance? Who wanted his estate restored, by means fair or foul? Even if he were a model of decorum, which I assure you the baron is not, no respectable woman calls on a bachelor household. Here I was thinking you a sensible female with legitimate reasons for your erratic behavior."

"My what?" she asked with a gasp. "I will have you know my actions at all times are well reasoned and respectable. I did not go to Strickland's house unaccompanied, nor unprotected."

She patted the large reticule that dangled by strings off her wrist. All Stony could hear was the rustling of paper. She thought to defend herself against an aging rake with what, a sermon? Or was she thinking to reform Strickland with religion, like the butler? The day prayers kept a man from visiting prostitutes, every wife in London would be on her knees. Or not.

The hundred pounds that now rested in Stony's pocket was suddenly not nearly enough pay for the headaches this female was going to cause him. He counted to ten. Twice. "All right. You went to Strickland's home and . . . ?"

"And he fled out the back door. The next time, yesterday, the house was shut up. He has flown like a thief in the night."

"Someone at the clubs will know where he's landed."

"That was exactly my thinking," Ellianne said with a smug tone to her voice, "which is why I decided to engage your services after all. I cannot enter the gentlemen's preserves on my own. Nor can I introduce myself to the young ladies who might have conversed with Isabelle at balls and such. You know, at supper, or in the ladies' retiring rooms, or between dances. Girls are prone to chatter, so one of them might recall something of use."

Stony well knew how young females prated on and on about nothing at all. If any one of them could recall a conversation ten minutes later, though, much less over a month ago, he'd be surprised. "I can ask Lady Valentina Pattendale. She had her come-out last year, and attended every function since."

Ellianne recognized the name from her lists, and from more current news in the *on dits* columns. "Will the lady help without gossiping about Isabelle? I mean to protect my sister's reputation as well as her fortune."

"I would not trust Lady Valentina with a bent soup spoon, much less a secret, but she does owe me a favor. And all anyone has to know is that Miss Isabelle Kane did indeed go north to help bury her aunt, then to visit friends nearby during a brief mourning period. As you mentioned, she could not stay on in Town unchaperoned, nor could she attend balls so soon after a death in the family, so no one will wonder at her leaving."

That sounded reasonable to Ellianne, more reasonable than entrusting her sister's good name to a young lady who had made micefeet of her own reputation.

"There are other girls I would like to interview. I made a chart." She opened the strings of her purse and withdrew a folded square of thick paper. She unfolded it to reveal the project she'd been gluing when Lord Wellstone came to Sloane Street. He leaned over her shoulder while she started to explain it to him. She tried not to be distracted by the closeness of his broad shoulder, or the soap-and-spice male scent of him.

Of course, she had to think about his strength and his smell in order to tell herself not to think about them. "Here, that is there . . . No, that piece was to cover a hole. This one? Perhaps the cream-colored scrap."

He took it from her and studied the opened page, filled with newspaper clippings and bits of expensive pressed papers, with arrows and circles connecting the various items, where dried glue had not obscured the markings. He hoped she was better at numbers than at making maps, or whatever the deuced thing was.

With him standing farther away, Ellianne found her wandering wits. "I gathered a stack of invitations from Aunt Augusta's desk, events she might have attended when Isabelle first came to Town. Then I ordered back issues of the various newspapers and cut out any mention of those parties. The papers often mention who attended, who danced with whom, that kind of thing. I was hoping to see my sister's name among them, but the journalists preferred to write about titled ladies, or ones whose conduct was questionable."

"Scandal sells more newspapers than news does, unfortunately."

"Yes, but I did manage to gather some names, names that occurred frequently enough that they must have been introduced to my sister at one time or another. You see, here is Lady Valentina's name, but there are others which appear more often. I have listed them on the back," Ellianne concluded, proud of her handiwork.

Stony studied the notations a moment, turned the page over, then tore it in half, then quarters.

Ellianne jumped to her feet, dropping her reticule, which landed with a heavy thud. She ignored it and reached for the pieces—now eight of them—of her once lovely chart. "Of all the high-handed, rude, obnoxious behavior! Why, you are exactly like those old dodderers at the bank. If something is not their idea, it must not have merit. If this is your notion of assisting me, belittling my efforts and—"

"She was not at any of those events."

"What?"

"I said, your sister was not at Lady Fanshawe's rout, nor at the Byington girl's betrothal ball. She could not have spoken to your list of young ladies, for she was not among them."

"How can you know that?"

"Because I was there, and I would have known if Lady Augusta was firing off a niece, or if a new heiress had come to Town. It was my job to know such things, you understand, my livelihood."

"Oh," was all Ellianne could think to say.

Stony saw the droop in her slim shoulders. "But it was a good effort on your part," he said to cheer her up. "Well conceived and, ah, well constructed."

"But a wasted effort. Now we will never find anyone who spoke to my sister."

"Nonsense. Of course we will. Lady Valentina might know, and, better still, Gwen will know who Lady Augusta's friends were."

"Gwen?" Ellianne was not happy that yet another stranger was going to be privy to her family's woes.

"My stepmama. But she is quite young. You'll adore her, everyone does, and she is an invaluable font of information about the beau monde. What she does not know, your aunt's cronies will."

"Aunt Augusta had no close friends when I was in Town last. She still received invitations, of course, although she rarely reciprocated, but she seldom had morning callers or guests for dinner. She balked at wasting her money at silver loo, and declined to sit on any charitable committees, places where her contemporaries congregated." Ellianne was still bitter that her aunt had refused to help fund the girls' training school, yet she died a wealthy woman. Like it or not, Aunt Augusta's money was going to add a new wing, Ellianne had decided, with her name on it. If her posthumous generosity annoyed the old miser, she could take it up with the marquess's ancestors. "She said the London ladies of her generation were all empty-headed ninnies, who spoke of nothing but their grandchildren, their health, and how to spend more of their husbands' money than the husbands could spend on their mistresses."

"Now there's a problem." Stony propped one booted foot up on the bench, resting his arm on his knee, thinking out loud. "We need more information. Usually the servants and the grande dames know everything. Featherbrained chits cannot be counted on to recall anything but their next dancing partner."

Ellianne did not like any of her gender being called featherbrained, but then her sister had gone off without leaving a note. She sighed. "I had another idea, in case the first ones did not work."

"I am sure you did," Stony muttered, almost too low for Ellianne to hear.

"Excuse me?"

"I said I am sure you devised a good one."

Ellianne's brow was furrowed, but she went on to explain: "You see, if Aunt Augusta was trying to promote the match with Strickland"—she grimaced worse—"she might have tried to keep other men away, not making introductions that she should have. Yet I know from my sister's letters that they did go out, that she did make new friends and met one gentleman in particular, before our aunt took ill, that is. That must be why you hadn't heard of my sister's presence, or encountered her at the more popular gatherings. But someone saw her, perhaps without learning her name."

"That makes sense."

She tilted her head in acknowledgment of the meager praise. "So we have to prod their memories. I thought perhaps I could attend some quiet functions, not to dance, of course, not while wearing mourning, but to be seen. That is where I need your assistance. Without Aunt Augusta, I have no social connections in London. I know various bankers and investors and other men of business, but they are of no help in this matter. The schoolmates I still consider friends are spread about the countryside, tending their ever-increasing nurseries." Ellianne kept a stock of silver rattles ready to be engraved. "And I made no lasting relationships in the short time I spent here for my own presentation." Well, she had made a lasting impression on Lord Strickland.

"You were presented at court?"

Ellianne bristled at the surprise in his voice. "Of course. Aunt Augusta insisted. After all, my father was knighted for service to the Crown, and my grandfather was a marquess. The queen was very gracious; the hoops and high feathers one had to wear were atrocious. Two days later I went home. So, you see, I have no one to call upon to seek invitations. I thought of attending the theater, but do not wish to encounter the kind of gentlemen who would approach me without an introduction."

"Invitations are no difficulty." Lud, once it was known that the heiress to the Kane kingdom was in Town, she would be deluged, introductions be damned. For that matter, her spindly looks and sometime lunacy were of no account, compared to her bank account. "My stepmama can host a small dinner in your honor," he volunteered, "and make you known to enough ladies that you will have engagements aplenty. I shall, naturally, escort you to whichever you choose. But I do not see what good that will do. If no one recalls your sister, why would your presence refresh their memories?"

"Oh, did I not say? We look remarkably alike, my sister and I, despite the age difference. Isabelle is an inch or so shorter, but otherwise we might have been twins."

Now that was a lot of help. Who was going to remember another nondescript young woman? The green eyes were nice enough, but nothing to stick in one's mind, especially when affixed to a stick of a figure. And if the sister kept her eyes lowered, like this one, or shielded by bonnets and lace, like Miss Kane, she would be no more memorable than the wallpaper. "I do not see—"

Ellianne went "Tsk" with her tongue. Then she looked to see that no one was near them except a nanny and a toddler. Even her maid seemed to be drowsing in the sun, paying no attention to Ellianne and the viscount. She stood up and untied the ribbons of her black bonnet. Then she lifted it off. Because she was simply going for a brief walk, then returning to wash her hair, Ellianne had not bothered with an intricate coiffure. She pulled out the two combs that held it piled on top of her head, letting her hair fall down, absolutely straight down, to below her waist.

The viscount's mouth was open. The foot that was resting on the bench dropped to the ground for better balance, so he did not fall over. "Great gods."

"Impossible, isn't it?" Ellianne said with a blush, the kind of blush that only a porcelain-skinned redhead could generate. She hurried to gather the mass of lurid, almost lewd red hair back into a knot.

"Don't. That is, please don't."

She let go, letting her hair fall back, then sat down and tilted her face up. To be without all that weight on her head, and the heavy bonnet, felt heavenly. So did the sun on her cheeks, especially since it was too weak to burn. The viscount still had not spoken, so she said, "I know it is thoroughly unfashionable, but people rarely forget the redheaded Kanes."

That was not red. That was living fire. Bits of gold, slivers of orange, but mostly glorious, gleaming flame, smoother than satin, as sensuous as sin. Siren-colored, scarlet woman-colored—on Miss Ellianne Kane, the banker's spinster daughter. Stony could have cried. In fact, he felt a tear in his left eye now, but that was from not blinking so long. Lord, no one could ever forget a woman with hair that ignited the senses, stirred the loins, spun carnal dreams. Miss Kane, by Jupiter!

She was not half as old as he'd guessed, definitely under thirty. She was still thin, with prominent cheekbones and that pointed chin, but she was stunning, if not classically beautiful. Her nose was straight, but a bit too short, and her eyelashes were too gold to be the proper frame for those fine green eyes, which were shadowed by worry, he supposed, or lack of sleep. They were staring at him in consternation now. Miss Kane, by George. Who would have imagined?

"Your sister, she looks like you?" he finally managed to ask through dry lips.

She nodded, sending ripples through the glorious sunset shades.

Stony could not take his own eyes away, although he knew she was becoming concerned, as well she might. Lud, no wonder someone had carried Miss Isabelle off, and her dowry be damned. For a minute he considered handing back Miss Ellianne Kane's hundred pounds, for there was no way in hell he was going to be able to keep this sister safe from the jackals. Then too, if he was not in her employ, he could join the horde of lust-filled, leering predators.

But he was in her employ. He had accepted her check, and she did need his help. He swallowed and suggested she put her hat back on, since the park was starting to fill. Meanwhile, he tried to gather his wandering thoughts. Since that proved almost impossible, he started to gather her possessions, the scraps of torn paper, her fallen reticule.

"Zeus, the thing must weigh more than you do. What is in here?" he asked. "A cannon?"

"No, only a pistol," she said, taking the reticule from him.

"You carry a pistol around with you?" The idea of a gun in any woman's hands was terrifying.

She nodded. "For protection. Especially now, not knowing what happened to Isabelle."

"And you let it drop like that? Good gods, ma'am, don't you know those things are notoriously unreliable, hair trigger or not?" He knew he was ranting, more to cover his licentious thoughts than anything else. In a way he was thankful that Miss Kane had reverted to being rattle-brained, which he could manage far better than her being ravishing. Ravishable, ravish-meant, rats! "By heaven, it could have gone off when it hit the ground. Thunderation, you might have shot yourself, or me! Of all the cockle-headed, caper-witted ideas, that one wins the—"

"It was not loaded."

He turned to look at her. It was safe now that her head was all covered in that crime against manhood. Of course, now he could not see her eyes or her expression. "Good grief, ma'am, how can an empty pistol be protection?"

"Oh, that is your job now," she said as she took his arm to walk toward her maid and the park exit. "Isn't it?"

Chapter Ten

"You could have hired a blasted bodyguard!"

"Yes, but he could not have helped find my sister." As they neared the bench where her maid sat, Ellianne asked, "Do you have siblings, my lord?"

"No, to my regret. Not even a half brother or sister. I do have a handful of cousins scattered across the country, mostly on my mother's side. I have barely seen them since her passing."

"Isabelle and Aunt Lally are all the family I have left now. I would do anything for my sister, pay any amount to have her returned. Or if she does not wish to come home, I would do anything in my power to see that she is safe and happy. Anything."

"Even hiring a vagrant viscount to parade you through polite society, which can be anything but polite?" He smiled at his own self-deprecation.

"If that is what it takes, my lord, then yes."

"I would feel more comfortable if you managed to forget the title part. Well, the vagrant part too, but I'd rather you called me by name. For both our sakes, we can give out that our families have some distant connection. No one needs to know that you had to hire yourself a gentleman escort."

"Or that you have to squire misfit misses about Town to pay your bills."

"Oh, I think everyone knows that by now," Stony said, "but they will accept the pretense of a long-standing friendship."

Ellianne had to laugh. "They cannot be such fools as to believe Ellis Kane and the former Viscount Wellstone were bosom bows."

"No, but your aunt might have introduced us years ago, as a distant cousin to my mother."

The notion of her penny-pinching Aunt Augusta introducing her to a profligate peer was almost as absurd as her egalitarian Aunt Lally making her known to a pockets-to-let lord. She laughed again, and Stony had to smile at the sound.

"So will you? Call me by name, that is. Nobody but Gwen addresses me as Aubrey, but Wellstone will do if you cannot bring yourself to call me Stony."

"I will think about it." The informality might raise other questions, fueling more gossip that she wished to avoid. She did not suggest that he call her by her given name, either.

By this time they had reached her maid. The attendant's presence a few steps behind them put an end to any personal, private exchanges, although they both knew their conversation was not concluded.

For Ellianne's part, she thought things had gone well so far, although Lord Wellstone was a bit more assertive than she might have liked. Ripping up her chart was certainly no act of a subservient employee, nor was shouting at her about the pistol. Alternatively, a docile, biddable man might not serve her purposes half as well. She simply had to be more forceful, so his lordship did not forget who was steering the ship, so to speak. Toward that end, she decided, she might stop using his honorifics, but she would not relinquish the dignity of Miss Kane. Let Lord—no, let plain Wellstone, although there was nothing plain about him, from his shining blond curls to his polished leather boots—remember that she was a woman of substance, of standing, of independence. Otherwise, she feared, he would be treating her like one of his silly protégées, or a pet pony on a leading string. Goodness, he'd be calling her Ellie next, or the dreaded Nell, or "my girl."

His girl? Where had that idea come from? Perhaps the sun had been stronger than Ellianne thought, for her cheeks were growing warm. She erased any notion of such familiarity from her mind on the instant. He was her hireling, that was all.

It was too bad that she could not call him Stony, though. The name suited him, not that there was anything gray or harsh or forbidding about his countenance or personality. The casual shortening of his title seemed to match both his open friendliness and the solid strength of his character, though. For a moment Ellianne regretted that they could never be friends, that an ocean of differences flowed between them, that she had to maintain her authority.

Ellianne thought she had conducted herself in a manner befitting her age and consequence. Except for when she screeched at him for destroying her chart, or when she dropped the reticule with the loaded pistol. Of course it was loaded. She was not fool enough to carry a weapon she could not fire—or to argue a minor point with an angry, officious gentleman. Oh, and she was not proud of herself for becoming moonstruck in the morning, just because an attentive, handsome, virile man had leaned close enough to her that she could breathe the same air he did.

Other than those few lapses, Ellianne told herself, she had done well. She had not been permanently reduced to schoolgirlish imbecility over a practiced charmer, and she had acquired the perfect colleague for her quest. Together—but with her in charge—they would find Isabelle. Ellianne felt comforted by the thump of the heavy reticule against her right thigh, and the firmly muscled arm under her left hand.

Stony liked the fact that he did not have to shorten his stride to accommodate a petite female. He liked too that Miss Kane's wider skirts, while not precisely unfashionable, allowed her free movement. For once he did not have to walk at a woman's mincing pace. He also liked the fact that he was one of the few people, so far, who knew what was concealed behind the obscuring black coverings. Half of him couldn't wait to see the *ton*'s reaction to the woman, sure to be dubbed an Original. Another half wanted to clasp her secret to himself like a precious jewel. A third half—he was that flummoxed—still wanted to clasp her, period.

He would not, of course. His job was to act as escort—and detective, it seemed—not seducer. With that check in his pocket, the woman was in his care, and out of bounds.

Of course, nothing in his personal code of honor said that he could not enjoy himself, or could not try to bring some pleasure to his client. He remembered her laugh, no titter, no giggle that grated on one's nerves, just a sound that had to make anyone near her smile in return. She should laugh more, and would, he swore, as soon as they found her sister.

He'd rather not examine why he should care so much about relieving her anxieties, but he thought any decent man would feel the same. The sister was in hugger-mugger up to her eyebrows, but his Miss Kane was innocent of anything more than devotion to her family, which he could understand and admire. As for understanding anything more of how the woman's muddled mind worked . . . Well, she was a female. There was no comprehending.

Contrary to his first impressions, Stony thought he might come to like her, when she came down off her high horse. Someone had to keep reminding her that she was a woman, an incredibly attractive one at that, not a financier. The gentlemen of her acquaintance must have made poor work of it, for the woman seemed oblivious to her allure. She thought her brilliant hair was impossible and unfashionable. Hah! When had glory been out of style? Stony thought he just might take on the job of proving that Miss Kane's worth did not lie in her wealth. Add that to the chore of finding the sister, and Stony was pleased with his new undertaking. Here was a far better challenge than choosing which waistcoat to wear, or which gentleman might make an acceptable dance partner for someone's spotty sister. He started to whistle a jaunty tune.

Amazingly enough, the parrot was singing the same tune when they arrived at Miss Kane's residence, if the squawking could be considered a song. Unfortunately, the parrot was singing the words, not whistling. Even more unfortunately, the verse to "The Mermaid's Ball" was not fit for the ears of a gentlewoman. Stony was left to wonder once more about the bird's former owner when the maid clapped her hands over her ears and fled for the servants' stairs, and Miss Kane hurried into the front parlor.

"To put Polly in his place," she said, slamming the parlor door behind her before Stony could follow. He stayed where he was, waiting for her return, so they might find a private place to continue their discussion. Stony had a few more queries to make, especially about the Bow Street man's investigation, so he did not repeat the other man's obviously futile search into coaching inns, et cetera.

Timms was not on duty in the entry hall, but Stony was not concerned at missing a conversation with the old man. Miss Kane had given him ample information to consider, answering a lot of the questions Stony would have put to the butler. If Timms was as forgetful as Miss Kane said, he'd be of no help anyway.

Except for fetching another bottle of that excellent Madeira.

Ah, there he came. But no, the wheezing breaths might have been Timms's, but that scrabbling sound was not the butler's slow footstep. It was claws on marble tile, tearing down the long hall, sliding on loose carpet runners, careening off walls and side tables, straight for Stony. "No, Atlas. No. Good dog, sit."

Atlas did not sit. He kept coming, barreling down the hall like an asthmatic ale keg on legs. Stony could not afford a new pair of boots, or gloves for that matter. He looked around, frantic to find something to—Aha! The huge bouquet of exotic blooms in the Chinese urn. He snatched out a huge red flower to throw.

"Silk? The flowers are made out of blasted silk? No, Atlas. Friends, boy. We are friends."

Atlas must have had a memory problem too. He did not seem to recall the viscount. He was steps away from Stony's boots, about to launch himself for an attack. Could he reach a man's throat? Could a toothless bulldog do any damage to a strong, fit man? Stony was not waiting to find out. He dove for the front door, pulled it open, and dashed through it. Atlas was on his heels. Atlas was out. Atlas was flying through the air. Before the dog's short legs touched the ground, Stony swiveled and was back inside, the door firmly closed behind him.

He adjusted his neckcloth and was placing the red flower back in the urn when Miss Kane came back to the entry. "Did I hear someone at the door?" she asked.

"Oh, that was Atlas. He seemed to want to go out, so I opened the door for him. He does know his way back in, doesn't he?"

"Yes, and how kind of you. I am more and more convinced that you are the perfect gentleman to assist me. I do have a few more items to discuss with you first, though. Will you come with me?"

So she was once more the banker's prim and proper maiden daughter, Stony thought as he followed her down the hall. She paused occasionally to kick a rug back into alignment with her foot, and once she bent to unfold a lifted corner. She'd removed the pelisse, though, and the black bonnet, leaving her hair loose except for two tortoiseshell combs at the sides. Her gown was crafted by a master seamstress, cradling what appeared to be ample breasts for such a thin woman, and the silk skirt, when she bent over, showed a nicely curved derriere. No starchy old spinster ever looked like this, he'd swear, a grin on his face.

"This is serious business, Wellstone," she said as they entered a well-stocked book room. She made sure the door was left partly open, for propriety's sake, then sat at a large desk, indicating that he should take the smaller, facing seat across the vast expanse.

He stayed on his feet.

"If you are worried that this is the desk that Aunt Augusta hit her head upon, you may rest easy. I had that one carted out and this one brought down from the attics in its place."

A jerk of her head signaled him to sit.

Stony looked at the wide desk, and the position of authority Miss Kane had claimed, and strolled about the room instead, admiring the depth of the collection on the shelves. A man could spend months here, visiting with old friends. And a woman could be taught not to play games with a professional.

Miss Kane cleared her throat. She had another piece of paper in her hand, another chart.

Stony knew he'd rather read the driest book of sermons than whatever she had written there. "Yes?"

She consulted the paper in front of her and cleared her throat again, as if to make way for some unpleasantness she had to relate. "I wish to discuss the terms and conditions of your employ, so that neither of us has unfounded expectations."

"But I agreed to help find your sister in whatever

manner is required. Finding Strickland, looking into whichever young ladies might have been her confidantes." Stony had other ideas of how to proceed, but Miss Kane did not need to know about his going to exclusive brothels, or asking around whether anyone had recently taken a new redheaded mistress into his keeping. If the girl looked like her sister . . .

Then again, if Isabelle had that poker up her backside like Miss Kane, he might save the effort. She had not flown the coop to fly with the birds of paradise.

"Yes," Miss Kane was saying, "and I have every confidence you will perform your part admirably. But these"—she tapped the list with one finger—"are more intangible aspects of my requirements. For instance, I must be assured of your discretion. I would be a fool to tell people that Isabelle is visiting relatives if you contradict me at a later date. In your clubs, perhaps, or in your cups."

"I do not drink to excess, if that is what you are tiptoeing around with your list. Nor do I gossip about my affairs. I would never be entrusted with a young woman again were I to bandy her name in smoke-filled rooms. For that matter, no lady would speak to me if I betrayed her confidences. Do you wish me to supply references, testimonies to my character? That might be difficult without divulging names, which, of course, I am sworn to keep private."

She ignored the sarcasm, and the angry tapping of his fingers on the bookshelves. "A young woman's reputation is invaluable."

"As is the reliability of a man's word."

"Quite." She checked the first item off her list. "Next is loyalty. You were known to, um, escort more than one young lady at a time. My sister is an extremely wealthy young woman. What if someone else offered you more money than I do to find her for his own reasons? Or to not find her?"

Now his booted toe joined Stony's fingers in a rapid tattoo. Was she really accusing him of turning traitor?

"I should wish to know that man's reasons. The young lady's welfare must come first."

"But if it were a friend of yours who had an interest in my sister and her fortune?"

"I count as friend no man who would run off with a gently bred female, damaging her reputation and wounding her family."

Ellianne's brows knitted. "I suppose that means I have your loyalty?"

"I suppose it does."

She read off the next item on her list. "Communication. We must have open conversations."

"Are we communicating now, Miss Kane?" Stony thought they were having an exercise in seeing how many insults she could offer him before he walked out.

"Well, yes, but I mean that if you discover any information, I wish to be advised instantly. I do not want to be protected from any unpleasantness, as gentlemen are wont to do with women. Nor do I wish you to take any actions without discussing them with me first."

He was supposed to tell her about the bordellos? Or his plan to visit hospitals and the morgue? The docks to see what ships left, and what cargo they carried? He'd tell her, all right. When pigs flew. He replaced the volume of Aristotle's *Poetics* back among its brethren and said, "Miss Isabelle is your sister. Of course you should be kept abreast of the investigation."

She smiled then and he almost forgave her for being a prig. Her features softened and golden flecks in her eyes danced when she smiled and said, "There, we are building an excellent understanding, are we not?"

He understood she was still a prig, who knew nothing of life and less about men. She did not know when enough was enough either. He went back to perusing the shelves, hoping the haughty hen-wit would get the hint, and let him get on with finding her sister.

"There is one other item on my list, an item of a somewhat . . . delicate nature."

That got his attention.

"You see," she began, "I know all about Lady Valentina and your friend Captain Brisbane, who is not the man she is presently engaged to wed."

"And?"

"And I should not like to be placed in any such awkward position. An unprincipled rogue could easily take advantage of my situation, thinking to better line his pockets. I need your word as a gentleman that—"

Plato slammed back onto the shelf. "Madam, if I am a gentleman, I would not betray a female in my care. If I am not a gentleman, my word is not worth tuppence. You must decide which I am."

She bit her lip. "I can see that I have offended you. I am not casting aspersions on your honor; I am simply trying to make it clear that I cannot be forced into marriage like Lady Valentina." She ignored his snort of derision. "Any attempt to destroy my reputation will fail, because I do not care. I can go home, where, scandal-touched or not, I cannot be denied. I own the bank, and I run the school. The people who matter know who and what I am."

"You mean you have paid for their loyalty also?"

"No! I have earned their—"

Stony held up his hand. "If it is assurance you want, Miss Kane, let me swear on my mother's grave that I have absolutely no desire to have you for a wife, at any price."

"Good." But for some reason his instant, absolute, heartfelt assertion did not feel good. Ellianne hurried on before she could think about it. "Then we are agreed. I am hiring you to help in finding my sister, because those of your social circles might have clues to her disappearance, and I require your entrée and your escort to those circles. I am not employing you to shower me with false gallantry or feigned affection."

"I assure you, my affections are not for hire." And affection was the last thing he was feeling for her at this moment.

"And there will be no flirting, no stolen kisses."

"I promise, if you do."

Her cheeks turned scarlet. "What? Me? Heavens, as if I would—"

"But you think I would? Trade favors for money? By heaven, I am no kept man, Miss Kane, and I would challenge any man who dared imply otherwise." He pounded his fist on the shelf for emphasis, and the parrot started squawking and the dog started barking. Someone must have let the cur in, and that someone would be in this room in a moment, checking to make sure another mistress was not bludgeoned in the book room.

It was a close call.

Stony sat down before he did commit mayhem, and Ellianne wiped her forehead. "Well. It appears we have only to discuss your payment."

"Miss Kane, gentlemen do not discuss money with ladies. In fact, they seldom mention remuneration."

"Which is why so many gentlemen end up in debt. Punting on River Tick, I believe they call it. I call it cork-brained. I am not a lady, however, even if I am accepted among your society's elite. No, I am Ellis Kane's daughter, of Kane Bank, and I would know the price of a pig before I purchase it."

"Now you are calling me a pig?" Stony was halfway to the door. "Good day, ma'am. And good luck. You will need it."

"Oh, botheration, Wellstone, come back. I did not mean to liken you to livestock. I just wished to ascertain what you expected to be paid, and how. By the week? By the month? You are the one doing the work, so you should be the one to make sure the payment is sufficient. Here, look at my chart. I tried to calculate a value for your time and another for your—"

Stony had stamped across to the desk. He leaned over, picked up her chart, and tore it to shreds. "If I work for you, you will pay me what my efforts are worth to you, no more, no less."

Ellianne looked at the scraps of paper on the desk. "I wish you would stop doing that. It is very rude, you know."

"So is treating me like an employee."

"But . . . but I thought that's what you were."

Chapter Eleven

The first order of business, when Stony and Ellianne were finished glaring at each other, was to introduce Miss Kane to Gwen, Lady Wellstone. At least that was what Stony decided had to come first. He could not take a marriageable—whether she chose to marry or not—woman out and about by himself without giving rise to a shower of gossip. The fact that Miss Kane was no young miss, but nearly on the shelf, would turn the shower into a pelter of hailstones. Hell, knowing that she was an heiress and he was an empty-coffers viscount, the ensuing deluge could drown both of them.

Once they had established that Wellstone's respectably widowed stepmama had taken Miss Kane under her wing, he tried to explain, then, and only then, could Stony take her for solitary drives, hold private conversations, escort her to unknown destinations. The *ton* might look askance at a single woman, even at Ellianne's advanced age, in public without a chaperon, but Gwen's approval would stifle the gossip. Besides, Stony predicted, Ellianne would instantly be labeled an Original, which was a polite term for a woman wealthy enough to be as eccentric as she deuced well chose. A poor woman, or one without such connections, would have been labeled Or Not. As in: She'd be invited places if there was an empty seat, or not invited. She'd be introduced to the eligible bachelors if no other girl needed a partner, or not be noticed at all.

Miss Kane could *not* not be noticed.

For her part, Ellianne saw no reason for visits to the shops with Lady Wellstone, ices at Gunter's in the viscountess's company, paying morning calls at her side. It was all a waste of her time. If she was not searching for her sister, she'd do better to read the newspapers, visit the new manufactories, tend to her investments.

What she'd rather be doing, what she thought Lord Wellstone should be helping her do, was breaking into Lord Strickland's house to see if the dastard was cowering under his bed. Or if he had Isabelle hidden there.

After a great deal of growling and gnashing of jaws—Atlas joined them, but Miss Kane had a cooked carrot in her pocket—Ellianne was convinced to let Wellstone track down the baron while she let herself be seen about Town. Someone might recognize her and inquire after her sister, but only if she were not hidden inside a black turtle shell of a bonnet.

"I'll have you know I paid a great deal of money for this bonnet."

"Which should prove that money cannot buy everything."

Ellianne had to bite her tongue before she reminded him that money had bought his company and cooperation. Wellstone seemed to be a bit sensitive on the subject of money, although Ellianne could not understand why. She saw no embarrassment in working for one's living, in earning an honest wage. There was nothing underhanded about what Lord Wellstone was doing, especially if he was not committing breaking and entering, as she wished. So what if he was being paid to escort a woman to a ball? He could have been the coachman driving, or the lackey cleaning the streets when the carriage passed. Of course, he could have gone into the army, or the church, or studied law, professions considered genteel enough for a member of the aristocracy, but at least he had shown initiative. Ellianne did not have any less respect for him. She did not have any more, either, for the prideful, officious, infuriating man.

She did let herself be convinced, however. He knew the beau monde far better than she did; she would not have hired him otherwise. So she dutifully went off to meet Gwen and to go shopping. Aunt Lally refused to go, out of Stony's hearing, of course. What, sit silent while the gentry morts swilled tea? Or pay some faker with a French accent six times what a hat was worth? By Saint Tarcisius's twig and berries, one bonnet was good enough for her, and she could get better yard goods, at better prices, from her late husband's friends, besides.

Ellianne went and enjoyed herself, to her surprise. She found Lady Wellstone a charming companion, as mutton-headed as Aunt Lally had predicted, but far more knowledgeable about fashion than anyone she had yet encountered. The viscountess truly believed that a woman should look her best at all times, for her own sake, not to please anyone else. Since such a pretty young widow could have rewed any time these past years, she must not be dressing merely to attract a man, Ellianne decided, and approved. Gwen—for they, at least, were quickly on a first-name basis—was also obviously devoted to her stepson, singing his praises, enumerating his accomplishments, deferring to his judgment . . . and likely planning his wedding. Which would have been fine with Ellianne, she told herself despite a peculiar pang, if she were not the chosen bride.

She had to nip such unfounded optimism in the bud,

especially if she were to be friends with Gwen. "You do know that Lord Wellstone is in my employ?"

"Oh, I wish you would not speak of it so. Polite company frowns on mention of trade, you know. Well, you might not, but just a hint, my dear, for you would not wish to be thought . . . Goodness, everyone knows your father was . . . so I suppose . . ."

Ellianne was beginning to understand her new acquaintance, ellipses or not. "But they will pretend I am one of them, if I do not keep reminding them."

Gwen beamed at her. "So clever. Just like my dear stepson. It is so lowering to think that dear Aubrey has to . . . That is, his father was not as careful as he should have been. And we do try to ignore the necessity, for there are those who might not be as understanding. Of course, they never had dressmakers dunning one for payment, or rooms shut up for economy's sake so that one's cousins had to . . ." Gwen let a slight frown mar her still-youthful loveliness, but only for a moment. She patted Ellianne's hand. "But I am sure that dear Aubrey would have helped you anyway, as a favor or out of gentlemanly duty, because he is so kind and caring."

Ellianne did not believe for an instant that a member of the *ton* would put himself out for Ellis Kane's daughter unless there were some gain in it for himself. Trying not to hurt her hostess's feelings, Ellianne merely smiled. "Lord Wellstone is a fine gentleman, indeed, but spoken aloud in company or not, ours is a matter of business. I hope you will not read anything more into our arrangement."

Hope sprang eternal in a mother's—or stepmother's—breast. "Ah, but you will be much in each other's company."

"But not keeping company, as they say." Ellianne was firm on the topic. "We are not stepping out together."

"But your steps fit so well. Most other ladies barely

come to his collarbone. Although I suppose I should not mention a gentleman's anatomy."

Neither should Aunt Lally, but that never stopped her. Ellianne smiled again, and agreed that height in a husband was much to be desired, especially for a bean stalk of a female like herself. "However, I do not want a husband. I do not plan to marry."

"What, never?" Gwen was aghast. Tears came to her eyes. "All those beautiful babies! My grandchildren!"

"Oh, heavens, I did not mean to upset you, just to warn you not to practice your matchmaking skills on me."

Gwen dabbed at her eyes. "I am rather good at it, you know. And Aubrey is—"

"Just the kind of man I would least consider: patronizing, pigheaded, and puffed up with his own supposed omnipotence."

"That does describe most men, I am afraid. I do believe their mothers teach it to them at birth, or their wet nurses do, for they start being bullies at quite an early age, you know. My cousin's boys . . . But no matter. If not dear Aubrey, what about—"

"No. No one. I am content in my present state, and have no desire to place myself under a gentleman's sway."

"Oh, dear, but they sway so nicely." Lady Wellstone gasped, then placed her hand over her mouth. "I should not have said that either. Dear Aubrey says my tongue runs on wheels, and you an unmarried . . . and bound to stay that way." She started weeping.

Lady Wellstone's favorite remedy for the blue devils, it seemed, was to go shopping, especially since she had a mission. Goodness, one look at Ellianne's ensemble was enough to launch a crusade.

Ellianne had never seen so many bonnets as went on and off her head that morning. At last she and Gwen agreed on an exorbitantly priced scrap of lace, properly black, but with red cherries at the side, drawing attention to her bright hair, instead of trying to hide it from sight. Gwen would not let her hide her feminine endowments under the high-necked gowns Ellianne favored either.

"What, have a friend of mine labeled a dowd?" Gwen was affronted. "Your appearance is a reflection on me, you know. When I introduce you as my young friend, I would be mortified if anyone titters behind their fans. They will already be nattering on about your fortune. That is, your father. And you and dear Aubrey, which is quite enough grist for the rumor mills, especially if you and he . . . Well, you will want to look your best when you face the world."

So Ellianne's new gowns were cut lower, in jewel-like shades of emerald or sapphire or amber, with black trimmings in memory of Aunt Augusta. She also ordered a black silk gown for evening that no one could mistake for mourning. Of course, the new gowns needed matching slippers, and new stockings and gloves to match. And new underpinnings, to make Ellianne's shape conform to the current fashion. While she was at it, she might as well order new night rails. Even if no one saw the bed gowns, Gwen insisted, Ellianne would have prettier dreams than when wearing serviceable flannel.

Shopping was exhausting work, Ellianne found, much harder than adding columns in her head or figuring interest rates. And more fun, especially when the shopkeepers learned she intended to pay cash.

"My dear, a lady does not ask the price of things," Gwen whispered at the first dressmaker's. "And they only pay for what their pin money covers."

"How does a lady manage to balance her books if she does not know the cost of things?"

The only books Gwen had balanced were those in school, atop her head, while she practiced perfect posture. "I am sure I do not know. Dear Aubrey . . . "

Ellianne was becoming thoroughly sick of Dear Aubrey. "Luckily I am not a lady, then, for look at the service we are receiving. Madame Journet would never have shown that watered silk she kept in the back if not for my money in her hand. I'd wager we are being treated far better than someone who waits three months to settle her accounts, if she has not already overspent that month's allowance. Which is another reason for a woman of independent means to stay unwed. Everything she owns becomes her spouse's. Can you imagine a stern-voiced husband telling me how much of my own money I am free to spend? Fustian."

"No, dear. That is bombazine."

So Ellianne filled the hearts of shopkeepers with her orders and filled the carriage with packages, including a new shawl for Aunt Lally and a silver filigree fan for Gwen, for helping. Two other gowns would be delivered to Lady Wellstone when completed, with the charges added to Ellianne's account, but those would be a surprise. She also purchased dress lengths for when Isabelle returned, summer-weight fabrics for new uniforms for the Sloane Street maids, and a pair of soft slippers for Timms.

Ellianne was having a delightful time. Shopping was a novel way to pass the hours, not half as boring as she'd imagined.

Stony, meanwhile, was having an adventurous day of his own. He'd even taken a page from Miss Kane's book—literally, while waiting in the library for her to fix her hair and don her pelisse—and made a list of possible avenues to investigate. So far, he had no results.

His first call was at Bow Street, to interview Edward Lattimer. The chap was brown-haired, with ears that stuck out. He could not have been much younger than Wellstone, yet his enthusiasm made the viscount feel old. The Runner was like an eager pup, tearing off in every direction. Every direction that Stony had felt so clever in writing down.

First, Lattimer wanted to ascertain his lordship's connection to the missing girl, for which Stony did not fault him. He would have complained to the man's superiors if Lattimer gave out information to any Paul Pry off the streets, or from the scandal sheets. Stony proved his bona fides by means of showing the check from Miss Kane made out in his name. Lattimer inspected the signature, whistled at the amount, compared the name to the one on the calling card Stony handed him, and finally consulted his occurrence book. The thing was almost as messy and indecipherable as one of Miss Kane's charts.

According to Lattimer's research, no redheaded female corpses had been found floating in the Thames recently. No unconscious or amnesiac redheaded women had landed in any of the nearby hospitals or lunatic asylums. No one recalled a red-haired lady taking a hackney from Sloane Street by herself. Or getting on a ship. Or purchasing a ticket at any of the coaching inns on the night in question.

"I can see you have been quite thorough in your investigation," Stony conceded, feeling not half as clever as he had an hour ago, and twice as old.

"I promised Miss Kane my best, and I always keep my word."

"Admirable, I am sure. The reward money would not have anything to do with your devotion to duty, would it?"

"The lady is already paying me handsomely. Not quite as handsomely as your lordship, it seems, but I expect you can perform other services for her."

Stony was prepared, his hands clenched into fists, to hear exactly what services the Runner thought he could perform. "Yes?"

Lattimer was innocent of insulting innuendo. "The other toffs'll talk to you."

Stony nodded, relaxing back in his seat at the Runner's desk. Damn, he was going to have to get used to the sly winks and knowing glances or he'd be defending his honor, and Miss Kane's, from morning till night.

The Runner was not finished. "Besides," he said with a heavy sigh, "money or not, I'd do anything I could for Miss Kane."

Lud, the chub was energetic, conscientious, and half in love with the woman! That was why he did not suspect Stony of low behavior: He could not suspect his inamorata of such licentiousness. "I take it that, in order to describe her missing sister, Miss Kane removed her bonnet?"

"Oh, yes." The Runner turned dreamy-eyed and forgot all about his copious notes, his illustrious guest, or the missing sister. Visions of long red hair cascading across snowy white sheets must be chasing all rational thoughts from the man's head. No, those were Stony's mind-pictures. Lattimer was likely picturing Miss Kane in a wedding gown, the righteous clunch.

"Did she take her hair down?" Stony had to ask.

"Of course not. No lady would be so immodest," the Runner said, confirming Stony's estimation of his infatuation and his intentions. And incidentally relieving Stony's unexpected and unwarranted jealousy that another man had seen Miss Kane in such a state. Zeus, he could not be jealous! Not over the banker's broomstick daughter. He must be suffering from brain fever, or else he'd risen from his bed too early.

Jealous or not, Stony was responsible for the woman. Now it was his turn to sigh. Lattimer was only the first of many, he supposed. "I daresay she can look as high as she wishes," he hinted.

The tips of Lattimer's jug-handle ears turned red. "Oh, I know the lady is far above my touch. Which is not to say any swell with a title before his name is free to take advantage of her sweetness." He glanced toward the black baton on his desk, in a not quite subtle warning.

Brain fever must be catching. Sweetness? Were they

speaking of the same woman? "Do not worry. The lady is safe with me."

And from me, Stony added, but only to himself.

Lord Charles Hammett, the recently and not very reluctantly betrothed friend of Stony's, was his next call. Charlie was one of the few gentlemen Stony felt he could question about the missing girl without his interest leading to more questions. Certainly Charlie was too involved in his wedding plans and his bride-to-be to care about any other woman.

He did not remember any stunning redheads, any available heiresses, or Lady Augusta Chansford's niece. He barely remembered to thank Stony for the engagement gift, what with hurrying to meet his betrothed at the jeweler's, his father-in-law-to-be at White's, and his solicitor at the bank. That was all right with the viscount. He was glad his friend was prospering so much better as a prospective son-in-law to an earl than he ever was as a younger son to a duke. Charlie thought he might even enter politics, with the earl's help. That would be after the wedding, of course, and after the yearlong bridal trip he and Lady Valentina were planning, with the earl's money.

Stony went along with Charlie to the jeweler's to inspect betrothal rings. Floating between velvet cases filled with gems of every size, shape, and color, Charlie's fiancée thought she did remember seeing a Miss Kane once, but was never formally introduced. The woman was certainly not on the wedding invitation list. It might have been at an afternoon tea, Lady Val guessed. No gentlemen were present that she could recall, and did he prefer the square shape to the oval?

Which left Strickland, who had definitely left his own residence. The baron had no country estate—not since losing it twenty-some years ago—so he could be anywhere. Stony tried the gentlemen's clubs, especially those with spare rooms a member could use in a temporary emergency. The doormen had seen

Strickland, so he was still in town, but no one could say where he was staying, not even for the coins Stony offered.

"I'm looking for the rum touch myself," one of the older members said, after Stony loosened his tongue with a glass of cognac. "What, does the bounder owe you money, too?"

Stony filed away the information that Strickland seemed to be in debt. A desperate man took desperate measures. "I merely need to speak with him on a minor matter. His house is shut up, vermin-infested, most likely. Do you know what hotel he patronizes?"

"A hotel? You'd do better to try the whorehouses!"

The hundred pounds, or what was left of it after Stony redeemed his watch and paid his outstanding bills, would not last long, not the way Stony had to slip coins into doorkeepers' hands to identify their patrons. Keeping the privacy of those within was precisely why such men were stationed there.

Stony went from perfumed bordello to gin-soaked brothel, from exclusive private club to half-hour harlotries. He had more convivial glasses of wine than he wanted, and slipped more coins down more bodices than he ever wished to explore, all for nothing. He had offers and invitations, a gratifying number of them for free, but no information. Of course, London had almost as many houses of prostitution as it had cobblestones, so he was not discouraged. Strickland would show up somewhere, perhaps at a mistress's cottage in Kensington. Someone would know. Stony left coins and his address with half the prostitutes in London, it seemed. They needed it far more than he did, or Miss Kane.

Meantime, he had to report to his employer. With his head aching from the wine, his mouth tasting the way the bulldog smelled, he called at Sloane Street. There was Miss Kane, every hair in place and covered with that black lace winding sheet. She sat as erect as a ramrod, and looked as eager to see him as she would the tooth drawer. The parrot was squawking his name, or something about stones, from the next room. He had no good tidings to give, no news of her sister or Strickland, no way to erase the frown or the shadows under her eyes. Worse, he had no intention of telling her where he'd been. Worst of all, he had no money.

Damn, he was used to having the expense of escorting a lady financed by her guardians, without a word spoken. He paid for flowers and carriage rides and tips to footmen—not fortunes in bribes. How could he tell this starched-up shrew sitting in morning sunshine that he'd given her blunt to women of the night? Hell, how could he ask a female, any female, but especially this distant, disapproving one, for money?

So he gave his report, lying through his teeth, and spoke to Timms instead.

Chapter Twelve

"Damn it to hell, Gwen, I had to ask for money!" Stony was in such a rage, he forgot to mind his language; then he forgot to apologize for the lapse.

Gwen was busy trimming an old bonnet with some new ribbons she had purchased while out shopping. Dear Aubrey could not complain of the expense of the ribbons, for look how much money she was saving over the purchase of a new hat. His curse words could not be for her, therefore, and were nothing she had not heard from his father, especially when money was mentioned. She looked up at her stepson over the rim of her detested spectacles, which she was wearing only because manufacturers were making the eyes of the needles so much smaller these days. Her beloved stepson was not an attractive sight, not with his neckcloth pulled awry, his fair hair standing on end as if he'd been tearing at it with his hands, and his handsome face wearing a black scowl. She set her gaze back on the old bonnet that would be as fetching as any in the shops when she was finished.

"Yes, dear."

"Like a blasted delivery boy!"

"You know, Aubrey, most people who work for a

living do expect to be paid." Lady Wellstone's eyes had been opened just that day to the plight of shopkeepers whose bills were in arrears. And here she'd thought only impoverished gentry had to worry about making ends meet.

"It was demeaning, that's what it was."

"Of course. But did you get the funds you need?" Pride was well and good, but cash in the bank was a great deal more comforting.

"An account was already established that I can draw on as necessary. You'd think the dratted woman could have told me, besides, without my having to beg, and from a prayer-book butler old enough to be my grandfather, by Jupiter. Next she'll be having me ask the dog if I can take a hackney, or do I have to walk."

Gwen set another stitch. "I am sure the dear woman would never expect you to walk her dog."

Now Stony was as exasperated with his inattentive relation as he was with his imperious employer. He kicked at a footstool that was in the way of his pacing. "I suppose I shall have to show vouchers to justify my expenses. As if abesses and back-alley bruisers handed out receipts!"

"You mean you won't be able to be so generous to those people." Gwen had never understood how dear Aubrey could give alms to the poor when they themselves were needy.

Stony ignored her and how well she knew him. Besides, he had a bone to pick with Gwen, too. "I thought you were going to take Miss Kane in hand and make her presentable. She still looked like a scarecrow this morning. The problem is, no one will be frightened; they'll only laugh."

"She has gowns on order. I guarantee no one will be laughing at our dinner party at the end of the week. If she comes."

"What do you mean, if she comes? The whole effort is to bring her to the attention of society."

"Yes, but she is shy."

"Shy? I have never met a woman more outspoken, more sure of herself, more determined to have her own way. Shy? A wild boar is shyer! Miss Ellianne Kane is a shrew!"

"Well, I like her. You told me I should, and I did. I found dear Ellianne excellent company and not at all overbearing."

"Dear Ellianne, is it? Then you have seen dear Ellianne the chameleon, not Miss Kane the queen. You would not have enjoyed her company this morning, I swear, not while she was scowling and stiff as a plank. She did not offer me her hand, nor a seat, nor a drop to drink, even though my mouth was as dry as day-old toast. I had to stand in front of her blasted desk like a failing student before the headmaster. No, like a debtor at the bank. I felt as if I were going to a foreclosure, not a friendly chat. She heard my report and then dismissed me, like a deuced servant."

"Oh, dear, she must still have been upset by something Lady Higgentham said yesterday. I know I should not have introduced that awful woman at the milliner's, but how could I not when she was right there, staring at dear Ellianne? And she was trying on an absolutely horrid bonnet, besides."

Stony raised his eyebrow. "And you were going to tell me that Miss Kane had been insulted . . . when?"

"When I first saw you, which is now. If you had not stayed out all night . . ."

"On Miss Kane's business. What did Lady Higgentham say that offended Miss Kane?" Stony might call the woman names; he'd be damned if he sat by and let others ridicule her.

"It was not precisely an insult, dear, more a friendly warning, although I doubt that crosspatch meant to be friendly. Mean people are rarely kind, and Lady Higgentham has those beady little eyes, which would lead me—"

"Gwen, what did she say to Miss Kane?"

"Oh. You do remember her daughter, do you not? The one we could not find a husband for, no matter how we tried?"

"The girl preferred her horses. And looked like them."

"But Lady Higgentham believes you ruined the girl's chances."

"How? I took her riding in the park, trying to show off the chit's only skill. And we went early, with her groom in attendance, so the conventions were observed. She wished to race, and I agreed, thinking to impress the chaps who were out exercising their mounts. The hoyden not only started early and bumped my horse, but she beat me to the finish by three lengths."

"And no gentleman likes a cheat."

"No gentleman likes a woman who can ride better than he can."

Gwen shook her head over men's foibles but said, "No, the horse race was not what had Lady Higgentham riled. She said you turned the girl's head with all your attention and spoiled her for any other man."

"What? I took her to Astley's to watch the trick riding because her father and brother flatly refused to go again after the fourth time. They begged me to drive with her in the park because they hated to be seen with a female at the ribbons. And I swear the only time that female turned her head was to look at a passing pair of matched chestnuts!"

"You just cannot help being charming, dear. At any rate, Lady Higgentham saw dear Ellianne at my side, and naturally assumed you might be escorting my friend on occasion. That horrid woman warned Miss Kane that you were nothing but a silver-tongued devil, out to collect as many ladies' hearts as you could, while their fathers were paying your tailors' bills. Then she said that perhaps Miss Kane would have better luck bringing you to heel with her fortune, for she recognized the name. And the bank, I suppose. I can tell you, I was so angry, I did not even warn Lady Higgentham how much she resembled a dragon in that lizard-skin hat!"

"But Miss Kane did believe her?"

"Oh, she said it made no difference, for she was not looking for a husband, and that she was long past falling for a handsome face and pretty compliments."

"She believed her. She thinks I am a cad, which was what had her on her uppers this morning."

"You have to understand, dear, that men have always been pursuing dear Ellianne, but always for her money, not for herself. Even when they do compliment her appearance, she does not believe them, since she believes her looks unfashionable. Red hair is considered unlucky, did you know that? And children can be cruel, so they made sport of her hair and her height and her thinness. I am afraid she fears you will do the same. Perhaps that was why she was a bit standoffish with you."

Damnation, he had never hurt a female's feelings on purpose, and he was not starting with Miss Kane. And she ought to know that. He'd agreed to her terms, hadn't he? Discretion, loyalty, no flirting, he'd agreed to it all, by George. He'd told her he was a man of honor, by heaven, and she should have believed him, not some harridan with a horse-faced daughter.

But what could he expect from a woman who carried a pistol in her purse, a potato in her pocket, and poppycock in her upper stories?

Stony turned and marched himself back to Sloane Street. He adjusted his neckcloth along the way and combed his hair into a semblance of order with his fingers. He stopped to buy a nosegay of violets from a flower seller on the corner, then decided he ought to bring one for Miss Kane too, not just her dog. He purchased a third for Mrs. Goudge, in case the silent aunt was feeling left out of the pleasures London offered.

He walked past Timms, who was sleeping beside the door, and past the dog, who was exercising his gums on the butler's fallen Bible. He briefly stopped by the parlor where the parrot was kept, hearing it screech out "Limp-rod lordlings, I say. Limp-rod lordlings."

Polly was obviously from the lower orders. If Stony had his way, the wretched bird would be lowered into the cookpot. The creature did not belong in a genteel household, and so he would tell Miss Kane, if she ever spoke to him again.

He kept going down the long hall until he reached the book room. After a brief, unanswered knock, he opened the door.

"I said I did not want to be dis—Oh."

There was Miss Kane behind her desk, almost where he had left her, but her head was bare. Her red locks were in a braided twist at the back of her neck, neat and proper, as decorous as flame-colored hair could be. Her green eyes were suspiciously red, but Stony convinced himself that was just a trick of the light, and he was seeing red everywhere. Why, the violets in his hand might turn crimson if he kept staring at her hair, willing some stray curl to loosen itself from the braid.

"Lord Wellstone," she said, straightening her thin shoulders. "I thought we had concluded our discussion."

Stony dragged his eyes from her hair to her ungloved fingers, which were long and narrow and clutching a handkerchief. He walked closer, to the side of the desk, not standing before it like a petitioner. "It seems we have unfinished business."

She did not say anything, just looked up at him, a crease between her eyes. He lowered himself until he was half sitting on the desk. He nodded when she did not rebuke him for the familiarity.

Then he said, "I do not want your fortune." That was a lie, of course.

"Nor do I want your body." He had never seen her body, only hints of soft curves among the angular bones, so that was not quite a lie. If she proved half as alluring as the image in his dreams, though . . .

"Or anything else from you." Now that was definitely a lie. He wanted to see her hair loose on his pillow; he wanted to erase the sadness from her eyes; he wanted enough of her brass that he never had to work for another woman again.

"Except to find your sister." That was not an untruth, and he was relieved. For a man who took great pride in the honor of his word, he felt he was perjuring his very soul. For a good cause, of course.

"Is that clear?"

"Very."

"Good, because I could not have continued in your employ otherwise." He held out the bouquet of violets.

Ellianne took the nosegay and brought it to her face, to breathe in the sweet fresh scent. It reminded her of home, where the air was clean and trees grew where their seeds fell, not just in parks. The people she knew there said what they meant, and did not say what was hurtful. They might talk among themselves—who did not?—but how could they be openly cruel to each other, when they had to deal together on a daily basis? Here no one seemed to care. They were all transient, all strangers, waiting for the Season to end so they could go somewhere else, with other people. They did not care about a missing girl who was not one of their own, or a well-to-do outsider, only what scandal they could find, what malicious gossip they could spread.

Yet here was Lord Wellstone, bringing violets. Asking her to trust him, to ignore the mean-spirited mouthings of a disgruntled mother, hateful words that would be, she knew, just the first of many once knowledge of her presence in London was more widespread. Her name would be in every *on dits* column, estimates of her annual income on every tongue. Her whole life would be on view.

Yet here was Lord Wellstone, leaning on her desk in such a comfortable, casual manner, swearing that he meant her no dishonor, that he had no base intentions, that he wished to find Isabelle. Fair value for her money. It was always about the money. Sometimes Ellianne wished she were poor—for a day or two, only; she was no fool—so she might know who were her true friends. Gwen, Lady Wellstone, had seemed genuinely kind, but she was Wellstone's stepmama, with ulterior motives of her own.

Yet here was Lord Wellstone, with angel-blue eyes and the devil's own smile. She inhaled another breath of the violets. "I am not after your title." That was no lie. Her deceased mother and her dead aunt might have desired she marry "up," but such considerations meant nothing to Ellianne.

"I am not after any man's ring on my finger, including yours." That was no lie, either. Wellstone would make a wretched husband, with every female from fourteen to fifty throwing him lures. Why, even Aunt Lally had been won over, temporarily. Who knew when the viscount would accept a pretty invitation, or let flirtation lead to infidelity? He'd never make a faithful, steady husband, if she were looking to wed, which she was not. Gentlemen of his class and upbringing seldom saw the need for constancy, despite their wedding vows. Ellianne already had enough disrespect from strangers; she did not need it from a husband.

"Or anything else from you." Here the line between truth and lie was not so clearly drawn. Ellianne had images of his lordship smiling at her, telling her she was pretty, letting her lean against his strength and borrow from his confidence. Those were only dreams, of course, although she had not been asleep.

"Except to find my sister. Is that clear?"

"Very."

"Good, because I could not continue to employ you otherwise."

Stony held his hand out to seal their understanding. She placed the violets in it. He supposed that was better than the wadded handkerchief, but shook his head. The woman was hopeless. He put the nosegay on the desk and took up her hand. He deliberated between shaking it and kissing it, but somehow kept holding it.

"One thing more. I am not an hourly wage earner. I help you find your sister, guiding you through the social maze if that is what is required, in exchange for financial consideration. Is that understood?"

As well as Sanskrit. "I do not see much difference, except in the words you use."

"To me there is. I am not a servant, a lackey, a hired man to do his mistress's bidding."

Ellianne understood it had to do with manly pride. She was willing to make concessions, especially when his manly hand felt so very nice holding hers, warm and a bit tingly, strong but gentle. What were a few words? "Very well. We are associates. Does that satisfy you?"

It did, but he did not want to let go of her hand. "Equals? My expertise, your expenditures?"

"I did not think you would consider any woman your equal."

He didn't. "Partners, then."

They were speaking of her sister, her money, and her reputation at stake. What kind of partnership was that? Ellianne took her hand back, so she could think better. "Why can we not be friends?"

Stony felt the loss, as if a rare butterfly had flown out of his palm. He looked at his empty hand. "Friends trust each other."

She placed her hand back in his and this time he did bring it to his lips.

"Friends," they both said.

And that was the biggest lie of all.

Chapter Thirteen

"So you will attend Gwen's dinner at the end of the week?" Stony asked before he left. When Ellianne hesitated he reminded her of her own earlier plan. "If even one person comments on your similarity to your sister, that is a start to finding her friends, or anyone who might know her plans."

"You are right. I will come." She did not look happy about the necessity, merely resigned.

"That's a wise choice," he teased, trying to cheer her up. "Otherwise I would have to charge you the price of Gwen's handkerchiefs."

"Lady Wellstone does seem a bit . . . lachrymose."

"Especially when her wishes are thwarted. She goes through three or four handkerchiefs on a good day, half of which are mine. I cannot imagine the stack required if her dinner plans are destroyed. We do not entertain as much as she would like."

"So she mentioned. I offered the services of my chef, if yours is not used to preparing for such increased numbers."

They had no chef at Wellstone House, just an everyday cook whose skills encompassed beef and breakfast. He nodded his head in thanks. "You will be happy you did, as will the other guests, although Cook does bake a delicious strawberry tart."

They discussed the guest list for a moment, Stony assuring Ellianne that these were neither the leading lights of high society nor the doyens who guarded the doors against intruders. No one at his table would find fault with her birth or her breeding. And no one, he swore to himself, would make her uncomfortable. The ladies were of kindly disposition, and the gentlemen were all respectably and reliably wed or betrothed, like Charlie. Not one raffish bachelor, roving husband, or randy widower was invited. He'd seen to that. Now he had to hope that Miss Kane did not dress in a sack, quote the cost of the china, or wrap green beans in her napkin to take home for the dog.

Gwen had promised him Miss Kane would not embarrass them, so he had to pray for the best, and help it along, like telling her she really did not need to carry her pistol to his home. "A weapon will absolutely destroy the well-mannered image we are striving for. We need these matrons to invite you to their own dinners and dances, not run away screaming. A pistol at your side will not do much for the new gown Gwen says you will wear, either. A fan or a vinaigrette is a much more fashionable accessory, I believe."

She finally smiled. "Ah, and here I thought I would set a new style. But speaking of gowns, I have ordered two new ones for Gwen, for her help. I hope you will not take umbrage, but she has been so kind to me, I felt that was the least I could do."

Stony hated that he could not buy Gwen all the fripperies she longed for, the luxuries that his father had cheated her out of by gambling away her dowry and her annuities. He hated that this heiress could buy Gwen a whole shopful of gowns if she wished, and was being so openhanded after knowing his stepmama for two days. Gwen was his responsibility, her needs his expense. He ought to refuse the gift, to tell Miss Kane that Wellstones did not accept charity. Yet he could not deny her generosity, and he could not spite poor Gwen to save his pride. He tipped his head. "That is extremely gracious of you. My stepmama already adores you. This will seal her approval."

Ellianne immediately bristled. "I am not purchasing her friendship."

"Of course not. I never implied you had any but the best of intentions. You must learn not to be so touchy, you know."

"Must I? What of yourself?"

His jaw clenched. He was not the least bit touchy. "What of myself?"

"That business account, for instance. I wished to enumerate the costs, but you were the one who said gentlemen did not discuss financial arrangements. Then you were offended that your expenses were not met, and went to Timms, not me."

"I was not offended. Merely concerned that you had, ah, miscalculated."

"I seldom make a mathematical error. And you were offended. Timmy told me so. Touchy."

"That is touché, madam. And now I had better be off to find Strickland for you, or else you will accuse me of being negligent of my duties. And that is being conscientious, not churlish."

Stony kissed her hand one last time before leaving. Touchy? By heaven, who was she to find fault with him? He'd never met a female so quick to raise her hackles. Why, she was like a kitten you'd be stroking, purring along, then she'd turn into a spitting, hissing hellcat. Touchy, hell. He'd like to touch . . . Well, he would.

He wondered, on his way home, if her skin could be as soft as it looked, if her prim little lips would soften in passion. He wondered if her hair would feel like spun satin, and if her legs were as long as he imagined. Lord, speak of prickly, she would scratch his eyes out if she knew what he was thinking!

Stony doubted she had an inkling. Between her

merchant's morality and her determination to stay unwed, he doubted Miss Kane had the least understanding of lust. If she caught a glimmer of what went on between a man and a woman, she'd only decide such base emotions did not apply to her, not with her bank-ledger brain.

He recalled their conversation. He'd sworn disinterest in her fortune and her body. She hadn't even blushed. Then she'd claimed she did not want his title or his ring. There was no mention of his body, as if she did not acknowledge his maleness or her possible response to it. Bah. Women like that were why married men kept mistresses. The sooner he found Strickland, and the sister, the better.

Ellianne had to change her clothes to go for a dress fitting. One of her new day gowns was ready, so she stripped down to her shift. Then she looked at herself in the mirror, turning to see her profile, then craning her neck over her shoulder to see her backside. What did he mean, he did not want her body? What was wrong with it? Granted, she was tall and thin, and little rounded dumplings of girls were in style, but other men ogled her. Other men tried to snatch kisses, and got their cheeks slapped, or worse. Wellstone was supposed to be a connoisseur of women, and he considered her beneath his notice?

She did not want him panting after her, of course, adjusting his trousers and breathing as heavily as a stag in rut. Of course not. What decent woman wanted to attract such untoward, embarrassing attention? Ellianne had been so disgusted she'd sworn off men entirely. Besides, theirs was a relationship built on mutual need. Not *that* kind of need, all hot and hurried, but her need for help and his for money. Desire had no place in their dealings with each other, none whatsoever.

Still, perhaps the necklines on her new gowns ought to be lower, after all.

* * *

Stony found Strickland that night. It was not an entirely felicitous meeting. Strickland was in his cups, in dishabille, and in need of a bath. He stank like a French tart, and Stony did not mean one of Cook's strawberry pastries. Nor was Stony surprised, since his paid informants had reported the man to be staying at Madame Mignon's Maison d'Amour.

Amour did not enter into the red-velvet-draped rooms. Strickland did not want to leave them.

"Don't see what we have to talk about, Wellstone. I don't owe you any blunt, do I?"

Stony shook his head. "No."

The baron looked hopeful, or as hopeful as an unshaven, bloodshot-eyed, middle-aged libertine could look. "You owe me money, then?"

"No."

"Then I was right. No reason to talk. I've better things to do, you know. There's Bettina and Lizbet and Betsy, for starters." He pulled one of the girls, Stony had no idea which, onto his lap. The whore giggled and wriggled and jiggled her uncovered breasts. Stony felt ill.

When he noticed that Stony had not gone away, Strickland stopped trying to raise the girl's skirts while she sat on them. "Still here? Young fellow like you ought to know better. If you need help choosing, Mimi used to be in the ballet corps, but Marie's tongue can touch her nose."

Stony was no prude, but this display was revolting. He was ashamed Strickland was a member of the titled class. He tossed the girl a coin and jerked his head to the side, indicating she should leave.

"Here, now, no call for that. You could have waited your turn if you wanted—"

"I merely want to talk, in private." Stony looked around the dimly lighted room. Most of the other "patrons" had gone off to the smaller chambers, and only a few of the girls were left sitting together at the far end, or were sprawled on sofas, drowsing. This seemed as private as he and Strickland were going to get. He lowered his voice anyway. "About Miss Kane."

Strickland pulled his wrinkled shirt down over his belly. "Now I know we have nothing to talk about."

"She wishes to speak to you."

"Well, I don't wish to speak to her. Obvious, ain't it, when a fellow has to leave his own house and move into a French nunnery to avoid the plaguey female?"

"Why would you do that? You had only to answer her questions."

"Hah! That proves you don't know the cursed woman, so it can't be any business of yours. But I'll warn you anyway, man to man. Dangerous, she is. You go near that witch at your own peril."

"What, you are afraid of Miss Kane, who is so thin a breeze could carry her away? I swear, her pistol is unloaded."

"I'm not talking about a gun. Damned female almost unmanned me. Besides, who are you to be calling me lily-livered? You're the one who refused to meet Earl Patten on the dueling field, aren't you?"

"That had nothing to do with bravery. It was a matter of principles."

"So is my not meeting the Kane creature. Deuced fond of my principles, I am, and I like 'em right between my legs."

"Good grief, man, what the devil did you do to the woman to make her so angry that she . . . ?" Stony couldn't even say it, and willpower alone kept him from checking his own best belongings.

"Hah! Do to her? I asked the fishwife to marry me, that's what I did!"

"And that's how she refused you? I thought ladies were taught to thank a gent for the honor, not cripple him."

"Well, she did thank me prettily enough the first time. I figured she was just playing coy. You know how they always say no at the beginning. So I tried to show her what a good time we could have together, in case she was worried I was too old."

Now Stony wished she'd used the pistol, after all. "You are only lucky she had no father or brother to come after you with a horsewhip." He supposed Strickland would never have taken such liberties if the poor female were better protected. No wonder she was so cautious around men.

Strickland was irate. "Lucky? I haven't fathered any bastards since then, not that I know of anyway."

"Lud, man, you had before, and you're proud of it?"

"Only one, and I paid for his schooling, so don't go getting righteous on me. But I haven't been so careful recently. Still, that woman's got a lot to answer for."

Stony decided it was best to move on, before he made sure Strickland couldn't move for days. "What about the sister?"

"Oh ho, so that's where you come on the scene. I was wondering. You're wise to avoid the older one, even if her portion is that much larger. Gives me the shudders just to think of her." He drank from a half-empty bottle by his side, then belched. "Did you know that she can add any string of numbers you can name, and come up with the correct total every time, right in her head? Scary, eh? Of course, she would have been useful when I took out that mortgage on Fairview. Didn't understand all those numbers, myself. I daresay she was hardly out of nappies, though. Brass ones, they must have put her in, to make her so mean."

"The younger sister?" Stony prompted when Strickland appeared ready to fall asleep. "Miss Isabelle?"

"What's that? Oh, she ain't half as ferocious. Handsome young chap like you ought to have no trouble winning her affections. Except the older sister acts as guardian, guards her like a dragon. I was surprised she let the chit come to town, out of her sight. Either way, the young gal's affections won't mean much if you don't meet the old maid's expectations. From what I hear, you don't fit the bill."

"But you met her here in the city, didn't you?"

"Never met her at Fairview, that's a fact. Never been invited back. Of course, I didn't take any chances with this one. Asked her in a moving carriage, don't you know, where she couldn't turn violent."

This licentious old sot had asked an innocent, sheltered, nineteen-year-old maiden to be his wife? Why, Strickland had to be fifty if he was a day. But it was night now, so Stony swallowed his disgust. "So you asked Miss Isabelle to marry you, too?"

The baron shrugged. "Thought the older one might give us Fairview as a wedding present, don't you know. What's a baron without a barony? The entail was broken ages ago, but a man's got to have his own piece of land, don't you know."

Stony did. He'd been working to reclaim and maintain his own estate forever, it seemed. "But Miss Isabelle also turned you down?"

"She might have come around if Lady Augusta hadn't stuck her spoon in the wall. I was making progress with the chit, you know. Taking her for rides and such. Felt sorry for the brat, cooped up in the house. Lady A wouldn't let her out with anyone else, so she'd have come around. I was sure of it. So was her aunt."

Stony asked the question that had been bothering him for days now, one of the many things that made no sense. "What did Lady Augusta see in you? That is, why ever would she favor your suit for one of her nieces?"

Strickland had another swig from the bottle. "My first wife's godmother, don't you know. She felt guilty for not doing more when Alice took sick. Hell, the old skint should have done more when we were losing Fairview. Wouldn't give us a shilling then, said I'd just gamble it away too. I haven't gambled since," he said, puffing out his flabby chest with pride.

It was strange, Stony thought. Timms gave up gambling and took up religion. This old rip took up wenching. One had hopes of heaven; the other had better pray he didn't have the pox.

"Anyway, Lady A said she'd help me get my estate back. In return, I was to restore the Cit niece to respectability."

Strickland was respectable? Stony looked around the smoke-filled room, with its sleeping doxies and wine-stained rugs and groans coming from side chambers. Since when? "So what happened to the girl when the aunt died?"

Strickland scratched under his arm. "Went home, I suppose. No use to me. The older one'd never give me the time of day, much less her sister's hand. And I wouldn't ask, not again. Fellow has to learn from the past, eh?"

"You haven't seen her since? Miss Isabelle, that is?"

"Is that what the bitch is saying, that I seduced her sister? No such thing. I meant to do it right and tight. The gal was going to be my wife, don't you know. I had to do it up proper, make her fit for Almack's, make Lady Augusta happy. No hope for that now." Strickland was staring at the nearly empty bottle in his hand. "Too late for it all. Gone, all of it's gone."

Lady Augusta, hopes for reclaiming his estate, or the cheap wine? Stony couldn't tell which loss the baron was bemoaning, but he knew he had to get out of here before Strickland turned even more maudlin. "Well, at least you can go home now. Miss Kane won't be bothering you anymore. I'll talk to her, explain about her sister."

Strickland shook his head. "Might as well stay here another day or so. Nothing waiting for me at home."

A bath was. But Stony was too late in leaving. Bloody hell, the baron was blubbering.

"Nobody there, nobody anywhere. No wife, no sons, no estate."

And no handkerchief, either. Stony swore and

handed his over, along with a few words of commiseration. Then he had to go explain to Miss Kane.

"You what?"

"He did not harm your sister, I am certain."

"But I do not see how you could trust anything that despicable man said. I told you what he did."

"And he told me what you did." Stony shifted in his seat. Ellianne blushed. "But he learned," Stony persisted. "And he tried to do things right with your sister. He felt sorry for her, under your aunt's thumb."

"Isabelle was never governed by Aunt Augusta. She could have come home at any time and she knew it. Despite the curtailment of her activities, she stayed on in London the last few months to be company for our aunt, who was ailing. I cannot believe you simply accepted Strickland's story. What kind of detective are you, anyway?"

"An inexperienced one, as you well know. But remember that your sister packed to leave Sloane Street. She was not carried away. Why would she run off with Strickland when he had your aunt's approval?"

"Perhaps he promised to drive her home."

"Without a chaperon? Your sister could not have been so cork-brained as to destroy her reputation by traveling for days alone with a man."

"But he might have convinced her I was sick, on my deathbed, and she had to rush home. He could have told her they were picking up his second cousin in Kensington, to act as companion."

"And he kidnaped her instead?" Stony looked around at the book room shelves. "You have been reading too many novels, Miss Kane."

"Well, Strickland could have done something! I would not put anything past the maggot."

"What would you have had me do, beat him bloody until he confessed to hauling her off to some love nest until she agreed to marry him?"

Ellianne did not answer that.

"Deuce take it, he is nothing but a weakling, and I am no bully. I could not strike a man of his age, in his condition. Besides, I do believe him. All Strickland wants is his estate back. Stealing your sister would never accomplish that, and he is not stupid enough to think it would. He is afraid of you, by George."

"Really?"

Stony could not tell if she was appalled or proud. "He most likely never came up against a woman with such strength . . . of character."

Ellianne's shoulders drooped. "Then we are no closer to finding my sister than we were before."

"No, but now we do not have to waste our efforts chasing down a dead-end alley. We can concentrate on finding who did help Isabelle leave, and why."

"I suppose," she conceded, then scowled at him. "But I still do not understand how you could have done what you did."

Stony did not pretend to misunderstand. "He is just a lonely man with neither friends nor family."

"You felt sorry for that scum?" Her voice was as harsh as the parrot's screech.

Stony shrugged. "He was weeping."

"So you invited him to your stepmother's dinner party? Gwen will kill you, Wellstone, if I don't."

Chapter Fourteen

Ellianne watched through the book room window as Wellstone left the house and set out down the street. She got a crick in her neck from craning to keep him in sight. As Aunt Lally said, he had a fine leg for a swell. Ellianne thought he had a fine leg for anyone, and the rest of him was not to be sniffed at. Of course, she had sniffed, surreptitiously, while he was leaning close. He smelled of soap and spices and something she could not quite put her finger on, but was positive she should not be thinking of touching.

She was thinking it, though, wondering for the first time in her life what it would feel like to touch the smooth, hard planes of a man. She would never do it, of course, but she rested her forehead against the pane of glass and imagined Wellstone beside her, his shirt loosened so she could put her bare hand against his bare chest.

It was her daydream; his shirt was on the floor. She knew some men had more hair on their chests than others, and she pictured him first with golden curls there, then with oiled muscles like a Roman athlete. She'd touch him ever so lightly with her fingertips, just to see. And then lay her palm against his heart to feel it beating. She might even rest her cheek there, to hear his life's blood pulsing. Would her heart beat as quicky? Surely it was galloping twice as fast as usual now, with the viscount around the corner, not under her covers.

Ellianne felt her skin grow warm at the thought. How had she gone from touching his chest to lying naked beside him? Lady Higgentham was right: Wellstone was dangerous. The man could turn a girl's head from three streets away. Not that Ellianne was smitten, of course. She was far too wise for that, she told herself, rubbing the back of her neck. But what if, just supposing, *he* were to touch *her*?

Other men had groped at her. She'd been repulsed. But Wellstone was no rough youth, no crude lecher, no sweaty-palmed suitor. He'd know how to treat a girl so she felt like a woman, and treat the woman like a lady.

Maybe she would like his hand on her bare skin, stroking, soothing, seeking. What then? Could she let him touch her here, and there, and that sensitive spot?

She had to rest her cheek against a different pane of glass to cool herself. The first one was fogged over with her breathing. Ellianne very much feared that she would like Wellstone's touch far too much, and let matters go far too far. Then what?

Ellianne did not think she could do it, take a man, even Wellstone, as a lover. Everything she believed, everything that she'd been taught, screamed in outrage at her wanton fantasies. But why should she not find some pleasure in life, experience what other women had? Because it was wrong, and because she had to live with herself long after he was gone.

She had no doubts he'd be gone. For that matter, she was uncertain if he'd come to her hypothetical bed at all. Wellstone had sworn he was not interested in her body. He'd vowed he was not after her fortune either, which he could get only by marrying her, and that was even more improbable. He was a confirmed bachelor, and she was a self-proclaimed spinster.

If her licentious thoughts could not turn into legitimate acts, then it was far better they took place in air castles than in reality. She stepped back from the window and sat at the desk, pretending to read the correspondence from one of her financial advisers. Ten minutes later, when she had not gone past the letter's salutation, she called herself a nitwit and a ninny. The imaginary affair had to be over before it began. There would be no wedding; therefore there must be no bedding, not even in her all-too-imaginative mind. As soon as they found Isabelle, she would never see Wellstone again. Never imagine golden chest curls tapering lower, never wonder at firm, horseman's thighs, never ponder what pleasure his strong hands could give. Never.

The reminder of Isabelle made her feel guilty that she was having improper thoughts, thinking about improper deeds, while her sister was still lost. She wished she could go back in time, back to Fairview with her bankbooks and her charities, and her sister safe beside her. She'd never had sleepless nights there, never cavorted through wicked, wanton, waking dreams of passion in a loving man's arms.

Loving? When had love entered into her fantasies? She firmly gave her errant wits a shake. She was not going to open that particular Pandora's box, not when it might prove impossible to close.

No, she would think about Isabelle instead. Ellianne took out her list, the dreadful one she'd made after speaking with Lattimer the first time. She crossed out Strickland's name. She had earlier made a mark through kidnaping, for Isabelle had packed, without any of the maids' help. A ransom note would have been delivered ages ago, besides.

Foul play? Again, she'd packed. Perhaps something dire had happened after Isabelle left Sloane Street, after she had sent the illegible letter, but surely one of the neighbors would have heard, or fellow passengers at the coaching inns.

If Isabelle had left Aunt Augusta's on her own, at night, she must have had good reason. Having heard Ellianne's suspicions about Strickland, Mr. Lattimer had suggested Isabelle feared being forced into marriage against her will, but Ellianne still rejected that theory. As she'd explained to Wellstone, their aunt held no authority over Isabelle, being neither guardian nor trustee of her fortune. Of course, if a wedding had taken place, Ellianne would have no choice but to honor it, or see her sister cast out in the streets.

Isabelle was no weak, watery-eyed miss. The only way a ceremony could take place without Ellianne's sister's consent was if they drugged her. Mr. Lattimer spoke of avaricious vicars who turned their eyes to the wall when the bride could not make her proper responses. But Strickland swore his innocence, and Aunt Augusta was too cheap to pay the necessary bribes.

If Aunt Augusta had refused to consider Isabelle's choice of husband, however, Isabelle might have decided an elopement was the only solution. She would have reached Gretna Green by now, though. She would have written to Ellianne, if only about her dowry, if not out of affection. Ellianne could not believe her beloved sister had not trusted her enough, had not written to her about the man, unless he was totally ineligible. Good grief, he could not be married, could he? No, Isabelle was not a fool.

Ellianne had never truly considered suicide, but Mr. Lattimer had brought it up as a possibility. That was a greater sin than adultery, and Isabelle was a good churchgoer. And she had packed. A girl did not take luggage to jump in the Thames.

A connection to Aunt Augusta's death was next on the list. Ellianne could not imagine how, unless Isabelle's suitor had shoved the old woman when she rejected his honorable offer, then fled with Isabelle. Again, Ellianne swore Isabelle was not fool enough to be attracted to such a cad.

Ellianne ignored her own temptations toward the primrose path and an unsuitable *parti.* No, Isabelle and her would-be betrothed would have come home to Fairview, anyway. Ellianne had always solved her sister's problems; she had never left her to fend for herself. Even if the man were far beneath Isabelle, a footman or a chimney sweep, anything, Ellianne could have fixed it, could have made things right, if that was the man Isabelle wanted to marry.

She knew what everyone was thinking, the last item on her too-short list, one of the few scenarios that fit the facts as they knew them: Isabelle had fled to her lover. Not to a border marriage at the blacksmith's, not to a ceremony at their own church witnessed by all their friends, not to marry, not at all.

No. Isabelle might have urges and curiosity and wanton dreams—Ellianne could understand those things, more since meeting Wellstone—but Isabelle was no trollop. She had the same morals, the same decency that Ellianne had, the same boundaries between right and wrong, between dreaming and doing.

The Kane sisters might not have been born ladies by right of title, but they were reared to be honorable. They would go as virgins to their marriage beds—or to their deathbeds.

Mr. Lattimer's note came later that morning. The body of an unidentified young woman had been discovered by a delivery boy in an alley. Did Miss Kane wish to go with him to the morgue?

No, no, no! It could not be Isabelle! It could not be! Not her baby sister, born when Ellianne was nine, hers to cherish when their mother died after so many miscarriages. Isabelle was hers to hold and protect, hers to die for if need be. Isabelle could not be dead, left in a dirt heap, lost forever.

Aunt Lally's lip was quivering. "Let the rabbit-ears Runner go by himself. He can tell us if—"

"No, if it is Isabelle, I cannot leave her there among strangers an instant longer. I have to go."

So she sent a reply back to Bow Street and a note to Lady Wellstone, telling Gwen that she had to cancel their engagement for that afternoon.

The Runner and Wellstone arrived at the same time.

"I shall escort Miss Kane."

"No, I shall. It's my job."

"It's what I was hired to do."

"I am the professional."

"The professional what?"

Then Stony heard someone say, "Just like mongrels, seeing which can piss higher." He looked around for Polly, or the precocious parrot's cage. The parlor was empty, though, except for himself and Lattimer and old Aunt Lally, Mrs. Goudge, busy with her needlework in the corner. That sweet old woman, so devoted to her husband's memory that she stopped speaking, could not have uttered those words, could she? No, he decided, she could not even have thought them. The walls must be thin, with the parrot close by. He went back to pissing—that is, pressing to accompany Miss Kane on this morbid mission.

"Deuce take it, man, the morgue is no place for a gently bred female! You should have gone yourself."

"Miss Kane wished to be informed of every possible development in the case."

"Which you could have done after you went to the morgue alone, by Jupiter!"

"As you would have done, Wellstone?" Ellianne asked from the doorway. "Without informing me?"

Stony cursed under his breath, both because she had overheard him and because she was wearing that horrid black coal-scuttle bonnet so he could not see her face or her expression. He bowed. "Good day to you,

Miss Kane. I am sorry you have to face such dread news and, yes, I would have spared you this."

"It was not your decision to make, my lord."

The "my lord' " was both an indication of her distress and her disapproval of him. Stony glared at the Runner and muttered, "It should have been."

"I believe we had an agreement about being partners."

"Circumstances have changed. Some things are simply better left to stronger shoulders."

"Like carrying in firewood, no doubt," she said. "But this is a matter of fortitude, not brute force. Shall we go, Mr. Lattimer?"

The Runner's ears turned red, but he held his arm out to her. "Indeed, I would have gone alone, Miss Kane, to save you the distress, but I doubted I could have made a positive identification."

"Why is that?" Stony asked, taking Miss Kane's pelisse from Timms's trembling hands and helping her into it. The damned Runner was not going to be allowed to get familiar with Stony's charge; neither was the viscount going to let her go alone with the chub to face the waiting misery. "Are you colorblind?" He gestured toward the unfortunate bonnet as he straightened the collar of Miss Kane's wrap. "How many redheads do you think are waiting to be identified?"

Lattimer stood by his guns. "The woman's hair was shaved off."

Stony's hand fell back to his side. "What, all of it?" The raised eyebrow that only Lattimer could see asked the question that was unspeakable in Miss Kane's presence.

The Runner's whole face was scarlet in embarrassment, but he nodded. "Yes, all of it. Shaved."

"I know there is still a market for women's hair for wigs and things," Ellianne was saying, oblivious to the by-play between her two escorts as she walked through the front door, "although less so than a few years past, but what kind of monster shaves a dead girl's head to get her hair?"

"The same kind of dirty dish what slit her throat in the first place, I'd guess," the Runner supposed, ignoring Miss Kane's gasp and Wellstone's faltering step.

"Good gods, man, you might try to be a bit more careful of a gentlewoman's delicate nerves," Stony said, his own shaken. He took Ellianne's arm. "Are you still sure you wish to go in person, ma'am? Surely the unfortunate woman is some female off the streets, a bawd who argued with her pimp, a light-fingered light-skirt who stole from the wrong patron."

"No, sir, she were a lady," Lattimer declared, despite Stony's scowl.

"How the devil can you deduce that?" the viscount asked. "Some new kind of detecting at a distance, by reading tea leaves, perhaps?"

Lattimer ignored the scowl and the scorn. He was being paid by the lady, after all, not the angry toff. He took his occurrence book out of his pocket and turned to the last page. "Right here, my lord, they say the unknown female has no calluses. No rough fingernails. That makes her a lady, all right and tight."

Not necessarily, Ellianne thought, glad for the gloves she wore. Her own fingers were ink-stained from the ledgers, with a callus from holding the pen so often. She left in such a hurry she might still have traces of cooked asparagus under her nails, from feeding the dog. She could not recall if Isabelle's hands were well manicured or not. Her sister used to suck her thumb as a toddler.

Ellianne hesitated alongside the coach, her lips moving in silent prayer.

Damnation, Stony thought as he handed Ellianne into her aunt's town carriage. He took the seat beside her, leaving Lattimer to ride backward, facing Miss Kane, for all the good it would do him, with that ugly bonnet in the way. "Pretty hands do not make the woman a lady. She might still have been a well-paid courtesan, one who had a falling-out with her protector. Those things happen frequently." When Miss Kane turned her head toward him, he added, "Or so I am given to understand."

"That's as may be," Lattimer said, "but you can see why I didn't go on my own to look at the corpse."

Stony could not see at all, nor why the blasted Redbreast had to use such language in front of a lady. He'd heard the whimper that escaped Miss Kane's lips at that hopeless word *corpse.* Stony grasped Ellianne's hand in his, hidden by her skirts. "Dash it, you should have gone!"

Lattimer was starting to get angry. He was doing his job, and this well-dressed nob was belittling him at every turn. "What was I supposed to do, guess?"

"To start with, you might have made note of her clothing, in case Miss Kane remembered similar attire, or if the dressmaker had left a mark."

"She was naked," Lattimer snapped back, "which I was not going to mention to Miss Kane."

"In that case, you could have looked to see if she had green eyes, for one, or if she was the right height, and slender, like Miss Kane. You could have discovered if she had any scars or birthmarks, anything that would prove the poor woman's identity, or disprove her connection to Miss Isabelle. You could have gone a great deal further on your own, without needlessly distressing Miss Kane."

Lattimer was frantically turning pages in his log book. "Green eyes, green eyes. Someone must have made a note of it. And the height, I was certain they said average length. Now where . . . ?"

Ellianne could not help smiling, even now. Trust Wellstone to look for the ray of hope. And trust him to try to protect her from whatever might happen. He could not shield her from the truth, no more than she could have kept Isabelle wrapped in cotton wool for her entire life, but he would try, the dear, pigheaded clunch. She did not think for a moment that his care of her had anything to do with money, for once. He was simply a genuine gentleman, and a nice one, too. Despite their gloves, Ellianne found his touch comforting and was glad he'd insisted on coming along, once he'd ceased insisting that she stay home. She squeezed his fingers, and was reassured by the answering pressure. It was good to have a friend nearby, not charging ahead without her, but at her side.

"I needed to come, Wellstone. Please try to understand that I have to see for myself, without the torture of waiting at home. Mr. Lattimer did right in asking me, no matter how terrible an ordeal it might be. I do appreciate your concern, and your support, but no one else can do this for me. No one else knows my sister half as well, and no one else cares as much. But maybe you are correct and the female is not Isabelle, after all. I pray that is so, and I pray for the soul of the woman, whoever she might be."

The rest of the ride was silent, except for the sounds of the horses' hooves and the carriage wheels.

Chapter Fifteen

When they arrived at their destination, Lattimer hopped out of the coach almost before it stopped. He put down the steps and stood, waiting to hand Miss Kane down. Then he led her into the dark building that housed the coroner's office and morgue, leaving Stony to follow, or not.

Inside, when Ellianne would have unbuttoned her pelisse, he cautioned her to keep it on. Where they were going was kept cold, of necessity. "I should have warned you to bring a scented cloth," he told her.

He should have taken up another line of work, Stony thought, frowning at the young man's back. In another borough. The one satisfying thought he had, the one that he grabbed on to instead of imagining what awaited them, was that Miss Kane was taller than the Runner. Not by much, and perhaps that inch was due to her hair or her bonnet, but she was definitely taller. Good.

They passed through a long corridor and several doors before reaching a long flight of stone steps that seemed to lead down into the very bowels of hell itself, lighted with oil lamps that were too far apart. Lattimer kept Miss Kane's arm in his, in case she missed her footing. Or Lattimer did, was Stony's uncharitable thought.

He could feel the dank cold start to seep into his bones despite the greatcoat he wore, and wondered how Ellianne was faring. The blasted Runner could have warned her to bring a heavy coat, too. Deuce take it, they must be tunneling under the river, in some ancient catacombs or ice house or dungeon.

At the bottom of the steps, Lattimer rapped on a thick door and then opened it, ushering in Miss Kane. Stony was hard on her heels, taking her arm and displacing the Runner. The temperature here was even colder, and the odor was sickening. Stony would have reached for a handkerchief to cover his nose, but Lattimer seemed unaffected. Worse, Miss Kane did not seem to notice the stench. Stony tried to breathe through his mouth.

While Lattimer spoke to a worker in a leather apron, the viscount slipped off his coat and placed it over Ellianne's shoulders. He couldn't tell if she was shivering from cold or from fear. She smiled weakly in thanks.

The worker disappeared through another closed door at the other side, leaving them in the vast room with platform tables at one end and gruesome stains on the floor. Stony was happy to stay right where he was. Eventually a gentleman came out and walked toward them. Nearly Stony's height, he did not have an athlete's build, but was neither cadaverous, as the viscount might have imagined, nor paunchy. He was forty-five, Stony estimated, in expensively tailored clothing, an intricately tied neckcloth, and highly polished boots. His brown hair was combed straight back, then pomaded to keep it in place, and his dark eyes had that same glisten to them. Stony supposed women would consider the man handsome, with his high forehead and prominent cheekbones. He did not appear to notice the chill or the smell, bowing low to Miss

Kane as if welcoming her to a ball. Stony hated him on sight.

"Sir John Thomasford," Lattimer proudly announced, as if he were personally responsible for getting a belted knight to assist on the case. "Elevated for service to the Crown in solving murders."

"Are you the coroner, then?" Stony wanted to know.

"Oh, no. I merely assist when I am able." The man smiled with one lip, as if anyone with more hair than wit could have guessed that he was a gentleman born, an educated man of good family and income, living a life of leisure. Sir John turned to Ellianne as soon as the introductions were complete. He raised her hand—she had no trouble holding it out for this grave robber, Stony noted—and brought it to his lips. "My dear lady, I was a witness for the coroner's jury held in relation to your aunt's death, so now I offer my deepest condolences. I am grieved that another such tragic event brings you here, but may I also offer my humble services?"

The man was anything but humble, Stony could swear. He was a dilettante dabbling in detective work, it seemed, as Sir John rattled on about his studies in Edinburgh, his research through classical tomes, his discoveries that were helping to advance medical knowledge and helping Bow Street to solve murder cases. Stony had no doubt that some of the man's detecting involved Miss Kane's bank account.

"Eventually," Sir John was saying, "we will be able to tell more about the killers simply from examining their victims. We will understand their minds, and why they commit such heinous acts. Science will outwit evil," he told Ellianne, his voice rising with near religious fervor and echoing off the high ceilings. "But not yet, unfortunately. There is only so much we can deduce thus far."

Ellianne said, "But how wonderful that dedicated

men like you are trying to unlock such mysteries. You must be proud of your work, and I am sure you are well deserving of the rewards it brings."

Sir John kissed her fingertips once more. "The best reward I get is seeing the killers hang. And helping find justice for lost souls."

Stony almost gagged.

Then the jumped-up mortician led them toward the far end of the room, where a body rested on a high platform, covered by a sheet. Stony made sure he was standing at Ellianne's side, near the head. He reached his hand out for hers, and felt hers shaking. He held it tightly.

"We do not have much evidence to examine, but we can tell something about the killer from our preliminary investigation. Identifying the remains will aid in uncovering motive and possible suspects. It all works together, you see."

Ellianne was staring at the shrouded body. Stony could feel her entire body trembling beside him. "Get on with it, man."

Sir John cleared his throat. "Quite." Without further speechifying, he slowly raised the white sheet, folding it back under the young woman's mouth.

One side of her face was bruised, but the other was so pale it would have made milk look healthy. Her lips had a purplish tint, and blue veins were a road map on her bare skull. Ellianne was silent, transfixed by the dead girl, perhaps in shock.

Stony thought the shape of the face was wrong, but swelling from injuries might be distorting it. The sheet covered what might have been a pointy chin like Miss Kane's, but he did not suggest lowering the fabric. Instead he asked, "What color are her eyes?" His mouth was so dry his question came out as a whisper.

"Ah, the lady's eyes." Sir John peeled back one translucent lid. They could all see a blue orb staring up at them, or perhaps seeing the image of her killer imprinted there forever.

"Blue. They are blue, Ellianne, not green. This is not your sister."

"No, it is not Isabelle," she echoed on a loud exhale, as if she had been holding her breath throughout. "It never was Isabelle."

"Too bad," Sir John said. "Of course, not for you and your sister, Miss Kane. My apologies. I was merely hoping we could give a name to this poor woman."

"I understand. And I am certain that you will do everything in your power to deliver the young lady back to her family and bring her killer to justice. You say you have some clues?"

"Why, yes, if you are interested. It is fascinating, really. Of course, we can tell her approximate age, the general state of her health, whether she ever bore a child or not, that type of thing. But here, let me show you. We can guess the killer was about my height by the angle at which he held the knife. He was right-handed, by the direction in which he wielded the weapon."

Sir John pulled the sheet down a bit farther, below the woman's chin. An ugly slash sliced across her throat. Dried blood was everywhere, on the woman, on the table, on the rags the coroner's staff were using to clear the area for their inspection. Ellianne leaned closer, letting go of Stony's hand.

Stony slowly sank to the floor.

Ellianne screamed.

"Nothing to be concerned over," Sir John reassured her, leaning over the corpse to see. "It happens all the time. Especially with those heroic types who will not admit to any weakness. At least this oaf did not hit his head, or fall on the body." He gestured for Lattimer and one of the assistants. "Just drag him to the side, out of the way."

"What, you are going to leave him there?"

Sir John shrugged. "No use in waving the smelling salts until we are finished. He'll only go off again."

Mr. Lattimer added, with a degree of satisfaction that Stony would have deplored, "And he's too big to carry up those stairs. We might drop him, you know, kind of accidentally."

The assistant grinned, showing two missing teeth.

Sir John was impatient with the delay, wanting to get on with impressing Miss Kane with his erudition. "He'll come around by himself by the time you are ready to leave."

Ellianne looked down at her fallen champion. Wellstone did not look like much of a hero, crumpled atop unspeakable stains. "No, please lift him. He will be too cold on the floor."

Lattimer and the worker dragged the viscount none too gently back to a wooden bench near the door to the stairs. Ellianne mentally added the cost of a new suit of clothes to Wellstone's account. She also placed his greatcoat over the unconscious man, and brushed a lock of blond hair back on his forehead.

Then she went back to Sir John and the murdered woman.

The medical examiner explained how they could tell which side of the woman's neck the killer slashed first by the shape and direction of the wound. Then he came to stand behind Ellianne, proving a left-handed man could not have made the same marks. Nor could a shorter one. "Of course, I am of average height, and most gentlemen are trained to be right-handed, no matter their inclinations, so that does not narrow our field of suspects by much."

"You called him a gentleman. Surely no gentleman would do such a thing."

"You would be surprised," Sir John told her, and Lattimer chimed in: "Especially if a nob's mistress gets too greedy, or claims to be with child, a brat that she threatens to leave on the toff's wife's doorstep, unless he pays up."

"But look here and you will see why I call the murderer a gentleman." Sir John pulled the sheet down lower, nearly to her breasts. "You see where he grabbed her shoulder, and left the mark of his fingers?"

Ellianne could make out four distinct bruises. "Yes," she said with less enthusiasm, positive that she had seen enough now. She looked over to check whether Wellstone was stirring yet.

"Look closer. You can see the seam of his glove."

"And that makes him a gentleman? Many men wear gloves." She looked at Sir John's own soft leather gloves, then back to Wellstone, whose left hand dangled off the bench, in York tan leather. Even Mr. Lattimer wore gloves down here in the cold. The assistant did not. Ellianne hurriedly looked away from the helper's filthy hands.

"Ah, but if you consider that the female is, or was, a healthy young specimen, attractive, not the least undernourished, with hands that did not know work . . . Do you wish to see her hands?"

Ellianne quickly shook her head. "No, thank you."

"A pity. They can tell us much. For instance, if she had blood under her fingernails, we might be able to search for a man with fresh claw marks on his face or hands."

"But they would not show on his hands if the man wore gloves."

"Excellent point, Miss Kane, excellent point. The killer might have been a lowborn brute, but clever enough to wear gloves. Still, I doubt this woman associated with ruffians of the lower orders. I pray we find out, and catch him before he acts again."

Ellianne gulped. "Again?"

"I fear so. The shaved . . . head leads me to believe that this was some kind of ritual murder."

"I do not understand."

"And why should you? I should not even be discussing such distressing facts with a gentlewoman like yourself. Your escort would not approve, I am certain."

Her escort was still unmoving.

"I seem to have a few more minutes to wait. Please, I wish to understand about the unfortunate woman's hair. Wasn't murdering her enough?"

Sir John rubbed his chin. "The simplest solution would be to assume the killer meant to sell her hair. But why the razor, not scissors? No, again we deduce that the killer did not need money. He had another motive. Perhaps he was trying to make identification more difficult. Or he wished to have a memento, something of hers to keep. I have read studies of the red Indians who collect the scalps of their fallen enemies, to prove their merit as mighty warriors."

Ellianne stepped back, appalled on top of horrified. "I think I should be going . . . Lord Wellstone. . . ."

Sir John shook his head, without dislodging a single strand of his own hair. "I apologize, again, for forgetting your refined sensibilities. I should not have responded so eagerly to your gratifying interest."

"No, please do not apologize. I have found your explanations . . . fascinating."

"I only wish we had more insight into the workings of a killer's mind. Alas, our science of the body, as limited as it is, far exceeds our understanding of the mental facilities."

"If it did not, learned gentlemen like yourself would be able to cure our poor mad king."

"Eventually, madam, eventually, I pray, we shall solve all the riddles, and eliminate such woes from the face of the earth. Not just for monarchs and the wealthy, but for all men, everywhere."

"And women?"

"Ah, we know even less about the workings of a woman's mind. What man aspires so high?" he asked with that sneering kind of smile. "But perhaps even the inscrutability of your gender will reveal itself to modern science."

"Let us hope so." They were walking toward the

door, near where Wellstone was still slumped on the bench. Ellianne looked back at the woman, whose face was once more covered. "What will happen to her?"

"Oh, they will hold her here as long as possible, in the ice room in the back, you know, hoping someone comes looking for her. Anyone missing a wife or daughter will be searching, as you are. Unfortunately, we have had no other concerned families come by as yet, and she has been here over twenty-four hours. The Runners have been alerted, and even the watch was notified, in case they hear of a woman gone missing. If, as I suspect, the victim is a courtesan, begging your pardon again for the mention of such a class of women, then I doubt anyone will come forth to claim her. Females of that trade seldom have families, you see, or anyone who will acknowledge them as a relation. She will go to the medical college then, so our young students can further their understanding."

That seemed the worst insult of all, to Ellianne. The woman was killed, barbered, and laid here in the cold for anyone to see—and she would not even be given a proper burial. How would her soul find rest?

"Would you please tell me if someone does come to claim her? I would feel better knowing she is spending eternity with her family."

"You dear, dear lady. Your tender sentiments become you. I thought it before, but now I am certain. You are a woman of great heart, Miss Kane. It has been a pleasure to have a beating one among us." His top lip quirked up again. "A little morgue humor, you understand. But it is easy to see your devotion to your sibling, and to discern your acumen by the intelligence of your questions and comments. Many women who come here for similar reasons as yours swoon, like your friend, or suffer paroxysms of the nerves, or collapse in uncontrollable weeping. You, Miss Kane, have been an exemplary guest."

Ellianne would not precisely label this a social call, but she made a slight curtsy and said, "I found it interesting, and your knowledge impressive. Thank you for sharing your insights with me."

"My pleasure. So few people appreciate what we are doing here, the benefits to come to all mankind, the strides we can take if we keep open minds. You are rare, indeed. In fact, may I call on you?"

Ellianne almost tripped on her own feet.

When Sir John saw how stunned she was, how taken aback, he quickly added, "To bring you news of our unfortunate victim, of course."

"Oh, of course."

"And to keep abreast of your own investigation, in case my expertise, as humble as it is, might be of assistance."

"How kind of you. I would be pleased to receive you, then. And if you do learn anything that might pertain to my sister's disappearance . . ."

"Without fail, my dear Miss Kane, without fail."

Stony was still somewhat disoriented as they climbed the stairs, but recovered fully once they reached the relatively clean air of the street to wait for the carriage. He handed Ellianne in, then took the seat opposite her when he saw that Lattimer was not coming along. As soon as the coach started to move, he leaned forward and took both of Ellianne's hands in his.

"That really wasn't your sister back there? Or is my brain so fogged that I imagined it?"

"It really was not Isabelle. Not even remotely similar to her, thank God."

"Thank God," he echoed, then let go of her hands to lean back against the leather cushions. He shut his eyes and shook his head. "What a help I was to you, and after insisting I act as your escort. Lud, I am mortified."

"Why? You had no control over your reaction. And I did feel better knowing you were nearby."

"Parked on a bench like an octogenarian, a blanket

on his knees. Thunderation! At least now you understand why I could never go into the army."

"What I do not understand is how you manage at the boxing parlor your stepmother says you frequent."

"Oh, I train in the side room with weights and a leather punching bag. If I do ever spar with a partner, we wear padded gloves. I have never watched an entire fisticuff match, a real match, in my life. Lud, can you imagine the laughter if one of the boxers got a bloody nose? I look away."

"It is a reprehensible sport anyway. Two grown men pummeling each other? I have always failed to see the attraction."

"Well, I could not see your interest in that ghoulish chap's blather back there. You and he appeared as close as inkle weavers, from what I could tell at such a distance."

"He was explaining his work, and it really is amazing. Did you know that they can tell whether someone is a suicide or a murder victim made to look like one, by the amount of the gunpowder residue at the site of the wound?"

"No, but since I am not thinking of doing away with myself, despite my recent humiliation, or anyone else, unless you threaten to tell the world, I can manage without the information."

"It is knowledge. I am always eager to learn new things."

"Well, I am interested in knowing what you said to keep Lattimer from coming back with us. I swear the clunch looked so disappointed he was going to need one of my spare handkerchiefs. For that matter, he seemed disappointed that the dead girl was not your sister."

"He wanted so badly to solve the crime. He is eager to advance, you know."

Stony knew the Runner wanted to advance right into Ellianne's bank vault. "Is that why you gave him a handful of coins?"

"I gave him money to see that the murdered woman had a proper burial, if her friends or family do not come forth. I sent him back inside to make sure Sir John knew, so he did not consign her to the surgeon's school."

"That was very goodhearted of you. Not that I am surprised, of course."

Ellianne twisted the strings of her reticule, in embarrassment at the praise. "That is what Sir John said too."

"Did he?" Stony asked with a growl in his voice. "What else did the ghoul have to say?"

Ellianne did not mention that Sir John asked if he could call, not after hearing that rough tone. "Oh, he mostly spoke of the dead woman, and what could be learned from a careful examination of her wounds. Did you know that Sir John thinks he knows the exact length and thickness of the blade that sliced her thr— Wellstone? Stony? My lord? Oh, dear."

Chapter Sixteen

Ellianne had a lot to smile at, that night in her bedroom.

Isabelle was not with Strickland, thank those lucky stars shining so brightly outside the window.

And she was not at the morgue, thank God, which Timms was taking care of at his evening church meeting.

And Ellianne's hero had feet of clay.

She liked Wellstone the better for it. He was no longer the perfect, poised gentleman, so intimidatingly far above her, like the stars. He was no awe-inspiring god on Mount Olympus, but a mere mortal, as human as she was, with human failings. He might be a titled gentleman of ancient lineage and impeccable manners, to say nothing of his good looks and his muscular physique and his social sangfroid, but he was flawed. Irretrievably. Irrationally. Irresistibly.

He was right not to marry, Ellianne told herself as she brushed her hair out of its coiled braids so she could weave it into a looser, more comfortable plait for sleeping. She liked to do this herself, without a maid's help, for she found the activity relaxing and conducive to thought before bed. If she settled the question of Wellstone and weddings, she would sleep better.

He'd make an even more dreadful husband than she'd thought before. Why, he could never help his wife deliver their children, if the midwife was late. And if they were lost in the countryside, isolated by a blizzard, perhaps, who knew if he could kill a hare, or butcher a hog. They'd have to become vegetarians, like Aunt Augusta and her dog. Ellianne wondered if he hunted at all. She'd have better regard for any man who refused to chase down foxes or deer, for whatever reason. And Wellstone was certainly not going to be a spectator at the revolting blood sports so many men enjoyed, like dogfights or bearbaitings. No, he'd only chase after women, or watch them tear at each other, vying for his attentions. He could slay with a dimpled smile, instead of a gun.

Bah. Her hair was crackling and clinging to her new satin robe, and Wellstone was still in her thoughts. He'd worried that she might suffer nightmares after the visit to the morgue. Nightmares? If he only knew her dreams, she'd never be able to face him again. He'd suggested a glass of brandy before bed. That would only give her a headache in the morning, though, after another night of tangling the bedclothes.

Not that Wellstone was the only thing on her mind, of course. She never forgot about Isabelle. Well, except for those rare moments, perhaps, when she pictured herself in his lordship's arms. In the waltz, of course. Not that she was much of a dancer, hating to appear gangly next to her usually shorter partners. Wellstone was just the right height.

She supposed he was a superb dancer, graceful, lithe, guiding a woman with gentle pressure. He was superb at so much—except for swooning. She laughed out loud and got into the bed.

Images of Wellstone kept dancing in her mind's eye. She'd never get to judge his abilities for herself, unfortunately, for she did not intend to take to the ballroom floor for the brief time she'd be in Town. She was still in mourning for her aunt, and still wary of bringing herself to the attention of oglers and opportunists. She did have to be out and about, she admitted to herself, to be seen and recognized as Isabelle's sister. Someone had to know where the girl had gone. Someone was giving her shelter somewhere. Whoever that someone was, he or she was more likely to confide in Isabelle's sister than any detective Ellianne could hire.

Lady Wellstone's dinner party in three days was the beginning. There would be no dancing, only food and conversation, perhaps cards or music afterward. A small, select group of Gwen's friends had been invited—and Strickland, plague take him. Ellianne had to go put herself on exhibit, so these people would invite her to their own gatherings. Then she would have to pay duty calls to thank them, and reciprocate eventually, playing the proper hostess. She could not provide lavish teas lest she remind the high-sticklers of Ellis Kane and his bank. She could not skimp, reminding anyone of Lady Augusta's parsimony and her problematic death.

What Ellianne most wanted to do, when she was not thinking of Lord Wellstone, was to stand at a busy street corner and call her sister's name at the top of her lungs: "Isabelle Kane, come home this instant," as if she were calling the dog, Atlas. That would end this nonsense before it began. One forthright effort, without finesse and finagling, and everyone would know she needed help finding her sister. Ellianne could not do it, of course, for such a public display would also end any hope of saving Isabelle's reputation. And would embarrass Gwen, who had been so kind. No, Ellianne would have to attend balls where the younger ladies congregated with their beaus, and position herself to gain introductions to them. That might be hard to do while she sat on the sidelines, watching Wellstone dance with every other woman in the room but her.

She hoped they served something stronger than punch. She'd need it.

Gwen was in a dither, trying to make up a seating chart for her dinner party. Stony offered to help.

"Just do not put Strickland next to Miss Kane," he warned. "The baron is liable to bolt. And the devil knows what she might do."

"Very well, but that leaves Sir John Thomasford as her dinner partner on her other side. She'll be to your right, of course, as guest of honor."

"The coroner? What the deuce is Sir John Thomasford doing on your invitation list?"

"Ellianne asked me. If you could add Lord Strickland, she wondered if she might add a gentleman who has been very helpful, she says, and has brought her books on criminal medicine."

"Who the devil wants to read about stabbings and stranglings?" Stony certainly did not, losing some of his healthy color at the very thought.

"Ellianne must, I suppose. I myself prefer a good Gothic romance, where the heroine is dangled off the edge of a cliff until the hero finds her, or she is given poisoned wine and carried to a dark tower in some misshapen ogre's castle. I have never understood how the hero always knows where she will be, or why he carries a ladder or a length of rope, but perhaps—"

"Gwen, about the mortician?"

"Oh, Sir John? Dear Ellianne says he is kind enough to bring her the latest news from Bow Street."

"Thunderation, that's what she has Lattimer for. Don't tell me the Runner is coming too?"

"No, only Sir John. I saw no reason not to honor dear Ellianne's request, even though the numbers will be uneven. I do not suppose it matters at such a small, intimate gathering as this."

Stony did not want to hear Sir John's name connected to Miss Kane's, especially not with the word *intimate* nearby.

"The man is nothing but a toadstool."

"No, dear, he is thoroughly respectable. And eligible."

Stony wanted to hear that even less than the other. He muttered an oath.

"I did inquire into his people, so you do not have to look like thunderclouds that he is sitting at our table. From the Dorset Thomasfords, don't you know. I believe my uncle Sidney's wife's brother married a Thomasford. Or was that a Thomas Jamesford? My cousins will know. They have accepted, of course, their hotel's food being sadly unappetizing. They dine away a great deal, of course, although we have not had them here yet in a formal manner. How could we, when we seldom entertain? But this was an excellent time to invite them, do you not think? Except for the children, naturally. You would not wish to dine with those unmannered beasts."

"I do not wish to dine with Sir John!"

"Oh, but he has accepted. And he is highly regarded in court circles, Aubrey dear. I should not like to recall the invitation. Why—"

"He is a bloody butcher, for heaven's sake!"

Gwen clucked her tongue and tapped her seating chart, wanting to get back to the troublesome chore. "Ellianne says he is an adviser to the coroner's office, I will have you know, not an employee. Detecting is a passion with him, dear Ellianne tells me, not a paying career. Sir John has made the study of crimes his life's work, to further the cause of justice, which is quite noble, I am sure, although I do not precisely see how knowing if someone has been struck by a brick or a bat makes any difference to the dead person. Oh, and I am certain he will wash the blood off before coming here."

Stony made a gagging sound. "Blood or not, I do not think I could eat a bite with him in the room."

"Of course you will, dear. The menu dear Ellianne's chef is providing could tempt a martyr's appetite. Besides, since when have you become so stuffy, dear, about gentlemen who work? You have always said that more of the aristocracy should dirty their hands, so they knew how hard their servants labor."

"This is not about working for a living, by George."

"That is good, because now that most people know how you are employed, that is, how you see your bills paid, a few doors have been shut to us. None that I wished to enter, of course, so you must not look so stricken. Still, Sir John will make an interesting addition to our little gathering. I am quite looking forward to meeting the dear man."

"The dear man?" Stony could not believe his ears. "Why are you so enamored of the gruesome bloke, Gwen?"

"Because Ellianne likes him, I suppose."

"Well, I do not."

"What has that to say to the purpose? The dinner is for dear Ellianne, is it not? If she is more comfortable among friends than total strangers, who is to blame her? Furthermore, I doubt you would like any man Ellianne does."

"What is that supposed to mean?"

"Nothing, dear. Nothing at all."

"Hell's bells, girl, you are rigging yourself out like a dockside doxy just to take grub with a crew of fancy fribbles! Your father would be spinning in his grave."

Ellianne turned her back on Aunt Lally and tugged up on the lace that bordered the minuscule bodice of her black gown. "But Lady Wellstone swears this style is all the rage."

"Among what those jackadandies call fashionable impures, maybe. I say a whore by any other name is still making money on her back."

Ellianne did not think the gown was quite that scandalous. The slim black silk skirt did cling to her legs, with the thinnest of silk petticoats beneath it, but the black lace overskirt veiled most of her anatomy. The high-waisted bodice did leave her breasts half revealed, but the matching black lace insert protected her modesty. The tiny puffed sleeves did leave her shoulders almost bare, but the long black kid gloves made up some of the lack. And no one would notice anyway. They'd be too busy ogling the large ruby that hung on a chain of diamonds right above her cleavage.

Gwen had insisted Ellianne wear the magnificent jewel that had been her mother's, to show she was no green girl. Aunt Lally had agreed, wanting Ellianne to thumb her nose at any silly rule that said unmarried women should not wear anything but pearls. She would have outfitted Ellianne in matching bracelets, ear bobs, brooches, and tiara, to show the useless swells her worth, and that she wasn't ashamed of her father and how Ellis Kane had made his riches.

Ellianne raised her chin. She was never embarrassed by her birth. Her looks, though, were another matter. The long, straight lines of the gown emphasized her height, and the new hairstyle added to it. Lady Wellstone had sent over her own coiffeur to arrange Ellianne's impossibly straight, unfashionably red tresses. Monsieur considered himself an artiste, and Ellianne his most challenging canvas. He sighed and he squinted and he snipped, and then he braided. He must have made twenty different plaits, it felt to Ellianne, sitting for hours on a low stool while monsieur worked above. He took the thin braids and brought them together into a pattern of swirls and loops that half resembled an opened rose, a very red rose, at the back of her head. Black silk leaves attached to combs at the base held the arrangement up, except for a few tendrils monsieur had cut to trail alongside Ellianne's cheeks. Ellianne's maid found a tiny diamond butterfly on a hairpin among her mistress's unused jewelry, earning the blushing woman a Gallic kiss on both cheeks. The Frenchman declared Miss Kane a flower of womanhood. The maid called her a blooming beauty. Timms said she belonged in the Garden of

Eden, and Aunt Lally called her a bird of paradise. She did not mean the exotic flower, either.

Ellianne nervously touched the ruby pendant that was cold against her bare skin. "Do you really think I look like a fallen woman, Aunt Lally?"

"Humph. If not fallen, then ready to tip over in a trice."

"Then come with me. Your respectability cannot be questioned. Unless you talk, of course. I'd feel better having you there, and I know Lady Wellstone will not mind." In fact, Ellianne knew, Gwen would go off in severe hysterics at having to change her seating arrangements at the last moment.

Her aunt refused. "Someone has to stay with old Timms, to make sure he doesn't fall asleep and set the house on fire."

"You won't play cards with him again, will you? You won all his pocket money last time, and he is really trying to reform."

"I'll keep him to the straight and narrow, never fear." The aisles of the wine cellar were just that, straight and narrow.

"Then you are sure you won't come tonight?"

"Chum buckets, girl! With me as ballast, your chances of finding a first mate would run aground afore you left the harbor."

"But you know I am going to ask about Isabelle, not to find a . . . first mate. I have told you a hundred times, I am not looking for a husband."

"No, but I have seen the way you've been looking at your hired man. He might be the bonniest lad on land or sea, but don't you go thinking you can taste the rum without buying the whole barrel. We might not be top-drawer like your new friends, but the Kanes have never had a bastard in their midst."

Ellianne gasped. "You know I would never do that. Why, I would never think of such a thing!"

"Cut line, girl. You think of every why and wherefore. Nothing gets away from that busy brainbox of yours."

"Exactly. I am too downy a bird to follow any handsome man tossing breadcrumbs my way."

"Begad, girl, I'm not talking about what's between your ears but what's between your legs."

"Aunt Lally!" Ellianne looking around to make sure none of the servants were within hearing. She decided it was a good thing her aunt was staying home after all, vow of silence or not.

"What, plain speaking not fitting for your delicate ears? Hah. You're a female, ain't you? And Wellstone's a male. A demmed fine-looking one at that. You've thought of climbing the mast, and no denying it."

Ellianne tried, her cheeks as red as the ruby pendant. "We are friends. And business partners, nothing else. Associates."

"Is that what they are calling it these days? Association? In my day they called it —"

"Aunt, please! Wellstone will be here any moment to drive me to the party. Besides, I thought you approved of him now. I know you thought him nothing but a parasite at first, but I could have sworn you grew to like him."

"Oh, I like him fine. In fact, were he a few years younger—not all that much younger, at that—I might hire him to escort me to a few places I never thought to see again. But for you? I still like him fine, even if he is a nob. But as a husband, my girl. Nothing else."

"That will never happen, Aunt Lally, so please stop speculating."

"What else has an old woman got to do? At least I am not meddling, like that goosecap Gwen."

"Lady Wellstone? But she is helping to find Isabelle."

"Like fish heads she is. Sending Wellstone to fetch you in their carriage when we have a perfectly good one of our own. Hah!"

"But she thought it would be safer."

"Safer from what, is what I want to know. Safer from some other bloke winning your dowry?"

"I am sure Lady Wellstone has no such intentions."

Aunt Lally went back to her needlework, muttering, "It's not her intentions I worry about in that dark carriage. You can tell your 'associate' for me that if he offers you a slip on the shoulders, Wellstone will be looking for his stones in the nearest well."

Stony brought flowers. White orchids, Gwen had declared, for Ellianne to carry.

He brought the carriage, freshly scrubbed with new straw laid on the floorboards. He was equally as neat, his blond hair still wet from his bath. He had a new dark blue superfine coat, and a new, more intricate knot to his snow-white neckcloth. He had his watch back on its fob chain across his new white marcella waistcoat, and a quizzing glass hanging from a ribbon.

He brought hope that someone tonight could lead them to Miss Isabelle.

What he hadn't brought was a cane to prop his bottom jaw shut when he got his first glimpse of his eccentric employer: Miss Ellianne Kane, the heiress, the Original, the most perfect rose he had ever seen.

Chapter Seventeen

Dropjaw was a common affliction at Lady Wellstone's gathering that evening. Almost every guest suffered from it when they were made known to the guest of honor, who had arrived earlier.

The young and lovely Lady Wellstone was not affected. Gwen wore a thoroughly smug, cat-in-the-cream-pot smile, especially when she introduced Miss Kane to that widowed in-law of her cousin's who had winkled an invitation out of her.

And Lord Wellstone's jaws were so tightly clenched—once he'd recovered from his own bout with the malady—after seeing the other gentlemen's reactions that he doubted he could unlock them by the time dinner was served.

Ellianne stood between them, her head held high. If she was on exhibit, she'd decided, she would put on a show worthy of her father, a man who owned his own bank. She would also prove herself worthy of her mother, the daughter of a marquess. If the results of such a match did not find favor with these members of the quality, then the devil take them all.

She smiled politely, she curtsied with the correct deference, but she showed no doubts of her own acceptability. In fact, that jealous widow was heard to comment, Miss Kane held herself like a queen, judging whether her subjects were worthy of notice or not. If Ellianne's knees were knocking together so badly she'd have bruises in the morning, no one could tell. The black lace overskirt hid that, too, rustling gently as if in a breeze. And Wellstone was close enough to catch her if her knees gave out altogether, thank goodness. In fact, Ellianne did not know how she could stand there being scrutinized at all if not for his solid, reassuring presence at her side.

"I say . . ." Lord Charles Hammett sputtered when Stony introduced his old friend to his new one. "I say . . ." What Charlie eventually said was "Ooph," when his new fiancée poked her elbow in his ribs.

Lady Valentina Pattendale was the only one to mention Isabelle. "I believe I met your sister, Miss Kane," was all she had time to say before she dragged poor Charlie as far away as possible, possibly saving him from being throttled by his host and former friend.

Stony shook his head when Ellianne sent him a questioning look. "No, she does not have any other information," he whispered between introductions, incidentally leaning closer to Ellianne's ear and to her long, graceful neck, her porcelain cheek, her silky tendrils of flame-colored hair, her heady perfume, her snowy bosom. If he leaned any closer, he was liable to scrape his nose on her ruby pendant. Gwen coughed and he straightened up. "I, ah, asked her before."

The guests kept coming. Gwen's intimate little gathering had turned into a dinner for twenty. They'd had to hire extra staff, but Stony had polished the heirloom silver himself, the stuff that was entailed and so could not be sold. The house hadn't looked as good in decades, he decided, this part of it, anyway. Two whole wings were shut up, but the company did not have to know that. He gazed around in satisfaction as the earlier arrivals chatted happily among themselves, glasses in hand. Charlie could not have been entirely happy, not with Lady Val rapping his knuckles with her closed fan. Stony smiled and Gwen smiled up at him from his other side.

Gwen had never looked better either, he thought, not even as a pretty young bride. In her social element, in a new rose-colored gown, she now had an elegance, a more mature, lasting beauty that could not help but please.

It pleased Lord Strickland, that was for sure. The baron had cleaned up nicely, just like the silver candlesticks under years of tarnish. His linen was spotless, and he must have bought himself a corset to hold in his paunch, for he creaked when he bowed over Gwen's hand. So taken with her smile of greeting was he, so grateful was he for her kind invitation—and so wary of Miss Kane, to whom he gave the briefest salute and "Good evening, ma'am"—that he swept Gwen away with him in search of a predinner sherry.

That left Stony and Ellianne waiting together near the drawing room door to receive the next guests.

To say that Gwen had never looked better was one thing. To say that Miss Kane had never looked better was such an understatement as to be ludicrous. She did not even look like Miss Kane! Lud, he wished he had an artist at hand to paint her portrait right now, in candlelight, in that scrap of silk and lace that was pretending to be a gown, with her hair rivaling the ruby for brilliance. He wished he could throw his coat over her, as he'd done at the morgue, so none of the other men could catch a glimpse of this exotic, entrancing Ellianne. Hell, he wished he could throw her over his shoulder and carry her up the stairs to his bedroom—no, to the closed wing, where no one would think to look for them for days. Five days might be enough so he could think straight again, without throbbing. Six days if her hair was as long and silky as he remembered. Better make that seven. He'd need a full twenty-four hours to smooth out all those tiny braids so her glorious hair lay across his pillow, across his chest, across her chest, playing hide and seek with her lovely, billowy breasts. They could be his pillow, his . . . They could be his.

Gwen would murder him.

Ellianne would do worse, judging from how gun-shy Strickland was.

And he would despise himself, instead of merely being ashamed of his brain's wicked imaginings and his body's wayward reactions. Damnation, when had Ellianne—he could not call her Miss Kane when he was calling on every ounce of his willpower not to kiss the inside of her arm, where her glove ended and the tiny sleeve of her gown began—when had Ellianne Kane gone from she-witch to siren? By George, it was deuced unfair. And dashed uncomfortable.

She was smiling now at the Duchess of Williston, who, it turned out, had known her mother. She'd also known his mother. Her Grace knew almost everyone and everything, in fact. Judging by her narrowed eyes, that included his dishonorable thoughts. How could he be censured for wanting to answer the most stunning invitation he'd ever seen? His body was ready to send a reply posthaste. In fact, he feared, more haste than post.

Her Grace did not say anything but give him a silent warning. She patted Ellianne's cheek and said, "Brava, my girl. Brava."

How come a duchess could touch her skin and a viscount couldn't? Hell and damnation, no one could blame him for wanting to. A man would have to be dead not to desire this woman.

Speaking of the dead, Sir John Thomasford was the next guest to be announced.

The coroner's adviser was impeccably dressed in dark formal wear, gleaming from his pomaded hair to the diamond stickpin in his neckcloth to the silver buckles on his shoes. His hair was slicked back from his high forehead again, as if all the scientific knowledge he spouted had swelled his brainbox. Then again, his forehead seemed a shade higher to Stony, as if the maggot from the morgue was losing his hair. Now wasn't that too bad?

Sir John oozed over Ellianne's fingers, and nearly left grease on Gwen's glove when she hurried over to meet the man Miss Kane liked enough to invite. Gwen gave the knight her brightest smile, and Stony almost gave his dear stepmama a shove back to Lord Strickland's side. As for Miss Kane, Stony was not letting her out of his sight or away from his side, not when he knew every man in the room had to be as bewitched as he was. Who knew what a man in lust might do? Stony knew what he wanted to do, and knew he would not do it, but who could predict the behavior of a man whose avocation was atrocities? He mistrusted that glint in Sir John's eyes and his curling lip that wasn't quite a smile.

According to Gwen, the man was single and respectable, with an adequate income to support a wife, not that anyone wedding the Kane heiress would have to worry about his income. He was of an age where a man had to think seriously of starting his nursery . . . and he sent Ellianne books about slayings. No, Sir John was not getting near Ellianne, not while Stony was acting as her escort.

As for Ellianne, she seemed pleased at the new arrival, as if counting him another friend among so many strangers. Stony could actually see her shoulders relax. The peagoose who considered herself so downy was too innocent to tell a vulture from a dove. Luckily she had Stony to play watch hawk. He all but sprouted beak and talons when Sir John held out his hand and asked, "Recovered now, are you?"

Even the man's voice sounded oily at such close quarters, deep but too smooth. Stony did not want to be in the same room with a man who dabbled in death, much less shake his hand. He could not refuse without causing a scene at Gwen's party, though. Ellianne was already looking at him quizzically. He straightened his thick blond curls before offering his hand in return. "Quite recovered," he said, giving his hair one last gloating pat. "That was a momentary weakness, don't you know. I had not yet broken my fast that day when Miss Kane's message arrived."

"Thank heaven," the man said as he stepped away, making room for the next arrival. Stony could swear he heard his companion giggle. Perhaps he ought to let the silly gudgeon swim with the sharks, after all. Or was that fly with the falcons?

By order of precedence, Stony was supposed to escort the duchess into dinner, once everyone had assembled. Miss Kane, as daughter of a knight, was far back, according to etiquette. She was to go in on Sir John's arm.

Like hell she would.

Stony managed to spill a drop of sherry on his shirt cuff, necessitating a delay while he dabbed at the spot with a dampened cloth. He begged Comte Villanoire, one of Gwen's steadfast but threadbare admirers, to escort Her Grace in his stead. Gwen was frantically reassigning dinner partners, trying to match fathers' titles and husbands' standings to the appropriate escort. This was precisely what she had slaved for hours over to get correct, so none of the matrons, dear Ellianne's would-be hostesses, could feel slighted. Now it was all higgledy-piggledy, a poor reflection on her hospitality.

Stony felt guilty when he saw her bottom lip start to quiver. Lud, was he reduced to upsetting Gwen over a thirty-foot walk to the dining room? Yes.

He finished his repairs in time to step in front of Sir John. "I seem to have made a mull of the entry order. Would you be a good fellow and escort Lady Valentina? I fear she'll be left with plain Mr. Camberly otherwise. Her father would be upset. Very high in the instep, Earl Patten is."

With Lady Valentina standing by the door, Sir John could not refuse. He bowed, said "My lady," and offered his arm. Which left Stony to escort Ellianne, which made Gwen's agitation almost forgivable, in his mind, at least. He got to listen to the swish of Ellianne's silk and lace skirts against his legs. He'd listen to Gwen's complaints later.

He could not do anything about the seating arrangements. The Duchess of Williston was on his right; Ellianne was on his left, with Sir John beyond her. Lud, Stony hoped the man was not going to discuss slaughters during the soup course.

Because the table was so long and so cluttered with candelabra and the monstrous silver epergne Stony had spent a day polishing, conversation could not be general. No one could see down the length of the linen cloth, much less converse across the middle of it, except at the head, deuce take it, and the foot, where Gwen sat between Strickland and Lord Aldershott, whose wife happened to be hosting a ball next week.

The duchess could be trusted to lead the talk at their end of the table, thank goodness, so Sir John could not chat about hangings over the halibut in oyster sauce. A kind woman, Her Grace was known for her ease at polite discourse with everyone, from the prince himself to the palest, most bashful young miss making her come-out. That was one of the reasons Stony and Gwen had invited her to meet Miss Kane. The dowager always knew what to say.

Not tonight. Tonight Her Grace uttered the worst possible comment: She praised the meal. "I cannot remember having a finer dinner, Wellstone. Your chef is to be complimented, and you for having the perspicacity to hire such an artist."

Stony hated to say it. The duchess had to know how matters stood with him, that he could never afford a high-priced French chef. Gads, he'd squired two of her grandnieces last year, and had a load of coal delivered, with her regards. The comte, on Her Grace's other side, was without a feather to fly with, so his opinion did not matter. The way he was eating was no credit to the cook; this might have been his only decent meal for the week. Miss Kane, of course, knew the truth. But Sir John Thomasford?

The eel in aspic turned to ashes in Stony's mouth. He swallowed anyway and admitted, "I wish I could accept your gracious flattery, Duchess, but, alas, the maestro is courtesy of Miss Kane. She was good enough to lend us her chef's services for the evening." The man had been in the kitchens here for days, cooking foods also provided, Stony supposed, by Miss Kane, with helpers from Miss Kane's household. Gwen had made the arrangements and the viscount had not wanted to inquire too closely, polishing the silver and his pride in the butler's pantry. Pride? His was as flattened now as the lobster patty on his plate. At least the dishes were his.

Ellianne quickly leaped into the quagmire of the awkward silence. "Oh, no. It was Lady Wellstone who did me the favor. The chef was threatening to leave my employ if I did not give him a chance to display his skills. We barely entertain at Sloane Street, since we are in mourning and know so few people, being new to town, so there was little enough for the man to do."

And because she ate like a bird, Stony thought, noting the sparse selection of food on her plate. Still, he was happy for Ellianne's sop to his *amour propre,* and pleased that she had thought to come to his defense.

"The man was *aux anges* at the opportunity to cook for a duchess," Ellianne concluded. "I'll be lucky if he returns home."

The duchess smiled, glad the unfortunate matter was so easily smoothed. Stony smiled at Ellianne in thanks, and she smiled back at him. Sir John curled his lip.

Stony ignored it, for it was Miss Kane's lip that had snared his attention. She had a little bit of custard from the sweets course at the corner of her mouth, a tiny drop, like nectar on a peach. Lud, what he wouldn't give to play honeybee and gather that confection to himself. He'd start at her lip, then see if her mouth tasted half as sweet. He'd . . . spill wine in his lap if he did not pay attention to his meal.

He turned to the duchess and entered into a lively—and proper—debate on the merits of the refreshments served at several recent gatherings they had both attended. Miss Kane and Sir John, Stony was glad to hear, without having to crane his neck too far, were discussing the various offerings at the London theaters. The theater? Stony interrupted Her Grace in midsentence to inform the jumped-up mortician that Miss Kane was already promised to him and Lady Wellstone for Drury Lane that week.

Before Ellianne could deny any such appointment, or the duchess could descry his manners, Gwen stood, signaling the end to the dinner, and time for the ladies to withdraw. Stony stood and held back Her Grace's chair, pleased to see an unfamiliar footman performing the same service for Miss Kane. He must be one of hers, then, helping for the night, but Stony did not mind that he wasn't paying the man's salary. In fact, he'd give the chap extra, for an exemplary job.

Stony did not sit back down, not near Sir John. He carried his port around to where his friend Lord Charles was lighting a cigar. Stony declined the offer to join him in blowing a cloud. Damn if his mind wasn't already befogged. He did raise his glass once more to Charlie and his engagement.

"Your lady is looking lovely tonight, Charlie." Lady Valentina was indeed looking prettier than ever. She still wore the virginal white of an unmarried maiden, but her gown was trimmed in flowing blue ribbons that matched her eyes and, not coincidentally, the forget-me-knots embroidered on Charlie's waistcoat. Charlie smiled his agreement through the smoke ring he blew. "A regular diamond of the first water."

"You've made an excellent choice." They both knew Lord Charles had been given few options, once Captain Brisbane decamped and Stony declined.

"I think so." Charlie took another puff, then looked to see that most of the other men were busy relieving themselves, or laughing over some ribald joke. "You know," he said when he was certain they would not be overheard, "I wondered why you gave Val up. She's beautiful."

Stony raised his glass to that.

"And wealthy."

Stony sipped again.

"And spirited."

Too spirited for Stony's taste, trapping a man into marriage, but he did not say so.

"She's wellborn and intelligent to boot, so I asked myself what was wrong with her, that you didn't want the lady."

"It was nothing like that. I—"

"After all, we all have to wed someday, and you even have that title to carry on. Val would have made the perfect bride for you. Yet you pushed her my way."

"I did not—"

Charlie stared up at the gray cloud rising above him. "No question but that Earl Patten wanted you for a son-in-law, not me. So I wondered, you know. Until now."

"Now?" What, had Charlie discovered his bride-to-be was a designing minx who'd try to rule his household?

"Yes, now that I have seen Miss Kane."

"You are far out there, old boy. The situations are nothing alike. You know I am acting as companion for the lady, nothing else."

Charlie ignored him. "What a woman! Not that I

am not happy with Lady Val, of course. Suits me to a cow's thumb. But your Miss Kane . . ."

"She is not my anything," Stony insisted. "Except a bit of escort duty."

"Hah. I saw the way you were looking at her, like she was on the menu. Not that I blame you. Any man would. Unless he is newly engaged, of course."

And newly under the cat's paw.

Out loud, Stony said, "Miss Kane is indeed an attractive female."

Charlie snorted. "My mother is an attractive female. Miss Kane is something else. Who would have thought to find such beauty in a banker's daughter? And he's dead, the father, so you do not even have to worry over a merchant's stain on your family escutcheon. You lucky dog."

"Devil take it, Charlie, I am not going to marry Miss Kane. She is wealthy and beautiful, educated and reasonably clever, for a woman. She is everything you say, and more." Stony recalled her loyal and thoughtful defense. She could have left him confessing to his dinner guests that he could barely afford the peas on their plates. "But she is not for me. I'd never live off my wife." Then he recalled to whom he was speaking. "That is, dash it, I am not in the market for a bride."

Charlie stubbed out his cigar and stood up. He looked back at his friend in regret. "Then you are a bigger fool, Stony, than I thought you were the day you turned down my Valentina."

Chapter Eighteen

Whoever dictated that the gentlemen should stay apart from the ladies after dinner anyway? Stony wanted go make sure Ellianne was faring all right among the women, but he could not. He was the host, and so had to make sure the wine kept flowing and the talk stayed convivial. Much longer and they wouldn't be able to see the door through the smoke, and Lord Aldershott might have to be carried out.

Stony kept checking his watch. The deuced thing must have stopped working while sojourning at the pawnshop, for the minute hand did not seem to be moving. He went to join a knot of gentlemen at the other end of the table, not seeing Strickland among them until it was too late. Like everyone else, the baron had enjoyed the meal. His neckcloth and waistcoat hadn't. Stony would rather speak with anyone else—except Sir John Thomasford, of course. The knighted night crawler was talking to Comte Villanoire over by the liquor tray, likely exchanging gory details about the guillotine.

Stony was about to find that helpful footman and tell him to offer Strickland a fresh cravat, from Stony's wardrobe. Before he could locate the servant in the smoke-filled corners of the dining room, Strickland called to him. "I say, Wellstone," he said in a voice made jovial by the fine meal and louder by the wine. "You had me fooled, you did."

It would not take much to fool the beef-witted baron. Stony reminded himself once more that he was the host. If the rule separating the sexes after dinner made no sense, the one about not insulting a guest in one's house made less. If he were offended, the lout might leave. But Stony had invited the man, on a whim that seemed worthy at the time, so he raised one blond eyebrow and asked, "How is that, sir?"

"I thought you were interested in the younger Kane gal, not the hellcat heiress. I'll admit she's looking better than I have ever seen her. Your stepmama's influence, I'd wager. Still, you ought to reconsider. This one ain't going to make a conformable wife."

Perhaps the man was not such a fool after all. Miss Ellianne Kane was one of the least conformable, least comfortable women Stony had ever encountered. She was a guest in his house too, though, and he would not have her name bandied about by an old whoremonger with creamed carrots on his cravat.

"That will be some other fellow's problem," Stony replied as casually as tightened jaw muscles would allow. "I am just helping my stepmother's young friend find her feet in Town, not a husband."

Strickland laughed. "I know what I saw. Daresay everyone in the drawing room saw. But I can tell by those daggers you're sending my way that you don't want to give away your plans too soon. Quite right, my boy, quite right. No formal announcement, nothing signed, no notice in the papers, means you can still back out. Take your time, lad. Once you get to know the harridan you'll be glad you didn't commit yourself. Else you'll commit yourself after the wedding, to Bedlam." He gave a hearty laugh that had half the men turning to look. "Of course, by then you won't need a wife, just a boys' choir to join."

He slapped his meaty thigh. For all Stony knew, it had veal and lamb and beef stains on it. Then, "By the way," Strickland said just before he would have found his teeth joining the carrots down his shirtfront, "did you ever locate the younger sister? Miss Isabelle Kane, that is?"

Stony looked around to make sure Sir John was not listening, to give him the lie. "Of course. A slight misunderstanding led to the confusion. Miss Isabelle is visiting family in the north. She left before receiving the note that her sister was coming to town, and Miss Kane left her home before hearing of Miss Isabelle's plans. I believe there are papers to sign concerning their aunt's estate, but they can wait. Gwen has convinced Miss Kane to participate in the Season a bit, rather than returning home to wait there for her sister's arrival from those relatives."

One of the other gentlemen nearby quipped, "I hope those kinfolks have harder heads than Lady Augusta."

Not even Strickland thought that was funny, remembering Lady Augusta with a surprising degree of fondness. Maybe the old clutchpurse had left Strickland something in her will, too. Changing the subject, the baron said, "I didn't know the chits were on terms with the Chansford side of their family. The old marquess swore he'd never recognize Ellis Kane or any of his brood."

"But the current Marquess of Chaston is the girls' uncle," Stony offered, lest anyone look too closely at his Banbury tale. "Perhaps he's had a change of heart."

"Or he sees a way to get hold of the younger gal's fortune. She's not even twenty yet, is she?"

Stony said, "I do not believe so, no."

"Well, Chaston would still be a better guardian for the chit than any of the Kane relatives. Smugglers, the lot of them. Lady Augusta swore that's where the brass to found the bank came from. Hell, if the girl went off visiting any of them, she'd come back sounding like a Billingsgate fishwife."

Or a pirate's parrot.

Stony checked his watch again. This time he rapped it on the table to get the blasted thing working.

Then Lord Aldershott shot the cat, casting his accounts on Stony's silver epergne.

Things were not much better in the drawing room.

First, Lady Valentina truly knew nothing about Isabelle. She was a few years older than Isabelle, more established in London society, and had a different circle of acquaintances than any Lady Augusta would encourage.

"No, I am sorry I cannot be of more assistance," Lady Val said, checking her hair for loose pins, after taking a place beside Ellianne on a sofa. "But why do you want to know your sister's friends? Young girls are all ninnyhammers," she said, as if Ellianne were in her dotage.

"I was hoping to plan a small gathering for when she returned," Ellianne explained. "Her trip could not have been pleasant, with Aunt Augusta's funeral and all, and I wished to give Isabelle a bit of gaiety before we left for home. There is not much room in the Sloane Street house, however, so I wanted to invite Isabelle's closest acquaintances. And mine, of course," she added, lest Lady Valentina thought Ellianne was rejecting her overtures of friendship. The younger woman was a frothy confection of fashion, snobbery, and pleasure-seeking; in other words, a typical London miss. She was still a lively, good-natured companion, it seemed, whose biggest concern was how many of her own dearest friends could fit into St. George's for her wedding. So far, it sounded to Ellianne as if half of London would be invited.

After giving Ellianne a thorough description of the wedding plans, from the gown she would wear to the flowers she would carry, Lady Valentina floated over toward the pianoforte, tuned for the occasion, and started to play a popular song.

Gwen's cousin's wife and her sister, Mrs. Collins, took up the vacated seats near Ellianne, beginning to quiz her about her connection to the Wellstones.

Ellianne looked around for her hostess, but Gwen and the duchess had their heads together at the opposite end of the room. Ellianne would give a month's income to know what those two charming connivers were up to, but she could not intrude. Lady Aldershott and another woman Ellianne had met earlier but had not spoken with since were examining a collection of Staffordshire dogs on the mantel. The last two female guests, also mere names to Ellianne so far, must be visiting the ladies' retiring rooms. No one was going to interrupt this rude inquisition.

Ellianne raised her chin. Stony would have recognized the sign of proud determination, but Mrs. Collins chose not to.

"Dear Gwen is always bear-leading some unfortunate girl or other," the widow was saying. "Never tell me you have no respectable female relative of your own? Of course there was the unpleasantness concerning Lady Augusta, wasn't there?"

Ellianne made the vaguest of comments.

"I am surprised a woman with your advantages does not hire herself a wellborn companion."

The cousin tittered, and Ellianne wondered if Mrs. Collins were applying for the position. Ellianne would rather take a boa constrictor into her house than this biddy. "My aunt Lavinia, Mrs. Goudge, is companion enough. Aunt Lally does not care for social gatherings, but Lady Wellstone has been kind enough to include me in some of her plans, such as shopping excursions, morning calls, and the theater."

Mrs. Collins fumed. Gwen had never invited her anywhere before this, and she was by way of being a relative. Well, a connection, anyway, by marriage. Speaking of marriage, the widow meant to enter that happy state again as soon as she found someone to pay off her bills. Living in shabby rooms on a pittance of an annuity, Mrs. Collins had ambitions far beyond her expectations. She'd been hoping to move into Wellstone House with her relatives, but they were putting up at a hotel. There was no room, and no invitation, even if she wished to put up with her beastly, bratty nieces and nephews.

There was still Wellstone himself. Everyone knew he was below hatches, playing the Fancy Fred to lonely ladies, but so what? He had this house, the pile in the country, the title, and a respected place in society. Mrs. Collins did not care how the viscount earned his keep, just that he share it. Besides, a gentleman who made his way from boudoir to boudoir could not be particular about his wife's little flirtations. Her first husband had been, and deuced unpleasant he had been about it, too, until he collapsed of a heart seizure in the middle of a jealous rage. Wellstone was young and fit and handsome, and Mrs. Collins would not mind in the least sharing his bed, at least until she had provided him with an heir. Which happy event, she knew, had better take place sooner rather than later, for while a gentleman could wait until middle age to start his nursery, a woman could not.

So Mrs. Collins had dressed with care this evening in her finest gown: a dark blue satin with scalloped hem and matching scalloped neckline, set off with her diamonds. Not even her sister knew the stones were paste. She was elegantly fashionable, she told herself, without looking fast. She did not want to give Wellstone the wrong idea, for she could find the other kind of offer on every street corner. No, she wanted a wedding band, not a bauble when he tired of her.

She had not given Wellstone the wrong impression. She had not given him any impression whatsoever. The man had eyes for no one but this mushroom, this banker's daughter. Next to her black silk, Mrs. Collins's dark blue satin might have been a servant's uniform, for all he noticed. Granted Miss Kane was dramatic looking, worth a fortune, and on good terms with the viscount's stepmother. So? She was no real lady, had no idea how to go on in the polite world, and who wanted red-haired children anyway?

Mrs. Collins waited until she could hear the men's footsteps and laughter in the hall. Then she gestured toward the pianoforte. "Such a lovely touch to an evening, musical entertainment and good conversation, don't you think?" At Ellianne's nod, she went on: "Lady Valentina must be growing weary of playing by now. Why do you not take her place, Miss Kane?"

Ellianne smiled. "I am afraid I have no skills on the pianoforte whatsoever."

"Another instrument, perhaps?"

"No, I am afraid not, to my sorrow, and that of numerous musical instructors. They did try, I swear."

"Then perhaps you might sing. I am sure we can convince Lady Valentina to accompany you. Such a talented, accommodating young lady."

Now Ellianne had to laugh. "I assure you, my singing would be no pleasure for anyone in the room. In fact, Gwen's guests would all leave before the tea tray was brought in."

"Oh, my," Mrs. Collins said, louder than before, "I thought all young women had some drawing room skills."

Gwen and the duchess were hurrying over, to reach Ellianne's side before the gentlemen entered. Before they arrived, Ellianne stood. She was enough taller than Mrs. Collins that she could look down on the slightly older woman, to note the few gray hairs her tweezer had missed. She pointedly touched the ruby on her chest, which glowed as it ought, not like the dull jewels around Mrs. Collins's neck. "I am afraid I was never one for useless pastimes. And before you ask, no, I am no needlewoman. I leave that to my aunt. I do not compose poetry, nor do I dabble in watercolors. I have never tried knotting a reticule, but I would likely make a mare's nest of that, too."

"Ah, you must be a reader then. A bluestocking."

"No, I read what interests me, nothing more. I am sure you are far more accomplished than I, Mrs. Collins."

Ellianne would have moved off then, to join Gwen or Lady Valentina, since she could not fly to the door to seek Wellstone's comforting presence. Before she left, though, the impertinent Mrs. Collins asked, in a tone sure to carry to the rest of the room, and the gentlemen just entering, "But what do you do, then?"

"What do I do?"

"Yes, you must do something to fill your days and nights. I am certain you do not do your own cooking and cleaning."

Gwen's cousin's wife smothered another titter with her hand.

Ellianne hardly had a moment free between the bank and meetings with her investment counselors, trying to keep up with all the papers they presented for her consideration, trying to stay abreast of the latest news that could affect the local and national economies. If she said she oversaw her investments, however, that she monitored the bank's workings to guarantee no one would swindle them again, she would be a pariah, a social outcast. Ladies did not lift their fingers to anything heavier than a teacup, certainly not a bank ledger. She was a banker, and proud of it, but tonight she had discovered she also enjoyed being a part of society, being a desirable woman, being her mother's daughter as well as her father's.

Gwen was wringing her handkerchief already. The duchess, usually the most kindhearted of ladies, was scowling. Ellianne raised her chin a notch higher. She was literally looking down her nose at the widow who so obviously wanted Wellstone for herself. "I do have one skill, Mrs. Collins, whether you consider it a lady-like virtue or not. I am good with numbers. Very good. So good, in fact, that I spend hours managing the charitable foundation I have established to aid less fortunate females. We now have a training school, a hospital, and a home for orphans. Perhaps you would wish to contribute? If not, we always need volunteers. But of course you already give a portion of your income and your time to the needy. All ladies do, don't they?"

Mrs. Collins turned three shades of purple that did not match her gown, and Gwen let out an audible sigh of relief. She instantly suggested they play a few hands of cards, rather than let the sharp-edged conversation continue.

Lord Strickland rushed to claim Ellianne as his partner.

Surprised and disappointed, for he wanted to be the one to ease Ellianne's tension, to tell her that one jealous cat should not destroy her enjoyment of the evening, Stony raised his brow.

"You heard her," the baron answered his unspoken question. "The gal is good with numbers. Deuced good, according to her aunt and Lady Augusta's man of business. Who would you rather have as a card partner? A pretty widgeon who can caterwaul and pound the keys, or one who can count?"

Stony thought the baron had given up gambling. He must have given up his fears of Miss Kane instead, although he did keep his chair as far from the table as possible. Or perhaps Strickland's self-imposed rules did not pertain to such low-stakes games as found in a lady's parlor. Or else he bet only on a sure thing.

They won. And won. And won.

Strickland had never been known for his proficiency with the pasteboards; he might not have lost his estate if he'd had half this much card sense. But it was not his mastery, nor even his luck, that kept the baron chortling over the point count. It was his partner who seemed to know every card that had been played and the odds of each other one appearing. The lady could calculate.

Hell, with Ellianne as a partner, Stony thought, he would not have to be in the escort business. Of course, if he was not in the squiring service, he would not have met this woman who continuously astounded him. A goddess and a cardsharp? Who ever would have thought that, meeting the dowdy, uppity heiress? Not the viscount. He'd thought he knew women. By George, he admitted to himself, he was as stupid as a stone.

He was not playing. The comte and the duchess were continuing a discussion started during dinner, of which Stony heartily approved. If Her Grace took pity on the Frenchman, then perhaps Stony wouldn't find the impoverished émigré at his own table so often. With Lord Aldershott resting in the library, the tables would have been uneven if Stony had participated. Instead of making his guests change partners with every hand, Stony volunteered to sit out. He truly did not care for games of chance, which they were, since he lacked Miss Kane's skill. And if he could not sit at the table with her—or on the couch or the love seat—then he could make certain that Strickland treated her with the proper courtesy, while the dreadful Mrs. Collins kept her distance. He maneuvered the widow into partnering Sir John Thomasford. The greedy and the ghoulish; they were the perfect match.

As the gracious host, Stony circulated among the four tables, seeing that the guests had fresh decks and fresh glasses of wine. He tried not to single out Strickland and Miss Kane's table, but somehow found himself watching their play far more often than he did, say, Lady Val's and Charlie's, who were already bickering over their bids like an old married couple.

By standing behind Miss Kane, looking over her shoulder, Stony could not only admire her skill, but he could admire her bosom, only half-hidden by the gauzy black lace. That narrow space between her ivory breasts was a great deal more fascinating than the back of Lord Strickland's balding head. And that red down at the nape of her neck, below the upswept style, was tantalizing. And her scent . . .

She threw out the wrong discard.

"Go away, Wellstone," Strickland ordered without modulating his voice, so half the card players turned to look. "Can't you see you're making the lady nervous hovering over her like a bee in a clover patch?"

Ellianne's blush started at her toes. She glared at Strickland, and then she glared at Stony for good measure while their opponents laughingly begged him to stay. Feeling like a schoolboy caught stealing tarts, Wellstone went to watch Gwen lose her monthly allowance.

As soon as her pin money was gone, Gwen called for an end to the card playing. As the various scores were tallied and debts settled, everyone could hear Strickland boasting of his winnings. He did give credit where it was due, showing Miss Kane more respect than he had when he was courting her. In fact, Stony feared he was thinking of putting his luck to the test again, she was that dab a hand at cards. Then she said, "Oh, I always give my winnings to charity. Shall I add yours to mine, Lord Strickland?"

The baron scurried over toward Gwen and the tea tray.

Stony was too late to get a seat near Ellianne. Lady Aldershott wanted to discuss the training school, and Mrs. Harkness-Smythe was inviting Miss Kane to her card party the following week.

There was a vacant seat next to Mrs. Collins on the sofa. The woman tilted her head and cooed. Stony took his tea and stood near the fireplace. He liked his pigeons baked in a pie, not stuffed in satin.

Deuce take it, he thought, he'd hardly had a chance to say three words in private to Ellianne all evening. Here she was in his own house, and he might be one of the china dogs on the mantel, for all the time they'd spent together. First she was being introduced, then sitting beside Sir John at dinner. Cards with Strickland, now this, surrounded by females and would-be card partners . . . and the undertaker.

She was a success, he thought, half with pride, half with regret that soon she would not be needing him anymore. Of course, they had not located her sister yet, but with Ellianne's success would come exposure to wider circles. Someone would mention Isabelle. They'd talk about it on the ride home, he planned, when he would have her all to himself. Whatever else Stony was planning for that short drive wasn't ready for words, just a smile of anticipation.

The duchess, unfortunately, saw that smile. She declared she would see Miss Kane home in her carriage. Since it was on her way, there was no need for Wellstone to call out his own coach for the short drive to Sloane Street.

"But I brought her." Damn if Stony didn't hear a whine in his own voice. He squared his shoulders and spoke with authority, not agony. "So I shall take the lady home. With one of our maids in attendance, of course." The servant was going to ride up with the driver this time, he promised himself.

"Well, your maids have enough to do, cleaning up." And then Her Grace issued the unkindest cut of all: "Who leaves the fox to guard the henhouse, anyway?"

Et tu, Duchy?

Chapter Nineteen

He wanted her. But what did that mean? Ellianne wondered. Did his heated looks mean he liked her, or that her gown was cut too low after all? Perhaps he admired her, or perhaps he believed that red hair went with loose morals. Surely he did not believe she would become his paramour, did he? Was he hoping to increase his earnings by increasing her dependency on him?

Of course not. He'd given his word. Lord Wellstone was a gazetted charmer, that was all. He could not help flirting with every woman he met. He'd even tried turning the duchess up sweet. Maybe he could not help desiring every new female who came his way, like some women craved every new bonnet they saw.

More likely, Ellianne thought, he did not truly want her but was just trying to bolster her confidence. Gwen must have told him about Ellianne's anxieties before the dinner, and he was trying to give her the strength that Gwen said came with knowing one looked one's best. That was it, and just like Wellstone, to be concerned with her emotions. She laughed off Her Grace's warnings. The viscount's warm regard meant nothing.

So what did her own warm feelings for him mean? Warm? She was practically fevered, thinking about the lingering kiss he had placed on her gloved hand as he handed her into the duchess's coach. Her blood was heated, if not to boiling then at least to simmering, stirring in secret, unexplored places. His scent lingered in her memory, and an image of his one ready dimple was indelibly imprinted on her mind. He was calling for her in the morning, and Ellianne was already planning what to wear and how to leave her maid behind. She might as well be planning, for she'd never sleep in anticipation.

Why? Nothing could come of this nonsense. She was not a light-skirt, and he was a gentleman. They were not adolescents who did not understand the pull of passion and its disastrous results. They were mature adults, with responsibilities and with respect for their good names.

So what did her growing attraction to Lord Wellstone mean? That she was a fool, that was what.

She was a success. Stony had known she would be, by the depth of her fortune, if nothing else, but this was beyond even his expectations. By the afternoon after Gwen's dinner, the Sloane Street house was under siege. Invitations arrived by the bushel, and old Timms was rebuilding his pension, accepting calling cards and coins from would-be gentlemen visitors. He gave them each a blessing and sent them on their way. Ellianne did meet with a few of the women who called, in hope they might mention Isabelle, but the ladies were merely hoping to snare the newest comet on the social horizon for their next affair.

They all claimed acquaintance with Lady Augusta or Ellianne's mother, to justify calling without an introduction. They all lied, according to Timms. Aunt Lally labeled them three-nippled ninnies and refused to sit in the parlor with the gossiping, gushing, gawking matrons. Ellianne was so grateful to Stony for his invitation to drive in the park that she almost hugged him, despite her firm resolve to ignore his all-too-masculine physicality. She might have ignored the ground under her feet more easily.

The park was not a good idea. Every horseman, every whip, every town beau out on the strut hailed their good friend Stony. If courtesy hadn't demanded he stop to make introductions, the clogged traffic paths did. He could not drive on, not through two half-pay officers, a threadbare third son on a second-rate hack, four confessed fortune-hunters, and one widower with five hopeful progeny. News of an unwed heiress spread faster than fleas on a dog, it seemed, and was just as uncomfortable to Ellianne.

None of the gentlemen spoke of meeting her sister. They only wanted to know where they could meet Miss Kane again. Did she attend this party or that one? Would she honor them with a dance? If she did not dance, perhaps she would prefer cards, or a trip to the Tower Menagerie or Vauxhall, a drive to Richmond . . . or to Scotland. No one spoke the last aloud, of course, but she could almost hear the gentlemen's minds calculating their chances of winning her consent, and her fortune. She did not need any grande dame's warnings about what else these London bucks were estimating, not when their eyes strayed below her collarbone and they licked their lips.

Ellianne's only consolation was that Lord Wellstone appeared as miserable as she felt.

"Sorry, gentlemen," he finally said, after trying to dislodge another contingent of rakes who'd rather be rich, "but my horses are growing restless, and Miss Kane's aunt made me promise that I would have her back in an hour."

The aunt had not said a word, of course, but he thought the parrot had screeched out something as they were leaving. It sounded like, "Keep your mind on the road, sonny, and not on your rod." He shook his head. He couldn't have heard that right.

He did have Ellianne back within the hour, though,

angry, frustrated, with energy to burn—and those were the horses' complaints. Stony's were a lot worse.

Ellianne was close to packing her bags and going home. She was no closer to finding her sister, and too close to the slavering jackals she feared and despised. Stony promised that evening would be better, and it was, at first.

They were attending the theater. Whether they went because Stony had claimed the prior engagement to Sir John, or because he thought she might enjoy it, made no difference. Ellianne was looking forward to a performance far beyond what she was used to in the shires. It was the audience here that put on the show, however.

No one watched the actors, it seemed, nor bothered to listen. Those in the pit constantly moved around, making assignations with the pretty orange sellers, tossing fruit to each other, or onto the stage. The box holders spent all their time gazing at each other, chattering like squirrels over who was with which widow, and which husband was in which courtesan's box.

Half the opera glasses, quizzing glasses, and lorgnettes were trained on the Wellstone box, it felt to Ellianne, weighing the carats in her diamonds, counting the black feathers in her hair. She edged a fraction of an inch closer to Stony's seat. Gwen was there too, with Lord Strickland, of all the escorts she could have selected, and Aunt Lally was sitting in the far rear corner. She did not say anything, thank goodness, but her gnarling disapproval of the audience's behavior resembled the bulldog Atlas more than any well-mannered lady. Ellianne could only hope the raucous crowd drowned out the noise.

She also hoped her ensemble did not offend Stony, for he was growling nearly as loudly. She was not flaunting her wealth with the diamonds, she told herself. She was wearing her mother's jewels tonight because that lady would have been proud of her daughter, taking her place in the beau monde.

As for Stony, his appearance tonight quite took Ellianne's breath away. He was wearing formal black satin knee breeches and black silk stockings that proved he had no need to pad his calves. The breeches clung to his muscular thighs like paint, so close to her that she could have reached out to see if the paint was dry. Her palms were not, under her gloves.

The noise—and Ellianne's quickened heartbeat—subsided as the play progressed and the audience finally became rapt in the drama. Now she could relax and enjoy someone else's tragedy.

The first intermission brought every needy gentleman who had not yet winkled out an introduction. Stony's mutterings grew louder, or were those Aunt Lally's? Ellianne tried to see past the dark coats that filled the box, wishing she had not insisted that her aunt join them for some innocent entertainment. She could not be certain if it was innocent, but one of the callers at the rear, suspiciously close to Aunt Lally and her cane, tripped and fell. His flailing legs kicked the gentleman in front of him, who lost his footing and collided with a third, who also fell, toppling two more. One of the men came up swinging.

Strickland gallantly stepped in front of Gwen to protect her, but then he started calling out odds on the match.

"Enough!" Stony shouted above the melee. "You are in the presence of ladies, blast your hides. Now act like gentlemen, bow, and get out. Whoever is still in my box when I count to ten had better be prepared to meet me at Gentleman Jackson's Boxing Parlor in the morning."

"I thought you don't really fight?" Ellianne whispered to him, from her secure place beyond his left shoulder.

He turned and winked at her. "But they don't know that, do they?"

Gwen wept through the next act, for the deaths onstage or the melee in her box, no one was certain. Aunt Lally chuckled.

Stony took no chances at the next intermission. He bustled Ellianne out and over to the Duchess of Williston's nearby box. No one would dare to misbehave in Her Grace's presence.

"In over your head, are you, my boy?" the duchess asked after seeing Ellianne seated, but not unkindly. "You go back to that watering pot Gwen before she scares Strickland off. He's not much, but she could do worse."

Worse? Stony wondered. How, by taking up with a coal heaver? Lud, he couldn't leave the peagoose alone with the old reprobate, but he belonged beside Ellianne.

"Go on," the duchess ordered. "I'll look after your heiress."

Lady Aldershott's ball was no better.

Ellianne spent as much time as she could in the room set aside for the ladies to refresh themselves. First, she wanted to ask if anyone knew her sister's friends, using that surprise party as pretense. Second, she wished to avoid the crush that surrounded her whenever she ventured into the ballroom or the supper room.

Half the time she could not spot Gwen in the crowd, to join her supposed chaperon. Lady Wellstone was busy on her behalf, she knew, trying to find not Isabelle's friends, but Lady Augusta's. Gwen was telling the dowager set that she wanted to introduce them to Miss Kane, so dear Ellianne could hear about her aunt's last days. So far Aunt Augusta seemed to have had no friends. No one wanted to recall her final hours, only her final bequests.

The one Ellianne really sought was Stony, but he had duty dances to perform, acquaintances to greet. He could not just lounge outside the ladies' retiring room for ages waiting for her, not without adding more gossip to her name.

Other men did not care about her reputation or her comfort. They rushed to her side when she appeared at the ballroom door, pressing too close, like pigs at a trough, she thought, squealing to get her attention. A promenade? A cup of punch? A stroll on the balcony or through the portrait gallery? She could not remember their names, or if she'd been properly introduced. They did not know Isabelle, and they did not know Ellianne, if they thought she would be impressed by their fulsome compliments or their absurdly high shirt collars and intricate neckcloths. They smelled of wine or heat or too much cologne. They talked too much and held her hand too long. They gave her a headache.

She fled back to the ladies' room.

From his superior height, Stony had seen her across the ballroom, but could not leave his dance partner in the middle of the set. He deposited the young lady back with her mother as quickly as decency permitted and hurried to rescue Ellianne from the worst pack of rakes, fortune-hunters, and hangers-on he'd ever seen gathered in one spot since Prinny's last gathering at Carlton House. Lady Aldershott had no daughters, so she did not care what kind of libertines she invited to her ball. The mothers in the ballroom cared, so they were vigilantly guarding the young misses—the way Stony should have been doing.

By the time he reached the spot where she'd been standing, Ellianne was gone. Lud, what if one of the cads had swept her off to a darkened alcove or a deserted room? The silly widgeon thought she could protect herself, telling him she could do better on her own. The young ladies would not look at her when he was present, she'd said with a laugh, much less talk about Isabelle.

But she had never met a determined seducer like any of the blackguards standing by the door telling ribald jokes. Stony recognized them all, half from his days as a gambler, half from his days escorting young women away from their influence. Sadly, not one of them was above coercing an heiress into a compromising position.

"What, did you lose your little red hen, Wellstone?" Godfrey Blanchard called out to him, making cackling sounds.

At least she wasn't with that dirty dish, Stony thought in relief. Blanchard was always on the lookout for a wealthy woman with a father mutton-headed enough to let him near the girl. He'd been shown more doors than a two-toothed tinker.

Sir Poindexter, who barely reached five feet, declared Miss Kane a maypole with red streamers, rather than a chicken.

Lord Durstan, who had already buried two wives, jerked his head toward the ladies' retiring room. "She must be a sickly thing, spending her night in there. You're welcome to the wench."

Since Durstan had to weigh more than the prince, and Miss Kane barely weighed more than a pullet, the others laughed as he walked away.

Stony ignored all of them. Let them laugh, he thought; they'd had their last chance at Miss Kane. He'd go into the ladies' withdrawing room himself if he had to, to keep a better eye on her.

He did not have to take such drastic measures, for Lady Valentina Pattendale hurried down the hall, holding up a torn flounce. Stony asked her to inform Miss Kane that he was waiting outside the door.

Lady Val saw no reason to hurry with the message. She was more than happy with her betrothal, but a tiny splinter of resentment still festered. Wellstone, who had a higher title than Lord Charles, better looks, and far more skill on the dance floor—the torn flounce being testimony to Charlie's clumsiness—had refused to marry her, Earl Patten's only daughter. Let him wait.

She asked Miss Kane to keep her company while a maid set hurried stitches in her hem. Ellianne was all too happy to see a friendly, familiar face . . . until the younger girl confessed that she'd almost become betrothed to Lord Wellstone.

"Oh, Charlie suits me fine, but he was my third choice, you know. Captain Brisbane was my first. So romantic with that limp. Of course, he could not dance at all, so I suppose I was lucky."

Ellianne was horrified. "You'd choose a husband because of his limp?"

"Of course not, silly. The captain seemed the most honorable of the three. I never thought he would turn craven."

"But you loved each of them?" Ellianne supposed such a thing were possible, although she could not imagine herself being struck with Cupid's arrows more than once in a lifetime, if that, certainly not thrice in one month. Lady Valentina must have mistaken girlish infatuation for the truer, permanent emotion.

The young lady laughed. "Heavens, love had nothing to do with it. My father would have married me off to a cabinet minister who was too old to dance the reels and too fusty to waltz. Can you believe it? Captain Brisbane was handsome, at least."

"But you did not love him?"

"Oh, I was fond enough of the man. I never expected to marry for love, you know. Most girls don't, especially when their fathers want to consolidate lands or fortunes or power. I always hoped love could come later. It never could have with that stodgy old lord my father chose because of his influence at court." She twirled around, to the dismay of the maid working on her hem. "I think I love Charlie already, and we are not even married. Isn't that grand?"

"Very . . . grand. And how lovely for you." This was marriage among the quality? Ellianne pitied the poor girls traded away like broodmares. Marriage was bad enough, but marriage without love? How could a woman share her home, her bed, her very body, with a man she did not love? Ellianne's stomach turned at the very thought. She wanted none of it.

"Wellstone has some silly romantic notion, I suppose," Lady Valentina was going on, to the seamstress's edification and Ellianne's embarrassment. She was not used to treating the servants as if they were wallpaper, simply there, without ears or thoughts. Lady Valentina was oblivious to the fact that whatever she said would be repeated in servants' halls throughout London. "Wellstone told Papa that he won't live off a rich wife, and won't step into parson's mousetrap until he can support a woman in comfort, but do you know what I think?"

Ellianne knew she was about to find out. She had to admit she was curious about any assessment of Stony's character, especially from the viewpoint of a young lady from his own circles.

"I think no man is ready to take a wife until the right woman tells him he is. I believe Wellstone would marry in a flash, money or not, if he found a woman to truly love."

"Do you?" Ellianne forgot about the maid. "Do you really?"

"I do, and so does Charlie. Oh, he's waiting outside."

"Charlie? That is, Lord Charles?"

Chapter Twenty

Ellianne wanted to leave town. Stony wanted to tie her to her desk in the book room to keep her from leaving because . . . because he wanted her to stay, that was all. He could not or would not put a name to the wrench in his gut at the thought of missing Miss Kane. "You can't go."

"But I hate it here."

The day after the Aldershott ball, Stony had come to persuade Ellianne to go for a curricle drive out to Richmond. Instead she kept staring out the window, where a boy was leading Stony's horses back and forth, talking of going home to Fairview in Devon.

"A lot of newcomers feel the same," he said, seeing more than his plans for a long drive out to Richmond evaporate like that morning's mist. "The noise, the bustle, the perpetual fog. But you'll get used to it. Everyone does."

"Does everyone get used to being stared at and discussed as if they were a bill of fare at a hotel's restaurant?"

He could only shrug. "Gossip is unavoidable wherever you go. The rumormongers simply make it into an art form here. You are new and exceptional, out of the ordinary. Of course they all want to get a look at you, gather tidbits about you to share with their neighbors. But I thought you said you did not care about the scandal sheets."

"And I don't." She waved her hand through the air, dismissing fashionable London's favorite pastime. "It's the bad manners I deplore, the sheer rudeness of people speaking behind one's back, when one's back is not turned."

"Not everyone is that awful."

"No, some of the shallow, selfish, mindless pleasure-seekers are worse. They have no values whatsoever, and are of value to no one but themselves."

"If you mean that coven of devil's spawn last night, that was my fault. I should have protected you better."

"Against what? Shoddy morals? Men who make overtures without the least affection? Why, two men proposed marriage to me last night, and I never caught their names."

They'd catch more than they bargained for, if Stony found out who they were.

"No, I shall never get used to the loose behavior here, or the way marriages are arranged, then disregarded by the husbands—and the wives also, sometimes—as if the wedding vows were merely a legal transaction, a transfer of funds."

"Not every married man, or woman, forsakes their oaths. I admit there were some choice spirits at the ball last evening, imbibing too much, finding those dark alcoves and willing partners, but not everyone at the Aldershotts' was a philanderer or a Paphian."

"Of course not, but enough were. I would be happier at home at Fairview. So would Aunt Lally."

Stony was willing to surrender his plans for Richmond, but that was all. "You cannot leave London. What about your sister?"

"I have to keep believing that she will send word as soon as she can, so I should be home to receive her message. Mr. Lattimer will keep looking here, of course. He says it was your suggestion that has Runners retracing every possible route between London and home, looking for a red-haired lady." She gestured to her bonnet dangling from its strings off the back of a chair. It was not the horrid black scuttle one, but it would hide enough of her head and her flame-colored hair. "He does not hold out much hope."

"He is a clunch. Your sister could not have vanished into thin air. And we have other avenues to pursue. You said Isabelle took her jewelry. She could be selling it when she runs out of money, or someone might have stolen it from her, so she cannot make her way back to Fairview. She might make it to London, though, so you ought to be here. Lattimer is having his men take your descriptions around to jewelers and pawnshops and fences, but they might need you to identify her belongings, so you cannot leave."

"Why didn't you tell me about the jewelry? Mr. Lattimer never mentioned that."

"There was no need to get your hopes up until we found something. And Gwen hasn't given up looking for associates of Lady Augusta's. She has enlisted Strickland, heaven help her, because he seems to have known your aunt best. You cannot leave until she has exhausted every possibility."

"That's all fine, but there is nothing for me to do now but wait. I could be doing that at Fairview. I swear I spoke to every unfledged miss in London last night, without learning anything."

"No, the high-sticklers were not there with their innocents. Hundreds more were at other balls last night, so you have to stay. And remember we discussed that a gentleman could recognize your likeness as easily as one of the young girls could."

"They all saw me at the theater, and no one said anything."

Stony was running out of arguments, so he just repeated, "You cannot leave!"

"If it's about your pay, I—"

"No, dash it, not everything is about money."

She gave a halfhearted laugh. "Tell that to your fortune-hunting friends, or the gamblers who already have my initials in the betting books at White's."

"Who the devil told you that?"

"Not you, although I thought we'd agreed to be honest with each other."

"Honesty has nothing to do with upsetting you over trifles. But that is not the issue here. You have seen the polite world at its least mannerly, but London has far more to offer than crowded ballrooms and rakes. I know you have seen the sights and the shops, but stay and let me show you the rest. Let me prove that not every Londoner is a gossip or a gambler or a grasping parasite. You'll find much to enjoy, I swear, and you deserve some pleasure, too. You'll have forever at Fairview. London is here, now. Please don't go."

Ellianne let herself be persuaded, not by Stony's logic, but by the look on his handsome face. His unvoiced words, the unspoken plea, touched her as no rational arguments could. It was as if he'd torn up another of her charts, her master plans, with "Please don't go" written in his clear blue eyes.

They drove to Richmond after Ellianne spoke a few words to her aunt and fed the dog the pansies Stony had brought. Her aunt said nothing, as usual, but as they were leaving, the parrot made its usual bawdy comment from the other room: "A maze, my arse."

Lord Wellstone, Miss Kane, and Timms all pretended to be hard of hearing, which was easy for the old butler, less so for the red-faced Ellianne.

The drive to Richmond was as lovely as the viscount had promised, with spring in its bright green glory. Wellstone was concentrating on his horses at first, navigating through the heavy traffic. With his groom up behind, they could not speak of weighty matters anyway, so Ellianne relaxed, without her aunt's grumbling, Gwen's chatter, or innuendo-filled flirtations.

For once she refused to worry about the bank or her investments or the charity school, or even Isabelle. What would be, would be, she thought, almost resigned to waiting, now that she had done everything she could. Of course, her resignation did not keep her from imagining her sister behind every hedge in the maze, or at the pretty little inn where they stopped for nuncheon. She stopped looking back, rather than have her hopes dashed time after time.

Wellstone was the perfect host—he even had the maze memorized so they did not get lost—and saw to her every comfort. It was not his fault that his closeness raised her temperature from balmy spring to sultry summer. She raised her parasol so he wouldn't notice her flush. But then she couldn't see his laughing eyes or his bright smile or that flashing dimple. She lowered the parasol. This was going to be one of her favorite memories to cherish; let it be complete. And let him pretend to have bad eyes as well as poor hearing.

Stony never once went over the line so carefully drawn between them. No matter if he found her blushes adorable when he lifted her into the curricle or handed her down. No matter if he was aware that she was aware of him as a man, not as a friend or an employee. No matter if all he wanted to do was hire a room at the inn and take her hair out of its neat braids and bury his face in it and bury himself in— No matter.

He was a gentleman, and she trusted herself with him as with no other. He'd burn in hell—worse than he was burning now, if possible—rather than betray that trust.

They were both getting to be experts at pretending.

The next night, Stony convinced Ellianne to attend Mrs. Harkness-Smythe's card party. The hardened gamesters like Blanchard would not be there, not for the paltry stakes permitted. Nor could any would-be Romeos get up a flirtation, not under Mrs. Harkness-Smythe's eagle eyes. She took her gaming seriously, and her strict sense of propriety more so. Besides, Stony claimed Ellianne for a partner.

"Are you prepared to give your winnings to charity?" she asked him when they were seated.

Lord Strickland grumbled. He was at a nearby table partnered with Gwen, who could barely remember the rules, much less what cards had been played. Mrs. Harkness-Smythe glared him into silence.

Stony smiled at the baron, but whispered to Ellianne, "Help me win and I'll show you."

They did win, despite Stony's mistakes when he was watching Ellianne's face instead of his opponents' discards. The next afternoon he drove her out of Mayfair again, but in a different direction. Here the houses were not set apart with parkland, and the carriages were not all crested. The streets were congested with donkey carts and drays and men with barrows and women toting babies and bundles. Beggars huddled in doorways, but the passersby were too hurried, and too poor themselves, to help. Litter was everywhere, and odors were also.

"Here is yet another side to London you should see before leaving," Stony said as he pulled up in front of a three-story brick building that was in better condition than its neighbors, but still had a boarded window and tiles missing from the roof. A roughly lettered sign on a gate proclaimed the place the Wellstone Home for Young Women.

"You support a charity home?" Ellianne asked in disbelief as the groom went to the horses's heads.

"Why not? You have a training school and a hospital and I don't know how many orphanages Gwen mentioned."

"But you don't have the funds!"

He gestured toward the door, where young women—

no more than girls, really, barely in their teens—were pouring out, calling his name. "They had less."

"But why?" Ellianne could not fathom why he hadn't made a donation somewhere, why a top-of-the-trees gentleman concerned himself with these waifs from London's stews and slums.

"Why? Because they came to London to find work, and there was none for them. Or their families tossed them out to make room for the younger children. Or their parents died of drink and disease. Who knows how they all landed in the streets."

"I meant, why did you take them in?" She waved her gloved hand at the building, the girls, her out-of-place escort. "Why here?"

"Oh, I won the house in a card game," he said, as if such magnanimity were an everyday thing. "No one would buy it in the condition it was in then, to my regret. So I decided to put it to good use, rather than let the rats and dry rot take it."

Ellianne was still shaking her head, her mind spinning with the knowledge that Wellstone, who had so little he had to betray his class by going to work, gave so much. Her own charitable contributions seemed less generous in comparison. Stony was going on, telling her how the girls were taught to read and write so they could find honest work, part of their earnings coming back to the home for the next crop of girls. They had nothing so ambitious as her training schools, he confessed, but perhaps she could offer some suggestions. Or financial assistance, he added with a smile, tossing the leather pouch containing their last night's winnings to a smiling black-clad matron who met them at the door.

After a tour, and after hearing from the girls that their Stony had hung the very moon, Ellianne promised to return with a banknote and a list of ideas to make the home more self-supporting.

"Why girls?" Ellianne asked when they were on

their way home. "Why not orphaned infants, or boys, or a hospital for wounded veterans?"

The need was endless, he explained, and his resources laughingly limited. His heart went out to the girls, though, because they seemed the most vulnerable. Without the Wellstone Home, they had nowhere to go and nothing left to sell but their bodies. "No one should be forced to that. No one."

Ellianne could not tell if he was speaking of his own experiences or not. She only knew that she could not go home now, not until Stony's girls had fresh pinafores and more instructors and new mattresses. She'd go make a chart of what needed doing.

As long as she was in Town, she might as well continue with her plan to be seen. A ball at Rockford House should have every member of the quality in attendance. If no one recognized her as Isabelle's relative there, she would have to conclude that her sister had made friends outside polite circles.

Stony was prepared this time. He found a sturdy cane, not any elegant walking stick, but a thick, polished tree limb. Then he found a small pebble to put in his shoe. Then he found a limp.

Finding a cause for his affliction was more difficult. He was too young for the gout, too old to be climbing trees. Claiming he'd fallen off his horse would have branded him an oaf; a carriage wheel running over his toes would have made him a fool. He decided that his horse had stepped on his foot. No, a runaway horse that he was trying to stop before it injured someone. That sounded wondrously heroic, but too much of a lie. In the end he decided to smile when someone asked and say it was a minor injury, a nasty sprain. Ellianne's aunt did not put much stock in his story. Neither did the too-predictable parrot: "Limp leg. Limp brain. Limp lord. Limp rod."

They hurried from the house as fast as the pebble permitted.

At the ball, he could walk but not dance. He could sit by Miss Kane but not promenade with the hostess's niece. He could go in to supper but not to fetch punch for every thirsty miss who batted her eyelashes at him. In other words, he was a limpet. Stuck to Miss Kane like a scrap on one of her charts, he was. He was not budging, and she was not leaving his side. No disappearing to the ladies' withdrawing room, he warned. He needed her protection from the solicitous mamas and their so-available daughters. There was to be no going off with strangers, no finding a quiet room where some prowling tomcat could pounce on her. He was taking his escort duties far more seriously this time.

Ellianne was almost giggling like one of the little moppets at his charity home by the time he finished his lecture. She stopped smiling when Lord Strickland approached them, looking for Gwen, who was dancing with the comte.

"Gads, she didn't kick you too?" the baron asked, too loudly.

Stony accidentally dropped his heavy cane. His would not be the only sore toes by the morning. Then he kept the area near them clear by twirling the gnarled wood, as if it were a wizard's wand. It worked, or his rudeness did.

"No, Durstan, the lady does not dance tonight. Can you not see she is wearing black gloves?"

Then: "No, Sir Poindexter, that seat is taken.

"No, the lady is not thirsty, Lord Hathaway, but perhaps your wife is.

"No, Miss Kane is not playing cards this evening, Major, but she will be pleased to accept donations for her favorite charities."

Ellianne was relieved that she did not have to face all these men on her own, that Stony's solid presence kept them at a distance. She did feel, though, that she could have spoken for herself, that she was no shrinking violet. She did not want him to think of her as another of his little girls, to be protected from the world. Besides, what if one of the men had news of her sister?

"Trust me," Stony told her, "your aunt would not have let one of these fortune-hunting rakes within a mile of Miss Isabelle."

Word must have gone out that Wellstone was declaring Miss Kane off-limits, for few others approached the gilt chairs where she and Stony sat with Gwen and whichever of her cisisbeos was around at the time. Ellianne was starting to recover from the viscount's high-handedness. He was only trying to protect her, she told herself.

A bit later, one of the handsomest men she had seen—not as good-looking as Lord Wellstone, of course—stopped in front of their seats. He was as tall as the viscount but thinner, not as broad-shouldered. He was dark-haired instead of fair, with the brooding look of a fallen angel. He might have been Stony's age, but his eyes seemed older, duller, harder.

He bowed and said, "I say, Lady Wellstone, I have been pining away, waiting for someone to introduce me to this goddess in our midst so I might worship at her feet. Will you perform the honors?"

Stony answered instead of Gwen: "No, Blanchard, she will not. The lady is not a goddess, her feet do not require adoration, and she is not going out on the balcony with you, so go find another pretty pigeon to pluck."

Ellianne felt a blush starting at those same feet. Gwen gasped and batted at Stony's sleeve with her closed fan, but Strickland laughed and said, "He's got you dead to rights. Takes a rake to know one, eh, Blanchard?"

Blanchard could have caused a scene. He could have demanded satisfaction for the insult, but not in Lady Rockford's ballroom. He was barely tolerated in society as it was, and could ill afford to lose his chances of finding an heiress. Not even a Cit would let Blanchard marry his daughter if he were banished from the *ton.* He had no choice but to bow to Gwen again, nod at Strickland, say, "Your servant, Miss Kane," even though they had not been introduced, and turn his back on Wellstone.

"That was dreadful!" Ellianne would have struck Stony with her fan, too, but too many eyes were watching them.

Stony's jaw was set. "He is not fit company for you."

Ellianne raised her chin. "I'll thank you to let me decide for myself. I am old enough to select my own friends."

"Friends? Do you really think that loose screw wanted to be your friend? Not even you could be so bacon-brained."

Gwen decided she had a sudden thirst for lemonade and fled on Lord Strickland's arm. Ellianne and Stony sat in angry silence. He tapped his cane on the floor. She stared at the dancers.

Then Sir John Thomasford bowed over Ellianne's hand. "Good evening, Miss Kane. It is a pleasure to see you again, and in such fine looks." He nodded in Stony's direction. "Wellstone."

Sir John was not looking so fine, Stony decided. He had always seemed slimy, but now he resembled something that had been dragged out of a cave into the light.

Another naked girl had been found murdered, this one with brown eyes, thank goodness, so Ellianne had not needed to go to the morgue. She'd made sure Lattimer went, though, to see that the woman was buried properly. She also paid for one of the Bow Street artists to draw a sketch of the dead female, and offered a reward for her identification. The young woman's landlady had come forth to claim the purse. The woman was, indeed, a lady of the night, but the landlady went to sleep early. She never saw her boarders' patrons.

The newspapers got wind of the story and were starting to clamor for action, so the coroner's office and Bow Street must both be under pressure to solve the case. The bloodsucker should have stayed at the morgue, then, or gone home for a good night's rest. Instead he was asking Miss Kane if she cared to stroll around the room with him.

Damnation, Stony thought, he should have put the pebble in Ellianne's shoe.

"I wish you'd stay so I can hear any new developments in the case." He lied. The last thing he wanted to hear was if this highflier had her throat slit, too.

"There are no new developments," Sir John answered curtly, holding out his arm to Ellianne.

Stony got up when she did. "I think I will join you on that walk. One gets stiff sitting around. How was that for a little morgue humor, eh? Stiff?" Ellianne glared and Sir John curled his lip. Stony could not tell if that was a smile or not.

The pebble in his shoe was deuced painful. So was watching that oily maggot touch Ellianne, lean his head closer to hers, whisper sweet forensics in her ear.

"Devil take it, I think my foot must be broken, after all. Your pardon, Sir John, we'll have to go home."

"I could see Miss Kane returned to her house," the man offered.

And the devil would wear ice skates before Stony let that happen. "What, alone? What are you thinking, man? Miss Kane is a young lady of impeccable virtue, not one of your dead demireps. You ought to apologize for speaking of her that way. In fact, I don't think you ought to be speaking to her at all, not after you've been mucking about at the morgue. Come, Miss Kane, I need your arm to lean on."

"How dare you?"

Chapter Twenty-one

"I have never been so embarrassed in my entire life."

That was doing it too brown, for a woman who walked around with boiled potatoes in her pocket. At least Ellianne had waited until she and Stony were alone in the carriage. Not that they should have been alone, of course. Gwen had taken one look at the pugnacious pair and chose to have one of her gentlemen friends drive her home. She mumbled words to the effect that they were old enough, and people were already talking, and if they were going to be tossing insults at each other, then she was not going to sit in the middle.

No one sat in the middle. Ellianne sat as far from Stony as possible, in the corner of the coach, as rigid as his cane. He was congratulating himself at separating her from the fortune-hunters and the funereal knight, not that Sir John's avocation precluded his avarice. He was also glad he'd had the foresight not to sit opposite Miss Kane in the carriage.

"You thoroughly offended a friend of mine," she was saying.

He could see by the coach lanterns that her brow

was lowered and her hands were tightly clasped around her beaded reticule. Lud, if she had the pistol in that thing, loaded or not, he should have ridden up with the driver. It was too late to turn tail now, so he spoke his thoughts out loud: "If you are referring to Sir John Thomasford, the man is not your friend."

"He has been kind to me, I will have you know."

"Of course he has. He wants your money. Not even he could think to win you over with his good looks. Unless you are attracted to eels, of course, all slimy and slithering. The man never bothered to attend social gatherings before. I doubt if he even likes women. Live ones, anyway. The fact that you show an interest in his pet projects puts ideas in his head that never existed before."

"Are you accusing me of flirting with Sir John? Of leading him on?"

"If the shoe fits . . ." Which reminded him. He removed the pebble from his evening pump.

Ellianne inhaled sharply. "That is insufferable!"

"That's what I was beginning to think. There is no permanent damage, though, I am certain."

"So you lied and you cheated and you made people feel sorry for you, just so you could insult them?"

Stony pretended to think a minute. "I cannot recall insulting anyone who showed me the least sympathy. In fact, most of the dirty dishes I sent off were wishing me to perdition, not a quick recovery."

"There was no reason to insult Sir John."

There was every reason: Ellianne liked him. "He was being too familiar."

"He kissed my hand! What about Mr. Blanchard? You would not permit that poor man to make my acquaintance."

"You said it: He is poor, but hoping to remedy that shortcoming with a wealthy wife. There have been so many ugly rumors about him accosting heiresses that I would have suspected him of carrying off your sister, except he never left London. I checked, and at his rooms at the Albany, too. He'd be after you like Atlas if he had her, besides, to get more of her blunt."

"Then you should have told me, and let me decide for myself if I wished to meet him. You should have asked me about those other men, and Sir John. Instead you had them all angry and upset."

"They will recover. In fact, I'd wager a guinea that Blanchard finds a way to be introduced before the end of the week."

"Then I shall get rid of him myself. Without your interference. And I shall treat Sir John as I see fit. Without your insults. Is that clear?"

As clear as the window beside Stony, fogged with his breathing. "You do not know men," was all he said.

"I know that I did not hire you to watch over me like a mother hen with one chick. You were supposed to help me meet people, not frighten them away. For that matter, you were not supposed to make arrangements with Mr. Lattimer on your own, either. We were supposed to deliberate together, if I recall. You never discussed visiting the jewelers with me, or hiring the additional Runners."

"Are you worried I am overspending your account?"

"Of course not. I am concerned that you do not consider me capable of managing anything."

"I took you to the Wellstone Home, didn't I? You have already made a difference there, I understand."

"That is not what I mean. Your patronizing attitude is. Even now, you relegate me to doing good deeds, while you decide the course of the investigation, the course of my London sojourn, and the course of my friendships. I will not have it, I say. I shall not be treated as an inferior being by one who . . ." Her voice trailed off.

"Yes? One who what? One who believes in protecting womenfolk? Or one who sells his soul for the price of a meal? One who cannot afford to keep his dependents in silk and furs and jewels? Just how inferior do you consider me, Miss Kane?"

"I was going to say one who spends his days and nights among the pleasure seekers of Town."

"Like hell you were. You consider me as dirt beneath your feet. You always have. You respect no man who cannot match your income."

"That is untrue! I admire what you have done with the home for girls, and how kind you are to Gwen."

He made a snorting sound, like Atlas having a bad dream, or downing a good cucumber sandwich.

"Well, I do. I believe I have shown you more respect from the very beginning than you have shown me."

Stony's patience was wearing thin. "If I did not respect you, Miss Kane, I'd have your skirts up to your ears right now and your hair down to your rear. And that is the honest truth."

Ellianne's imagination was wearing silk garters, to her dismay. That was his fault, too. "How dare you! You are exactly what Aunt Lally said, a lewd and licentious, good-for-nothing lordling!"

"Aha! She does speak!"

"That is not the point! Your superior attitude is reprehensible, and your rakish thoughts are repugnant."

"As opposed to your holier-than-thou airs?"

"I do not have airs," she said, her chin so far in the atmosphere she might have bumped it on the carriage roof if they hit a rut.

The carriage interior was only dimly lighted by the lanterns and the street lamps as they passed, to Stony's regret, because a redhead in a rant was a magnificent sight. Next time he'd make sure to aggravate her in the afternoon. She sure as Hades was ruining his night, going on about respect and evil thoughts, as if a man could control his mind. Stony had enough trouble governing his body, when he could hear her breath coming in quick rasps, as if she were in the throes of a different kind of emotion. Her chest was heaving, as it would if she were making love. Her words were making as much sense as the hungry murmurings of a woman at pleasure. He could almost see her vibrating with anger—or passion. He fought to get those images out of his mind while she raged on, condemning him for everything since Adam got Eve thrown out of Eden by eating the apple.

He lost the battle. "Oh, hell." Before Ellianne could say another word, or raise her hand—or her knee—he slid across the seat, pulled her closer, and kissed her. At first it was as if he were kissing his cane. She was stiff and bony and cold. What the deuce had he been thinking? But he held her tighter, pressing her body against his until he could feel lush femininity against chest. He used his tongue to soften her lips and his breath to warm her. "Please," he whispered, or perhaps pleaded.

Tentatively, reluctantly, but inevitably, Ellianne brought her hands up to wrap around his shoulders, to touch his firm back, his neck, his wavy hair. She tilted her head to a different angle, sliding her lips against his even as her body leaned into his. She stopped thinking, stopped breathing, stopped being Miss Ellianne Kane. She was a cloud, a river, a rainbow. She could fly; she could float.

She would pass out if she did not get air. Ellianne pulled back, and Stony's arms instantly released her. He was breathing hard, too, with a sheen of moisture on his brow. He put more distance between them, eyeing her cautiously, as if wondering if he should leap to his death from the moving carriage or wait for her to shoot him. When she made no move toward violence, he reached up to straighten his cravat.

His neckcloth was not the only thing askew.

"I . . ." she began, but had to wait for her heart to stop pounding louder than her voice. "I shall not be needing your services any longer."

"You need me," he stated unequivocally. "A lot of

other men would not have stopped there. Do you wish me to apologize?"

She shook her head, completing the damage to her hairdo that his eager fingers had begun. She tried to gather some of the loose pins. "No, I would not trust your sincerity. How many times have you sworn that I was safe from your blandishments?"

He tried to make her smile. "One kiss is not exactly a blandishment. A minor beguilement, maybe, but definitely not a blandishment."

She saw no humor in the situation. "I do not need you or your lust. That was not part of our agreement."

"My lust? Am I the only one with fevered blood? I distinctly recall hearing some tiny mews of pleasure during our little embrace."

Little embrace? Ellianne did not think she could survive anything bigger. "You must have heard the carriage springs. But that is irrelevant. I am not paying you for sexual services."

Now he grew angry. "My 'sexual services,' as you say, are not now and never have been for sale. Or did you believe I put a price on my kisses? How much do you think your sighs were worth? Forgive me, Miss Kane, the carriage springs. A pound? I wonder what you would be willing to pay for completion. Perhaps I could retire after a night of total satiation."

"Stop that! You are being vulgar and hateful, as if you were the one who was offended."

"I was. I am. I thought you knew me better than that, dash it."

"And I thought you knew me better than to think I would enjoy being mauled in a carriage!"

"I did. And you did. Enjoy it, that is, until you remembered to be the prim and proper Miss Kane, with everything under your cool command, as if you had one of your lists in hand and emotion was not on it."

"There is nothing wrong with being prim and proper, or organized, or in control of one's emotions."

"Except that it is a lie. You are a living, breathing woman, not a marvelous counting pig, not a beautiful glass figurine, not a blasted army general."

"You dare accuse me of lying? You with your clumsy cane? You don't even have a limp!"

"Well, you don't have a parrot."

Miss Kane hopped out of the coach before he could assist her down. She opened the front door herself, without waiting for either Stony to knock or Timms to hobble to the front hall.

She did not slam the door in Stony's face, which he took for the best invitation he was going to get. They had to finish their discussion, which meant, he supposed, another apology. He followed her into the parlor, trying to decide which sin to apologize for first. Lying was bad. Calling her names was worse. Kissing her was . . .

"Snake eyes!"

Timms was on his knees, but he was not praying. Ellianne's aunt and the butler were throwing dice in front of the sofa. When they heard the arrivals at the parlor door, Timms crawled to his slippered feet and kicked the dice cup and some coins under the furniture. Mrs. Goudge snatched open her tapestry workbag, stashed the wine bottle inside, and took out some knitting.

Adjusting his spectacles, Timms begged Miss Kane's forgiveness. "Tempted by the devil, I was."

Ellianne glared at both of them, but especially at her aunt. "The devil does not wear silk petticoats."

Aunt Lally glared right back, her lips pursed shut.

Ellianne could feel Wellstone's presence right behind her. The dratted man was most likely laughing at her and her household. Without looking in his direction, she told her aunt she might as well speak, for his lordship knew they had no parrot.

"And not above time, I'll have you know," Aunt Lally said. Once started, she intended to have her say, company present or not. "As for Timms, he promised you he'd stay away from the racetrack and the pubs. By Saint Aloysius's swive-sacks, what more do you want? The bloke's too old for the sheets, so what's he supposed to do for fun?"

Stony was grinning until Mrs. Goudge raised her knitting needle like an épée and advanced on her niece. Before he could step in front of Ellianne as a shield, the older woman lifted a lock of red hair on the needle's tip. That lock was trailing down Ellianne's shoulder, not tucked into the neatly pinned arrangement she'd worn when she left the Sloane Street house.

"As for you, missy, you're a fine one to talk, coming home from some swell's do looking like you've been done, all right. I warned you to watch out for silver-tongued toffs, didn't I?"

Stony looked around. He was the only toff, or titled gentleman, present. He thought of running, but he was too late. That knitting needle, with half an unfinished glove dangling off one end, was poking into his midsection.

"As for you, you Romeo for rent"—the needle jabbed an inch lower—"we don't have any parrots." Another inch. "And we don't have any soiled doves here, either." One more inch and his manhood would be wearing a mitten. "Understand?"

How could he not, when Mrs. Goudge was so eloquently persuasive? He glanced at Ellianne, whose turn it was to smile. He stepped back, out of danger, bowed, and said, "It will not happen again."

"Damn well it won't. We don't need your kind around here. Tell him, Ellianne."

"I already did, Aunt Lally. I already did."

Stony bowed again and left, following behind the butler, who was shaking his head in sorrow. Stony felt he had to say something. The old man was more part of the family than a mere servant. "I am sorry if I have disappointed you too, Timms. I meant no disrespect to Miss Kane."

"Oh, I'm not worried about my lady. She can take care of herself. It's Mrs. Goudge what has me disheartened. Tell me, my lord, do you think I am too old for sex?"

They didn't need him, like hell! Miss Ellianne Kane needed a man's protection more than any woman he knew. An infant would be safer on the streets of London than the heiress would be in the parlors of polite society. Why, the girls at his home had more sense than that ninnyhammer. At least they recognized the dangers.

With flaming hair, a fortune in the bank, and a standoffish manner, Miss Kane was nothing but a dashed challenge to a man with shifting principles. Hell, his own scruples were solid as rock, and he couldn't keep his hands off her.

She didn't need him? Didn't need a man's escort or affection, didn't need a husband or a lover or a friend? What, did she think her diamonds and her dividends would keep her warm? Dratted, dunderheaded woman!

Stony had half a mind to let her see what would happen without a trustworthy gentleman's presence at her side.

Unfortunately, the other half of his mind had a different problem. He didn't know if he could be all that trustworthy anymore. Having tasted her lips once, he worried that he could not live without tasting them again. Need? He needed a cold bath.

Aunt Lally was right. They did not need him. Ellianne did not need him. The entire world did not need an insolent, overbearing, immoral churl. Well, Gwen needed him, to be fair, and the young girls he rescued needed him.

Ellianne most assuredly did not. Bow Street could expand its search for Isabelle. For herself, she had her thoroughly satisfactory life waiting for her at Fairview, where she was the one who was needed. No one likened her to a performing pig there, or a statue, or an army officer. No one made her melt there, either, and that was as it should be.

Unfortunately, if she went home he would think she was running away, that she could not stay in town without his support. Worse, he'd think that his kiss had her in such a quake that she had to flee to save her virtue. He was wrong, of course. She was never in danger of succumbing to his charm and his practiced skills. No, never.

Ellianne decided to stay in London, just to prove him wrong. She'd stay as long as it suited her, becoming the darling of society Gwen thought she could be. She would have a different gentleman for escort every night, and, yes, she might even sample a few more kisses, just to prove that Wellstone's were nothing out of the ordinary. She would enjoy herself, by heaven, even if it killed her.

No, she did not need Viscount Wellstone.

She needed a dry handkerchief.

Chapter Twenty-two

A well-to-do woman of pleasing mien and passable birth could find at least a tepid acceptance among the *ton*. An astronomically wealthy female of astounding looks and good enough connections on the maternal side, to say nothing of the approval of the Duchess of Williston, was warmly welcomed. Ellianne did not require any pockets-to-let peer securing her invitations or introductions. She had only to choose the best among the various entertainments.

First was the opera, in Her Grace's box. Ellianne wore her pearls this time, a magnificent strand ending with a priceless, perfect pearl of enormous size. Another string was wound through her intricately braided hair, causing one top-gallant chap in the pit to shout out that she was a mermaid.

"That ain't no Neptune's daughter," his chum said, standing on his chair, inspecting Ellianne through his opera glasses. "That's a nabob's daughter. Miss Coin."

"Ignore them, my dear," Her Grace advised, patting Ellianne's trembling hand. "You wished to be noticed, did you not?"

After that evening no one in London could be unaware of Ellianne's presence in town. If they had not attended the opera, they had only to read the *on dits* columns with their morning chocolate. The newspapers estimated the price of her pearls, her gown, and her dowry.

"And it is good for you to be seen without Viscount Wellstone at your side. You would not wish to be considered one of his charity cases. Or have him deemed your divertissement," she added politely.

The papers were also filled with speculation about Ellianne's marital prospects, noting that her usual escort was absent at the opera. They also dredged up the story of Aunt Augusta's death, nearly two months ago now, mentioning that the lady's younger niece had been the last to see her alive. And where was Miss Isabelle Kane?

Ellianne was desperate to know that, too, since the Runners were reporting back that Isabelle had not gone north with Aunt Augusta's remains, or anywhere else they could discover. No one else came forward with any information or inquiry, despite Ellianne's notoriety.

Since her goal of being seen had been so successful, and so unpleasant, having all those eyes on her, all those tongues wagging, Ellianne declared a holiday. She and Aunt Lally and Timms went out to Sadler's Wells to see the clowns. Ellianne invited Mr. Lattimer to accompany them as a reward for the Bow Street man's efforts, despite their lack of progress. Despite a certain gentleman's opinion, Ellianne did know how to have a good time for herself. She did not spend all of her hours with bank ledgers and account books, merely what was necessary.

Timms enjoyed the pantomime. Aunt Lally, whose fickle vow of silence was becoming as faded as her husband's memory, cheered at the farce. Ellianne was happy to have the performers on display, not herself. Here only Mr. Lattimer watched her instead of the stage.

Ellianne thought of starting her experiments in kissing with the Runner, but decided that would be beneath contempt. She feared the young man was already unduly encouraged by her invitation to the comedy. Heavens knew what the mooncalf might dream of after a kiss. No wishes she was prepared to grant, that was certain.

He was a pleasant enough young man, although no laughing, lively, well-read companion, and he was attractive enough, if one ignored his somewhat elephantine ears. Ellianne had never held a man's work against him, not even her departed uncle Goudge's, although she did have reservations about smuggling. Ladies of the *ton* would deem a Runner, any Bow Street officer, beneath their consideration as an eligible bachelor, but Ellianne was not looking for a husband, only a gentleman to weigh Wellstone's kisses against. There was nothing wrong with Mr. Lattimer, nothing except the fact that she simply did not find him, or the idea of any intimacy with him, appealing.

Ellianne had not changed her mind about marriage, although she did have a new understanding that parts of the bargain might not be entirely distasteful. Which was to say—which she would never say, of course—that Lord Wellstone's embrace had left her wanting more. But not with Mr. Lattimer.

Or with Sir John Thomasford. The man's devotion to his chosen career was admirable, but a trifle macabre for Ellianne's comfort. She did not find him as ghoulish as Wellstone did, but his fascination with solving crimes through science did seem a bit fanatic. And his appearance seemed to be deteriorating with each successive murder he could not unravel.

Yet another young woman had been discovered slain, naked and hairless. This one had hazel eyes and was short and plump. Someone recognized her from Ellianne's poster as a chorus girl at the opera house, so her body was claimed for burial by her friends and coworkers. At least this woman would not go unmourned, and someone beside Ellianne would see that flowers were placed on her grave. Ellianne could not help thinking that she might have been at the young woman's final performance, sitting in the duchess's box looking to see if Stony was in attendance instead of watching the performers.

She also could not help thinking that the unsolved deaths were weighing heavily on Sir John, too. He was obviously losing weight, his formerly well-tailored clothes hanging loosely on his frame. His eyes seemed more sunken in his head, as if he never slept, yet they maintained the glitter that Wellstone had called a feral gleam. His hair was still carefully swept back from his face, but now the strands were separated, lank, and dull, as if he had not washed off yesterday's pomade.

Ellianne felt sorry for the poor man, working so hard his health was suffering, so she accepted his invitation to a lecture at the Medical Society. Aunt Lally snored beside her, but Sir John seemed to find the subject of bloodletting engrossing. Ellianne found it off-putting enough that her appetite was gone by the time they went to dinner at the Clarendon after the lecture. She had no desire to taste the prawns in butter Aunt Lally was devouring, and no desire to taste Sir John's kisses.

She thought of experimenting to see if Lord Strickland's kiss was as repulsive as she remembered. Perhaps her new awareness and appreciation of a man's physicality could alter her view. Ellianne knew she could have the baron on one knee in an instant; all she had to do was dangle Fairview in front of him. But she did not want Lord Strickland. She only wanted to see if another man's touch could make her blood sing and her bones melt. If just any man would do, then Lord Wellstone was nothing out of the ordinary, and she could put him from her mind once and for all.

Besides, Gwen seemed taken with the thick-bellied baron. She was taken with the notion of reforming him, at any rate. If Strickland was busy, Lady Wellstone reasoned, he would have no time to visit the brothels and bordellos. If he was exhausted from dancing and driving and doing the pretty at four different entertainments a night, he might not need any additional female companionship. He might turn out to be a decent enough gentleman of middle age, Ellianne was forced to concede, now that his linen was clean and his nose hair was trimmed, if his heart did not give out before then.

He was more comfortable in her company now too, especially when card playing was part of the evening's activities. She agreed to accompany him and Gwen to Lady MacAfee's small gathering rather than attend one of the larger balls. Ellianne was not particularly fond of cards, but neither was she brazen enough to walk into an assembly without some chaperon or escort. Besides, there was little chance of encountering Wellstone at such a tame affair.

As Ellianne discovered, she was still unused to the vocabulary of London society. By a small gathering, they meant a mere hundred guests or so, not the three hundred or more that ambitious hostesses crammed into their ballrooms. She was happy enough to take a seat in the card room, rather than suffer through more introductions and importunings.

Gwen waved her off gaily, happy among her court of old bachelors and widowers, where she could dance and gossip and sip champagne. As long as Miss Kane was in the card room with Strickland, Gwen decided, she could relax the vigilance her dear, mutton-headed stepson had decreed.

With her hand on Strickland's arm, Ellianne proceeded across the ballroom. She knew everyone was watching her, and she knew she looked worthy of their regard. Her gown was the most expensive she had ever owned, of dark gray shot silk with jet beads worked into filigree patterns across the bosom and the hem. It was worth the price of having each bead painstakingly sewn in place, for she felt like a queen in it. With it she wore her ruby pendant, and a black feather in her coiled hair that curled down against her cheek. She must be getting used to being the focus of so much attention, for she did not even blush. See, she told herself, she did not need the confidence of Stony's support. She could do fine on her own.

She smiled at Strickland, and he almost tripped. "I say, I don't have gravy down my chin, do I?"

"No, nothing like that. I was just wondering . . ."

So was the baron. He was wondering if she'd know how much of the winnings he kept instead of donating it to plaguey charities.

Ellianne looked around and spotted the door to the supper room, which was empty at this time. She pulled Lord Strickland inside.

"Eh? What's this? If you are hungry, girl, you'll have to wait. Though you don't look like you eat more'n a hummingbird. All skin and bones, eh?"

So much for thinking she looked pretty in the new gown. Ellianne was determined, though. "No, my lord. I am not hungry. I am curious. I wish to know if you still want to kiss me."

Strickland took three steps back, eyeing the distance to the door. "Can't say as I do. Unless you're fixing to hand over Fairview. Then I'd kiss your arse if you wanted. That is, begging your pardon, I'd be grateful."

"But you no longer want to marry me?"

"Devil take it, I never wanted to marry you! I want the estate your blasted bank won from me."

Ellianne tapped her foot. This was not going at all as she expected. "Once and for all, the bank did not win it; you forfeited your lands by not paying your loans."

"Then what is this argle-bargle about? Kisses and marrying, eh?" He wiped at his forehead with a handkerchief. "Don't tell me you are looking to get hitched and you've chosen me?"

"Good grief, no."

"Well, you don't have to sound so shocked. It was you who brought up the subject, wasn't it? Kisses, my big toe. No proper young miss talks about such things. Indecent, it is."

Gwen ought to be proud of her handiwork. She'd taken a perfectly loathsome philander and turned him into a prig. "You are quite right," Ellianne said. "Shall we proceed to the card room?"

Stony was watching.

He'd been at the opera, watching Her Grace's box in case any bounder tried to lure Ellianne off for lemonade or licentiousness. He'd followed her party to Sadler's Wells at a distance, not trusting the Bow Street man to keep her safe. He'd trailed the carriage through the park when she and Gwen took a drive, and he'd window-shopped on Bond Street when they went for fittings.

He had not gone to the medical lecture on bloodletting. There were limits to even his loyalty. Furthermore, Sir John was morbid, not immoral. And Mrs. Goudge carried her sewing bag with her.

But tonight he couldn't take his eyes off Ellianne. The beads on her gown caught the candlelight and shimmered like fireworks. The black feather against her face emphasized her fine cheekbones and porcelain complexion. The ruby at her décolletage emphasized her high, milky breasts. She was magnificent.

She was a fool. Everything about her emphasized her damned wealth. And what was she doing, going off with Strickland like that? No matter what Gwen said, the man wanted her property. He'd already proved he'd do almost anything to get it.

Stony followed them to the door of the supper room, then laughed at himself. Strickland was most likely looking for Dutch courage just to sit at the card table with Ellianne. He was in a sweat when they came out minutes later, and walked as far from her as possible on their way to the game room. Stony watched them take their seats, then stepped out to the balcony to blow a cloud. He was satisfied. Miss Kane was safe for now.

When he returned, glancing in from the door, they were still at it. Ellianne was looking bored, watching the other players while her opponents deliberated. Strickland was grinning, and no wonder, at the stack of coins piling up in front of him. Stony supposed the baron was resigned to giving his portion to charity, but played now for the sport of winning. With all the blunt he was saving by not visiting the houses of accommodation, he could afford to be generous.

He left them in mid-deal to check on Gwen in the ballroom. She was standing with their hostess and a number of other ladies, likely planning some poor bachelor's fate. He headed in the other direction.

Charlie's betrothed was sitting by herself next to a drooping aspidistra. Lady Valentina looked just as unhappy as the potted plant.

Stony sat beside her. "What, never tell me Lord Charles has deserted you already, and the engagement ring still new on your finger?"

Lady Val looked up at him and smiled in relief that she would not be forced to sit out the entire dance set by herself, like some unfortunate wallflower. Instead she would have the best looking man in the room at her side. "Hallo, Wellstone. Your friend is upstairs making repairs. The clumsy oaf tripped again during the quadrille. At least he tore his own sleeve this time and not my gown. He made us both look embarrassingly awkward."

Stony laughed at her petulance. "It could have been worse. He could have ripped his trousers. Yellow pantaloons, weren't they?"

Lady Val smoothed out a matching yellow ribbon trailing from her high waist. Wellstone was in dark blue and buff, and as handsome as a storybook hero. "You really do have a nice smile, you know. And you are a much better dancer than poor Charlie."

"While you are engaged to him, minx, and happily so."

"I am," she confessed with a sigh, "but I do love to waltz."

How could he not respond to that plea in her voice, that dramatic exhale, that manipulation? So they waltzed, and he wondered if Miss Kane was a graceful dancer. At least he would not be looking down at the top of her head, or be trying to push a sack of lard into a turn.

They waltzed around the ballroom, avoiding other couples on the crowded floor. One of those couples was Godfrey Blanchard and Mrs. Collins, the widowed connection of Gwen's. Now there was a marriage of true minds, Stony thought, but a match that would never come about. The union might be consummated, all right, but no wedding lines would be spoken. Blanchard's gaming debts were too high to wed a dowerless woman, and Mrs. Collins was too ambitious to settle on a gamester at the fringes of society.

Stony was glad neither was his problem.

Somehow, though, that other couple ended the dance at the same spot as Stony and Lady Val, where Charlie was waiting to claim his bride. They went off to find refreshments, and Blanchard went with them. Stony was left with Mrs. Collins, and another dance starting up.

"Perhaps you would like to follow the others and procure a glass of wine?" he offered out of politeness, and hope.

He was not surprised when she replied, "Oh, I would much rather dance."

He'd been manipulated again. Damnation, was every woman devious and conniving? He knew of only one who was not, who said what she thought, who was not forever laying traps.

. . . Who was not in the card room when the interminable dance with Mrs. Collins was finally over.

Ellianne was tired of playing. "Surely it must be close to the supper hour," she told Lord Strickland at the conclusion of one hand. "We must not leave Lady Wellstone to go in alone, you know."

The sweet little viscountess was a temptation. So were the lobster patties usually served at these affairs. Strickland pushed himself to his feet and started to rake in his winnings. Ellianne cleared her throat. He passed half the coins over to her, daring her to claim the rest. "For the orphans and widows, don't you know," he said to the losers and the players at the nearby tables. A lot of them handed Ellianne their winnings too, or some coins from their own pockets. She poured them all into her drawstring purse. Decorated with black jet and a beaded fringe to match her gown, the reticule was much smaller than her usual one, which was at home with her pistol. This one was nearly full to bursting with the coins, and pulled on the bare flesh above her gloves.

She stopped to adjust the strings, and managed to lose sight of Strickland in the crowd leaving the card room to find their supper partners. No matter. She could find Gwen on her own.

Then a smooth voice spoke so close to her that the sound tickled her ear: "May I offer my escort, Miss Kane?"

Chapter Twenty-three

It was Mr. Godfrey Blanchard, the man Stony had refused to introduce to her. He was as attractive as she recalled, with his dark, brooding eyes. She could see where he might be dangerous to a weak, vulnerable woman, or to a silly young girl who might mistake his intentions. Ellianne was much too wise.

He was bowing over her hand. "Godfrey Blanchard at your service, Miss Kane. Your partner seems to have deserted you, and for once your watchdog appears to have strayed. Forgive me for the impertinence, but I had to take the opportunity to make your acquaintance."

"Had to?" she asked, raising her brow.

He smiled, showing even white teeth. But no dimple, and no laughter in his eyes. "Wished to, then. I was struck by your beauty the first time I saw you, in the park. And again at the theater and Rockford House, and at the opera. Your loveliness grows every time. Word of your kindness and your intelligence was on everyone's lips, and I promised myself an introduction to this paragon of feminine virtues."

He knew everywhere she'd been? Ellianne was flattered, despite herself. "Thank you, you are too kind."

"Nothing of the sort. I would consider it an honor to escort you to Lady Wellstone's side."

She nodded, and they walked slowly down the long corridor of closed doors toward what Ellianne supposed was the supper room. Most of the other guests had gone in by now, or were in the ballroom, in the opposite direction.

His arm was firm under hers, and his conversation everything proper. He spoke of the king's sorry condition and the latest novel, nothing anyone could take exception to. Ellianne was glad he'd stopped pouring the butter boat over her, for that she would have mistrusted. Now he was just an attractive man with an attentive air. She saw nothing to deserve Stony's contempt.

Blanchard's reputation must be formed on his success, she decided. Perhaps other men were jealous of his good looks or his ease with women. He might be living on a small competence from his family, as Gwen informed her, but that did not make him a blackguard. Every bachelor in the ballroom who was looking for a bride sought to marry a wealthy one, urged on by their own mamas. Indeed, half of them could not afford to keep a wife otherwise, so Blanchard's motives for seeking her out were no worse than any other gentleman's.

Or perhaps they were.

The room he led her to was not the supper room at all. It was dark, lit by a single candle, obviously not meant for public use this evening.

"I believe you have made a mistake," she said after taking two steps inside the door. He'd chosen the wrong room, and the wrong woman for dalliance. She turned back to leave but found the door shut.

He was in front of her, blocking the doorway. "Please stay a moment."

She eyed the closed door. "This is highly improper."

"But no one will be looking for you yet."

Gwen would be, if she remembered. "Please open

the door and step aside, sir." Ellianne did not want to have to scream, creating an ugly scene and more gossip.

"I am afraid I cannot do that, Miss Kane. You see, I have fallen so deeply in love with you that I will expire if I cannot express my deepest sentiments. I have worshiped you from afar for far too long."

"Chum buckets," Ellianne said, borrowing from Aunt Lally.

"Excuse me?"

"Never mind, Mr. Blanchard. Just open the door or step aside so that I may do so. Save your deepest sentiments for your tombstone, where they belong."

"You wound me, fair lady. Do you not believe in love at first sight?"

"I do not believe a gentleman would so ill use the object of his affections. An honorable suitor would have found a way to meet his beloved under the eyes of her guardians, not jeopardize her reputation in some hole-in-corner seduction."

"What, do you doubt my intentions? I swear they are entirely honorable."

"Oh, I am sure marriage to me would suit you well, coming as it does with a substantial dowry, to say nothing of my personal fortune. Marriage to you, however, does not suit me. Now please let me pass before I am forced to do something we shall both regret."

"I was afraid you would not cooperate, my dear. I am sorry for that."

He advanced on her but Ellianne would not back up. He would only follow, she knew. This way she was still close to the door. She was almost his height, and stared straight into his eyes. "It will not work, you know. For one thing, most of my wealth is tied to trusts, which will not come into my husband's keeping. For another, I am already an outsider, recall, daughter of a mere knight, a banker, not a blue blood." She snapped her fingers. "That is how much the approval of the *ton* matters to me. I do not care enough about my standing in London society to worry about being discovered in here with you."

He began to look less assured, but still showed his teeth in a smile. "But what if your hair was mussed and your gown torn?"

"Then I suppose I would have to shoot you." She dangled her reticule, missing her pistol. "If not tonight, then the next time I saw you. I am a very good shot. You would then be a dead bachelor instead of simply a destitute one. Or else I could hire certain gentlemen I know who are of a naval persuasion. For a small purse, less than I have in my reticule right now, they could see that you disappeared. My uncle was a pirate, you know, and a smuggler. In fact, his first mate, Uncle Nathan, would conduct a short swimming lesson for free for any gentleman who dared such a transgression. Very short."

Blanchard took a step backward, losing his smile. "Surely you would not . . . ?"

"Surely I would, rather than marry you. You might ask Lord Strickland to what lengths I might go, rather than be forced against my will. I do believe he has recovered all of his, ah, facilities by now. He must have, to visit his convenients."

One more step backward and Blanchard bumped into the door. He did not open it, though.

"Oh," Ellianne went on, "if you are thinking that I will pay you to keep quiet about this embarrassing and unpleasant little contretemps, think again. Not only will I not pay silence money, but I will buy up all of your outstanding debts." She looked at him from carefully barbered head to expensively shod toe, and sneered. "Gentlemen of your ilk seldom pay their servants or their tailors or their bootmakers. It will be a moment's work to gather enough past-due bills to see you in Newgate."

Blanchard . . . blanched. There was no other word for the color fading from his face. "But—"

"No, sir. No buts. No betrothals, no blackmail. Now I believe we have no further business, so—"

"I have another proposal. What if I take Wellstone's place?"

"As my escort?" she asked, confused. "I have recently decided I no longer require his services."

"All the more reason for me to step in."

"But I do not need a gentleman escort. Between Lady Wellstone and Her Grace of Williston—"

"No one believes that rot about Wellstone acting like a pageboy, so don't try to convince me. I'd take his place as your lover. I'll accept whatever you pay him."

She slapped his face.

"Bitch."

Ellianne's cheeks flared with the color his seemed to have lost, except for the imprint of her palm. She did not say anything.

Neither did he. He grabbed her shoulders and pulled her close, grinding his lips into hers.

Ellianne stood still, not giving him the satisfaction of fighting or trembling or crying out, although she wanted to do all three, and vomit besides. So much for experimenting with kisses.

"You see?" Blanchard asked when he finally pulled back. "I can give you whatever Wellstone can. Better."

Ellianne staggered but somehow found her balance on jelly-boned legs. She heard voices in the hall—Gwen and Strickland, she thought. They would be here soon, thank heaven. Maybe Stony, she prayed. She took a deep breath, ready to call out.

Blanchard heard the voices, too, and his last chance to compromise the heiress beyond repair except with a ring. Perhaps he hadn't believed her threats, or else he believed his own sexual prowess was great enough to overcome her misgivings. Or else he was desperate. He reached for her again.

This time Ellianne was not going to submit tamely. She was a free and full-grown woman, no helpless child, no serf without recourse or defense. She would not let her friends see her cowering in front of this bully. Stony would not get to say, "I told you so."

The door opened.

Stony was calling her name.

Blanchard grasped the back of Ellianne's neck.

Gwen screamed.

Stony was cursing.

Strickland said, "What the devil?"

Stony was pushing past both of them.

Ellianne grabbed her reticule, the weighty little purse filled with coins. She swung it right at Blanchard's descending face, connecting with a satisfying crack. He staggered back, clutching his nose.

Stony was at Ellianne's side. "Are you all right? I'll murder that bastard."

Then he looked at Blanchard, with the bright red blood streaming, gushing, flowing down his chin.

Stony was at Ellianne's feet, out cold.

He returned to consciousness with a start, jerking away from the vinaigrette Gwen was waving in front of his face. He would have leaped to his feet, off the Axminster carpet, but his head appeared to be cushioned in Ellianne's lap, so he put it back down. He looked up to see her green eyes awash in tears.

"Oh, lord, Ellianne, don't cry. Scream or kick the furniture if you want. Just don't cry."

She sniffled and wiped her nose, but nodded.

He looked around. Strickland seemed to be guarding the door, but Blanchard was not in the room. There was a stain on Lady MacAfee's carpet that Stony would not look at, but the blackguard was gone.

"He went out the window," Gwen volunteered. "I hoped he'd break his neck, but no such luck. We said that dear Ellianne took ill and found her way here to rest. No one needs to know the cad was in the room at all. I might not be able to explain why, to protect dear Ellianne's reputation, you know, but Godfrey Blanchard will never be invited to a decent home again, I swear."

He would be invited to pistols at dawn the next time Stony saw his face in town. "But how did you explain my presence on the floor? I assume others came to look when they heard a commotion."

"Oh, you tripped over the cat, dear."

"Does Lady MacAfee have a cat?"

Ellianne answered with a weak chuckle. "She will by tomorrow morning."

He returned her smile, still making no effort to rise. Why should he, when he was more comfortable than he'd been in years? In fact, he pretended to be weaker than he was. He groaned and said, "Gwen, why don't you ask for a pot of tea? I think I would recover faster then, rather than with a glass of wine." Which would take less time to fetch. "It is cool here on the floor."

"Heavens, we can have tea at home, dear. And if you are cold, perhaps you should get up before you wrinkle dear Ellianne's gown. Do you not think we should . . . ? Oh, I see. Tea, of course. I'll just go find one of the servants, shall I?"

"Leave Strickland at the door, will you? The other side of the door."

When she left, leaving the door slightly ajar to prevent any more gossip, Stony reached up and brushed a tear from Ellianne's cheek.

"You are the bravest woman I know. A regular trooper, my friend Captain Brisbane would have said."

She bit her lip to keep it from quivering. "No, I am not brave at all. My knees were shaking so hard I shall have bruises in the morning."

"But you never let that dastard see your fear."

She started to sniffle again. "I wouldn't give him the satisfaction."

"That's the Miss Kane I know. Tough as steel. A lot prettier, of course."

She shook her head. "But I am not tough at all; you know that."

He knew, all right. His head was resting on a lilac-scented cloud, not a bed of nails. "Of course you are. You've got bottom, my girl. And that's pretty too."

Not even his teasing could keep her eyes from filling up.

Still on the floor, his head still in her lap, Stony fished in his pocket for a handkerchief. He always carried an extra when he was with his stepmama. "Please, sweetings, don't cry. I don't know which is worse, the sight of blood or the sight of a woman's tears."

She reached for the smelling salts Gwen had left behind. "You are not going to swoon again, are you?"

He laughed. "I should think I have humiliated myself enough for one night."

"You were very brave when you needed to be."

"Until the Blanchard bastard spilled his claret. That was a flush hit, incidentally. Excellent science, my dear."

"Excellent card playing, you mean. If not for the generosity of the others, my reticule would never have weighed enough. But you would have rescued me."

"If I had been in time. Lud, you thought I was brave? I nearly panicked when I saw Gwen and Strickland without you. If a footman had not seen a tall red-haired lady come this way . . ." He did not want to think what might have happened otherwise, if he had been five minutes later, or her purse five shillings lighter.

Neither did Ellianne. "Will you kiss me?"

Stony feared he was still light-headed. "I must have hit my head on the way down. I thought you said—"

"I did. I need to replace a terrible memory with a

better one. I want to believe that not all kisses are brutal assaults."

"In that case, for the sake of your future recollections, I suppose I can make the sacrifice." He flashed a bright grin. "Better yet, why do you not kiss me?"

"Me? I couldn't." The idea was appalling—and exciting.

"Of course you can. You'll see; you'll do just what you want. Make your own memories, sweetings."

She leaned over and brushed his lips with hers.

He smiled. "That won't stick in your mind for an hour. Try again. I'll shut my eyes if that will help."

This time when she bent her head, he rose to meet her. His mouth was partly open, warm, soft, gentle, with no threats, no pressure, no sense that he was taking, only giving. No, he was sharing, sharing the magic, sharing the current that flowed between them like tender lightning.

Ellianne put her arm under his head, supporting him, and he wrapped his around her neck, warming her with his body, with his heat. His lips parted further, so she let hers open more and their tongues touched, a surprise, a shock, a shiver that coursed through her. She let her own tongue explore, licking at the wine taste, the slight trace of smoke. She stroked his teeth, the corner of his mouth, the softest flesh at the inside of his bottom lip.

Stony groaned and met her tongue with his, darting, dueling, defeating his intentions of letting her be the leader. He must not force her, must not rush her. God, he must have her!

His tongue showed her what he craved, the ancient rhythm and eternal joining. She met his thrusts with groans of her own, with a hand stroking over his chest and his neck and his cheek. His other hand crept up her side until he touched the top of one perfect breast, above the low neckline of her gown.

She gasped, but did not halt the kiss or pull back or push his hand away. She let her own hand wander, touching his brow, learning the shape of his ear, feeling the slight roughness at his jaw where his beard would soon need shaving again. Still, their tongues met in the dance of love.

His fingers pushed beneath the fabric of her gown, beneath her shift, beneath her corset, so he could touch the peak of her breast, making the nipple as hard as he was. She was making those little mews of pleasure, right in his mouth, and the sound was reverberating through his bloodstream, pooling in his groin until he worried that he could, indeed, humiliate himself worse this night.

Ellianne's bones were melting; her brains were rattling in her head. No, that was Gwen, diplomatically rattling the tea tray outside the door. Ellianne quickly sat up, letting Stony's head sink back into her lap and his hand fall to his side.

Before the door opened all the way, Stony reached up and brushed back a stray lock of her flame-colored hair, then let his fingers stay to caress her satiny cheek. "You see? You do need me."

Ellianne stood up so suddenly his head bounced on the carpet. "I knew you'd say that!"

Chapter Twenty-four

London was in a taking. No one was speaking of anything else. Ellianne and Stony and Lady MacAfee's cat were hardly mentioned. It was the murders that were on everyone's lips, in all the newspapers. They were even mentioned in Parliament as a disgrace and a call for an official police force.

Another woman had been found, her throat slit, her hair shaved off. Wig shops were searched, known bladesmen were rounded up, to no avail.

This fourth young female was a serving girl at Lord Sandercroft's. He was screaming loudest for the instant capture of the fiend. He had daughters, he said; he had maids who went on errands at night. He had a pretty young mistress who was too afraid to unlock her door, but he did not say that. He added to the reward money.

The other servants at his house reported that Maisy had been walking out with a toff, a swell, a gentleman. The girl had been secretive about her lover, meeting him around the corner, but she'd boasted of his gentility.

A gentleman committing these heinous crimes? One of the quality's own? Impossible!

Sir John Thomasford did not think so. A title was no guarantee against brutality, he told Ellianne, and she had to agree, thinking of Blanchard. High birth certainly did not exclude low behavior. Goodness, her own actions—and her own desires, even if she never acted upon them—were of questionable morality. Her mother would never have condoned such unladylike behavior as smashing a gentleman's nose, although her father would have applauded heartily.

Her conduct with Blanchard was the least of it. Ellianne blushed just thinking about the rest. Her father would not have approved, not at all. Ellianne did not even approve, and she was relishing the memory even as she took tea with Sir John in his office, her maid waiting properly just outside.

He mistook the shiver that ran through her. "There is nothing for you to fear, my dear Miss Kane," he told her. "The killer does not prey on decent women. The four victims were all females who sold their favors, not innocent maidens."

Ellianne was feeling less innocent by the day, but she ignored those qualms to say, "But what of the serving girl? Her friends said she believed her gentleman suitor had honorable intentions."

"What, a gentleman marry a mobcapped trull? The wedding bells rang only in her ambitious mind, I'd swear. The wench was taking money, by Jupiter. She was nothing but a whore."

Sir John's vehemence surprised Ellianne, and so did the way he spoke of the poor murdered girl. Whatever Maisy may have done in her life, she did not deserve such a death. Still, Ellianne could sympathize with Sir John, too. His frustrations must be eating away at him like a tumor. All his knowledge, all his science, all his examinations of the victims could not give Bow Street a solid lead to follow.

They knew the killer was above average height. He was right-handed, and owned a stiletto. He knew his victims, so he must have enough blunt to hire the expensive doxies. Oh, and he had a steady hand, for the women's shorn heads had fewer cuts and scrapes than a gentleman received from his valet during his morning shave. In fact, one of the newspapers was demanding that Bow Street investigate every barber and gentleman's gentleman in town. Sir John said that was a waste of time, but he could give no other avenues for them to pursue, and the defeat was killing him, too.

He was gaunt and hollow-eyed, and his long hair hung against his waxen cheeks in stringy locks. He smelled of the morgue, and used words a gentlewoman was never supposed to hear.

Perhaps, Ellianne thought, Sir John had to convince himself the dead girls were unworthy of his regard in order to excuse his failure to find their killer. He had to blame the women for their deaths, rather than blame himself for not stopping the murders. She also considered that, if the victims were beneath contempt, Sir John did not have to feel so sorry for them, the way Ellianne did.

Every woman deserved some respect, in life and in death. Stony had shown her that. Not all women who plied the trade had a choice, other than casting themselves into the Thames or starving in the gutter. Some were even led astray by passion. The serving girl might have accepted a few coins from her beau, but what if she really loved him, really thought he would marry her? Then he was the unscrupulous one for stealing her chastity, not she. She was guilty of poor judgment, surely not an offense to die for. Half the women in Town could be accused of the same stupidity, trusting a man's words when his sexual satisfaction was at stake.

Ellianne felt sorry for them all, and sorry for the dedicated scientist whose investigations bore so little fruit. Even now, he could not seem to warm his hands, cradling the hot teacup instead of drinking the sweetened brew.

Ellianne could sympathize, but she could not make

herself accept his invitation to dinner the next day. She was promised to Lady Wellstone, thank goodness, so she did not have to lie. She felt guilty enough planning to attend Vauxhall Pleasure Gardens while Sir John was immersed in death.

Gwen thought they ought to be seen, to counter any gossip that might have arisen from her supposed illness and Stony's supposed fall. Ellianne was looking forward to the evening of music and fireworks and the famous, heady punch served in the private boxes. Although the dark walks were closed for the safety of the highfliers who nested there, Ellianne imagined Stony asking to accompany her down one of the less traveled paths. Who knew what fireworks might follow? No, she could not think of such things, not now, not ever.

She shook herself, and endured more remorse at her wayward thoughts. Her troubled feelings were no help to the murdered girls, though, or to the killer's next victim. Instead of guilt and useless grieving, she added still more to the reward at Bow Street. Then she spent the rest of the afternoon at the Wellstone Home for Girls, where she really could make a difference. Aunt Lally was already there, teaching some of the girls to knit. There was always a need for caps and mittens, she swore. And money.

Speaking of which, Mr. Lattimer called later that afternoon. He apologized, but he could not pursue her private investigation any further. Every available Bow Street man was being assigned to the Barber Murders, as they were being called.

As Ellianne wrote a final check, she told the Runner that she was not ready to give up hope.

Neither was Mr. Lattimer. He asked if he could call on Miss Kane.

"If you have news of my sister, certainly. Otherwise, thank you for your assistance, and I wish you godspeed in finding that madman."

Lattimer stammered something about her generosity while staring at his shoes. Now Ellianne had something else to feel guilty about. She could not have said anything else, though, or offered false encouragement. Mr. Lattimer was a fine young man. He just did not make her pulse quicken. The thought of merely seeing Stony tomorrow had more effect on her heart rate than did sitting across the tea table from the Runner today.

While Lattimer could not relieve her raw, raveled emotions, he could relieve one of her worries over Isabelle.

"No, I don't think your sister ran afoul of the fiend," he told her, referring to his occurrence book rather than look her in the eyes after her rejection. "Miss Isabelle disappeared over a month before the first corpse was discovered, and that's a good sign. What's more, we would have come upon her body by now, because the killer puts his victims where they can be found. I think he likes the fame, getting talked about in all the papers. My superior says he is taunting us, or that he wants to be caught." He scratched his head. "I don't know about that. If he wanted so badly to get nabbed, he could knock on the door at Bow Street. Anyways, he could have hidden the bodies out on Hounslow Heath if he wanted, or dumped them in the Thames with weights. But he didn't, so I think your sister is still alive. Unless some other villain got her, of course."

That was not exactly comforting, but Ellianne was glad to hear someone else say Isabelle was not dead. Aunt Lally was ready to give up and go home to mourn. Gwen's eyes filled up with tears whenever Isabelle's name was mentioned, and Strickland, who had been taken into their confidence, asked the inescapable question: "If the gal ain't dead, where is she? Why hasn't she written to you again?"

Ellianne wanted to know what Stony thought, but was afraid to ask. If he believed Isabelle was dead, then Ellianne might as well return to Fairview. She had accomplished everything she could, becoming almost as notorious as the murderer, and no one had mentioned more than a vague recollection of her sister.

She wasn't ready to go home yet. There was Vauxhall, for one thing, Wellstone's home for girls for another. And his laughing blue eyes. Ellianne wanted to store a few more memories away, like a squirrel storing nuts for the winter. She feared it might be a very long winter indeed. She'd have ample time when she left London to examine her roiled feelings, to try to make sense of the alien emotions. For one of the first times in her life, Ellianne did not know what she wanted. She only knew that it was not waiting for her at home at Fairview.

Stony was more than a little confused himself. In fact, for a man who thought he understood women, he was confounded. What in Hades did the woman want from him, and was he prepared to give it?

He didn't even know if she would expect or accept an apology. But she was the one who had asked for the kiss, he reasoned to himself over a glass of cognac. Of course, she had not asked to be fondled, but that was immaterial, part of the overall cataclysmic event. Hell, he had not asked to be so aroused that he could not exit the room gracefully, not without thinking of her knee and Strickland's knobs.

Thunderation, he could not think of her now without his body turning as satyrlike as a schoolboy's. He hadn't asked for that, by George, not from a skinny spinster heiress. So what was he going to do about it, besides have another cold bath?

Absolutely nothing.

He worked for the woman, by Jupiter. She was still an innocent, by some miracle. She was wealthy beyond counting, by her father's grace and her own wits. By any reckoning, she was not for him.

He could not, would not, should not, think of Miss

Ellianne Kane as anything but an employer. Every fiber of his being—except the traitor between his legs, of course—was clamoring for him to recall his honor, his dignity, his pride. All he recalled was his head cushioned in her lap, her tongue so sweetly meeting his.

No. He was not a trifler, damn it. He'd spent years building a reputation for trustworthy integrity. He was not going to throw it away for a moment's pleasure, not even if Ellianne were willing.

Whom was he fooling? A moment would not be nearly long enough. He doubted a lifetime would be long enough. And she would never be willing. She'd said herself that she would not wed; women of her age and upbringing did not have affairs. That left him . . . where?

On one of the dark paths at Vauxhall, all night, in his dreams.

They traveled to the pleasure gardens by river, on a starlit spring night that was meant for lovers. The Chinese lanterns, the artificial waterfall, the acrobats and tightrope walkers, the gypsy fortune-tellers, all added to the magic of being in a different time, a different place. Vauxhall was two-faced: part sophisticated elegance, part country fair. Everyone was laughing, dancing, calling to friends, dressed in their silks and satins. Ellianne wore a green hooded cape, like a forest sprite, Stony thought.

The music played; the wine flowed. Every sense was sent reeling by the sights and sounds and scents and tastes.

Stony had hired a box for them, a private area in the tiered pavilion to view the activities without being jostled by the crowds. Painted partitions separated them from their neighboring revelers, and waiters hurried back and forth with Vauxhall's famous arrack punch and shaved ham.

Acquaintances strolled by, some to stop for a conversation with Gwen, some to finally be introduced to the heiress in this less formal setting. Friends of Stony's arrived in waves, making their bows, then laughing as he sent them on their way with a wish that they would disappear. No, Miss Kane was not going to dance after supper. No, she was not going to watch the fireworks with this rake, or go have her fortune read with that fortune-hunter.

All was in good sport, with the festive air and gay laughter aided by the heady punch, until Sir John Thomasford approached.

Looking like a death's-head figurine, he stopped in front of their box, ending all conversation.

No one said anything after Ellianne's polite "Good evening, Sir John. How do you go on?"

He went on like one of his corpses, Stony thought, stiff, silent, unsmiling. Out loud he said, "I did not suppose such lively activities would appeal to one of your nature."

"No, they do not. I came to make sure Miss Kane was safe. A killer is loose, you know."

Everyone knew. No one wanted to be reminded, not that night. "I will look after her," Stony said, dismissing the older man with a nod. "I would invite you to join us, but the box is filled, as you can see."

Strickland was there—he seemed to be forever underfoot these days, Stony realized—as were Lord Charles and Lady Valentina, and Gwen's cousins. The harpy Mrs. Collins was not included, at Stony's insistence. He did not trust the widow, not around Miss Kane, not around him. The social-climbing cousins were not impossible, until they started talking about their progeny. So far Stony had avoided meeting the unlovely children. He fully intended to continue his good fortune, despite hints from the cousins about visiting this summer in Norfolk, if he and Gwen were going to take up residence at Wellstone Park. The gray stones it was made of would crumble first.

Ellianne felt sorry for Sir John. The man looked

like he needed a meal and a bit of laughter. She told him, "Perhaps another night, then?"

"Wednesday?"

Ellianne looked to Gwen for an excuse, but Lady Wellstone was fixing her turban, which had tipped over her eye. "Yes, Wednesday will be fine."

Before Sir John had taken ten steps away, Stony was berating Ellianne. He did not trust the man, and she should not be accepting invitations from a coroner as queer as a two-headed hen.

Ellianne was ready to climb on her high horse to retort that it was none of Stony's business whom she conversed with, when they heard another conversation, this one coming from the next box.

The men spoke loudly, slurring their words, and the women giggled too shrilly.

"Do not listen," Gwen ordered. "They are not fit for polite company." Which meant, of course, that Lady Valentina and Gwen's cousin's wife strained their ears to hear. Lord Charles peered over the partition to confirm what both Ellianne and Stony suspected: Godfrey Blanchard and a group of like-minded maggots and their doxies occupied the next supper box.

Blanchard must have known they were close, for he spoke to be heard and to be offensive. "That's right. That's the bitch who broke my nose. Ellis Kane's daughter. Rich as sin and mean as a snake."

"I thought it was Wellstone who broke your nose?" one of his fellows asked, laughing uproariously. One of the women squealed as the man dropped a piece of shaved ham down her gown, then went after it.

"What, that coward?" Blanchard answered. "He passed out at the first hint of a fight. Just like his friend Brisbane fled rather than face Earl Patten on the dueling grounds. Lily-livered cowards, all of them. And those highborn bitches? Whores, all of them. Give me an honest slut any day."

Stony was on his feet, but Ellianne grabbed his coattails. "Let it be. He only wishes to make trouble."

Stony sat, sharing glances with his friend Charlie that promised retribution on Blanchard when the ladies were not present. Gwen was chattering to her cousins, trying to drown out the dreadful talk, but Lady Valentina's lip was trembling. Ellianne was pale but composed. "He is not worth having our lovely evening ruined over."

But Blanchard was not finished. "Wellstone can keep the shrew, and good riddance. I'd wager his pockets are empty, else he'd find greener pastures to graze. I don't know what the Kane bitch is paying him, but she couldn't offer me enough. The woman's so cold, it'd be like screwing an ice sculpture. Freeze a man's rod right off. Some chaps will do anything for money, I suppose."

Stony was halfway out of the box, Charlie beside him. "Take the women home," he told Strickland and the cousin.

"I am not going." Ellianne clutched her reticule, a large one tonight.

"Take them home, Strickland," Stony ordered again, not looking at her.

The women in Blanchard's box ran off, screaming, when Stony burst in, Charlie at his heels. Two of the men pushed out past them. "Not our fight, don't you know." They'd seen Wellstone working out at the boxing parlor.

Blanchard sneered. "What, have you come to challenge me to a duel? What's it to be, Wellstone, vinaigrette at twenty paces? Or you, Hammett." His lip curled at the sight of Lord Charles's yellow Cossack trousers. "Quizzing glasses at dawn?"

"No," Stony said. "Duels are for gentlemen, not scurvy swine like you." He lunged in a move that would have made Ellianne's bulldog proud, straight for Blanchard's throat. He grabbed a fistful of neckcloth in one hand, and drew his other arm back. He wasn't about to aim for the dastard's nose. It was already broken anyway. The man's jaw offered too many possibilities for cut lips, broken teeth. So he swung as he did at practice, straight for Blanchard's midsection. The rotter's gut was not half as hard as the leather punching bag, but the sound he made was a whole lot more satisfying.

Stony hit him again, to make sure all the air was out of the blowhard. Then, still holding him upright, he shook the cur like a dirty rug. "If I ever see you in Town again, Blanchard, or hear one word from your filthy mouth, I will finish this, for once and for all. Do you understand?" Just in case he did not, Stony drove home his point with another blow to Blanchard's middle, just below his ribs. Well, maybe not far below, for Stony heard a distinct crack when his fist connected.

Blanchard's friend started to drag him away. "He'll go, he'll go. Don't kill him, for God's sake. He owes me money!"

Charlie called after them, "And if Wellstone doesn't pound you into the ground, I will lay charges of slander against you, and see that your creditors call in their bills. I might even tell Bow Street to look in your rooms for a stiletto and a wig or two. Who knows what they might find, eh? And whose word do you think they are going to believe, the son of a duke, or a son of a bitch?"

Stony quickly wrapped a handkerchief around his knuckles, scraped on Blanchard's buttons and fob chains; then he and Charlie strolled back to their own box, for all the world like gentlemen returning from blowing a cloud.

Ellianne and Lady Valentina were sitting there alone, holding hands.

Stony viewed Ellianne with aggravation. "I told you to go home. What was the matter? Didn't you trust me to shut him up?"

"Of course I trusted you, but someone had to be ready with the smelling salts."

Chapter Twenty-five

"There will be talk."

"Should I hope another young woman gets murdered to displace the gossip about me and my escort?"

Stony winced, and not just from the ointment Ellianne was rubbing on his knuckles. They were in the butler's pantry at Sloane Street, the butler, her aunt, and the rest of the household having sought their beds hours ago. Stony was sitting at a sturdy worktable very like the one at his own house, where he'd sat polishing the heirloom silver not many days past. Ellianne worked on his hand by the light of the single candle they'd brought with them, along with a bottle of wine and two glasses.

Her green cloak was folded over the back of his chair, and she was leaning over, far enough that Stony could see right down her gray silk bodice to the vee that formed between her breasts. The fact that he noticed, and that his mouth went dry despite the wine, was one reason they shouldn't be alone here like this. Another reason was that the rumor mill would be working overtime as it was.

If anyone saw Wellstone bring Miss Kane home sans chaperon, the tongues would wag even harder. If one of the neighbors saw him escort Ellianne to her door—and not come out—there would be hell to pay in the morning.

Thanks to Blanchard, Ellianne's reputation was already hanging on to respectability by a thread. It might be a golden thread, but it was still fragile.

"Stop fretting about what society is going to say," she told him when he repeated his concerns. "I do not. And I have no relations other than Isabelle to be embarrassed by a stain on the family name. My mother's family is already ashamed of the Kane connection, so whatever I do cannot affect them. I'll go home, that's all. I never intended to stay in London this long, and I never need to come again."

"But what about me?" He looked away while she wound a strip of linen around his hand. "My honor is at stake, too, you know, and I have to stay here. So does Gwen, who will be crushed that her friend is exiled. As for me, my reputation does matter, especially when no one wants to entrust their sisters or daughters to my care after all the recent blunders."

"Do you have to do that? Work as an escort?"

"What other employment is there for a gentleman trained to be an idler? I did try gambling, but I do not have your head for numbers, and my lands do not earn enough yet to support themselves, if I had enough experience to manage them properly. The army is obviously out of the question, so what would you have me do, turn highwayman?"

Ellianne was not one to see romance in road pirates. Nor could she envision the viscount's sunny smile hidden behind a mask, threatening, "Your money or your life." Goodness, what if he shot someone? His victim's carriage could roll right over him as he lay on the ground. "No, I do not think you are suited to the life of crime."

"I only need to work for a short while more, at

any rate. Then my father's debts will all be paid and Wellstone Park will start earning income instead of taking every farthing I make."

"That you don't give to the girls' home." She nodded in understanding and approval. "What are we supposed to do, then, to restore your good name? Get married? Lady Val was hinting about such a course while we waited for the carriages to take us home. Of course, that would be a moot question, since marriage to me would mean an instant end to your financial difficulties. You would not need a good name to find work, for you would not be seeking a position."

"A man always wishes to be proud of his name. If he is not known as an honorable gentleman, he is nothing." He tried to see her face, but her head was turned away as she rewound the roll of bandage. "Would it be such a bad idea?"

"What, an end to your employment or our marriage?"

"The match, of course. We rub along well, for the most part."

"When you are not trying to act superior."

"And when you are not trying to rule the roost."

She acknowledged their competition for the upper hand with a smile. "But you do not wish to marry. You have said it many times."

He was not so closed-minded, Stony told himself, that he could not consider another position. "Neither do you. You have said it as often."

Ellianne was beginning to think she could change her mind, under the right conditions. Marrying to save her reputation and his pride was not one of those conditions, however. She pushed the candle aside, now that she did not need its light to see his injured hand. She did not need for him to see the disappointment on her face. "But there is still the money."

He did not pretend to misunderstand. "Of course. The money. You would always worry that I was wedding you for your fortune."

"And you would always worry that I wed you because I was desperate for a title. Besides, you would resent that I had most of my funds tied up, out of your control."

"That would show a lack of trust, wouldn't it?"

"Or caution."

"Or wisdom, knowing my father's history. I would not blame you. But that makes no difference. I have never believed a man should live off his wife's income."

"Well, I certainly do not believe he should! Nor do I think a woman requires a title to prove her worth."

"Fine, then we are agreed. We should not marry." Stony did not know if the decision relieved him or wrung his innards. He was certainly feeling an ache that was not from his bruised knuckles.

"Fine," Ellianne concurred. "We shall weather the storm of gossip without setting sail on the sea of matrimony." Now if only someone would toss her a lifeline before she drowned. She tried to sound happy, or at least keep her voice steady past the lump in her throat. "If the talk gets too uncomfortable here, you can always come visit Fairview on a repairing lease, to see how my schools are run. And bring Gwen too, of course, for I shall miss her most severely."

She had not mentioned missing him, Stony thought.

"She will enjoy herself, I promise," Ellianne was going on, hoping to convince him to visit, "for we are not entirely isolated. There are the local assemblies, and the finest families in the neighborhood would delight in having a viscountess at their entertainments. We do not make such a business out of socializing as you do in the city, but we do hold frequent dinner parties and dances."

"Would you dance?"

"At small gatherings, yes, for enough time has passed to show respect for Aunt Augusta. Besides, how could I resist, when I would have the handsomest, most elegant escort the county has ever seen? Why, it would be worth every shilling I had to pay, to see the look on the old tabbies' faces."

"You would not have to pay me," he said in a low voice, pouring himself another glass of wine. "The money truly does not always matter."

"Have I hurt your feelings once again? I did not mean to. I only wished to encourage you to come. If that is the only way . . ."

"Some things are worth doing for free."

"Like dancing with me?" She laughed. "But you have no idea if I am a competent dancer. After all, what if I wished to lead in the waltz?"

He laughed back, showing the smile that captivated females from six to sixty. "I'd be surprised if you did not. Come." He held his arms out. "May I have this dance, Miss Kane?"

"What, here? Now?"

"Why not? We are already accused of far worse." He began humming, and Ellianne stepped into his embrace, hiding her blushes by lowering her head. They waltzed around the worktable, barely having space to twirl in the long, narrow room. They managed.

None of the gentlemen at home ever held her this closely. No couples she'd seen dance in London let their bodies touch this way, her bosom to his solid chest, her legs to his firm thighs. The dowagers would have conniptions. Ellianne would have another memory to take home with her.

She pressed daringly closer, her cheek nestled against his chin, breathing in the scent of him, the spices and soap and a bit of sweat from the fight with Blanchard. No wine's bouquet was more intoxicating.

Stony sighed and brushed her hair with his lips, feeling the satiny texture. He sighed again, which threw off the tempo of his humming, which had Ellianne swaying when she should have been turning, which made them bump into the table.

"I warned you I was not a proficient dancer," she said, laughing, with her backside against the wooden table.

"You are perfect." He did not step away or release her, but pulled closer, so that his lower body was hard against hers and his legs pressed against either side of hers. He began to pull pins out of her hair, then comb through the freed braids with his fingers, smoothing and stroking. "Perfect."

Ellianne could feel her long hair fall to her shoulders and down her back. She shut her eyes, entranced by his motion, by his so-evident appreciation tight against her. Stony might not love her and might not want to marry her, but heaven—and Ellianne—knew he wanted her.

Almost as much as she wanted him. She was a spinster virgin of impeccable morals . . . and immediate, inexplicable, indescribable needs. "Closer," she murmured.

"Any closer and we'll both get splinters from the table."

Timms would never permit rough edges on his work surface, and what were a few splinters anyway? Ellianne pulled Stony closer, wrapping her own fingers in his golden curls.

"A man can resist only so much temptation, sweetings."

How much was too much? His touch on her hair was Ellianne's limit. She did not want to resist her own inclinations anymore. "Closer," she insisted.

He smiled and lowered his head for a brief kiss. A smiling kiss, a happy kiss, but not the earth-shattering kiss they had shared before. Ellianne wanted the ground to tremble, at the very least.

"What Blanchard said, you know, was not true."

He was back to drawing his fingers through her hair, watching the carmine colors shift in the candlelight. He thought he would never grow tired of touching her hair, watching it float around her like a scarlet veil.

He could only imagine how it would look against her bare skin; Lud knew he could not grow any harder.

"Stony," Ellianne said with a tinge of impatience.

"Hmm?"

"Blanchard lied about me."

"Of course he did, and about Captain Brisbane and Lady Val and me. I don't think the dastard cared a whit for the veracity of his statements, only how much trouble he could stir up."

"But what he said, that I am as cold as an ice sculpture, that was not true at all, you know."

Now he laughed outright. "Oh, I know that full well, my dear. How could I not know it, when you are setting off sparks that a typhoon's rains could not extinguish? When you are starting a conflagration in my brain that nothing but your lips can quench? You, Miss Ellianne Kane, are a fraud. Under that prim and proper exterior of a banker's daughter beats the heart of a wanton. A beautiful, alluring wanton, who can heat a man's blood with one green-eyed glance. But you are still a lady, not a mare in heat, twitching her tail. And I, unfortunately, am still a gentleman, not a stag in rut. I do not despoil innocent maidens, especially not ones who have endured an emotional evening and perhaps a surfeit of wine. I should be going."

"No." She moved her hips against him. "I am neither in shock nor inebriated. Stay, please."

Stony could not have left if the roof collapsed around them. He kissed her again, a long, searing kiss this time. The earth might not have moved, but the heavy table certainly did. "You, cold? Hades should be this cold."

Ellianne was unwrapping his neckcloth, aching to touch his bare skin. Stony pulled her hands away. "No, sweetings. You are playing with fire."

"I am not playing."

"Deuce take it, we cannot."

"Why? I am old enough to know my own mind, and now I seek the experience other women have enjoyed for years by my age. Or do you not wish to . . . ?"

"Wish to? I must have used up a hundred shooting stars, fifty Christmas puddings, and thirty birthday candles wishing for you in my arms." He placed her hand between them, on the front of his trousers, to reassure her of her desirability, or perhaps frighten her. "Do you understand how much I wish to continue?"

Instead of being frightened, she left her hand where it was, learning the shape of him. He was learning what being boiled in oil must feel like. He did not know whether he was coming or going. Literally. "This is wrong."

"Just this once cannot be so wrong, just so I know what I am missing. Goodness knows I do not want to be your mistress, waiting for you to grow tired of me, or having to share you with any number of girls. Oh, and I swear there will never be recriminations."

"There might be consequences, dash it."

"A baby?" she asked with a sense of wonder, squeezing the source of the possibility. "I never expected to be a mother."

"And you won't be expecting now, if I have any say in the matter. Ellianne, we cannot do this!"

To move her hand and that sweet torment, he pressed her back down on the table. Now her legs straddled his, though, which was no less torturous for him. "We cannot," he repeated once more, leaning forward to kiss her eyelids, her nose, her mouth, her neck, and that damned vee at her neckline that he'd been watching all night. Her arms wound around his neck and his back, holding him so tightly he was strangling. No, that was his neckcloth. He pulled it off and threw it to the floor. Ellianne started to wrap her legs around him too, to keep him close to her, close to the need she could not express, but she was sure it bore Stony's name.

He groaned. How in heaven was he supposed to

walk away when the devil was dancing in his brain, and below? To stop her long, slender, graceful legs from driving him past endurance, he touched one. That was a mistake. Her skirts were in disorder, and his hand touched silk stocking, taut over smooth muscles. He raised his hand—and her skirts—higher, to feel the satin garter, which he deftly removed. It joined his cravat on the floor. He had to feel her skin, just an inch of it, just for a minute, that was all. He might expire right in the butler's pantry if he didn't.

Stony started to tug down the loosened stocking, but his hand had a will of its own—likely the same will that had him pressing kisses to her breasts—and moved higher, to the skin on the back of her knee, the inside of her thigh. So smooth, so soft, just as he'd imagined.

Now she groaned. And wriggled. Lud, his hand slipped higher than he'd intended, almost to . . .

"Oh hell, we cannot." He took his hand away and cupped her face in his hands. "I work for you!"

"This is not part of the job."

"But I swore never to dally with one of my charges. It's wrong, taking advantage of them. Of you. Men trust me with their innocent daughters. Gads, I cannot even trust myself with you!" His hands were pulling at the top of her gown to free her breasts. He almost cried at the sight of those perfect round globes with their rosy centers, knowing they could never be his to fondle, to suckle, to tease into hardness. Why, the merest touch of his lips on her nipple had it rigid and waiting. "Damnation!"

Ellianne was gasping. "So quit. No, do not quit that." *Never that,* she prayed. "Quit my employ, so you won't have to suffer such qualms."

"I think I have quit caring," he murmured as his tongue found her other nipple, and his hand reached again to find nirvana. "I'll worry about it in the morning."

"No, you'll only feel . . . remorse," she said between

labored breaths while her hands reached into the opening of his shirt to touch wiry curls and hard muscles. "So I'll get rid of your plaguey principals for you. You are fired." She lowered one hand between them, to find the fastenings on his trousers.

"No, I am on fire."

"I am, too. I have never felt this way, so heated, so consumed by burning need, as if my very soul were waiting to erupt like a volcano. There is fever in my blood and—"

"I really am on fire." His arm had brushed against the candle, and the lace of his shirt sleeve was starting to smoke.

Ellianne screamed and pushed against him, jumping off the table, knocking over one of the wineglasses, the tin of ointment, and Stony. She grabbed up his neckcloth and knelt beside him on the floor where he'd landed. She started beating the length of fabric against his hand.

"Stop that, you goose." He took the cloth from her and used it to smother the incipient fire. "You're just fanning the flames, which is no surprise. You've been doing it this past hour."

"I? I did not have my hand up your . . ." She helped him shrug out of his jacket, then pull his shirt over his head.

"You were trying."

"I was not." She turned his wrist this way and that, to see if any skin had been burned. It hadn't, but she put her lips to the spot anyway, just to make sure it did not feel hot. It did, but not from the candle burn. She had to kiss his bare chest, to compare. He moaned, but not from the candle burn either.

This time she was on top, trying to touch every inch of naked skin while his hands were busy loosening the tapes at the back of her gown. Meanwhile they kissed, joining together in fevered anticipation of another joining.

This time he stopped uttering protests he did not mean.

This time the floor really did tremble . . . under the heavy pounding of running feet.

Chapter Twenty-six

"He was on fire."

"I'd wager he was," Timms said with an old man's envy.

Aunt Lally picked up Ellianne's garter from the floor and waved it. "And what were you going to do with your skirts up and your stockings down, piss on him to put the fire out?"

The two had coming barreling into the butler's pantry. By then Stony had his shirt on, but no jacket, waistcoat, or cravat. Ellianne had the top of her gown pulled up, with her long hair covering the unfastened opening in the back. Timms, in nightcap and gown, had an ancient blunderbuss but not his false teeth or his spectacles. Aunt Lally's gray-streaked red hair was in a long braid, and her night rail had delicate violets embroidered on it, surprisingly. Less surprisingly, she had a long-handled copper warming pan in her hand and immediately started beating at Wellstone's head.

Ellianne shouted at her to stop, as soon as she took the blunderbuss from the old butler before he fired at one of them by mistake. "It is not his fault. Lord Wellstone has done nothing wrong, nothing I haven't asked him to do."

So Aunt Lally started beating at Ellianne's head. She might have the language of a dockside laborer, but she had the morals of a vicar when it came to her family.

Stony wrested the warming pan away from her. "You are making more of this than need be," he said, looking to see if any other servants has heard the commotion and were coming to find out if they were under attack. Luckily, the rest of the staff slept in the attics, far enough away to dampen the sounds. "Nothing happened." By the grace of God and a single candle.

"More than need be?" Aunt Lally yelled, fighting him for the weapon. "By Saint Sylvester's stones, I'll give you what need be, you jackanapes."

They all knew what needed to be done. Ellianne's aged butler and her widowed aunt waited for Stony to speak.

"I would be honored—" he began, resigned, relieved, almost in raptures that the decision was out of his hands.

But Ellianne interrupted. "Lord Wellstone would be honored if you shared a glass of wine with him before he leaves, in case we do not see him before we depart. We'll start packing tomorrow to return to Fairview."

She could so calmly, so casually dismiss what had happened? Stony was almost as angry as Mrs. Goudge. Ellianne really had been using him to satisfy her curiosity, to scratch an itch, nothing more. Blanchard was correct, but misguided: Miss Kane was not cold; she was coldhearted. He poured wine into crystal glasses Timms took out of one of the cabinets.

He could so cheerfully, so unconcernedly accept her interruption? Ellianne's heart was breaking at Stony's cavalier behavior. The least he could have done was try a little harder to finish the proposal so she could have refused it in form. He did not even want to marry her enough to finish the blasted sentence. Well, she did not want to marry him either, she told herself, accepting the glass he handed her. If she drank enough, perhaps she would believe it. Wed a man who did not love her? Never. She should have listened to his pleas to go. He had not wanted her, Ellianne Kane, at all, only a physical release. Any woman would have done as well. Once she paid him his wages, he could pick his own woman, his own wife if he chose, a real lady this time, one of his own kind. She drank the wine and held out her glass for more.

By Jupiter, she was celebrating her escape, Stony thought, tucking in his shirt and putting on his coat. A man should get drunk in private.

By heaven, he couldn't wait to leave, Ellianne thought, mortified now that she'd urged him on when he was so unwilling. She handed him his crumpled cravat from the floor, hoping her cheeks weren't scarlet with shame that she'd help rip it off his neck.

Aunt Lally's mouth was clamped shut, as if she'd taken another vow of silence, or was too aggravated with the pair of ninnyhammers to speak.

The butler's mouth was shut too, because he was embarrassed by Mrs. Goudge's seeing him without his teeth.

Then they heard another sound, the scrabble of clawed feet on the bare floor in the hallway.

"Oh, no," Ellianne cried, searching the pockets of her green cloak for a bonbon or a boiled carrot.

"That's just what this night needs to be complete." Stony started for the door, thinking that if he could slam it shut, he'd rather spend the night in here with the bitch, the witch, and the butler than encounter the hound from hell. He bumped into Timms, though, who'd had the same intent. Stony almost knocked the old fellow off his slippered feet. By the time he'd pushed Timms into the chair, the bulldog was careening around the doorpost, into the room. His wrinkled head swung from side to side, until his bloodshot eyes focused on Wellstone, the intruder.

The dog started to gather itself for a leap, a snarl in his throat, but no teeth in his gaping jaws.

Stony leaped first, for the bottle of wine on the table.

"Don't hurt him!" Ellianne shouted.

"Damnation, what about me?" Stony shouted back. But he wasn't holding the bottle by the neck, like a club; he was showering wine out onto the wooden floor.

"My floor!" Timms whined.

"My wine!" Aunt Lally wailed.

"My word," Ellianne whispered. "I think it's working."

At first the dog skidded in the liquid; then he sniffed. Then he put his big, ugly head down and began to slurp. The nubbin of a tail on his rear end began to wag.

Ellianne let out the breath she'd been holding. "I wish we had thought of doing that before."

"I wish we hadn't drunk so much," Stony said, setting down the empty bottle and looking at Ellianne accusingly for having that second glass. He began to sidle toward the door, thinking to make his getaway before the floor was dry.

Timms had unearthed another bottle, of even better vintage, from a different cabinet. He poured an inch of it into a gleaming silver finger bowl and set it on the floor. "I do believe Lady Augusta and the beast shared a libation now and again."

"I wonder if dogs suffer from overindulgence," Ellianne mused as the slurping continued. "And what they call the morning's remedy. The hair of the cat?"

"I'll leave you to find out. I deem it the better part of valor to depart while Atlas is imbibing," Stony told the others, bowing slightly, trying to look dignified despite his disarray.

"I'll see you out," Ellianne said, ignoring her aunt's glare and Timms's throat clearing. "I won't be long. A minute or two."

Aunt Lally picked up the blunderbuss, not the warming pan. "I'll be counting."

When they reached the front door, Ellianne told Stony that she would send a bank draft over in the morning.

Stony nodded. He could not afford to refuse her payment, the way his pride wanted. "All business as usual, Miss Kane?"

"Our business is concluded, Lord Wellstone."

So he kissed her. Stony did not like being dismissed, did not like thinking that their heated exchange meant so little to Ellianne that she could brush him aside like a dog hair on her hem. He did not like thinking that the passionate interlude would never be repeated, either. So he kissed her with fervor and feeling and every fiber of his being.

She kissed him back. Heavens, she kissed him back as if she could sink into his skin, becoming part of him, a part that he could not simply walk away from. Let him take his freedom home, she thought, but let him take the memory of what could have been, if he had cared for her at all.

They kissed, and Ellianne could no longer feel her feet touch the floor. She was up in his arms, she realized with the two bits of her brain still working, off the ground. He was holding her so they touched everywhere. Everywhere they touched was another glowing ember about to catch on fire.

They kissed, and Stony was ready to burst, ready to lay her down on the marble tiles, or carry her up to her bedroom. He could not move, though. He could not breathe or think or do anything but what he was doing, kissing Ellianne—not like he'd ever kissed any other woman. Hell, there was no other woman but Ellianne.

They kissed and time stood still. Aunt Lally did not. She and her blunderbuss appeared in the hall.

Stony opened the door; then he raised one gold eyebrow in inquiry.

"I still will not marry you," Ellianne said, understanding the question.

"I still have not asked."

According to Gwen, Ellianne was not planning on leaving for two days. She was not going out except for her engagement with Sir John Thomasford, because of the gossip. Dear Ellianne could not like being stared at or whispered about, Gwen said, eyeing Stony with accusation, as if he could have prevented Blanchard's vile rant. He could not have foreseen the depth of the cad's hatred, any more than he could have foreseen the heights of his own folly afterward, of which, thank goodness, Gwen was ignorant.

He could, however, make certain neither happened again. He guaranteed Blanchard's departure from Town by having friends call in the dastard's markers. Blanchard could flee, or he could face debtor's prison. He'd never be welcome at the gentlemen's clubs or the polite drawing rooms again, not a loose screw who insulted women and, worse, reneged on debts of honor. Someone, perhaps Lord Charles, dropped a hint that the man might have cheated at cards. Blanchard wouldn't be showing his face, broken nose and all, at the gaming parlors, either.

As for Stony's lack of control where Miss Ellianne Kane was concerned, he solved the problem by staying away from her. He could not overstep the bounds of propriety if he did not step over her doorstop. He was not certain he could see her, otherwise, without making a worse fool of himself. Even knowing she was a heartless jade, he still wanted her. Desperately.

Of course, one word from her would have brought Lord Wellstone to Sloane Street before the ink on her note was dry. The note never came, though. The draft on Miss Kane's bank did, more generous than he deserved, considering, but not so high that he would be offended. No message was included. So be it: He no longer worked for her. He did not have to follow her dictates or cater to her whims. He could stop worrying over fortune hunters or her future in whatever narrow society she chose to live.

On the other hand, he no longer worked for her. His uncomfortable scruples about mixing employment and enjoyment, finances and flirtations, were not relevant anymore. Of course, he still believed no woman should be wed merely for her wealth, and no man should be a parasite on his bride's bank account. If he were a rich man, though, Stony could now present himself as a legitimate suitor for Ellianne's hand, freed from the restraints of his guardianship. Not that she would accept him under any conditions, but he would feel better about asking. If he were inclined to make the offer.

Lud, a wife. Living with the same willful woman for the rest of one's life? Hell could not be worse. Of course, living without Ellianne was already torture, and barely twelve hours had passed. He looked at the clock, then at the check in his hand. He and Gwen could live comfortably—if not happily, on Gwen's part—at Wellstone Park in Norfolk now, but he would never be wealthy, never be considered an advantageous match for anyone but a vicar's daughter, a Cit's niece, or a title-hungry widow.

Stony decided to call on Miss Kane anyway. He had legitimate reasons, after all, he told himself. He had to thank her for the check, ask about the dog, make a last report on the search for her sister, and express his concern about the lint-brained female's engagement with the leech.

"I really wish you would reconsider accepting Sir John's escort," he told her, after caching his breath at the sight of the radiant smile she gave him in welcome.

Ellianne was smiling from the inside out. He'd come. He did not have to, was under no obligation to do so, was not being paid to do so, but he had come to call. On her. What a beautiful, glorious day. One could almost hear the birds singing, if one ignored the rain and the wind and the street traffic noise. He had come, and he was expressing concern for her welfare—for free.

"I know you thought I was merely acting like a dog with a meaty bone," Stony was going on, "but I cannot trust Thomasford or his motives."

Ellianne did not want to talk about Sir John. "He is simply a dedicated scientist. Would you like more tea?"

Stony shook his head and persisted in his warning. "Being dedicated to dead people is freakish enough, but the man seems to grow more peculiar by the day. That night at Vauxhall he was decidedly queer. You must have noticed."

"I did feel he was somewhat distracted, but I believe Sir John has cause for his perturbation. We are all worried about the murders, but he feels personally responsible, in his position of authority. That is admirable, rather than odd. Besides, I feel sorry for the man."

"So send him a tin of biscuits or a bottle of wine. You do not have to share an evening with the fellow to show your sympathy."

"It would be rude to back out at this late date."

"You could claim a headache. Women do that all the time. Or say you are leaving town and have to finish your packing. Say anything, but do not go with him."

She smiled. Stony was jealous. "Now you are sounding like Aunt Lally, who declares Sir John sends chills down her spine. She finds him so unsettling that she is making me take my maid instead of going with us as chaperon. She will not walk past a cemetery at night either, though, or walk under a ladder. I was always amazed that she stepped foot on her husband's boats, for women aboard ship are supposed to be unlucky."

"Perhaps they were, for Mr. Goudge. He died, didn't he?"

"Of choking on a cherry pit, I believe, safe at home. Anyway, Sir John's unique calling is gruesome, I do admit, but that is all one can hold against him. He is a gentleman and harmless, and he needs the relief of an evening away from his work."

Stony needed relief, too, and he was not likely to get it, not while Ellianne was busy defending that slimy creature. Considering Miss Kane's face and fortune, Stony was not convinced the man was so innocuous either, but he realized he was wasting his breath. Miss Kane's head was as hard as her heart.

"Very well, I can see that you are adamant about going. What merry entertainment does the coroner have planned for the evening, anyway?" Stony thought he might meet them there, for his own peace of mind.

"He is taking me to dinner after another lecture. This one is about amputations at field hospitals on the Peninsula."

Stony rethought his plans. He also reconsidered his regard for Miss Kane. Any woman who could listen to such a talk, much less eat dinner afterward, was not natural. Perhaps she and the morguemaggot could make a match of it after all. The wedding could take place in an insane asylum.

She was continuing, as if Stony had expressed interest instead of half gagging. "Did you know how many more soldiers would have died of infection if their wounds were left to fester? Why, pieces of his own uniform could kill a man if they stayed imbedded in his flesh."

Stony quickly dropped his napkin, so he could put his head between his knees before he fainted. "I . . . I am sure you will find the lecture . . . informative."

"I suppose, but I am mostly going in hopes of locating a qualified surgeon for the hospital I am building."

"And after the lecture?" Stony asked, recovering with the aid of another cup of hot tea that Ellianne silently handed him.

"Dinner at the Pulteney Hotel. I thought of inviting Sir John here, but decided against it in light of Aunt Lally's animosity. She was a trifle . . . vocal about taking mutton with a mortician. Not that Sir John is one, of course," she added defensively. "He is an eminent research scientist, and so I told my aunt. And Gwen. Lady Wellstone refused to come, if I made a small dinner party of the occasion, and Lady Valentina and Lord Charles are busy. I did not feel Her Grace would be interested in Sir John's research either."

Good gods, the Duchess of Williston dining with a connoisseur of crime corpses? "I should think not."

"I could have asked Lord and Lady Aldershott, Mrs. Harkness-Smythe, and the other hostesses who were kind enough to invite me to their gatherings, but I do not think Sir John is in a frame of mind to endure strangers and small talk. Neither did I wish him to think I was holding an intimate dinner party for the two of us. So, you see, you need not worry that I am entirely unaware of the awkwardness of the situation."

Not worry? He'd stop worrying when she was tucked in her bed, alone. Better yet, with himself beside her in case a lust-crazed lunatic climbed up to her window. Stony thanked heaven that the peagoose showed a little sense, not inviting a bloodsucking vampire into her home without the protection of company. Stony knew all too well what could happen there, with Mrs. Goudge's lax chaperonage. At the hotel, even if Thomasford hired a private dining parlor, they would never be entirely alone. Her maid would be present, the hotel's servants would be underfoot, and the other patrons would be nearby.

So would Stony.

Chapter Twenty-seven

Stony had a bad feeling about that night. Perhaps he was coming down with a quinsy from yesterday's rain, or he'd had too much to drink last evening, sitting alone in his book room. Or perhaps he would have distrusted any chap sharing a dinner with Ellianne. No matter the cause, Stony felt uneasy.

He was so unsettled that he went to speak with Lattimer at Bow Street.

The Runner was too busy to listen to Stony's vague, niggling suspicions. "The man's a bit daft, of course. He'd have to be, in that line of work. But he's a brilliant anatomist, you know. Knighted for his advances in the field and all that."

Lattimer went on to say that they were all being harried by the press and haunted by the dead girls. Everyone connected with the magistrate's office was going without sleep or baths or proper meals, trying to nab the Barber before he struck again. So it was no wonder Sir John was not looking his finest. Lattimer glanced at Stony's spotless, elegant attire in disdain.

"Some of us are trying to catch a killer, not the eye of every damsel in Town. I consider Sir John a lucky dog to have Miss Kane's company tonight, a reward he richly deserves."

Stony wondered how much the reward money was influencing Lattimer's zeal. He read a posted handbill outside the door at Bow Street that named an astronomical price for the murderer's apprehension. Some of the money was Ellianne's, he knew, but pounds had poured in from other concerned citizens, the government, the slain maidservant's employer, the murdered actress's friends. A group of Covent Garden doves had donated their pence to make the streets safer for their sisters. Now the reward was nearly a king's ransom. Lattimer would go without a few more hours of sleep to find the stiletto wielder. He would not take the time to help guard Miss Kane.

Stony was not reassured by the Runner's opinion of Sir John Thomasford. He still felt Aunt Lally's shivers up his spine, and not from the damp, drizzly day. His friend Captain Brisbane had always said that a soldier's best defense was the inner voice of instinct. Stony's intuition was yelling, "Danger! Danger!" in his ear.

So he rode back to Sloane Street early that evening and waited in the saddle, in the shadows and the rain, huddled in his caped riding coat. Dusk fell late this time of year, but there were enough clouds and trees between houses to offer some concealment, if not much protection from the cold drops that ran off his beaver hat and down his neck. With every drip he asked himself what the devil he was doing here.

He merely wished to make sure, Stony answered himself, that Sir John did not find some excuse to leave Ellianne's maid behind. Who knew what a knave could do in a moving carriage? Stony did, and intended to make certain Ellianne never found out, at least not with the carrion crow.

Eventually the gray-clad maid got into a modest coach, all right and tight. So did Miss Kane, wearing her green cloak and a black ruched bonnet trimmed with sprigs of green silk ivy that Stony had never seen before. She wore sensible half-boots, he noted as she stepped up into the carriage, showing trim ankles. She handed her umbrella to Sir John to fold for her before she took her seat.

She was smiling, Stony could see from his position, and he felt like a fool. A jealous fool, besides. He'd go home, have a hot bath, then take Gwen to a pleasant dinner at the Pulteney, as he'd arranged. That was likely another wasted effort, but at least the food was good.

The problem was, Sir John's coach headed east on Sloane Street. The hall where the medical lecture was to be given was west of Sloane Street. He stared after the black carriage, feeling the shiver down his spine turn into a sharp pain, as if someone held a knife to his back. Or else he'd been out in the rain too long, sitting too stiffly on his horse.

Home, a hot bath, and a good meal . . . or a dismal wet ride following the coach on another fool's errand? Hmm.

Ellianne was surprised that the coach did not turn around, too.

When she asked if the driver had the address wrong, Sir John reached across the carriage and placed his gloved hand over hers. "My dear Miss Kane, I fear I have ill tidings for you. I wanted to wait to tell you until we were closer to our destination, so that you had less time to fret."

"Oh, heavens, my sister?"

"I cannot be certain, of course, without your identification. But this latest victim does have green eyes and light eyelashes, like yours. I knew you would not want to wait until tomorrow, and I could not let you read about this in the newspapers, or sit through a lecture, not knowing."

"Of course not. Thank you. That was very kind."

Ellianne wondered why Mr. Lattimer or another Bow Street minion had not come to tell her. She also wondered why she did not feel more distraught, as if she had accepted that Isabelle was lost to her forever. She only wished that Stony were with her instead of this gentleman who seemed more affected by the newest murder than ever.

He was dressed correctly in evening wear, bathed and shaved, but his clothing hung on his increasingly thinner frame. His neckcloth was badly creased, and his hair was hanging in damp, greasy locks from the rain. His lips were thinner, the creases on his forehead were deeper, but his brown eyes were still glimmering, as if with a fever. The poor man was obviously distraught that he had not been able to prevent yet another killing. Ellianne let her hand rest under his a moment longer before moving it away.

On the way to the morgue, Ellianne made no attempt at polite conversation, and Sir John respected her silence. She was trying not to think about the latest murder victim, but found herself recalling Isabelle as a toddler, red hair like a halo as she held her hands out to be picked up by her older sister. No, that was too painful. She would have years to grieve, to take out each cherished memory in turn. She would not think about Isabelle, and the dead girl would not be Isabelle.

Ellianne thought about Stony instead, and how sincere his concern for her had been. He did care for her, undeniably, and maybe that was enough. A great many successful marriages were based on far less. He was to call in the morning, and Ellianne was determined to discover his true feelings, even if she had to hit the clunch over the head with her reticule as she had done to Blanchard. Not that she would clobber Stony with the purse she carried tonight. After his visit, she'd decided to carry her larger reticule this evening, so she could carry the small pistol. She held the bag close to her now, as if it could protect her from bad news. At least it could keep her fingers from trembling, as Sir John's hand on hers had not.

The coroner's office was nearly deserted at this time of night. Only one clerk remained at his desk, writing reports by an oil lamp. He stood when Ellianne passed by and silently bowed his head toward Sir John before getting back to his work. Otherwise the place was as quiet as the tomb it was.

Ellianne's maid was wide-eyed and quaking, clutching the umbrella.

"Perhaps your maid would feel better waiting above stairs?" Sir John suggested. "Jenkins can look after her."

"Oh, yes, Miss Kane, please. I don't want to see no dead bodies! Especially none what's been murdered."

Ellianne agreed, and Sir John seated the girl at an empty desk near the door. Then he took up a lantern and led Ellianne to the stone steps that went down to the bowels of the building and the vast, frigid chamber that was the morgue itself.

Ellianne pulled her cloak more tightly around her and clutched her reticule to her chest for warmth and comfort. She followed Sir John across the expanse, their footsteps echoing in the high-ceilinged room. Wall lamps were left burning, but she was glad for the lantern, to dispel some of the shadows.

Sir John guided her toward another table, another sheeted form. Ellianne was certain he could hear her teeth chattering, but Sir John did not seem to notice the cold or the gloom or her misery. He was intent on the dead woman and what secrets she could tell.

"You'll see that the modus operandi is the same. The method, that is. The blade was of similar length and width, if not identical. We'll know better tomorrow, after further examination."

Ellianne wanted to shout for him to stop, that she did not want to know the terrible details, just if the woman was her sister or not. She wanted to tell him to pull the sheet down now, this instant, so she would have the dreadful anticipation over, one way or the other. She could face the truth, but not the uncertainty, not the waiting.

Just when Ellianne was about to reach for a corner of the sheet, Sir John stopped his monologue about the barbering done to the woman. Then he raised the covering from the woman's face.

She was not Isabelle. Ellianne felt her knees grow weak in relief. Then she grew confused. "This woman is far older than my sister. She appears to be closer to forty than to twenty, and her face is round. She has a dark complexion, and a mole on her chin. How could you have thought this female might be my sister?" Ellianne grew angry next. "You could not have believed she was Isabelle, not for a moment. Bringing me here, telling me about her, was cruel, Sir John, and unworthy of you."

"No, no. Never that, dear lady, never cruel. I thought I saw something similar in her looks. I needed your verification. The green eyes, you see." He reached out to open one of the woman's lids, but Ellianne stopped him.

"No, I have seen enough. This is not my sister. I wish to leave."

"Of course, of course. In a minute. I must fetch some papers from my office before we go." He indicated a closed door to the side of the room. "And I think you could use some wine. This has been a blow to your nerves, for which I humbly apologize. And the cold, of course. Please, let me pour you a small glass of sherry, or Madeira if you prefer. I think, yes, I think I need a drop of spirits myself."

Ellianne's knees still felt weak, and the chill was indeed seeping up through her feet and into her bones. She could use a restorative. Sir John looked so abjectly crestfallen that she agreed. Perhaps a drink would put some color back in his complexion before someone mistook him for one of his corpses.

She waited at the door to the office while he lit a lamp, then pulled open a drawer on his desk to find two wineglasses. A decanter already rested on the dark wood surface. As Ellianne walked into the small room she noticed that he kept his desk in perfect order, unlike Jenkins, upstairs. She set her reticule down on a chair near the door and came closer, to accept the glass he was filling. She also noticed that, while Sir John seemed to have developed a tic in one of his eyes, his hand was perfectly steady.

A steady hand? Wasn't that what they'd said about the killer? Ellianne looked back at her purse, then laughed at her own skittishness. Of course his hand was steady. He was trained in surgery. It did not matter that his patients could not complain if his hand slipped, she told herself, smiling at the thought.

"Ah, I can see that you are recovered already. What an admirable trait in a lady, such composure, such emotional control."

He had not seen her with Stony, Ellianne reflected, still smiling at the memory.

Encouraged, Sir John went on: "In fact, I find much that is admirable in you, dear lady. Your intelligence, your steadfast character, your lack of the appalling levity so common among young women. And your interest in those less fortunate, of course, your consideration—"

"Stop, please do. You will turn my head with your praise." She drank some of her wine quickly, hoping to end this conversation.

"Ah, and modesty. I forgot modesty, another fine trait in a woman. I can see I embarrass you with my compliments, but they are true ones. I would not have spoken so precipitously, but for fear that you might leave Town after the unfortunate gossip."

"Yes, I was planning to leave tomorrow or the next day, as soon as I make arrangements with my solicitor about continuing the search for my sister." She set her half-empty glass down on the desk, beside the decanter. "So you must see I have a great deal to do to get ready."

He ignored her hint, reaching out and grasping her hand tightly. "Then I must speak tonight. I realize that I cannot match you in fortune. Who could? But I am not a poor man by any means, and my knighthood is as good as your father's. I have been led to believe I might expect a baronetcy eventually. Who knows after that? My birth is not despicable, and my—"

Ellianne tried to pull her hand back but he would not release it. "Please do not go on, Sir John."

"I must." To Ellianne's dismay, he dropped to his knees, still clutching her fingers, almost painfully. "I must, for how else am I to convince you that I am worthy of your regard? Worthy of your hand in marriage? My dear Miss Kane, I knew the minute I saw you that we were destined to spend eternity together. Do make me the happiest of men and agree to be my wife."

"I . . . I cannot, sir. Please get up." She tugged on his hand, which now felt like a vise around hers. All she could think of was that Stony was right again. She should never have agreed to meet with Sir John. She took a deep breath and said, "You do me great honor, and I am certain any other female would be thrilled to accept your honorable offer. I, however, have determined to remain unwed."

"You cannot! That is against the natural order of things, an abomination."

"Surely it is my decision, no sin against humanity." She tried to make light of the situation: "I am certain the good Lord will forgive me for not being fruitful and multiplying, but the world has enough redheads."

He did not find any humor in her words, but he did get to his feet, still clutching her hand. "No, you have to marry me! I planned it all."

Now she was beginning to grow annoyed, both at his insistence and at his continued refusal to release her. "I do not have to do anything, sir, but go home to finish my packing. You had no right to make any plans without consulting me, so I do not feel responsible for your disappointment."

"But you smiled at me. You had Lady Wellstone invite me to the dinner in your honor. You accepted my invitations!"

"Your invitations to lectures, not any proposals of marriage. I was being polite, nothing more. Now cease this foolishness before we both say things we shall regret."

"No! You are mine!" He pulled her toward him, almost jerking her off her feet with a strength that surprised her, and frightened her a bit, Ellianne had to admit. He kissed her, if pushing one's lips against another's could be considered a kiss, which she doubted. His lips were dry, chapped, harsh, hurtful against hers, forcing her lips against her teeth. She could taste blood on her tongue. This was an assault, not an embrace, and she would not permit it, no matter how sorry she felt for the misguided man. She pushed against him, and he released her, panting heavily.

"You see? You are mine!"

"I see nothing of the sort." She wiped her mouth with the back of her glove. Then, when he would have reached for her again, she picked up her wineglass and dashed its contents in his face.

"You bitch!" he screamed, scrubbing at the liquid dripping into his eyes.

Ellianne took her chance to flee. She was inches from the door—and her reticule—when he grabbed her from behind. He pressed her back against his bony chest, one wiry arm clamped across her waist, pinning her arms there as he dragged her away from the door, toward the desk, with surprising strength for one so thin. Her kicks availed nothing but a tighter squeeze, so she could hardly breathe. Then his other arm was at her throat, holding a long, gleaming knife. A stiletto. Its point was pressed against her neck so tightly Ellianne dared not struggle.

"You?" She gasped.

He laughed, or it might have been a snarl. "Of course. Who else could ensure the crimes were never solved?"

"If you hurt me, they will know. My maid, Jenkins. They saw us. You cannot hope to escape."

He made that low sound again. "Do you think I am so stupid?" He dragged her around until she faced another door that she had not noticed. "Another exit. I have only to kill you, run outside shouting that the killer was waiting for us here, that he was getting away down the street. Or I could keep going. We are close to the docks, you know. I have a ship there, a yacht, but you could not know that. No one does. I have been careful, using a different name to hire a crew. I was going to take you away with me, a joyous bridal sail. Now I see that will not do, for you are not the woman I thought you to be. I could go, yes, I could be at sea before they discovered your body."

"You are mad!" Ellianne said, which was not, she instantly realized, a wise thing to say to a maniac with a knife to one's throat.

He did not seem to take offense. "Madness is a relative term. Why, once we were wed, I could have had you declared insane and placed in an asylum for the rest of your life. Then the money would have all been mine. But I need to think." He prodded her bare throat with the knife point, to keep her silent.

Ellianne could not imagine how his irrational plotting could benefit her in any way, so she spoke: "What if I gave you the money? I could give you a draft on my bank."

"And have the magistrates waiting for me to cash it? You would tell them as soon as I set you free."

"No, I swear I would not!"

"You would let a criminal go free, with your fortune, to boot?" He shook her, the blade drawing blood she could feel trickling down her neck. She was too numb with fear to feel any pain. "I am not a fool!"

"Of course you are no fool." She was, and was going to pay for it with her life unless she could offer him an alternative. "You were knighted for your brilliance, after all. But surely there is some way for you to have the money and me to live."

"Both! I almost had both!" he said, half crying. "Now I cannot trust you, even if you promise to wed me."

Which had been Ellianne's next offer.

"No, you have to die."

Which was not the option Ellianne would have picked.

Chapter Twenty-eight

Before Sir John could act, Ellianne tried to distract him. Surely her maid would notice and come investigate if they were gone so long. If she were not brave enough to come down, she might send Jenkins if enough time passed.

It already seemed like hours to Ellianne.

"What about the women?" she asked, stalling for time. "The other women. Why did you . . . ?"

"The first was an accident. The rest were your fault. Yes, your fault."

"How could I be responsible? I did not even know their names! I never saw them before they arrived here."

"But I wanted you to come back. You were so interested and so polite. I had to keep you interested in them, in me."

"You killed four—no, five—women to bring me here to look at them, in case one was my sister?" Ellianne had never known such madness, had no idea that such depravity existed, or how to deal with it.

Sir John nodded, and Ellianne could feel the motion against the back of her head, but the knife did not waver. "I knew from the very first, you see, that we were well suited. Until you . . ."

Ellianne might not understand his tortured mind, but she knew she did not wish to remind him of her rejection. His arm at her midsection was pressing more tightly, and his voice was higher pitched. His breathing seemed to come harder, and she could smell the stench of his sweat.

She had to keep him speaking of something else, then.

"You said an accident? Could you not have explained to the magistrate? I am certain a man of your distinguished reputation would be believed that it was self-defense or some other factor beyond your control."

"Do you think I wished anyone to know that I visited that kind of woman? Filth, she was, for all her airs and graces and expensive demands. Filth, I say!"

His spittle wet Ellianne's cheek. Obviously the first murdered woman was not a good topic either. "But there was an accident?"

"She laughed at me."

So his hand slipped? He just happened to be holding a razor-sharp blade to the woman's throat at the time? Ellianne had to keep reminding herself that the man was insane; he did not have to make sense. He had a knife instead. "But . . . ?"

He needed no prompting now. "She called me a little man. I did not mean to kill her, just frighten her, I was so angry. Then she laughed. I had to stop her then, or she would have kept laughing, not believing me man enough for that, either."

That was not Ellianne's definition of an accident, not by half, but if it kept the madman talking, it kept her alive. She vowed not to laugh—if by chance anything funny occurred to her. "What about her hair? Why did you shave it off?"

"Why, to make her ugly, so no other man would want her."

"When she was already dead?"

"I had been seen with the Cyprian, although none of her neighbors knew me. I had to make her harder to identify, so no one came here looking. You were the one who insisted Bow Street put out posters with the other ones' pictures."

"I do not understand. If you did not wish her identified, you could have hidden her body instead. Why did you let her be found at all?"

"Why, so I could conduct the investigation, of course," he said matter-of-factly, as if gentlemen killed their mistresses every day, just so they could carve them up afterward, officially. Ellianne was growing nauseated, both by the pressure on her stomach and the cold-blooded derangement of her captor. At least she was not dead yet.

She kept talking. "What did you do with her hair?"

"I have it, all of it, in a box. Now she is mine, you know. I can touch it anytime I wish, and she cannot laugh. She did, you see, when I asked to comb it. Lovely hair, it is, honey-colored and wavy. I made sure there were no knots."

Ellianne squeezed her eyes shut to keep from crying at the horror that was creeping over her with every word he spoke. She needed to maintain her wits, but how could she hope to reason with a Bedlamite? A sob escaped from her throat.

He took that for encouragement. "I did not see your hair the first time we met. You wore an ugly black bonnet, but you said your sister's was red, like yours. I had to see for myself."

"I could take my bonnet off now, so you could see it. I have a comb in my reticule. Let me fetch it and you can comb my hair, see how long it is." She prayed he would release her long enough to get her purse, to run or scream or kick or claw, to do anything but die, helpless in his arms.

Heaven ignored her prayers, and Sir John ignored her offer. With a flick of his wrist he neatly sliced her bonnet strings, tipping it to the floor. The knife was back at Ellianne's throat before she could blink, much less act. "I wanted to have it for myself, but now I won't have time," he mourned, nuzzling his nose in the braided coil she wore at the back of her neck.

He would not have time? That meant she would not have time. "Of course there is time. Let me take it down and you can see." She'd cut it off herself and give it to him, in exchange for a few more minutes.

He pulled out a hairpin with his teeth, and she almost retched. When he did not reply with anything but another moaning sound because he could not unfasten the rest without using his hands, she asked, "What about the other women? Surely you could not have killed so many innocent girls just to get my attention."

"They were whores," he said, as if prostitutes were as disposable as ants at a picnic. "And I could not stop."

"Not Maisy, the serving girl," she said, desperate to stall for another minute, or sixty. How long did her maid think it took to identify a body? "She was a hardworking maidservant, no courtesan."

"She offered herself to me. She thought I would wed her if I had a sample of her wares. She was no better than those others who put a price on their favors. Whores, the lot of them. Filthy, foul sluts, going from man to man. But lovely hair. They had to have nice hair. Except this last one. I did not have time to be so particular, you see, and had to find a green-eyed doxy so you would come tonight."

Ellianne was truly sick now that another poor woman had died for such a stupid, senseless reason. She could not give in to that weakness any more than she could give in to tears. "But I am not like that! I do not sell my body."

The knife moved a hairbreadth away from her skin while Sir John thought. "But you will not have me." The point returned to press deeper than ever. "After giving yourself to that cad Blanchard. Or did you think I would not hear all the talk?"

"I did not give myself to that dirty dish. It was all talk, all his braggadocio. No one believed it, and he was forced to leave Town."

"What about Wellstone? You would raise your skirts for him, I'd swear, if you have not already."

"No, I am not like those other women. I would not lie with a man who was not my husband."

He did not believe her, perhaps because she no longer believed it herself. Oh, how she wished she had begged Stony to stay with her, or fly away with her. He did not love her? She could live with that, for however long they had together. He did not want marriage? She could stifle her scruples and live with that too, to have him. She could not live here, not with a madman's knife at her throat. "I never have, I vow."

He made that rasping laugh sound.

"I am a virgin," Ellianne cried, weeping in earnest now. "I swear on my sister's name. You cannot kill an honest woman, sir, you cannot."

He could. Sir John drew the blade away, ready to turn it sideways to slice across her throat, severing the veins and arteries and sinews whose names he knew in Latin. "Too bad I will not get to perform an autopsy."

Ellianne could not see through her tears, and she could not think of any prayers but "Please, please, please."

This time her pleas were answered. She heard the sweetest sound in all of creation: Stony, from the doorway. "I say, am I interrupting?"

Stony had followed the black coach in the rain for ages, it seemed, in the direction of the harbor, until he began to wonder if Thomasford was planning on forcing Ellianne and her maid on board a ship. He could carry them off to Scotland or Nova Scotia, for all Stony knew.

Then the carriage pulled up in front of the government building that housed the coroner's office and one of the city's morgues. Perhaps he had misjudged the maw-worm after all, Stony thought, and they were holding the lecture here. But there would be other coaches, crowds of other corpse lovers. Or maybe the benighted knacker had to fetch some papers before going on. But why take Ellianne out in the rain?

There must be a hundred good reasons why Miss Kane would go with Sir John into a nearly deserted building after dark with no protection but a maid. Stony could think of none.

She was not being forced. He could see that from the alley he waited in. Sir John held the umbrella, not a weapon, as they entered the building side by side, the maid following. Stony waited. And waited. Whatever errand they had there could not take this long, not if they were to go to the lecture, or to dinner. He waited a few minutes more, then tied his horse to a railing under an overhanging roof, out of the rain.

Remembering his last visit to this place, Stony faced the door with dread in his heart. He'd rather be anywhere than here, the tooth-drawer's, Newgate Prison, even Almack's. But here was where Ellianne went, so here was where he had to follow.

He pushed the unlocked door open and walked in. There was the maid, sitting at a desk, anxiously shredding her handkerchief, watching a clock that hung on the wall. Some kind of clerk was asleep at another desk, his head on his arms.

The maid was ecstatic to see Stony. She did not like this place; Miss Kane had been gone too long; and Jenkins, the man at the desk, snored. Stony told her that he would go down to fetch her mistress. If, however, they had not returned in five minutes, she was to sound the alarm. "Wake up Jenkins, stand in the street, and scream for the watch. Send a hackney to Bow Street. Anything, but bring help."

The maid agreed and Stony went down those cold

stone stairs. He opened his coat and removed the pistol from the waist of his breeches as he descended into Thomasford's private hell.

No one was there. No one still breathing, at least. Stony averted his eyes from the sheet-draped bodies as he stopped to listen. Yes, he could hear voices, and more light was coming from the side chamber where Thomasford must have his office. Stony walked across the vast central room as quietly as he could and paused outside the narrow door, which was slightly ajar. He recognized the voices as Sir John's and Ellianne's, but he could not make out the conversation.

He peered around the door, then instantly drew back against the wall, cursing at himself. Fool, fool, fool. He was twenty times a fool. This was a tryst, not an abduction. They were embracing, by Harry. And by lantern light, with wine.

Stony flattened himself against the wall, trying to catch his breath past the cannonball lodged in his throat, waiting for it to sink to his stomach so he could go home. Lud, she was even making those little mewing whimpers! For a loose fish forensics expert.

Or was that a real whimper? He peeked around the door again, then jerked back.

Bloody hell.

Lud, he'd rather she'd been kissing the cad.

Options, his mind screamed. He had to have a plan. He could not shoot, for Ellianne was in front of Thomasford. She was so blasted tall, not enough of the dastard showed to make a target. He could not lunge at the man, for that shining, sinister blade was already at Ellianne's throat. Zeus, he did not want to startle the blackguard into any sudden moves.

Then she sobbed. To hell with a plan. Stony walked into the room, his pistol pointing at whatever he could see of Sir John's head. "I say," he drawled. "Am I interrupting?"

"You." Thomasford's lips were pulled so taut he

could not raise so much as a corner of one in his habitual sneer. "I should have known you would turn up."

"Yes, you should have. Your typical bad penny, that's what I am. But what are you?" he asked, as casually as if he were offering port or cognac.

"I am the man who holds a knife to the throat of your bit of muslin. Put the pistol down."

"I think not. Why do you not release Miss Kane and we can all go home."

"Only I would go on a plank. Unless you are too missish to shoot. I heard about your cowardice. Everyone did. And there would be blood," he reminded Stony, as if the viscount did not know his own weakness.

Stony answered: "Yet I am not the one hiding behind a woman's skirts."

Sir John licked his lips. "No, you would not shoot now anyway. Too much chance of hitting your paramour. So put the gun down, I say."

When Stony still hesitated, Sir John pressed the point of his blade into Ellianne's tender flesh. She winced, and a drop of blood welled beneath her chin. Stony would not look. He trained his gaze on the glitter in the villain's eyes instead, weighing his chances, Ellianne's chances. Low, too low.

"No, Stony," she cried. "Don't put it down. Shoot him. He is going to kill me anyway."

"No, he knows he cannot kill both of us with one knife. He'll never get away."

"Yes, he can," she insisted. "There is another exit, and he has a yacht in the harbor. Shoot him, Stony! You have to! He is the Barber, the madman who has been killing all those women."

"Yes, sweetings, I guessed that. I did not think he was demonstrating lessons in surgical procedures with that blade at your pretty throat."

More tears ran down her cheeks. "But he is mad, Stony."

"I never thought otherwise, my love."

"Enough!" Sir John yelled. "Put the gun down or I kill her now!"

Stony looked around, saw Ellianne's reticule on the nearby chair. Her eyes widened when she saw where he was looking. She whispered, "Yes."

He put the pistol down and picked up her reticule. Yes, it was satisfactorily heavy, so she was still carrying her useless weapon. It would have to do.

He swung the purse by its strings, trying to make it appear less heavy. Thomasford watched it, distracted as Stony had hoped. Ellianne's eyes almost crossed, trying to send a message. Stony nodded, knowing she would be ready to act on his signal. Now he had to make an opportunity.

Still swinging the bag like a pendulum, Stony took a step closer to Ellianne and Thomasford. He addressed the crackbrained coroner, watching his weasel eyes as they followed the motion. "If you are such a downy cove, why do you think I will let you kill my . . . lover, then scurry out your side door, like a fox leaving its barrow when the hounds come digging? I will not, you know. A gentleman defends what is his." He took another step in Thomasford's direction, swinging the purse.

"She is mine now!" The man's eyes were shifting from side to side. "And do not come any closer! I know what you are trying to do, and it will not work."

It had already worked for a few feet. "Do you know how handy I am with my fives? Was that part of the gossip you heard? It should have been. I have been training at Gentleman Jackson's Boxing Parlor since my university days. I boxed there, too. I'd say I have the advantage in height, weight, reach, and science. Perhaps stamina, from the look of you. Are you willing to chance killing my woman, and making it to the door?"

"I am a dead man anyway."

"Not if you let her go. I will not follow you. Word

of a gentleman." Stony would send out the militia, but he would not follow.

Thomasford licked his lips again.

Stony took another step, holding the drawstring purse by the bottom now, not the strings. "Our little heiress must have a fortune in here, the thing is so heavy. What say I toss you the reticule and you toss me the girl?"

"No!" Ellianne screamed.

Stony raised his eyebrow. "I know money means a great deal to you, my love, but surely you can spare your pocket change."

"I lied!"

"You are not one of the wealthiest women in England? No matter. There is bound to be a tidy amount here." He shook the purse and they all heard the jingle of coins, or something, over Ellianne's moan. "What say you, Sir John, a trade?"

"You won't follow?"

"I gave my word. On the count of three then?" Ellianne's eyes were squeezed shut, and Stony prayed she'd open them in time to move when she had to. He doubted they would have another chance. "One." He swung the purse once more, took another step, and took a solid grip on the weight inside it. "Two." Ellianne groaned. "Sorry, pet. You shall just have to foreclose on another mortgage. Three."

He swung the bag with all his might at Thomasford's head.

At the same instant, Ellianne stomped her sturdy sole down on her captor's toes.

The reticule connected. The pistol in the purse exploded. Sir John's hands relaxed. Ellianne leaped sideways. Sir John fell forward, at Stony's feet.

And Stony said, "Bloody hell. That's what you lied about?"

Chapter Twenty-nine

"You mean it was loaded all the time?"

"Of course. I am not fool enough to carry an unloaded pistol."

They would discuss the depth of her foolishness later. For now Stony was staring at the smoking fabric in his hands. "You mean I shot a man with a lady's reticule?"

Ellianne brushed plaster dust off her nose. "No, I think you shot the ceiling. Sir John might not be dead, only concussed. Someone ought to look, I suppose." She did not sound eager for the job.

"Not dead? Damnation!" Stony leaped to the chair where his own pistol rested. Keeping it aimed at the murderer's greasy head, he prodded Thomasford over with his foot. He was dead, all right, impaled on his own stiletto. There was not much blood, thank goodness, but Stony shrugged out of his coat and tossed it over the still form anyway. He turned away, saying, "Good riddance."

Then he looked at Ellianne. Tears ran down her cheeks. If ever a woman had earned a bout of crying, Ellianne had. After all his years with Gwen, he could manage tears. But then he saw her neck. Blood was running from under her chin down to the collar of her cloak. He could never manage—

"Don't you dare, Wellstone. I need you with me now. I swear, if you swoon and leave me here alone with him, I will take your gun and shoot you myself. I can say he did it before he died. I promise you I will."

Stony swallowed, his eyes closed, and breathed deeply. "You won't be alone long. Help is coming."

She raised his chin. "No, look at me. At my face, Stony. What do you see?"

"Red. Red hair, the color of—"

"No! Look at my eyes. Green, Stony. They are green." She didn't want to search her exploded reticule for a handkerchief, so she pulled at his loose neckcloth until it was untied, then used it to stanch the blood she could feel already drying on her neck. She wrapped the white linen around twice, so Stony could not see the marks left by the madman's blade. "There. Now look more closely. What else do you see, Stony?"

"The bravest, most beautiful woman in the world."

Then she was in his arms, and he was stroking her back, her hair, her shoulders, everything he could touch while she wept in relief. He showed his own relief by murmuring to her, "When I think how close I came to losing you I could cry, too, sweetings. Lud, I almost did not follow you. Then I thought . . . Well, it does not matter what I thought. I did follow, and in time, thank heaven. We'll never know for certain what might have happened, but I would have died along with you, you know. My heart was ready to shatter in a million pieces. Maybe part of it did, for I swear it is beating triple time. Can you hear it, my sweet?" He placed her hand on his chest. "Can you feel it?"

She could feel life flowing through him, through both of them. They were safe now, and she was not going to waste another minute in roundaboutation.

She nodded and put his hand on her chest. "My heart, too. It almost stopped working when I thought you could shoot yourself with the pistol."

"Gads, I could have shot you!"

They stood like that a minute, marveling that they had survived, together. Then Ellianne dabbed at her watery eyes with the ends of his neckcloth and looked into his sky-blue ones. "What else do you see in my eyes, Stony?"

He saw love, pure and shining, and his heart almost burst all over again with the wonder of it. He lowered his lips to hers—and tasted blood from where Sir John had cut her lip. He instantly pulled back, lest he add to her injuries. "That bastard died too easy a death."

"I think he suffered a hard enough life, being as disturbed as he was."

"I think you are too forgiving. When I think of what he—"

She placed her fingers over his lips. "No, don't think of that now. Later is soon enough. I know I will have nightmares without any reminders. But, Stony, why did you let him go on thinking that we were lovers? I was trying to convince him I was still a virtuous maiden."

She was right: There would be ample time to revisit the horror. For now he could gladly exchange the mental image of Thomasford licking his lips for a fonder memory. He thought of Ellianne atop the worktable in the butler's pantry and grinned. "A maiden perhaps, but virtuous? You are every man's dream companion: suitable lady on the outside, seductress on the inside."

She blushed, but was pleased with Stony's assessment. "But Sir John could not have known that."

"He is—he was—a man. We live in hope of finding that perfect mate."

Ellianne was not ready to let herself hope for more than she had. She was alive and in Stony's arms. That had to be enough for now. "But I am a virgin!"

Not for long, if Stony's grin had anything to say about it. "Thomasford would never have believed we were not lovers, not when I came after you with a weapon in my hand, so I saw no reason to waste the effort of arguing with him. Besides, I liked the sound of it. Lovers."

"Lovers." Ellianne sighed, repeating the word. Making love and being in love were two separate activities, though. Not always, and not in fairy tales, but not the same. "Does that mean . . . ?"

She was not destined to hear Stony's definition, for shouts and running footsteps could be heard on the steps.

"Later, my sweet. Later." He brushed off her bonnet and placed it on her head. There was no reason for anyone else to see Miss Kane's hair coming undone. Lud, it was enough to make lunatics of them all. Even now, amid the mayhem and misery, he wanted to take down those last pins, unplait the last braids, and spread it out, a living fire to warm the chill in his blood from this place of death. He could not, not now.

"In here," he called. "We are in here."

Stony's explanation, demonstration, supplication of "lovers" had to wait much longer than he wished.

Bow Street arrived in force, led by Mr. Lattimer, who was full of regrets. Of course he was. He hadn't listened to Wellstone's suspicions, hadn't been the one to rescue Miss Kane. Not only was he not going to collect any part of the huge reward, but he might be collecting his last paycheck, to judge from his superior's scowl.

The magistrate came, and the coroner's inquest panel, mortified that one of their own was suspected of such heinous acts. They looked at Stony as if he were the murderer, trying to foist his dastardly deeds onto the most respected member of their fraternity. Even Lattimer had to protest that.

Official recorders for the courts came to hear Ellianne repeat her story yet again. Reporters from the newspapers came, too, and artists who bribed the guards outside for a glimpse of the beauty, the Barber, and his bête noire. Napoleon's defeat would have been a bigger story, but not tonight.

Stony tried to shield Ellianne as much as possible, insisting they go elsewhere to give their depositions, calling for pots of hot tea, and brandy to add to it. He made them send a messenger to Sloane Street so no one would worry, another to Gwen canceling their dinner, and one to a groom to stable his poor horse. He demanded Lattimer send for a physician to look at Miss Kane's neck and the prostrate maid, while Runners went to Sir John's rooms in search of the evidence Ellianne told them would be there.

They found the hair, all neatly collected in hatboxes, one atop the other. They found knives and razors and shaving soap, and the deed to a yacht in the harbor. They found diaries in Sir John's handwriting, and clothing that could only belong to ladies of the night. Even his mother, if the fiend was indeed spawned by a creature of this world, would have to believe in Thomasford's guilt.

They were free to go.

By the time Stony walked Ellianne to her door, she was staggering on her feet. He saw her into her aunt's care, but kissed her forehead before he left and promised, "Tomorrow."

Tomorrow was impossible. Miss Kane was a heroine. So many flowers were delivered that her house looked like a country garden, with narrow pathways between banks of bouquets. No one could have walked the aisles anyway, they were so filled with callers eager to congratulate her on surviving, commiserate with her at the ordeal, and capture a bit of her glory for themselves. They were friends of the amazing Miss Kane, guests told themselves, although they had never shared two words before. The ladies delightedly clutched their vinaigrettes at sight of the sticking plaster her high collar could not conceal, and the gentlemen clutched her hand. Everyone wanted to speak with her, touch her, have her at their affairs, like a prized trophy.

Timms had to find a replacement for the overflowing silver salver that held calling cards and invitations. He chose a much larger basket. The dog had slept in it only once, far preferring Lady Augusta's bed.

So many invitations arrived, Ellianne could not think of leaving London, not when one of them came from the prince regent himself. Refusal would have been near to treason, Gwen insisted. Prinny wanted to throw a fete at Carlton House in her honor. After all, London was safe for all women now, because of her.

She was brave. She was a celebrity. She was overwhelmed.

And Stony was . . . rich.

Ellianne wanted no part of the bountiful reward money. After all, she was paying a big portion of it. Besides, she had not suspected Sir John, had not overpowered him, or rendered him helpless. In fact, she insisted, without Viscount Wellstone she would have died at the murderer's hand instead of being any kind of heroic Amazon warrior. His lordship deserved every pound of the generous bounty, and more.

He got more, a lot more. The coroner added to the already huge reward, in hope of deflecting criticism of his office, and the home secretary added a heavy purse from a grateful government. A newspaper offered a handsome sum, just for an interview, and a broadside printer paid for a portrait. Relieved women sent him coins, sometimes anonymously, sometimes with a perfumed note. Those last he returned, but the rest he kept and counted and put to good use.

His bills would all be paid as soon as his solicitors

could tally them. Repairs to Wellstone Park would be under way, new farming equipment ordered, laborers hired. Gwen's annuity would be restored so that if, by the grace of God, she chose to rewed, she had something to bring to her new husband. Careful investments could be made so some of the money would earn him more. His home for girls would get a new roof.

He was not wealthy, not by Ellianne's standards, but he was well-off. He was instantly retired, never again to escort a female for money, unless he was taking a mare to sell at Tattersall's. He could have his fields and his sheep and his stud farm. The shipbuilding enterprise could come later, if he wished. If not, he could still live nicely at Wellstone Park, and keep the London town house open for Gwen. Or he could stay in the city, if that was what his wife wanted. He shut the accounts books and put on his hat and gloves.

He could afford a wife. He could not afford to miss another chance at having the right wife.

He needed Ellianne, and not just because he could make neither heads nor tails out of the ledgers and wanted her advice on the investments. He knew that without her he was poorer than any beggar in the street, no matter what he had in the bank. He just had to convince her that she was the prize, not her fortune. He took the top ledger with him, to prove he was a man of means. He meant to succeed this time.

Ten other fellows were ahead of him, with posies and bonbons and bad poetry. None had brought their account books, though. Ellianne dismissed them with a wave and a smile, telling Timms that she was no longer receiving guests. The old butler thanked her and the good Lord, sat down, and removed his shoes. Ellianne led Stony to her book room.

Just looking at him in his dark blue jacket and doeskin breeches and high-topped boots made her forget all those other men. They left her yawning; he almost took her breath away. She knew what she wanted to say but, suddenly shy, waited for him to speak. She knew what she wanted to hear.

She did not want to hear a financial report. She frowned.

She did not want to hear a summary of investments. She scowled.

Most of all, she did not want to hear a bloodcurdling screech from her aunt in the front parlor. She jumped to her feet and raced past Stony and his foolish lists. He dropped the ledger and followed her.

Aunt Lally was screaming, and barefoot Timms was on his knees, praying. No, he was shaking the dog, who, on his side, was gasping for air.

"I gave him a piece of a turnip!" Aunt Lally wailed. "It was cooked soft enough, I swear. But he started choking and gagging and wheezing; then he fell over, just like my husband did when he swallowed that cherry pit. By Saint Jerome's jewels, I have killed someone else!"

The dog was barely breathing. "Do something!" Ellianne cried.

"You want me to save the miserable creature's life? Why?" But Stony was already on the floor, with his hands—reluctantly—prying open the dog's mouth and putting one hand—regrettably ungloved—down Atlas's throat. He could not feel anything but a few teeth in the back of the jaw. He looked over at Aunt Lally and the knitting she'd dropped, and thought of sticking one of the long needles down his throat. Or hers, if she did not stop caterwauling enough for him to think. That would be a last resort.

Ellianne was looking at him beseechingly. Damn. He had not yet proposed, and he was already failing her.

Stony hauled the dog off the floor and dangled him upside down, shaking him hard enough to rattle those last few teeth. Nothing happened. Then he bounced him against the padded armrest of the sofa. Again nothing happened. Recalling the bout with Blanchard, Stony punched the dog in what he took to be the animal's midsection. Ellianne gasped; Aunt Lally cursed; Timms prayed, but the same thing happened as occurred with Blanchard. Whatever air remained in the dog was expelled in one whoosh, along with the turnip. Stony laid the beast down, then bent to put his ear to his chest, listening for a heartbeat. He'd heard of the kiss of life, of breathing air into the mouth of a drowning victim. Good grief, Ellianne did not expect that of him, did she?

Yes, it seemed, from her pleading look. He would have to rethink this proposal business later. A woman who asked a man to move mountains was one thing, but this . . . "Yes! He is breathing! Yes! No, damn you, do not lick my face!"

Then Aunt Lally threw herself into Stony's arms, almost bowling him over. "You saved my niece, now the dog! And here I thought you had no bottom! By all the saints, Wellstone, you've got stones!" She kissed him on both cheeks, which was almost worse than the dog's show of gratitude.

Timms was weeping tears of joy, not out of any fondness for the dog, Stony knew, but because his prayers had been answered: He didn't have to kiss the cur. Stony shoved Ellianne's aunt in the butler's direction. Let them comfort and congratulate each other. He had waited long enough.

He held his empty arms open. Ellianne walked into them.

Before he could speak, she stopped him with a kiss, then said, "No, I have waited too long to say this, and I might not find the courage again. But you truly are my hero, Stony, the finest man I know. I do not care if you don't love me. I want to be yours anyway. If you do not wish to be married, I can try to accept that too, for however long I can share your life, your bed, your thoughts. I do not think I could bear it if you wed someone else, but until then we can have whatever kind of life you wish. You can be the richest consort in the kingdom, for I would give every shilling I own to be in your arms like this forever, or you can be the poorest, living on love alone, for I would give the money to charity if you wanted."

Stony kissed her eyelids, both of them. "Whoa, sweetings. Who said I did not love you?"

"You do?"

"No, he does not!" came a commanding voice from the hallway. A scarlet-uniformed officer had come to call but, finding no one at the door, he had limped toward the voices. Now he stood leaning on his cane, but evidently ready to use it on Stony's head. "Unhand my fiancée, you cad!"

Stony looked at him. "Brisbane?"

Ellianne looked at him. "Fiancée?"

He looked at Ellianne. "Isabelle?"

Chapter Thirty

Stony's friend Daniel, Captain Brisbane, had met Isabelle on her way to Town, it seemed, months ago.

He had been returning to London after accompanying the dowager countess Hargeave to her daughter's lying-in. Stony recalled the trip, for he had made the arrangements himself. Lady Hargeave did not like traveling without a male escort, even if she had to pay for it, since innkeepers gave better service, rooms, horses, and meals to a female under a gentleman's protection. And she liked to flirt.

Brisbane rode beside the carriage for the most part, offending the lady, but seeing her handed safely into the care of her son-in-law, who rewarded him generously, since the man was elated at the birth of his first son.

With coins in his pocket, the captain was in no hurry to return to London. He stopped off at a pleasant inn, but a commotion disturbed his rest. A carriage had arrived, a private hired coach, but the groom, the lady's maid, and an older chaperon were ill, and the driver not much better. At first the innkeeper tried to turn them away for fear of contagion, until a beautiful young lady swore they had eaten bad fish the previous night, of which she had not partaken. Being a gentleman, of course, Brisbane came to the young woman's assistance. He made sure she had rooms, and her servants were cared for. He rode for the apothecary himself, since the village had neither surgeon nor physician.

"She never told me any of this, merely that the journey was delayed." Ellianne was dismayed. She had sent her sister off with ample protection against everything except bad fish . . . and handsome, injured young officers. "What else did you do for my sister, sir?" she demanded.

Stony said, "Hush, my dear. There is more to the story."

Brisbane nodded. "The apothecary said the patients needed five days' rest, at the least. The inn was not the finest, catering more to the local drovers than the carriage trade. I could not leave a young miss there on her own, could I?"

"Of course not," Stony agreed, when Ellianne would have suggested any number of alternatives.

Sensing her disapproval, Brisbane turned to her. "I swear I did not know she was an heiress, ma'am. She was dressed simply, like a sweet country lass, not in the height of fashion. She said she was coming to London because her old auntie wanted her to contract a decent marriage. I thought that meant into a bit of money, never thinking her aunt was related to a marquess, or that Lady Augusta intended her to wed a title. Miss Isabelle said she did not care about making an advantageous match; she just wanted to see the sights."

"I told her there was no hurry in picking a husband, simply to enjoy herself."

Brisbane nodded. "I told her where to go first, which buildings and exhibits and views she should not miss. She took notes and made lists."

Stony glanced at Ellianne. "A family trait?"

"We are all organized, efficient people. I cannot believe Isabelle did not hire another coach, after making provision for the servants at the inn, of course. It would have been far less dangerous for her to complete the journey on her own than stay at a second-rate inn with no chaperon whatsoever."

Brisbane colored. Miss Kane was correct, of course. He could have begged the vicar's wife or the innkeeper's daughter to accompany Miss Isabelle while he rode alongside the coach himself. But he had not wanted her to go, and she was reluctant to leave. So they talked and they walked, as best he could with his limp, and shared meals in the private parlor. Otherwise, he claimed, she would have to eat in her small bedroom, or alone.

"Heaven forfend," Ellianne muttered, knowing what was coming.

"She was so sweet and kind, never once belittling my awkward gait, as many of the flighty London girls do, thinking that a lame man is beneath their notice. Miss Isabelle thought I was a hero, injured in my country's defense. She did not believe my life was ended with my army career, but was just beginning. I could be anything I wanted, she said."

"And you wanted to be . . . ?"

"Her husband. Belle is perfect, beautiful yet modest, intelligent but not opinionated. How could I not adore her, not want to care for her the rest of my days, have her beside me, bear my children?"

Stony took Ellianne's hand. "How indeed?"

"And she returned my regard, to my delight. I never believed in love at first sight, but I do now."

Ellianne did not want to discuss falling into love. "What happened then?"

Then the servants recovered, and they all left for London. Brisbane skipped over the intervening days, the rest of the journey, the nights at various inns or whether he rode alongside the carriage or within. He thought it sufficient to say they arrived safely in London, more in love, and determined to wed.

Then he discovered her connections and her consequences. Worse, Lady Augusta discovered his lack of both. She forbade him the house. Isabelle told him not to worry, that her sister was different, and her sister was the only one whose approval mattered, to Belle or to the courts.

"She said you always judged a man on his own merits, not his title or his purse," Captain Brisbane told Ellianne. "She said you would give us your blessings, because you only wanted her happiness, and she could be happy only with me."

Stony handed Ellianne his handkerchief, but not the one with which he had wiped his face following the dog's resurrection.

But the young couple could not wait for Isabelle to return to Fairview. They met, in secret, in the back garden or at the various museums, galleries, and cathedrals on Isabelle's list. As Lady Augusta's health deteriorated, so did their hopes of Isabelle's early departure from London. They tried again to convince the old woman that true love mattered more than social position, that Isabelle's portion was so large she could marry a beggar if she wanted, much less a half-pay officer. Lady Augusta was more and more adamant. Belle and Brisbane were more and more desperate. They were in love and impatient. They did not want to wait.

Lady Augusta stopped going out. Isabelle did not. With so few servants in the old miser's house, and those busy caring for their mistress, or incapacitated, like Timms, it was easy for them to meet. Other times they visited in the parlor. Atlas was their only chaperon, often. Too often, to Ellianne's way of thinking.

Then Captain Brisbane urged his darling to confront her aunt. He wanted an official betrothal, not a shameful, hole-in-corner affair. It was bad enough that he was wooing an heiress; he did not want her reputation destroyed, too. He was not ashamed of Isabelle or his love for her, and wanted the entire world to know of it, of the miracle that she loved him in return. Besides, he was tired of having to spend time with other young ladies, escorting spoiled misses to tedious events when he wished only to sit next to Belle at a fireside.

Isabelle was going to speak to her aunt the night of the Pattendale debacle. She was gone in the morning when he came to Sloane Street. The house was in an uproar, Lady Augusta was dead, and no one knew where Isabelle had gone.

"Didn't you try to find her?" Ellianne demanded.

"Of course I did. I checked inns, posting houses, and hotels. No one had seen her. She had no friends that I knew of, so all I could do was return to my lodgings to wait. She never came. At last I decided that they must have argued about the betrothal, and that the harridan threw her out. When Lady Augusta died, Isabelle must have been afraid, so she went home, to you, Miss Kane, who could fix anything, she said. So I followed."

"I never saw you at Fairview," Ellianne said with suspicion.

"No, I did not make good time," Brisbane answered with chagrin. First his horse came up lame right out of London and he had to walk to the closest inn, aggravating his wounded leg. He did not have the blunt to hire a carriage, so had to take the brute the sullen hostler offered. The man-hater tossed the captain as soon as they left the livery, and nearly broke his good leg, so he could not ride for two days. Then the horse tried scraping the determined rider off under a low-lying tree limb. The officer was concussed and lay on the cold, damp ground overnight, until a flock of sheep almost trampled him in the morning. The shepherd dragged him off the roadway, but had no horse or wagon to take him farther. Finally a farmer came by with his load of cabbages. By that time Brisbane had contracted an inflammation of the lungs. Two more weeks passed before he could resume the journey, begging rides in donkey carts and peddlers' wagons, because his purse had gone missing while he was ill.

By the time he reached Fairview, Miss Ellianne Kane had left for London to settle her aunt's affairs, the servants told him. Miss Isabelle Kane had gone north for the funeral. So the captain sold his watch and his silver buttons and trekked across the country to the Marquess of Chaston's estate in Yorkshire. Isabelle was not there, never had been there, and was never going to be invited there. When he asked for an interview with the marquess, to offer for his niece's hand in marriage, Brisbane was thrown off the property.

With nothing left to sell, he was lucky enough to find a ride back to London with a band of circus performers, in exchange for his help with their horses. They stopped at every market square and village green to perform, though, so he might have made better time if he had walked, if his leg had permitted.

But now he was back in Town, in a fresh uniform after a visit to his bank, and calling on Isabelle. He begged Miss Kane's apology for mistaking her for his beloved—Miss Kane was too tall and too old, at closer inspection—but where was Isabelle?

After a look toward Ellianne to make sure he could speak what the poor man already suspected, Stony said, "That's the problem. We have no idea. We thought she'd be with you, whoever her gentleman friend turned out to be, on her way to Gretna Green."

Brisbane drew himself erect. "I will marry my darling properly, in a church with our friends and family nearby. She deserves nothing less."

Her sister deserved more than a crippled soldier who could not manage a simple journey, Ellianne thought, but the man did seem sincere in his affection for Isabelle. "We have to find her before you can marry her anywhere. Perhaps you have another idea where we can look?"

Brisbane did not. Stony sent him home to rest and think about it. He and Ellianne had unfinished business first.

He had hardly finished taking the pins from her hair when Timms cleared his throat outside the book room door. "You have a caller, miss."

"Tell him to go away."

"It is Lady Wellstone, and she is upset."

"My stepmama is always upset about something," Stony answered. "Give her a handkerchief and then tell her to go away."

He knew that would not work, so he sighed and said, "Later, my sweet."

Gwen was in the parlor, in a taking. She embraced Ellianne, crying, "You were right; that man is a rake! I have been offered the worst insult of my life."

Stony cursed. He was not in the mood for any more high drama. All he wanted was ten minutes alone with Ellianne, not another confrontation.

"Wellstone will make it right," Ellianne told the older woman, making Stony feel as if he could face a fire-breathing dragon, much less whatever gudgeon had offended silly Gwen.

"Which rake would that be, Gwen, and do I have to call him out?" The sooner he got rid of Gwen, the sooner he could have his time with Ellianne.

"Strickland!"

Ellianne was aghast. "He did not try to molest you, too, did he? I'll run him through myself."

Gwen sniffled. "Worse. He took me to his love nest!"

A man should not be shot for trying to steal a little private time with the object of his affections, Stony firmly believed, wishing he had some quiet place to take Ellianne. On the other hand, he did not appreciate the baron playing fast and loose with Gwen. "I thought you said he was reformed. In fact, I thought his intentions were entirely honorable."

"So did I," Gwen wailed, throwing herself into his arms and dampening his shirtfront with her tears.

Then Brisbane's words echoed from the doorway again: "Unhand my fiancée, you cad!" Only this time the red-faced baron was in the entry, not a red-coated soldier.

"Fiancée?" Gwen and Stony asked at once.

But Ellianne was not paying attention. "Cad? Who are you to be calling Lord Wellstone a cad?" She advanced on Lord Strickland, who scurried behind an armchair for safety. "You accost young women, you keep low company, drink and gamble to excess, and now you offer a respectable widow a slip on the shoulder. You should be ashamed of yourself, sir."

Strickland looked toward Stony, begging for rescue, but the viscount had his arms crossed over his broad, damp chest and a smile on his face, enjoying Ellianne at her most majestic.

Gwen was still asking: "Fiancée? Did he say fiancée?"

No one answered her.

Ellianne tapped her foot. "Well? What do you have to say for yourself?"

Strickland frowned at Stony for his lack of intervention. Gentlemen should stick together, after all. All Stony did was raise an eyebrow and wait. "I'd be interested in your answer myself, as the head of Lady Wellstone's household, you understand."

"What, I should have asked your permission first, a man half my age?" the baron blustered. "And that's not the way of it a'tall. I admit I made some mistakes in the past, missy, and I've suffered for them, I have. Lost my lands, and almost lost my family jewels. But I already begged your pardon, and I ain't doing it again. Whatever company I kept is nothing a lady should acknowledge nor mention, but since you did, I can say I ain't been back in ages. As for my place in

Richmond, I haven't kept a mistress there in years. I wanted to show Gwennie that I wasn't entirely without property, so she wouldn't think she was marrying any caper merchant."

Stony asked, "Gwennie?"

Gwen asked, "Marrying?"

But Ellianne asked, "Richmond? Isabelle said you took her for a drive there, too. Did you show her your house also, in hope of convincing her to marry you?"

Strickland kept his eyes from meeting Gwen's. "Might have. It's a pretty place. We didn't go in, mind you. No one there but the caretaker and his wife, so it wouldn't have been at all the thing."

Ellianne turned to Stony. "She's in Richmond! I know it. My sister is at Lord Strickland's house in Richmond. I don't know why she's there, but it's the perfect place to hide."

There went Stony's chance to have Ellianne to himself again. Later was seeming like forever to him, but he understood that she had to go see now.

Strickland went with Gwen in her carriage, and they stopped to pick up Brisbane. Stony took Ellianne in his faster curricle, but they could not get too far ahead, needing the baron's directions. He directed the coach to pull up at a charming stone and timber cottage set in a well-maintained park. No one was stirring.

Ellianne hardly dared breathe, she was hoping so hard. She held Stony's hand as they walked up the pathway to the house. When they were halfway there, the door flew open and a whirlwind with red hair rushed down the stairs.

"Oh, I knew you would come! What took you so long?"

First she was in Brisbane's arms; then she was in Ellianne's. She even kissed Stony's cheek for driving Ellianne. "I do not know who you are, sir, but you brought my sister, so I am grateful." She hugged a blushing Strickland for letting her use his lovely cottage, even though he had not known. After hasty introductions she invited him—and the rest, of course, since she had not released Captain Brisbane's arm—inside his own house for refreshments.

Ellianne was wiping her eyes with Stony's last handkerchief, but her joy was tempered with curiosity and a tinge of aggravation. Her sister was radiant, while she had been frantic with worry. She had a hundred questions. "But why are you here, Isabelle? Why did you leave Aunt Augusta's? And why did you not come home, or tell anyone where you were? I have been turning London upside down, and half of England."

"You mean you never got my letters? You neither, Daniel? That's why you did not come for me?" Isabelle started weeping, but Stony did not flinch. She was Brisbane's problem now, wetting the captain's clothes. "Oh, I knew I should not have trusted that tinker! He swore he would take my letters to the posting house. I'd wager he took my coins and never delivered them!"

Ellianne felt better knowing that her sister had not forsaken her loyalty entirely, only her wits. "I got one, but could not read it. But why, love, why?"

"Because Aunt Augusta would not let me marry my dear captain. There was a terrible row, and then she told me to leave her house. You see, I told her I was breeding so she would have to let us announce the betrothal so we could go about together. But she washed her hands of me instead. She was so angry, I feared for her heart, so I packed and went to Daniel's rooms. His landlady would not let me in, however, so I left a note and went to a hotel. Do you know most will not rent rooms to a single woman?"

Brisbane was in despair. "I never got that note, either! My poor darling, lost and alone!"

"Oh, I hired an old woman to pretend to be my second cousin, so the next hotel manager let me stay. The next afternoon, though, you still had not come. I read the newspapers, and they spoke of Aunt Augusta's death, and that I might have had a hand in it. I swear, Ellie, I didn't."

"I never thought you did, love. And she was a horrid old woman anyway, throwing her own niece out in the night! But do go on. How did you come to be here?"

"I was afraid others might suspect me. And . . . and that Daniel did not wish to be connected to such a scandal."

Brisbane groaned. "How could you doubt my love?"

"Because you did not come to the hotel, silly. Then I remembered this place, and thought I could stay here, with no one the wiser, while I decided what to do. I told the old couple that I was your mistress, Lord Strickland, and I am sorry."

"Nothing to be sorry over. Glad I could help." And proud that someone might think the pretty redhead was in his keeping. He wiped away his grin when Gwen poked him in the ribs.

Ellianne was shaking her head. "But I still do not understand. Why didn't you just come home? If your young man truly loved you he would have followed."

"I was ashamed and afraid." Isabelle clutched Brisbane's hand, but she also touched her stomach. "You see, I really am breeding."

Gwen swooned. Strickland caught her.

"Fainting is a family trait, I daresay," Ellianne said, before she started beating Captain Brisbane about the head with her reticule. Since she no longer carried her pistol, her fury had almost no effect.

Stony pulled her away anyhow. "Remember he was concussed. And you need him to give your new niece or nephew a name."

"And I love him," Isabelle stated. "I knew it was wrong, but I do not regret giving myself to the only man I will ever love. I know Aunt Lally would never approve, but I hope you can forgive me someday."

"Aunt Lally is back in town dallying with Timms, so you can forget about her censure."

"Really? Anyway, I know you cannot understand, Ellie, never having known a grand passion, but it is wonderful and overwhelming and irresistible. I regret nothing."

Ellianne did understand. And she regretted that she and Stony could not stay on in the Richmond cottage when the others drove back to town.

Chapter Thirty-one

Stony had had enough. He had waited long enough, watching all the happy reunions. Now it was his turn.

He pulled the curricle off the London road and headed toward a small inn he knew in a nearby village.

"But the others will not know where we are," Ellianne protested.

"Good."

"But Isabelle will worry."

"After leaving you fretting for months? Good." Besides, he doubted the captain and his bride-to-be would notice if the entire population of the south of England went missing, since they were alone in the carriage. Gwen and Strickland had decided to stay on in Richmond, after all, so Gwen could make some refurbishing decisions. Hah! The only thing she was deciding was whether she should marry by special license or have the banns called. Brisbane and Isabelle had no choice. A messenger was already on his way to procure a hasty permit from the archbishop's office. This was one messenger who would not go astray, not with what Ellianne was paying him.

Stony knew that as soon as they reached Sloane

Street, Ellianne would be busy celebrating her sister's return, then planning the removal to Fairview for the wedding. He would not have a moment of her time for days or weeks. Another hour was fifty minutes too long.

"Besides," he told her, "I am starving."

"I suppose we did miss nuncheon, but Isabelle offered us tea."

"I am not hungry for a meal."

Ellianne untied her hat when he feathered the corner into the inn yard. Dessert sounded just fine.

The innkeeper was reluctant to give them a private parlor. "I don't hold with no loose goings-on, and that's a fact, viscount or not, my lord."

Stony whispered, but loudly enough for Ellianne to hear, "I hope to make an honest woman of her eventually."

The innkeeper was still dubious. He looked at Ellianne, all ablush and her hair blowing down her back. "Redheaded women are nothing but trouble."

"Amen to that," Stony said, not bothering to lower his voice at all. "But she is rich. Very rich."

"That's all right, then, I suppose."

"More than all right. She is perfect."

The parlor was small but clean and sunny, with a table that could have seated six, and a sofa that was just right for two. The landlord warned that he would be back with tea and ale in a flash, but he winked at Stony on his way out.

Ellianne turned to Stony, ready to find his arms, more than ready to find his lips on hers. Instead he stepped away and led her to a cane-backed chair. "No, I will never get this done if we start that. Here, you sit where I won't be so tempted."

Ellianne folded her hands in her lap, but her smile was anything but prim. "Yes?"

"Deuce take it, I had this all worked out in my head."

"You should have made a chart."

Stony could not help himself; he reached out to stroke one loose lock of her hair, to let it ripple through his fingers like molten fire. Like lava, the touch burned. He went farther away and removed his coat, he was suddenly so warm. "Gads, this is harder than I thought." So was he.

Ellianne looked at the door, praying the innkeeper took his time. "Just say it."

"Yes, well, I would have taken a page from Strickland's book and taken you to see Wellstone Park, to prove I am a man of substance, too, but that might have frightened you away altogether."

"I am not easily frightened."

"No, I have learned that, haven't I? I have also learned that we are not so far apart as we both thought. You have a fortune, but I have enough money to live on, without needing yours. You have a fine estate, but mine is larger, even if it is ramshackle right now, and has been in the family for centuries, not a few decades."

"You have a title," she put in, still concerned over the discrepancy.

"The title of heiress is not to be scorned. Or heroine."

"You have a higher social standing," she persisted.

"But you are on terms with the prince himself. We both have work. Your bank and my breeding farm."

"And charities. We both care about those less fortunate. But I have inconvenient and scandalous relatives."

"I have Gwen's cousins. And Strickland, it would appear. We both like dogs," he added, trying to recall all the points he had intended to make.

"No, I don't really like dogs," Ellianne admitted.

"Good, neither do I, not in the house, anyway."

"What about children?" she wanted to know.

"Oh, they definitely belong in the house. My house. Our house. Lots of them, all with red hair."

"Truly, Stony? Not just because I am hopelessly

compromised, or you feel responsible for me? Or . . . or because you are physically attracted to me?"

"Truly, my sweet, because I am hopelessly in love with you." He reached for her hand, then sank to his knees beside her chair. "All of that. I want you, and I want to take care of you, yes, but I want you next to me forever, although if I do not have you in my arms soon, I might expire. I thought I could take any acceptable female to wife, eventually. How wrong I was. I doubt I could take another woman to a dance, much less to my bed. You are the only one I see when I enter a room, the only one I want to talk to, be with, make love with. When I almost lost you—gads, was it just a few days ago? It seems like ages—I realized that I would not be losing a woman or a friend. I would be losing a part of myself, Ellianne, the best part."

"And you will not mind being faithful to one woman? For I could not bear it if you missed your bachelor life."

"The only woman I will ever want to escort again is you, down the aisle. Will you marry me, Miss Ellianne Kane, and make me a whole man? The happiest man in all of England?"

"Ah, my love, I thought you would never ask, and I would have to do it." She dabbed tears of joy from her eyes with a lace-edged handkerchief. "Of course I will marry you, for I cannot imagine surviving a day without you in it."

"Truly?" he asked, his own eyes suspiciously damp. Ellianne handed him her handkerchief, and he kissed her hand. "No one has ever offered me a handkerchief before, you know."

"No one has ever loved you this much before. I have adored you forever, my dearest, and the differences between us are as nothing now, except that I am a woman and you are a man."

"That's the finest difference. Come, let me show you."

Soon they were on the sofa, lost in each other's arms, when the innkeeper came in with the tray.

They never heard him. "Redheads," he muttered, shaking his head on the way out. "Trouble every time."

About the Author

The author of over thirty romance novels, **Barbara Metzger** is the proud recipient of two *Romantic Times* Career Achievement Awards for Regencies and a RITA award from the Romance Writers of America. When not writing romances or reading them, she paints, gardens, volunteers at the local library, and goes beachcombing on the beautiful Long Island shore with her little dog, Hero. She love to hear from readers care of Signet or through her Web site, www.BarbaraMetzger.com.